Praise for delightful novels of

Donna Kauffman

Sleeping With Beauty

"Wonderful . . . a good time involving laughter, tears and romance. What more could you ask for?"

—*Rendezvous*

Dear Prince Charming

"*Dear Prince Charming* kept me up all night and left me satisfied in the morning. For pure fun served piping hot, get yourself a book by Donna Kauffman!"

—Vicki Lewis Thompson, *New York Times* bestselling author of *Nerd In Shining Armor*

"Sports reporter spars with ditzy publicist. Kauffman has a wonderful knack for turning nothing into sparkling fun."

—*Kirkus Reviews*

"Sexy, funny, entertaining . . . *Dear Prince Charming* may not solve real-life romantic dilemmas, but it will certainly bring a smile to your face."

—America Online's Romance Fiction Forum

"Laughter, passion, and friendship combine in *Dear Prince Charming* to create an enjoyable, fast, and highly entertaining read. *Prince Charming* will entertain and enchant the reader with its cast of captivating characters, humorous dialogue, and heartfelt romance. For a story that's guaranteed to find a place on your keeper shelf, grab *Dear Prince Charming*!"

—*Romance Reviews Today*

"*Dear Prince Charming* is campy, ridiculous fun. Kauffman plays happily with gender stereotypes and sexual chemistry, offering manly men for boys and girls alike. Her zippy prose and direct sensibility are a breeze to read, perfectly suited to romantic comedy. There's a bit of substance to complement the fluff, making for the perfect afternoon read."

—*Contra Costa Times*

"Ms. Kauffman writes a savvy, no-nonsense story with a strong heroine and a sexy hero. Fast-paced and witty, this story is a must-read."

—*BestReviews.com*

"Kauffman does it again. [*Dear Prince Charming*] is light and fun, filled with zingers and humorous scenes."

—*The Facts, Texas*

"*Dear Prince Charming* is a fun-filled story with characters that will touch your heart and lift your spirits. Filled with a lot of humor, romance, and sensitive situations, the book is a fast read and a perfect solution to a lonely day."

—*Inglewood News*

The Cinderalla Rules

"Fun banter and sizzling sex."

—*Entertainment Weekly*

"Kauffman writes with warmth, wit and swashbuckling energy."

—*Publishers Weekly*

"*The Cinderella Rules* is a captivating, modern day fairytale that will delight readers from beginning to end. Well written with humor, passion and a dash of mystery, *The Cinderella Rules* delivers."

—*Romance Reviews Today, America Online*

"A sexy, spicy romp." —*Booklist*

"Kauffman has written an action-packed, sexy, humorous, intricate story with zany characters who will touch your heart, tickle your funny bone and leave you wanting more. Smart, with sizzling romance and a captivating plot. It will make every woman want to follow *The Cinderella Rules*."

—*Old Book Barn Gazette*

The Big Bad Wolf Tells All

"Women everywhere will be taking *Big Bad Wolf* to bed with them. Donna Kauffman writes smart and sexy, with sizzle to spare . . . and no batteries required!"

—Janet Evanovich

"Deftly spun . . . with a zippy style." —*Kirkus Reviews*

"Entertaining . . . sure to find an audience with the beach-reading crowd." —*Booklist*

"Humor and suspense . . . fans of Laura Zigman will enjoy this book." —*Library Journal*

"This is one sheepish tale that stands out from the flock of chick-lit patter with a unique zest and fire all its own."
—*Bookpage*

The Charm Stone

"Give me more!" —Linda Howard

The Royal Hunter

"Kauffman . . . anchors her readers with sensuality, humor and compassion."
—*Publishers Weekly*

"Action packed adventure, steamy sensuality, and a bewitching plot all come together in a surprising and dramatic ending."
—*Rendezvous*

Your Wish Is My Command

"Whimsical and sexy!" —Jennifer Crusie

Legend of the Sorcerer

"Kauffman has written a spellbinding romance that is so hot it near sizzles when the pages are turned... a superb book to curl up with and get lost in."

—*New Age Bookshelf*

"Kauffman knows how to set our hearts afire with passion and romance."

—*Rendezvous*

"Ms. Kauffman is an amazing talent."

—*Affaire du Coeur*

The Legend MacKinnon

"Intricately woven together . . . a terrific read."

—*Rendezvous*

"A uniquely exciting, captivating and sensational read."

—*Romantic Times*

Also by Donna Kauffman

Sleeping with Beauty
Dear Prince Charming
The Cinderella Rules
The Big Bad Wolf Tells All
The Charm Stone
The Royal Hunter
Your Wish Is My Command
Legend of the Sorcerer
The Legend MacKinnon

Yours 2 Keep
With Kay Hooper, Marilyn Pappano,
Jill Shalvis, and Michelle Martin

Not So Snow White

Donna Kauffman

Bantam Books

NOT SO SNOW WHITE
A Bantam Book / June 2006

Published by
Bantam Dell
A Division of Random House, Inc.
New York, New York

Cover design by Lynn Andreozzi

Book design by Lynn Newmark

Library of Congress Cataloging-in-Publication Data

Kauffman, Donna.
Not so snow white / Donna Kauffman.
p. cm.
ISBN-13: 978-0-553-38309-6
ISBN-10: 0-553-38309-4
1. Women tennis players—Fiction. 2. London (England)—Fiction.
I. Title.
PS3561.A816 N68 2006
813.'54 22 2006040664

Printed in the United States of America
Published simultaneously in Canada

www.bantamdell.com

BVG 10 9 8 7 6 5 4 3 2 1

This book is dedicated with love to Mitch and Spence.
Being your mom is the best thing that's ever happened to me.

Acknowledgments

As a longtime fan of the green lawns of the All England Club, this was a very special book for me to write. I couldn't have done it without the generous and exceedingly patient assistance of the staff there. Not only did they provide me with insight and information I'd never have gotten elsewhere, they made a few personal dreams come true, as well. Centre Court will never look the same to me. Now it's intimate and personal. Saying thank you doesn't seem like enough.

I must also take this opportunity to beg forgiveness for the creative license I took with some of the details surrounding the Championships. Where it mattered most, I tried to stay true to the tradition and honor of this most revered British event.

I would also like to thank those who helped me in numerous other ways. For the tennis background, personal instruction, and insight into life on the pro tour, thank you to Sonya, Osiris, and John. For keeping my head in the game when it mattered most, and for support above and beyond the call of duty, a very special thank-you to my agent Karen Solem, and my editor Micahlyn Whitt. Everyone at Bantam, from sales and publicity, to marketing, to the great creative souls in the art department, thank you for your unwavering support. You all are the unsung heroes in this business. Thank you to Sharon and Betsy. And as always, thank you, Nita. Your support through the years—we won't mention how many!—means the world to me.

And for those who have been in the trenches with me, and they've been deep this past year, I hope you realize just how much you're appreciated, and how much you all mean to me. I couldn't have finished this book without each and every one of you.

Not So Snow White

Chapter 1

"Yes, Alden, I know I'm no longer on the tour, but—" Tess Hamilton bit her lip and, more firmly, her tongue as the Nike marketing rep continued talking over her. For Tess, not talking when she had something to say—and she had a whole lot of things to say at the moment—was like trying not to breathe.

She ripped her Boxster S convertible across three lanes of traffic on I-4, ignoring the honks and shouted commentary regarding her driving skills. She had to make her exit, right? Besides, at the moment, she had far bigger things to worry about than instigating inadvertent road rage. Lord knew she'd been responsible for far worse and lived to tell the tale.

The rep paused for an infinitesimal breath and Tess leaped in. "I appreciate what you're saying, really, I do, but this is shortsighted thinking." She raised her voice to be heard over the rush of road noise. God, she loved driving with the top down. Of course, shouting suited her rising temper at the moment, too.

"We're moving in new directions, Tess. So we're looking for a different kind of image. We need to stay fresh. I'm sure you understand."

No, she didn't understand. She refused to understand. She was no longer fresh? Well, shit, how mortifying was that? Not even thirty years old, and her shelf life had already expired?

She accelerated, going way too fast down the winding suburban road leading to her home in the elite, gated, Boca Raton community of Sea Spar. A home she loved. A home she'd bought and paid for with her own hard-earned income. Income which, since her career-ending injury the summer before last, had rapidly ceased to match her outgo. Mostly because of shortsighted morons like the marketing rep currently droning on in her headset about focus groups and future percentages.

She took a sharp turn without decelerating, leaving rubber behind as she fought to keep her temper in check. Unlike past run-ins with various sponsors and marketing reps, this wasn't about some stupid tabloid headline or missed promotional event. She could have talked her way out of that... and often had. Too often. No, this time her entire life was on the line. What was left of it, anyway.

And okay, sure, maybe that was partly due to the fact that she so often had spoken out when it would have been smarter to shut up. Financially smarter, at least. She was a firm believer that if more people spoke their mind instead of blowing smoke up people's asses and saying what they thought everyone wanted to hear, the world would be a much better place. But it wasn't like her sponsors hadn't known that when they signed on the dotted line with her. It hadn't mattered to them then.

However, as the condescending, very annoying man on the other end of the phone was making unavoidably and quite painfully clear, it mattered a whole hell of a lot right now.

She tapped her horn as she turned into the lavishly landscaped, stone-and-wrought-iron entrance, alerting Saul, the gate guard, of her impending arrival. She barely slowed as the bar began to rise, having to duck her head just slightly to keep it from catching on the brim of her tennis hat. She caught a glimpse of Saul, shaking his balding head as he always did when she zipped past, a blur of midnight blue and chrome. This time she didn't wave or blow an apologetic kiss they both knew was completely insincere. Not that she didn't have a soft spot for Saul, she just wasn't particularly remorseful about her no-prisoners style of driving. And she was pretty sure Saul secretly admired her for that.

She passed a string of long, winding driveways leading to this sprawling mansion or that, paying them no attention whatsoever, until she finally turned into her own drive. She slowed slightly, her attention snagging as it always did now, on the two pristine tennis courts laid out so perfectly behind her equally beautiful, perfect house. She'd spent countless hours on those courts.

Alden took another breath and Tess took advantage again, struggling mightily to keep her voice calm, her tone even. "Your company originally signed on with me, in part, because I *was* media bait!" Okay, so maybe she needed to work a little harder on the calm, even part. But honestly, had there ever really been a chance that she'd have kept her cool? The man was robbing her blind here.

And hell, she still hadn't recovered from the mauling she'd taken at the hands of good old Uncle Sam over that whole income tax fiasco last year. Then there was this past April's tab . . . yeesh. She might as well have been bending over when she saw the figure on the bottom line. She didn't even want to think about next year . . . and she wouldn't have to if Alden here would just get with the program.

It wasn't like it was her fault she hadn't exactly been up on the latest tax codes, or knew anything about what payment was due when. That was her accountant's job. Yes, yes, she had fired the man before the extension due date last summer—well, he claimed he quit, but that was semantics, really. And she hadn't even known about the damn extension, much less the due date. Of course, it was true he'd been pestering her for some time about a number of things that needed her attention, but she'd been focused on rehabbing her shoulder, mentally grappling with not being on the tour, dealing with the dawning reality that she'd probably never be going back, with having to retire before she was ready . . .

Suffice it to say, it had been a really rough year. And the government had *so* not been understanding about that fact. A lot like certain members of her family.

And now May was almost over, a new year almost half done, and this one wasn't going much better. Her life was still upside down, emotionally and financially, and she couldn't seem to find a way to balance it again. Which, admittedly, was why she and her accountant had had the falling out in the first place. He'd actually had the nerve to lecture her on developing proper postretirement spending habits! She'd laughed.

Well, she wasn't laughing now. And restraining her natural spirit—okay, temper—wasn't what put those ten grand-slam trophies on her mantelpiece, now, was it? "Alden, you know as well as I do that it was *my* face, *my* temperament on court and off, and *my* winning record that lined *your* company's pockets all those years." Gripping her cell phone so tightly it was a miracle it didn't snap in two, she slammed out of her car and stalked past the other three vehicles filling her four-car garage, before automatically punching in the security code and striding into her house. She stopped at the floor-to-ceiling picture window that made up the back wall on the main floor. "It's only been a little over a year."

"Almost two years," Alden mildly corrected.

"Twenty-one months since the injury," she shot back. "I only officially retired last September." That press conference had been exactly two days before the first lovely letter from the IRS had shown up. Talk about a bad week.

"You've been off the tour for two seasons, Tess. Two years in the tennis world is a long time when you're never coming back."

"I was number one for sixty-one straight weeks, and still top five when I went out, against girls a decade younger than me. People haven't exactly forgotten me."

"Martina Hingis," he said, adopting a slightly harder edge to his tone. "Monica Seles. Both former number ones, both multiple grand-slam winners, both retired before their time. How long afterward were you seeing their faces launching new ad campaigns?" He didn't wait for her to answer. "You didn't, because they weren't. It's a very competitive marketplace, Tess, you know that. We have to stay on the cutting edge of whatever sport we're associating with our product. And that means—"

"Snagging fresh meat," Tess snapped. "I get that. I know this is business, Alden. It's business for me, too. Something you seem to have overlooked here. I've held up my end all these years. Whatever happened to loyalty?"

Alden sighed deeply. "The fact that I'm speaking to you directly, and not your agent or manager, should tell you all you need to know."

"My management team didn't drop me, I dropped them!" Okay, so maybe that was stretching things a little. The official word was that they'd amicably agreed to part ways. What that really meant was that they'd found out about the heavy hit she'd taken as a result of last year's tax debacle—which she'd paid in full, thank you very much. Mostly to keep word of it out of the press, but still, it shouldn't have affected her viability as an asset to the agency. So what if she'd had to liquidate a few assets? Okay, more than a few. Okay, almost all of them. But honestly, some of them she hadn't even remembered she'd owned. An indication right there—outwardly, anyway—that things weren't that bad.

Maybe to some people's way of thinking, the tax debt had been kind of big... okay, so it had been close to eight figures. Her accountant hadn't been kidding about her neglect of certain business issues. Still, to her, that wasn't as big a deal as it might have been to some. Lesson learned. She'd just earn it back and be smarter next time. Offers poured in every day. Or they used to, but still, it would happen, she'd recover. And didn't she deserve some credit for paying it all off? Hell, it had been like having a giant international yard sale to come up with that kind of money. Did they have any idea how personally humiliating that had been? How hard to keep it out of the public eye? Like she needed more stress.

And yes, so her continued tangled financial picture hadn't been encouraging, what with April 15 rolling around almost right after she'd gotten done making the first payoff. With nothing new coming in, she'd had another little liquidation sale, and yes, it had zapped pretty much everything she had left. But all she needed was one or two little endorsement deals to get started, not too much to ask, to her way of thinking. She just wanted to keep a roof over her head. One roof! She'd sold all the others, hadn't she? Was it her fault the deals weren't being renewed? She'd placed that blame squarely on the agency. It was their job to get them to sign her, wasn't it? And they were mad at *her*?

Unfortunately, they hadn't appreciated her logic.

The bottom line was that they'd amicably agreed to sign a confidentiality statement saying they'd keep her less-than-flattering financial picture under wraps... as long as she agreed to terminate her contract with them effective immediately.

Almost a year before it was due to expire. Of course, she'd left their offices smugly certain she'd find new representation immediately. She always had before. So she'd lost a few contracts, so what? When the big boys came calling, renewing her major endorsement deals, every agency on both coasts would be begging to represent her again.

Which would have been supremely satisfying if it had happened that way. But here she was, still without representation. And Alden as her last hope. Yippee. And he was making it sound like, during the short time span from her injury to now, an entire era had passed her by.

So. Time to change tactics. She was all for histrionics if they were going to pay off, or if they simply made her feel better. But, just like on the court, when something wasn't working, you either changed your game, or you went home early. Perhaps now was the time to be a tad more conciliatory. Show that she understood the gravity of the situation. Lord knows it was pretty damn grave. "Alden," she said, forcing sweetness into her voice, "what if I fly to New York and we all sit down and discuss this, toss around a few ideas. Your company is known for being innovative. We just need to think outside the box a little. Shake things up."

"I don't think that's going to work for us, Tess. I'm sorry."

Staring down at her empty tennis courts, she finally ducked her chin and squeezed her eyes shut as she tried to come up with the right thing to say. She rubbed her fingers across her eyes, surprised to find they came away damp. Which pissed her off all over again. Panic wasn't a part of her makeup. She'd never been a handwringer and she didn't plan on starting now. She was a fighter, dammit.

"You're walking away from a good thing, Alden," she said firmly, hoping he mistook the slight hoarse edge in her voice for restrained temper. She tried to convince herself of that, too.

"Now that I'm a free agent, someone else is going to step up and reap those rewards."

"I wish you all the best, Tess," was all he said. "I really do." Then the line went dead.

Tess clicked the phone off, and barely resisted the urge to fling it full force at the plate glass. It was quite probable that Alden knew damn well there wasn't anyone else waiting in the wings to snap her up for a new deal. For all its international stature, the tennis industry was a tight little community. One where everybody knew everybody else's business, not to mention their dirty laundry. Since announcing her retirement, she'd worked her ass off to make damn sure nobody knew hers.

Judging by the questions the media shouted her way when she attended this event or that, she'd been mostly successful. But that couldn't last much longer. It was all about appearances and public perception. As long as the public thought she was still a winner, still a success story, still a hot property, then she was one. It was as simple as that, and as complicated as that. But she'd always been a winner. That part had been easy for her.

Only now there was nothing for her to win. And the companies who'd signed her to represent their products for the past decade were naming new faces. Fresher faces. Her window of income opportunity was rapidly shrinking and public perception could shift on a dime. Maybe she'd been shortsighted in assuming her endorsement deals would continue to finance her cash flow, but it was too late to shift gears now. Besides, what else was there?

Two years ago, at the age of twenty-seven, retirement had been relatively imminent, but not immediate. She'd thought she'd have a few years to plan things out, to think ahead, make sure she was secure when she left the tour behind, future plans all laid out. Well, her shoulder had had other ideas. One flying lunge on the hard courts at the U.S. Open the summer before last had changed everything. She'd landed smack down on her right shoulder, her serving shoulder, decimating the previous three repair jobs and abruptly ending her career. Not that she'd initially accepted that assessment. Or that of the surgeon who had tried his best to repair the damage one more time. It had taken nine months of grueling, heartbreaking rehabilitation before she'd finally been forced to admit that her shoulder wasn't ever going to recover to the point where she could compete on a world-class level again. The damage was too extensive.

She'd wanted it so badly, had focused so exclusively on returning, refusing to believe otherwise, she'd sort of let everything else go. Assuming, wrongly as it turned out, that she'd get it all back on track when she returned to the tour. To the only life she'd known since turning pro at sixteen years of age. And now she was on the verge of losing everything.

She looked at the small silver plate currently sitting on the second shelf in a glass trophy case that took up a fair amount of wall space on the front wall of her living room. It was the last one she'd ever earn, but it was a big one. There were four others just like it, each a smaller replica of the actual Wimbledon trophy, the Rosewater Dish, which stayed at the All England Club. With her name engraved on it five times, next to and around some of the all-time greats of the game.

All of whom probably invested their winnings, she thought with a scowl, *and were still comfortably living off of them today.* Still clutching the phone, she turned her gaze back to the courts below and once again tried to ignore the painful pang. Not the lingering one in her shoulder. The new one, somewhere in the vicinity of her heart. "You need to handle this better, dammit," she whispered, putting voice to a fear that had been growing rapidly as one sponsor after another walked away.

Fear was not in her vocabulary.

Yet here she was, scared shitless. And not a soul to turn to.

The one thing she still had in her favor was that the world at large generally assumed she'd wisely invested the multimillion-dollar fortune she'd amassed over the decade she'd spent in the pros. She'd bought this place for her twenty-third birthday and felt quite the grown-up at the time. There followed the flat in Paris, the summer house in the Hamptons, and that quaint little place outside of London that was so perfect and private when she was warming up for the grass-court season. And, of course, there were the cars. Some women collected shoes or jewelry, and they certainly had their place. But Tess was of the decided opinion that houses needed accessorizing, too. Every home should have one or two flashy vehicles parked out front. Sometimes three. Matching luggage was optional. But heavily recommended.

All of it, except the property on which she stood, was now gone. She pressed her forehead against the glass. So fast. It had all happened so damn fast. If her father or her older brother Wade ever found out? She shuddered. How often had they hounded her about long-term financial security? About hiring investment counselors and building a strong stock portfolio? But honestly, she'd made the money, why should she give it to someone else to spend for her? Spending it was half the fun. Okay, almost all of the fun. Next to actually winning it.

And her family certainly knew that when anyone tried to tell her what to do, she'd almost always do the opposite. Which made keeping a finance manager about as hard as keeping a coach. She was stubborn to a fault and a rebel to the end.

"Well, rebel," she muttered as she caught her reflection in the plate glass, "the end is currently staring you in the face. Not a real attractive picture, is it?"

Her cell phone rang just then, startling her. She didn't want to talk to anyone right at the moment. Maybe ever. She resolutely turned away from the view of the courts . . . and that lingering twinge of instinctive guilt she still felt because she wasn't out there right now practicing. There were no more tournaments. No more escaping from life's more serious issues by immersing herself in a hectic tour schedule. For some it was grueling, an impossible pace to maintain without burning out. Not for Tess. For her it had always felt like her private domain, her own little kingdom, which she thoroughly enjoyed ruling. Just her and her racket.

Tennis was the love of her life. Her absolute soul mate. Whether it be hard courts, grass, or clay, standing at the base line, looking across the net at the only thing standing between her and yet another victory, was the only time she felt completely, utterly at home.

So how dare her soul mate abandon her like that?

Shopping, she decided instantly. That's what she needed. A little retail therapy. Window shopping, she amended, remembering her maxed-out credit cards. She glanced down as her cell phone continued to chirp the theme from Pink Panther and noticed the incoming number. She hurriedly flipped it open, a smile already curving her lips. There was one person in the world she always wanted to talk to, no matter what.

"Hey there, brat, what's happening? Whipping asses and taking names like your big sister taught ya?"

"Not everyone considers a tennis court a battlefield." Bobby chuckled and she immediately felt herself relax. "But aye, aye, *mon generale,* the enemy has fallen again this week."

"That's my baby brother! Where are you, anyway?" She knew exactly where he was. In London, playing the Queen's Club tournament, a tune-up for Wimbledon. Why she bothered to pretend otherwise, especially with Bobby, she didn't know. Habit at this point, she supposed. A good part of last year had been spent solely focused on trying to heal enough to get back to the game, and it had been emotionally difficult keeping track of the tour results, knowing her ranking was sliding into oblivion as each week passed her by and everyone was accumulating points but her.

But when she'd realized last fall that her withdrawal from the tour was permanent... she'd gallivanted around the globe as if she hadn't a care in the world, as if she barely had time in her oh-so-busy life to keep track of something as mundane as tennis stats. That was *so* last year, after all.

But privately, she'd watched. And kept track. Still did. And it was like a dagger in her heart even now, every week when the rankings came out... and her name wasn't on the list. And wouldn't be ever again.

The outside world believed her life was a whirlwind of excitement, with offers simply pouring in. She'd read rumors of advertising campaigns, book deals in New York, Hollywood calling, begging her to consider a movie role she'd be perfect for. And she did her damnedest to let everyone think it was the truth, too.

If only. The sad thing was, that scenario was exactly what she'd expected her retired life to be all about. She'd honestly had visions of sitting back and sifting through the mountain of offers that would surely come cascading in, having the luxury of picking and choosing the best project for her. She'd be booked at least six months in advance, of course, right down to every lunch and every dinner.

Instead, she was sweating bullets day and night, praying for a solution to her money problems before the truth came out... and ruined any chance she had to ever get her life back on track.

"Actually, that's why I'm calling you," Bobby said.

Tess heard uncertainty in his tone, and immediately tensed. "What happened? You're not hurt are you? Does Wade or Dad know?"

He laughed again. "Jeez, you're worse than Mom was, you know that? Who'd have thought? If the world knew that beneath that tough bully exterior you were really just a big mushy marshmallow—"

Maybe she'd still have an income, she thought morosely. "They wouldn't believe it," she told him flatly. "And I bitch because I care. Besides, you know I promised Mom I'd look after you on tour."

"Yeah, I made her the same promise about you."

"Oh?" Tess said, honestly surprised. "First I've heard of that little deal." Their mother, Cissy McNamara, a young phenom herself, had briefly been a top-ten player back in the day. She'd retired from the tour only a few years after joining it, shortly after marrying Senator Frank Hamilton and getting pregnant with Wade. With a few trophies of her own already lining the mantel, she'd happily spent her remaining years raising her three kids, watching with enormous pride as her only daughter took up where she'd left off. She'd succumbed to ovarian cancer six years ago, right as Bobby was entering college, forgoing the pro tour until after he got his degree.

Every member of her family, in their own way, still suffered from the loss. Cissy had been the center cog from which all Hamilton family members operated; the determined, grounding force that held her strong and too-independent-to-her-way-of-thinking clan together. She'd been right, as it turned out. With her gone, they'd been cast adrift, and were pretty much making it up as they went along.

If she knew the mess Tess had made of her life...well, she wouldn't be exactly shocked. She was the only one, save for Bobby, who'd really understood Tess and accepted her faults and all. Had Cissy not married and left the tour early on, chances were she'd have been the Tess of her generation. Still, Tess hated feeling like she'd let any of her family down, especially her mom.

"So," she asked, forcing a bright note into her voice, "Mom asked *you* to watch after *me*? Sort of like putting the canary in charge of the cat."

"Yeah, I know." Bobby's dry laugh lifted her spirits like nothing else could. "Like I had a hope in hell of living up to it. You're not exactly baby-sitter-able. Hell, if Wade or Dad can't keep you pinned down, what chance do I have?"

Little did he know he was probably the only one who did have any sway over her. He was the biggest soft spot she had. Of course, she wasn't going to tell him that. "She was probably just trying to make you feel more mature. Give the baby of the family some responsibility."

"Hey now, I can be responsible."

Like she hadn't already gotten that earful from Wade and her father. It didn't matter that she wasn't playing anymore. *Bobby already has a financial manager, you should see his portfolio. Bobby has kept the same coach now for eighteen months and look how his game has improved.* Yeah, she knew how responsible he was. A shame she couldn't hate him for it. "Well, I'm still gonna boss you around no matter how much bigger your portfolio is than mine."

"Actually, that's why I'm calling."

Her stomach squeezed. Had he found out? She forced a laugh. "I don't need stock tips, Bobby." She needed an income before she could worry about how to invest it. "But thanks—"

"This isn't about money." She tried not to let him hear her major sigh of relief. "What, then? Oh, God, what'd I do now?" She'd long since learned that she didn't have to actually *do* anything to get blamed for something. Hell, she didn't even have to be on the same continent half the time. Trouble had a way of finding her even when she wasn't looking for it. Admittedly, this was probably because there had been a number of years when she had been. "I swear, I haven't left the area in days. It wasn't me. I didn't do it. I've never even met him. The baby isn't mine. Whatever."

He laughed. "Relax, you didn't do anything." He paused. "This week, anyway."

"Har har. So spill it already."

"I was calling to tell you that your baby-sitting, bossy-older-sister days are numbered. Someone else has applied for the job of telling me what to do."

"Oh? What, Wade is going to be the boss of you now? This can't be true. He'd have to lighten his client load so he only has to try twice as many cases as a mere mortal. Or does Dad have an offspring we're not aware of?" She could make the joke because there was no way the "esteemed gentleman from California" had ever done, or would ever do, anything remotely untoward. The craziest thing he'd ever done was marry the little darling of tennis, Cissy McNamara, emerging phenom and party-circuit regular.

Bobby snorted. "Oh yeah, that's it. And even if aliens did inhabit his body long enough for him to do something that unlikely, Mom would prove there is such a thing as reincarnation, just so she could come back and kick his cheating, lying ass. He'd never have risked it, anyway. Think of the damage to his pristine, much vaunted political career."

Tess smiled briefly, picturing it. "How true. So then, who is this amazing paragon of virtue with an unfortunate bent for self-torture?" There was a short pause, but Tess could feel the tension crackling through the phone lines. Her smile dipped. "Bobby? You're not in some kind of trouble are you?" Because that would shock her almost more than her father doing something illicit.

Bobby was the golden child of the Hamilton clan. Wade had

the smarts and the Hamilton drive and determination, but he was kind of an ass about it. Tess was brilliant on the court, but off the court, well, her faults had been well documented. On several continents. Leaving the youngest Hamilton to claim the cherished center-of-attention spot. Which he'd always done quite effortlessly. It was hard to hold it against him, though. He was charming, good-looking, smart, and accomplished, not to mention always quick with a smile or a selfless gesture. If he wasn't so damn adorable and sincere, he'd be disgusting.

At twenty-five he had a college degree from Stanford, a top-fifty ranking in the ATP, a gorgeous British girlfriend, and several major endorsement deals—which was almost unheard of for a doubles player. It was the dimples. She was convinced. It didn't hurt that he never yelled at referees or tournament directors. And never got his picture splashed all over the tabloids for being where he wasn't supposed to be, with someone he definitely wasn't supposed to be with.

There came a nervous chuckle on the other end that sounded nothing like her happy-go-lucky brother.

"For God's sake, tell me already!"

"Andrea and I are getting married," he blurted out in a rush. "I proposed last night and she said yes."

Her first reaction was to laugh. "You know, you said that like it comes as some great shock to you! Of course she said yes, you dolt." Andrea was gorgeous, talented, and quite successful in her own right—and she'd have been a fool to pass up her baby brother. Bobby Hamilton was a total catch. Just ask any female on the planet. "But I can't believe you popped the question right before Wimbledon. You've got Queen's Club, then two slams back-to-back, *and* she's getting ready to launch her new line after the Open, in the fall, right? When are you guys gonna have time to—"

"That's the other reason I'm calling," he broke in. "We don't want a long engagement. And since everyone we both know will be in London for the tournament, we figured—"

"You're getting married *now?*"

"After Queen's, before Wimbledon, yeah."

"As in, before *this coming* Wimbledon? The one next month?" Tess struggled to assimilate it all. "Now I understand your shock that she accepted your ridiculous proposal. I can't believe Andrea is agreeing to this. You have told her your crazy idea, right? Because men can be really stupid, but I always had higher hopes for you, B.S."

Bobby groaned at the reviled nickname. "It's all fine, really."

"She's a fashion designer and you're rushing her to the altar? Are you kidding me? It's not all fine, trust me."

"She designs sportswear," Bobby said, as if that made a difference.

"The woman's whole life revolves around clothes," Tess pointed out. "And you want her to toss together a wedding in less than a month." She snorted. "Honestly. Men."

"It was her idea!"

That stopped her. "Really?"

"Yeah, really."

"Well, hold on to this one, because that's blind love right there."

"Har har," he said now. "So you gonna lay off me and hop a plane over here or what?"

"Gee, with an invite like that, I can hardly say no," she said dryly. "What did Dad and Wade say? Are they going to be able to juggle their schedules to get over there in time?"

"I'm not sure. I, uh, I called you first, T."

And she'd given him a hard time. Tess's heart melted. Bobby might make her crazy with his easy perfection, but there was a reason everybody loved him. He was so damn earnest. He'd never have to worry about his postretirement lifestyle. With or without his investment portfolio, people naturally gravitated toward Bobby Hamilton. Well, they gravitated toward his sister, too. But with Bobby, it was for all the good reasons. "Thank you," she said more quietly. "I, uh . . ."

"God, I can't stand it when you're speechless. It scares me," he teased, clearly happy with himself for doing it to her anyway. "Just say you'll be there."

"Of course I will." Even if she had to hock something to pay for airfare. Which she very well might. "Wait a minute," she said, alarm and dread suddenly swamping her. "I don't have to actually be *in* this thing, do I?"

"Now you sound like Wade. Can't be bothered to put out a little effort when there isn't anything in it for you. And since when haven't you liked putting out?"

"Oh, you want me not to be speechless, you keep making comments like that. I'll ring Andrea right up and tell her all about your little run-in with my friend Bambi Sutherland the summer of your freshman year. I'm sure I still have my yearbook around here somewhere where she wrote on your picture, and I quote—"

"Okay, okay, you win."

She grinned. "Don't I always? You should know better by now."

"Yeah, yeah."

"And I wasn't balking at being in the wedding, in a general way. Surely Andrea of all people would pick out something not entirely horrific for her bridesmaids to wear. It's just that . . . well, you know how it is with me. Something bad will happen. And in London of all places. The tabs over there look for reasons to trash me. They hate me."

"They love you. You sell papers. Hell, you've put half the paparazzi's children through college by now."

She snorted. "Yeah, well, that kind of dysfunctional love I do not need. And neither do you on your wedding day."

"Not to worry. We're not having all the hoopla. Andrea has no family to speak of, just close friends and professional contacts. It will probably be a civil ceremony, small, no attendants and all that stuff. We just want the people we love and care about to share the moment with us. So say you'll be there and shut up already."

"You shut up already."

"You."

"You." She smiled, hearing her mother's *"Come on, you two!"* echo clearly through her mind. "Of course I'll be there."

"And you'll call Dad and Wade and tell them, get them to come?"

"Bobby!"

"You're the best. I knew I could count on you. Love you!"

And then he was gone.

Tess sighed and clicked off, but she was smiling as she shook her head. It would be so much easier if she could just get mad at the guy. She didn't relish being the one to tell the rest of the family about the sudden wedding. Not that Dad or Wade would be upset about the engagement. They'd known it was probably heading that way, as she had. The abbreviated time frame, on the other hand, would be an issue. Both her father and big brother lived by their BlackBerry schedulers. This would disrupt the routine. Where Wade and her father were concerned, rule number one was never disrupt the routine!

Ah well. She grinned as she flipped her phone back open. She might have learned that lesson at an early age, but that didn't mean she'd ever paid any particular attention to it. Hell, if she wasn't around to rattle the esteemed senator's carefully maintained cage every once in a while, who would? Her little rebellions with her father used to exasperate her mom to no end. But privately, Tess was pretty sure her mother thought it was a good thing that life didn't always go by Dad's schedule.

She snapped the phone shut a second later as another thought occurred to her. She sank down on the arm of her Harry Braxton davenport. She always thought of the piece that way. Not that she'd had a clue who Harry Braxton was—or that davenport was a fancy name for couch—but the stylist who'd done her house assured her in no uncertain terms that he was the second coming of modern retro furniture design. All she knew was that it was comfortable and didn't stain.

At the moment, however, she wasn't thinking about furniture durability, she was more concerned with her own. London. Wimbledon. Everybody who was anybody in the industry would be there.

On the one hand she wanted to be pretty much anywhere else on earth than around the very people who, when they found out she was broke and unemployable, would quite enjoy seeing her taken down a peg or six. But on the other hand, those very people were also her only viable source pool when it came to reversing said bank account and job status. Unlike her brother, she didn't have a degree to fall back on. Tennis—and being a tennis celebrity—was all she knew. And to be honest, all she really wanted to know.

The trick was going to be figuring out how to make the rounds, schmooze... and at the same time not let the media or, more important, her family find out about the predicament she'd gotten herself into. Then there was that other sticky little issue. She was going to have to maintain a certain lifestyle while in town. You had to be money to make money. Or something like that, anyway. Nobody wanted to latch on to a star that was descending, as Alden and all the reps before him had made so abundantly clear. She'd have to hit the town and the party circuit with stilettos blazing, and somehow—discreetly—find someone who was still willing to sign her to a deal. Any kind of deal. She'd hawk just about anything at this point.

All she had to do now was figure out how to finance her little plan.

Chapter 2

Gabrielle Fontaine's eyebrows shot up. "You want me to go *where?"*

Max Fontaine watched his younger sister flounce across their hotel room and flop onto the couch with the kind of drama only a sixteen-year-old girl could evoke. He struggled to keep his tone even. "Think of it as a vacation."

"I don't *need* a vacation. I need a coach, dammit."

"Don't swear."

She merely rolled her eyes at him, then huffed as she crossed her arms across her chest.

"And I think we need to take a short break before we recruit someone new."

She looked at him as if he'd sprouted another head. He wished. Two brains would come in handy when dealing with a recalcitrant, bullheaded, thinks-she-knows-every-damn-thing teenager. Especially when said teenager knew exactly what buttons to push.

"I know you're still disappointed that I didn't go further in Paris," she told him, "but give me a break. I drew Serena in the first round, so are you kidding me? My first grand slam and I get Wonder Woman on Day One. All that hard work to qualify and then, wham-bam-thank-you-ma'am, I'm gone."

Max shot her a warning look. "You know damn—darn—well that I'm not disappointed in you. Not everyone plays their first match of their first grand slam on a stadium court in front of sixteen thousand screaming fans. And you pushed her to three sets, Gaby, something even the top-ten players haven't been able to do since sometime during the middle of last year. Everybody's talking about it."

"Then I came here and made it exactly one round further in Birmingham. Oh yeah, everybody's talking. And what they're saying is that the junior-circuit phenom isn't so phenomenal when playing against the big girls. Some of whom are barely a year or two older than me."

"And have already been playing on tour for a year or more."

"And whose fault is it I haven't been on tour for the past year?" she groused, even though she knew that was a dead-end argument.

Max didn't even go there. Gaby had known for a long time that he had no intentions of putting her on tour before she finished school. Even then he thought that was too young. He'd have liked to see her play through college, earn a degree. But he'd known that was unlikely. She had such a fire in her, a burning passion to play, and she was just too damn good. To top it off, she'd worked just as hard off the courts, finishing her tutoring and getting her GED early, leaving him little choice but to cut her loose this year and let her try her hand on the pro circuit. And even now she was still in a hurry.

"Cut yourself some slack, Gabrielle. You're doing exactly what we hoped you'd do."

"*We* meaning you and stupid Sven. You might not care, but I wanted to go further in Paris. And I certainly expected to this week. I know I can do it. I just need a coach who understands me." She glared at him, all accusation and daring him to say otherwise.

Like he was the one who threw temper tantrums on and off the court. Like he was the one who had to make every little damn thing some huge melodramatic event. As a junior, the only reason he could get the top coaches to agree to work with her was because, as an athlete, she had a ridiculous amount of natural talent. He tried to blame it on hormones, or some other mysterious becoming-a-woman estrogen thing. But it didn't really matter why. What mattered was that he find some way to deal with it. To deal with her.

With more patience than he thought he still possessed, he took a steadying breath and crossed the room, taking a seat next to her. "Come on, Gaby," he said calmly, focusing all of his attention on her.

She kept her gaze averted, but he just waited. He knew a few buttons, too. Finally she shifted her steely, unrepentant gaze to him. It was a small capitulation, but a telling one for anybody who knew her. And no one knew Gabrielle Fontaine better than her big brother.

"You convinced me you were ready to move up, but—"

"I am," she said with absolute certainty. "You and I both know it."

He did know it. She'd obliterated the juniors to the point where there was nowhere else for her to go but pro. Truth be told, he was the one who hadn't been ready. He'd held her back as long as he could, keeping her as protected as possible from the big bad world of the women's tour. Not that competing on the junior level was a walk in the park. She'd been an international attention-getter for some time now, but on a much smaller scale.

Only the tennis world really paid attention to the junior phenoms. Now she was on the main stage, with the whole world watching. An enormous amount of pressure had been brought to bear on her as the next great hope for the American women's game.

He'd prepared her for that as much as he could, and carefully selected the initial events she would play in, keeping them well paced and her overall schedule light for her first year. Professional tennis was a sport populated by teenagers, so she was far from alone out there, but he'd seen too many burn out or end their careers early due to injury from overextending themselves and putting too much of a strain on their still growing bodies. On top of that, they had the international media paying attention now since her debut in Paris. It didn't hurt that she was beautiful, flamboyant, and confident bordering on cocky. Okay, maybe not bordering. She was making quite the splash already and it scared the hell out of him in ways he hadn't been prepared for.

He'd been almost relieved when she'd lost early this week. London media was the worst and he was thankful she was out of the spotlight for now. She'd been given a wild card into Wimbledon, her second grand slam of the year, starting in a few weeks. They could both use the break.

He'd been more worried about the tour pressures than the media attention, but her very confidence in herself insulated her somewhat. Gaby was so sure of her abilities that the pressures and international-scale expectations didn't seem to faze her. It seemed normal to her for people to expect great things of her, since she expected them from herself, as well. She only seemed to get bent out of shape with her assumptions about *his* expectations of her.

As brother, mentor, manager, guidance counselor, and most important, the only family she had left in the world, he worried constantly about whether he was making the right choices for her. Especially lately when her temperament careened from typical teenager, to tyrant, to woman-wise-beyond-her-years. Often in a breathtakingly short time span.

Now more than ever he wished Gaby had a female influence in her life, someone to maybe soften her up a little. Even a female coach would be welcome, but Gaby had gone through the few they'd tried like water through a sieve. Male coaches had slightly better luck, but didn't last much longer. And while they'd had varying degrees of success in molding her game, none of them had forged any inroads into molding her temperament. That job, apparently, was destined to remain his and his alone. Lucky him.

"I just don't see why I'm being punished with this stupid spa thing," Gaby insisted, drawing him from his thoughts.

"You know," he gently chided, "most people wouldn't view a few weeks stay at a place called Glass Slipper as punishment."

Gaby snorted. "Glass Slipper. I'm no princess."

"You're telling me," Max muttered before he could catch himself.

But rather than flip out, Gaby laughed, though it was totally sardonic in tone. The going-on-thirty-year-old surfaced once more. He wished he was better at predicting that, but he knew it was a fairly hopeless expectation.

"Exactly," she said airily. "So why try to pretend otherwise? No amount of time spent at some posh spa is going to magically transform me into the lovely, obedient young lady you so yearn for me to be."

"That's not true."

She leveled an amused smile at him. "Which? About it taking more than two weeks? Or you yearning for me to find my inner good girl?"

"Both, actually," he said, momentarily surprising her. He immediately capitalized on gaining the rare edge. "I don't want them to change you, I want them to help you." He held up a hand to stall her, surprised when she respected it. "And I don't want you turned into something you're not, no matter what you think." He leaned forward and took her hands, squeezing them together between his own. "You've been amazing these past couple of months. Most girls your age couldn't handle a tenth of what you have. I couldn't be more proud of you and how you've handled the tour so far."

Instead of being touched by his sincere proclamation, she snorted and tugged her hands free. The tyrant had returned. "Don't bullshit me, Max. Just tell me the real reason you want to dump me in this stupid, godforsaken 'life spa' for two weeks. Vacation plans of your own? Haven't been laid in a while? Because I have no problem with that. Really. You work too hard, you have no life. In case you haven't noticed, I can take perfectly good care of myself. I don't need baby-sitting." She flicked her hand at him. "So go on and have your little fling. You have my blessing."

Max clenched his jaw. "First of all, enough with the swearing already. And you know perfectly well that I'd never just take off and—"

Gaby barked a laugh. "Exactly!" She slapped her hands on her thighs and shoved to a stand. "God, Max, you're so uptight you don't even know how repressed you are."

"I'm not repressed!" he spluttered as he shot off the couch after her, wondering once again just where and when he'd lost control of this conversation.

"When was the last time you got laid? Hell, when was the last time you even went on a date? And I mean with a woman who wasn't tour personnel, a marketing rep, or a sponsor? In other words, not a business dinner? Honestly, I have more fun than you, and I have no social life."

Max stood there, hands on his hips, fully prepared to deliver a perfectly worded, stinging retort guaranteed to shut down this particular subject. Only nothing came to mind. Mostly because there was a hint of a chance that she actually had a point. But he'd let her pummel him physically if necessary before he'd give her that kind of power.

"If you don't have plans for the next few weeks, maybe you should make some," she went on, goaded by his uncharacteristic silence. "Go pick someone up. Everyone thinks you're kind of a hottie. For an old guy, anyway. Though if they saw you in those ratty old sweats you insist on—"

"They're my fraternity sweats, and I'd hardly wear them out on—wait a minute, I'm a *what*? What did you just say?" Max raked his hands through his hair, completely lost now. "Who says that about me?"

Gaby sighed in teenaged disgust. "You are so hopeless. Of course, that you're so totally oblivious to it is part of what gets them, you know? I mean, I know it's because you're too anal about every last detail of my every living and breathing moment. But to them it comes off like this cute, endearing sort of earnestness."

"*Them?* Who the hell is 'them'?"

"Don't swear," she said, smiling broadly, vastly amused at his complete consternation. "I could give you a list. But do me one favor, okay? You're thirty, so no hitting on anyone under, like, twenty-five. It would be so embarrassing." She lowered her gaze. "For both of us."

"I'm not going to hit on anybody," he insisted, his mind still racing along this surprising, if unbelievable, new path.

She crossed the sitting room that connected their two bedrooms. "You know, the more I think about it, the more I think you should. Date, I mean. Might do us both some good. Give me a little room to breathe, and loosen up that tight-assed, overprotective tendency of yours, all in one shot." With a grin and a wiggle of her fingers, she disappeared into her room. Once again, having the last word.

He couldn't help it. She'd left him with his mouth hanging open. What was it the Brits called it? Gobsmacked? Didn't he have enough to deal with? She was just being ridiculous, but even if it were true, it was more than he was prepared to deal with.

God, life had been so much easier before she grew breasts and started realizing boys were good for more than beating on the tennis court.

With a confused sigh, Max walked to her still open bedroom door. He leaned on the frame and watched as she flopped across the bed, magazine in one hand, while booting up her laptop with the other. If he didn't know better, he'd think she was just a typical teenager with nothing more on her mind than boys and the latest fashion tips. If only.

He let the room fall silent, save for the clicking sound as she typed on her keyboard. Perhaps it was time he admitted that cajoling and psychology were never going to work with her. She'd always been too sharp to fall for that. Maybe it was time to try something completely new. *Desperate times called for desperate measures,* he thought, then plunged ahead with plan B. Okay, so it was more like plan X, version 7.0, but who was keeping track?

Instead of thinking of her as a naive sixteen-year-old—which she obviously wasn't—maybe he'd have more success if he appealed to the older-than-her-years side of her. What the hell did he have to lose? "You've grown up fast, Gaby. You're light-years past most girls your age. I know that and respect it. But if you think about it, I know you'd agree that it's been an insulated life, too, in a lot of ways. Playing tennis full-time, learning from tutors, constantly traveling. And now things are changing even faster. You're going to face things on tour I can't prepare you for."

"Your point?" she said, not breaking stride in her keyboard tapping.

"I'm asking you to be mature enough to recognize that we all need help from time to time. I think you could stand a little life coaching from the Glass Slipper people." He stuck his hands in the pockets of his jeans. "And yeah, maybe I do need a break for a little life coaching of my own."

That had her rolling to her back, eyes wide in surprise. "What is this? Saint Max admitting that maybe he's not perfect?"

Now it was Max's turn to snort. "I've never pretended to be perfect or a saint." He smiled. "In fact, I feel far from that most every minute of every day."

Surprising him, Gaby's quicksilver mood changed yet again and her expression immediately softened. She scooted off the bed, came over, and wrapped her arms around him, putting her head on his shoulder. "God, I'm a horrible sister, aren't I?" she said, completely sincere in that sudden way only she could be. "I'm sorry I'm such a bitch."

Max's heart melted, as it always did when this side of Gaby—just as real as all the others, only making increasingly rarer appearances of late—surfaced. He smiled tiredly and pressed a kiss against her hair as he hugged her back. "Not horrible, no. But on the bitch thing? Totally," he said, in a teen-speak accent.

She laughed even as she half-jokingly sucker punched him. "You *so* do not do that right. Please don't try to impress younger women with your mad slang skills. They won't be able to reject you because they'll be laughing too hard. But they will reject you."

He rubbed his abs with one hand, but pulled her close with the other. "I think I'd figure it out, anyway. But thanks."

He hugged her with one arm, which she returned, before looking up and catching his eye. It was moments like this, when her guard was down, and he saw all the love and fear and hope in her eyes—all thrust directly at him, trusting that he'd take care of it, take care of her, no matter what she did, what she said—that terrified him most. He hadn't been kidding a moment ago. Eight years into it, fully half of her life, and he felt more unqualified than ever to be responsible for her upbringing.

Max had been twenty-two and fresh out of college when his father and Gaby's mother had been killed in a car accident while touring Italy. Overwhelmed by the suddenness of it, and all the attendant details that had been left to him to resolve as Trenton Fontaine's only son, when it had come to Gabrielle, he'd done the only thing he could do. Take care of her.

Max's mother—Trenton Fontaine's first wife—hadn't been any help. Already on husband number four, she'd wanted nothing to do with the offspring of the woman her first husband had left her for. Through most of high school and all of college, Max had been largely estranged from his international financier father, and consequently knew next to nothing about his much younger half sister other than she was already something of a budding tennis prodigy even at such a young age.

Their first meeting had been at the funeral and it hadn't gone especially well. A little darling she was not, but then, she'd just lost the only family she'd ever known, so he hadn't expected much to begin with. Then he'd learned that Gaby's mother had no family, and as the only legal adult and next of kin in his father's family, Max either accepted taking on guardianship of his little sister . . . or allowed her to be shipped off into the state system. Which meant there was no other choice.

The only blessing—if there was one in all that mess—was that Trenton Fontaine had left the two of them quite well taken care of financially. So at least Max hadn't had to worry about that while figuring out what the hell to do about his talented, snotty, eight-year-old precocious sister's welfare. His father's lawyer had suggested he enroll her in a private girls' boarding school, so Max could get on with his life. They'd only have to see each other during holidays and summer breaks.

Admittedly, it had been a tempting idea, for about two seconds. But it would have meant abandoning her all over again. Having been largely abandoned by his own father, and his mother, as well, seeing as she had always been more focused on finding her next husband than worrying too much about whatever Max was doing . . . he couldn't do that to Gabrielle.

For all that his father and his young second wife had traveled extensively, from what he could tell, they had doted on their only child. Perhaps too much. Private lessons, private tutors, private coaches. She was both an athlete and debutante-in-the-making. Part of Max was a bit jealous, but there was little use in nursing old grudges, and besides, it was hardly Gaby's fault.

Looking at her now, it was impossible to imagine what life would have been like without her. And he didn't want to. Come what may, they were family. It might not be the kind of family he'd yearned for growing up, but for better or worse, it was the one he'd been handed. And it was a damn sight better than having none at all. Which was probably why he was so protective of it, of her. He wanted to do right by her in the way he wished his parents had done right by him.

He pushed her dark, fringy bangs off her forehead. She was still too wise for her years. Her body, her brains, and her talent had all matured at a far-too-rapid pace. But sometimes those dark eyes were still the same ones staring up at him out of that eight-year-old's tearstained face. Defiant and terrified all at the same time, as she demanded to know what in the hell he was going to do with her.

In retrospect, he supposed he should have given up trying to get her not to swear right then.

"Humor me these next two weeks, 'kay?" he asked softly. "Worst case is you'll be pampered and get a little rest." A smile kicked up one corner of his mouth. "Best case is you'll get a break from your pain-in-the-ass brother."

Her own smile was dry. "That just might be worth being poked and prodded at." The smile faded and those gray eyes went old soul on him, but she kept her arms looped around his waist. "But I need to gear up for Wimbledon. I don't want a break right now."

She said it so earnestly, with such honest conviction, he wavered. But only for a second. "This is your first time. Not your last. And you have plenty of time to prepare. You'll get court time while you're gone, too. I know you can't take a complete break."

She sighed, but she didn't rebel again. "So what exactly are they going to do with me?"

Max tried not to sink back against the door in relief. The battle was over. He didn't bother bullshitting her. "They specialize in helping people reach their potential. From personal changes to professional ones."

Gaby gave him a look of wary surprise. But he didn't miss the curiosity. Good. Max was banking on that last part being what got her to open up enough to let the ladies at Glass Slipper do their thing.

"Pro athletes, too?" she asked.

Max shrugged. "All walks. What sets them apart is that they focus in on the specific needs of their clients . . . and do whatever they need to in order to get them the exact help they need."

Gaby frowned now and Max felt her tense. "Just what kind of 'help' do you think I need? Because if you're hiring some kind of shrink to psychoanalyze my game—"

"Your biggest strength, outside that wicked slice serve to the outside, is that you have the most naturally focused mental game on the planet. So the last thing you need is anyone screwing with your head."

Gaby's mouth opened in automatic retort, then closed again as his words sank in. "Uh. Wow. Thanks," she said, favoring him with a sheepish smile.

He tapped a finger to her cheek. "You should do that more often."

"What, be humble?" she said, only half-teasing. "I know I can be a brat. And yes, maybe I have a teeny little problem with anger management, but it's part of what helps me stay focused on the court. If I vent as I go, I stay tuned in."

" 'Teeny little problem'?" Max just gave her a look. "But that wasn't what I was referring to." He framed her face with his hands and pushed his palms up so the corners of her mouth curved. "You need to smile more. Looks good on you."

"I smile all the time," she said through her contorted lips.

Max grinned. "I don't mean that bloodlust victory smile."

Gaby pulled away and gave him a shot of the very smile he was talking about.

"Yeah, that one," he said as she stuck her tongue out at him.

"So when am I being committed?" she asked, flopping back on the bed, all sixteen-year-old once again.

"Tomorrow morning. Oh-nine-hundred."

She groaned, but was already clacking away at her keyboard. "No boot-camp references. I'm already boycotting this whole thing, anyway."

"Gaby—"

"Oh, I'm going. But no one says I have to make it easy on them."

Max just groaned, but he knew better than to take the bait. She'd go, and she might pout about it, but he knew she wouldn't intentionally make life a living hell for the Glass Slipper folks. At least, he hoped she wouldn't.

She tossed him a glance. "And just so you know, I'm only agreeing to do this on one condition."

"Which is?"

"That while I'm making a concerted effort to learn . . . whatever the hell it is they're supposed to be teaching me . . . you have to make a concerted effort to go out there and get some action."

"I'm not making some kind of sordid deal about my sex life with my sixteen-year-old sister."

"Um, ew?" she told him, making a face. "I'm not asking for details. Just promise me you'll get out there and . . . you know." She lowered her chin and stared at him. "You do know, right? I mean, you went to college. Do I have to have 'the talk' with you?"

Now Max rolled his eyes. "I am not having this conversation with you." He backed out of the room to the sounds of Gaby's laughter.

"Just promise me you'll use protection," she called out.

"Not listening," he shouted back.

"And you wonder where I get it from!"

Chapter 3

Comfortably ensconced in the Admiral's Lounge at Miami International Airport, Wade Hamilton leaned back in the padded leather chair and propped his ankle on his other knee. His immaculately tailored suit moved easily on his large, lean frame. A fact Tess knew he was well aware of and played to his advantage whenever possible. The prodigal son incarnate. Currently starring in the lifetime role of black sheep, Tess tried hard not to be bitter. Occasionally she was even successful.

"So, how's retired life treating you, Tess?" Wade asked, his I'm-harmless-really courtroom smile firmly in place. "Looking forward to the buzz of London, I bet. Make the rounds."

Many a jury had been fooled by that easygoing smile. Not that they should feel bad at being duped. It was the same smile that invited a person to share everything from insider stock tips to where the bodies were buried. And they often did. Much to the district attorney's dismay.

Tess, of course, knew better than to offer up any tidbit of her life to him. Her shark of a defense attorney older brother had never respected her career choice. To him, playing tennis for a living was something along the lines of having a glorified hobby that happened to occasionally hit pay dirt. Of course, he realized their beloved mother had played professionally, too, but she'd also retired young and "done the right thing" by marrying and starting a family. Now that Tess had retired, with no husband waiting in the wings to settle down and procreate with, Wade was constantly on her to finally get a real job.

"Yes, Wade," she said, a patently false smile curving her lips. "What would us party girls do if we didn't have the nightlife to focus all our dreams and aspirations on? Not to mention a place to show off our latest Dooney & Bourke clutch."

"I wasn't aware that you had any left. Dreams or aspirations," he clarified. "We all know you have enough accessories to fill a small boutique of your own." He lifted his eyebrows in faux inspiration. "Perhaps that is something you could do with all your spare time. Lord knows you're as much a professional shopper as you were a tennis player. Surely women everywhere could use your expertise in selecting just the right shoes to go with their eye color."

Tess clasped her hands beneath her chin in equally faux excitement. "Why, Wade, darling, what a marvelous idea! It would be like getting to play dress up every day. Oh, goody!" She dropped her hands and her pretense. "I'll keep it in mind for when I get truly desperate."

He shrugged, his smile steady as he spread his hands in a pretend gesture of admiration. "I can't imagine what it must be like having fulfilled all of my goals before reaching thirty."

She didn't bother to respond. She knew he wasn't done with his cross yet. No point in feeding him any more ammo than she already had. As usual, she was right.

"No matter how many titles you collected, now you're staring down the rest of your life and . . . what is there?" he asked, seemingly all concerned about her well-being, but she knew better. He just liked one-upping her in front of their father. "You have to be asking yourself how fulfilling it really was, all that time spent trophy collecting," he continued.

Why didn't juries see just how smug and condescending he was? Infuriating, really. It was so obvious to her.

"What can you take from that into the rest of your life? And I'm not talking about the money, Tess. I'm talking about a sense of purpose. All you know is tennis. Where are those trophies going to take you now except on an occasional trip down memory lane? You know what I mean?" He folded his hands across his stomach and leaned back.

And . . . the defense rests. Slice backhand serve into her court.

She glanced across the table at her father, whose nose was still buried in his copy of *The New Yorker.* How convenient. *Thanks again, Dad,* she thought silently. And yes, she knew exactly what her lovely, oh-so-benevolent older brother meant, all right. Lord knows she'd heard it in one form or another from him for years. Of course, in the past, her healthy annual income had usually shut him up. They both knew that despite his amazing success as a trial attorney, she'd still outearned him for years. But Wade was smart enough not to try cases he couldn't win, especially with her. It was tempting to toss that in his face once again. But she wasn't quite sure even she had the moxie to pull off a bravura performance like that at the moment. And if, God forbid, he got even a whiff of a suspicion about the current state of her finances . . . well, it simply didn't bear contemplating.

Still, she wasn't about to start off several days of enforced close familial contact by letting him get an edge on her. She had other weapons she could use. Tess mentally wound up for the return passing shot, right down the line, but her father cut them both off.

"Now, now," their father said, not bothering to look up. "You two settle down." Like they were both twelve or something.

Which, come to think of it, probably wasn't that far off the mark. That had been one of the main reasons she'd left California to live and train three thousand miles away in Florida. But she wasn't going to let Wade get away with this. He was insufferable enough. He rarely underestimated his opponent, but he did it with her all the time. One thing earning those trophies had taught her was how to win at any cost. If she couldn't outserve or outhit her opponent, the occasional drop shot wasn't beneath her. She sent her brother a smile that to anyone else would have looked affectionate bordering on adoring. Wade, of all people, should have known better.

She waited until he reached for his drink, then turned her attention to their father, and said, "It's sort of hard to believe that Bobby is going to be the first one of us down the aisle, isn't it?"

Tess savored a very pleasurable moment or two, enjoying the sound of Wade trying not to choke on the sip he'd just taken. She didn't have to look at him to know he was shooting invisible daggers of death her way. She was well aware of the Pandora's box she'd just opened. *Open a boutique, my ass,* she thought, a tad smug now that she'd leveled the playing field.

Wade's continued eligible-bachelor status was his one Achilles' heel with their father. Who wasn't all that happy about her lack of spousal prospects, either, but the crucial difference was, she didn't care if their father lectured her until he was blue in the face about her inability to settle down and pop out grandbabies. Or red in the face, as was the more accurate description. Another bonus to living three thousand miles away. She didn't have to endure the Senator Hamilton parental filibusters except on holidays and the very occasional family event.

Wade, on the other hand, got an earful constantly. And smarted mightily over it. As the gifted, perfect oldest child, that was one area where he continually let his father down. Tess could have told Wade what his problem was, if he'd ever bothered to ask. Like that would happen. Her brother was movie-star good-looking, had a career that was on a track so upwardly mobile it would hit zero gravity any day now, and a bank account that reflected his enormous success as one of the best defense attorneys in Monterey County. Hell, the whole West Coast most likely.

The problem with Wade was, he was so busy being successful, building his golden portfolio, and becoming the shining beacon of litigation for one and all, that he'd forgotten to have a life. Sure, he played golf and racquetball and regularly attended social functions, but all of those were merely extensions of his office. He was as apt to be doing business on the sixteenth green or with a squash racket in his hand, as he was in his well-appointed offices in Carmel. Not only did the women in his life come in second to his job, it was a distant, poor second, at best. Wade wasn't attracted to doormats or gold diggers, which was a shame, really, because it would take a rare specimen of a successful, bright, attractive woman, to put up with being second. So rare, in fact, she'd yet to be discovered. And just like that, one of the state's most eligible bachelors was known around town as a rather undesirable catch.

Franklin Hamilton carefully folded the corner of the page he was reading, marking it for future perusing, before laying the magazine down on the table and gifting his two oldest children with his wisdom.

Tess tried not to smirk as she awaited his speech. She loved it when a game plan paid off. It had been her idea for her father and older brother to meet her in Miami so they could fly together to Heathrow. Not because she wanted to spend family time together, as they'd assumed, but because she'd known her father would have his secretary book all three tickets and pick up the tab. Quite clever of her, really.

And first-class airfare was well worth sitting through a lecture she'd heard many times before. He'd been all but chomping at the bit to deliver his little speech about their inadequacy when it came to providing him with a legacy. Or as most people called them, grandchildren. Ever the dutiful daughter—all right, all right, so that was an overstatement of epic proportions, but she did give back when she could—she was quite happy to give him an opening.

Tess picked up her dry martini and settled back in her chair. Frank Hamilton never gave short speeches. Just ask his constituents and fellow politicians. Or his children. She crossed one leg over the other, mirroring her brother, even if her faded low-riders and beat-up Nikes didn't provide quite the same picture of aplomb and success his Armani suit and Bruno Magli loafers did. Something Wade would have definitely made a comment on at any other time, and about which she'd have enjoyed badgering him right back. But neither of them dared, not when the Esteemed Gentleman from California had the floor.

"You know, Tess," her father began, turning his craggy, tanned face to her, his eyes still a laser-sharp, icy blue.

She could feel Wade's smug smile next to her, as he basked in the glow of not being the one singled out first. That was okay, she'd make sure he got his.

"It's been a while now, going on two years, in fact—"

"I didn't decide to retire for certain until just this past September," she corrected him, knowing better, but saying it anyway. "You can't count the first year. I was rehabbing my shoulder."

There was a long pause where he censured her with nothing more than an extended stare. She held her own, knowing that, to some degree, he expected this of her. As always, she did her best not to disappoint. The dutiful daughter, indeed. Just like she'd been the dutiful enfante terrible on tour. Giving the fans and her opponents exactly what they expected. They could say what they wanted to about her on-court theatrics, and often did, but one thing they were all in agreement on: she rarely disappointed. She rarely lost, either.

As her father continued to perfect his guilt trip via laser-beam glare, Tess found herself absently wondering what would happen if she just stopped. Stopped doing what people expected of her. Stopped behaving according to pattern, for pattern's sake. Hmm. But then her father was talking and the rather bold idea faded without taking any real shape.

"Long enough," he said, "for you to have found your new direction."

This was the exact moment she'd been preparing for since Bobby had called her a week before. It was imperative she pull this off. London was her last chance to get something going and pull her financial hide out of the fire. It was bad enough that her father thought she was lazy. If he knew she was broke, too? Well, as with Wade, it simply didn't bear contemplating. But if all went well, neither one of them would ever have to know. By the time Wimbledon was over, she would have everything in place. She firmly believed that.

She kind of had to.

"What are your plans?" he asked her directly.

She smiled. It was her bright and shiny facing-a-throng-of-media-when-they-all-knew-she'd-just-screwed-up smile. Needless to say, she nailed it. "I'm fielding offers," she said. Okay, lied. She wasn't proud of it, of course, but she was in a bind here. "You've always told me not to jump into something before examining all the angles. I want to make sure I choose wisely."

"What sort of offers? Perhaps I can give you some guidance."

She had to fight to keep her mouth from dropping open. Beside her, Wade took another leisurely sip of his drink. Probably to hide his smile. Jerkface. She hadn't expected this particular turn of events. Apparently some of her surprise must have shown, because her father cleared his throat and sat forward.

"I realize you feel very strongly about making your own way, and I've respected that. As much as I may have wanted to over the years, you know I don't get involved in those kinds of decisions."

Privately Tess fought not to snort. It was true that he'd left her alone to manage her own life as she'd requested, but he'd hardly done so silently. Yet there was a thread of something in his voice that was unfamiliar to her. He'd almost sounded like, well, a regular dad there for a moment. She took another careful sip of her drink, trying to decide if her father was really grappling with child-rearing worries, or playing some political angle to get her to do what he wanted her to do.

"However," he went on, "you're presently at a crossroads of sorts. And I wonder if perhaps I shouldn't be so cavalier about leaving you to find your own way in such uncharted territory." He glanced down for a moment, and she was struck by just how out of character this particular little speech was. He sighed a little, and looked up again. His silver hair was as shiny and perfectly groomed as ever, framing his wide, tanned face. The deep grooves in his forehead and bracketing his mouth still made him look imposing and authoritative, just as the wrinkles fanning out from his blue eyes softened that imperiousness just enough to make him look dashing. And yet, despite all that, he looked . . . older somehow.

And she found herself wondering how many of those silver hairs and wrinkled lines were there because of her. More than a few, she knew. More than her two brothers combined, for sure.

"Your mother would have been far better equipped to handle this sort of thing, guide you through this change in your life, but, well . . ." He trailed off. It was such an uncustomary thing for him to do, great orator that he was, that they all three basically froze in place. Silently hoping it was some kind of technical glitch with his internal TelePrompTer or something, and if they just held their breath long enough, it would pop back on again and all would be right and normal in their world. Such as it was.

Instead, the silence stretched further. So Tess did the only thing she could think to do, which was as out of character for her as his fumbling speech was for him. She wasn't sure who she shocked more when she awkwardly put her hand over her father's and squeezed lightly. "I appreciate what you're offering." And, further shocking herself and quite probably him, as well, she meant it. They'd all pretty much let Cissy Hamilton run their lives, thankful for her natural expertise. Even six years later, they still stumbled when left to handle things on their own. "If it gets down to where I can't decide, we'll talk it over. Okay?"

He cleared his throat and slid his hand from hers and moved back, but not before giving her arm an equally awkward little pat.

Tess's throat tightened up a little, which was totally not cool. What was in those drinks, anyway? She glanced down into hers, as if she'd find the answer there. It was probably the impending wedding making them all act so uncharacteristically mushy. Yeah, that was it. Forcing a smile, she looked up at both of them, unwilling to let any moment with the men in her family—well, these two men, anyway—turn remotely maudlin. "You know Mom is up there right now having a good laugh over how ridiculously hopeless we are without her."

Her father instantly retreated back into his senatorial demeanor. Which was exactly what she'd aimed for. This man she understood. More important, this man she could handle. What hit her for the first time was the possibility that he escaped there himself for the very same reason. With his wife gone, perhaps that was the only world he understood, too.

The very idea humanized him almost too much in her eyes. So a somewhat confused Tess was intensely grateful when he started talking in his filibuster voice once more.

"In the interim," he said, his customary gruffness firmly back in place, "it wouldn't hurt you to consider giving some of your time to a charitable foundation. Use the media attention you garnered with your fame to do some good."

Thereby bringing positive media attention to the Hamilton name, for a change, she silently finished for him.

"I'll have Hilary send you a list of the foundations we work with."

Hilary was her father's assistant, his right hand, his keeper, and pretty much the only thing that kept him up and running. Fortunately he knew this and made damn sure she was paid well enough to stick around, no matter how difficult he was to deal with.

"That sounds like a good idea," Tess replied, surprised to discover she kind of meant that, too. Well, she was just full of surprises today. She'd been involved with several charities while on tour, but those were typically invitational benefit things that she'd just shown up for to help out. She didn't have a dedicated cause, per se. Had never thought about it, really. Maybe she should. She swore in that moment she could feel her mother's celestial gaze of approval beaming directly down on her head. "Have her note on there which organizations you're most involved with."

Her father gave her the closest thing she ever got to approval—a curt nod—then tossed in the blessed relief of shifting his attention to Wade. Double bonus.

"I ran into Mariella Robson at a fund-raiser last week," he began.

Ever the defense attorney, the only sign that Wade had just been put in a supremely uncomfortable situation was the way his hand tightened ever so slightly on his glass. Tess settled back, hiding her smile behind the rim of her own. Maybe she should look into joining the current poker craze as a way to enhance her bottom line. Years of playing tennis had taught her to ferret out her opponents' "tells" quickly, then capitalize on what they telegraphed to her. She could probably reverse her financial situation completely with one good weekend in Vegas.

As her father grilled her older brother on why it was that he'd let one of the most successful, beautiful, and most important, available, women in San Francisco get away, she took another sip of her martini and wished like hell she didn't feel so discombobulated. She needed to keep her head entirely in the game for the next couple of weeks. Far more than another title and trophy were at stake.

"So, will you be staying at your little place in the village?"

Lost in her thoughts, Tess glanced up to find them both looking expectantly at her. "I'm sorry, what did you say?"

Wade responded. "Dad and I are staying at the Connaught in Hyde Park. We assumed you'd stay in Wimbledon, so we didn't book you in."

Tess's mouth opened, then shut again. She'd just assumed they'd booked her room along with theirs. Had sort of been counting on it, in fact. Caught off guard, it took her a second to rally her thoughts. "I, uh, actually, with Bobby getting married and all the wedding stuff, I thought it would be better to stay in London. I sublet the village house, anyway." Which was kind of close to the truth. There *were* other people living there now.

Just thinking about that sent a little pang through her heart. Wimbledon was a quaint, traditional English village just outside of London, and one of her very favorite places on earth. And not just because she'd won five championships there. Walking through town and down Wimbledon Park, one would never suspect that just around the bend was one of the world's most venerable institutions. Quiet for most of the year, it turned into a massive tourist mecca during the fortnight of the Championships. Many owners of the houses along the main road rented out their places to players and fans alike, and even went so far as to rent out their driveways and lawns to vendors looking to hawk food and memorabilia to the throngs who walked daily from the subway stop in the village proper down the hill to the grounds themselves. She'd always liked staying close by, loved the feel and sounds and just the hum of activity that surrounded the event. London was close enough that she could easily get into town for shopping and an occasional evening of fun.

In fact, she was going to miss—terribly—not having her little village *pied-à-terre. Head in the game, Tess. Head in the game.*

"Where did you book?" her father inquired.

"I'm, ah, staying with some friends." She hadn't meant to sound so wishy-washy, but she was scrambling here.

Wade, of course, picked up on it immediately. "Ah," he said knowingly. "Shacking up in the city, huh? Anyone we know?" His smile grew. "Anyone we need to do a little background check on before you're both splashed all over Page Six?"

"Wade." Their father's censure was automatic, but didn't carry much weight. Especially given the equally disappointed glance he sent her way.

Wade would make a good poker player, too, Tess thought. And oh, what she wouldn't give to take his ass to the cleaners. Wipe that stupid smug smile off his face. But at the moment, as she didn't exactly have a good backup story in place, it behooved her—once again—to live down to her reputation. Would it never end?

She let her smile curve slowly, careful to keep her father to the very edge of her peripheral vision. "Jealous?"

Before Wade could retort, or their father could step in, they were called to board their flight. Armed with enough magazines and her handy little sleep mask, Tess scooted out in front of them and boarded first. She had every intention of burying herself in a few magazines, then sleeping her way across the Atlantic.

If she was going to launch an all-out assault on the collective unsuspecting tennis consortium hovering about London for the next couple of weeks, she had to have a base of operations. Maybe by the time they landed in Heathrow, she'd have figured out where in the hell that was going to be . . . and how she was going to finance it.

Chapter 4

"Well, there you are, my dear boy!" Aurora Favreaux waved across the crowded suite at the groom-to-be, enjoying, as she always did, the musical way the thin gold bracelets on her wrist clinked together. The recessed lighting, though tastefully muted, still created a dazzling effect as it bounced off the rings lining her fingers.

She smiled easily and nodded at several acquaintances as she expertly wove her way through the clusters of guests who'd come to congratulate the lucky couple. She loved parties. Especially engagement parties. The warm chatter, the hum of excitement, the room was simply infused with sincere happiness. That the two lovebirds were surrounded by such love and affection was a testimony that they'd both chosen well.

Aurora fussed with the chiffon scarves she'd loosely tied at her neck as she finally approached the always-charming Bobby Hamilton and his lovely bride-to-be, Andrea. Aurora reached out with both hands, taking one of Bobby's and one of Andrea's, before squeezing them both together. "I couldn't be more delighted for you two. Look how adorable you are!"

"Thank you, Aurora," Bobby said sincerely, perfect teeth gleaming, blue eyes, so like his father's, twinkling.

Unlike Frank Hamilton, who'd never seemed quite comfortable with himself and the gifts he'd been born with, his younger son, Bobby, was a completely natural charmer. Such a doll. Always had been.

Proving the point, he lifted Aurora's hand and placed a gallant kiss on the back, shooting her a quick wink as he did so, which, even at her somewhat advanced age, had her blushing. He then turned to his bride-to-be and Aurora sighed the sigh of a truly hopeless romantic as she saw his entire expression melt when Andrea smiled at him. Like he couldn't believe how incredibly lucky he was that this beautiful woman had consented to be his wife.

"Aurora, I'd like to introduce you to my fiancée, Andrea Nestor. Andrea, this is Aurora Favreaux. Her late husband Way served with my dad in the Senate for many years."

Andrea, with her soft brown hair, beautifully smooth English skin, and light green eyes, was quite the beauty. And, gauging from her quick glance at her husband-to-be and the stunning way it made her cheeks warm up, she apparently was just as besotted with the young Mr. Hamilton as he was with her. Ah, young love, wasn't it just the best?

She turned to Aurora. "It's a pleasure to meet you. Bobby has spoken of you."

Aurora's face lit up with a surprised smile. "Has he, now?" She glanced at Bobby and winked. "All flattering, I'm hoping?"

Bobby's winning smile grew wider and he gently squeezed the hand he still held. "Of course. Besides," he added wryly, "I'd risk the wrath of the godmothers if I were to say otherwise."

"Oh, right!" Andrea's smile grew even brighter. "You're one

of the owners of Glass Slipper, aren't you?" The lilt in her voice was ever so lovely. "You've made quite a splash opening up your new place here in London. Very posh, I hear." She laughed lightly. "There are more than a few of us here, trodding about, in dire need of your services."

"Present company excepted," Bobby said, pulling Andrea closer as another rosy blush bloomed to life in her cheeks.

"Most definitely," Aurora chimed in, a bit rosy herself. Almost had to fan herself at the heat those two put off. "I understand you design sportswear," she said to Andrea, who nodded.

"My new line comes out in the fall. We're going to launch it in conjunction with the U.S. Open."

"So much going on with you two, what with Bobby playing Wimbledon and you with your exciting launch. You amaze me, attempting a wedding in the midst of it all."

"It's not so hard as all that, really. Everyone we love is here for the Championships," Andrea said. She glanced at Bobby and beamed. "And all that matters is that we say our vows with those who mean the most to us present." She glanced at Aurora. "I'm not at all fussy about the rest."

Bobby laughed. "Now you know why I proposed."

"Well," Aurora said, "if you need any help with even the smallest of details, please don't hesitate to contact me, Vivian, or Mercedes," she said, referring to her two partners. "We're not heading back to Washington for another few weeks yet. You know we'd be more than happy to do anything for you both."

"That is so kind of you," Andrea said, quite sincerely. "It's lovely just knowing we have your support."

Aurora's expression shifted to one of fond memory. "I wish Cissy were here to see this. I know she's just thrilled for you."

"Thank you. Mom is definitely here in spirit." His mouth quirked a little. "She wouldn't dream of missing a wedding in the family."

"No doubt, my dear." Aurora looked about. "Speaking of spirit, where is that sister of yours? Don't tell me she couldn't make it."

Just then there was the sound of raised voices from somewhere near the suite vestibule.

"It is not my fault they followed us all the way here from the airport. I only made that one tiny little comment by the baggage carousel."

" 'Tiny little comment'? Tess, you all but lunged at the man!"

"He was stealing my bag!"

"You don't know that. It might have been an honest mistake."

"Honestly, Wade, we both know there was no way he was carrying Louis Vuitton, the man had no sense of style."

"And you're the height of fashion?"

"I'm traveling incognito!"

"Right. We've been hounded, harassed, and all but chased here by a pack of camera-wielding wolves. I don't know how you put up with it, Tess. You obviously enjoy that kind of attention, but I doubt seriously Bobby and . . . and—"

"Andrea. Perhaps you should put that in your BlackBerry. Then maybe you'll remember her name before their fifth wedding anniversary. And you wonder why women leave your bed before the sheets are cold."

"For God's sake, lower your voice! And please tell me you're going to change clothes before everyone—"

"If we hadn't gotten stuck in customs during that ridiculous dog search—want to bet it was the same luggage-stealing jerk who triggered that whole deal? I wouldn't be a bit surprised—anyway, I was planning on changing before leaving Heathrow. It's not my fault we had a little trouble."

" 'Little trouble'? *Little trouble?*"

Heads were turning, and Bobby smiled with affectionate resignation before looking back at Aurora. "I believe she's arrived."

Aurora laughed. "You have to love a woman who knows how to make an entrance, darling."

"It's part of her DNA," Bobby said as the conversation between his brother and sister continued to escalate. He grinned. "And they call me the baby of the family."

"The world can always use a little extra excitement." Aurora patted his arm. "I'll go say hello and see if I can diffuse things a little, let you get back to your guests."

"That's okay. I'll go with you. Andrea and Tess have met, but I want her to meet Wade." He glanced back at his fiancée with a wry grin. "I think I do, anyway. If we can get the two of them apart, things will settle down."

"A good idea from the looks of things." Aurora swept the soft, filmy layers of her floor-length caftan aside and made her way to the foyer and the bickering siblings. Wade was a strapping, handsomely gifted man, and quite the successful attorney. She'd always privately believed he'd follow his father's footsteps into public office someday. Frank would be enormously proud, of course, although, frankly, Aurora always wished Wade had gotten a bit more of his mother's flair for life in him.

The same could be said of Tess and her father. A bit of Frank's calm-in-a-storm attitude might have done his daughter a world of good. Aurora's smile deepened as Tess spied her and her face split into a wide, instantly sparkling grin. On second thought, why on earth would anybody want to dim the electric intensity that was Tess Hamilton?

"Aurora! I didn't know you'd be here."

Tess, so lovely and graceful with her lanky height and athletic form, swept Aurora—who was much smaller, if not quite diminutive—into a close hug. Aurora was so happy to receive the heartfelt squeeze of affection that she barely worried about mussing her perfectly coiffed updo, complete with age-softening ringlets framing her face. She kissed Tess on the cheek, then reached up to rub off the lipstick imprint.

"It's so fantastic to see you!" Tess exclaimed, taking Aurora's hands in her own. "What a wonderful surprise. It's been, wow, a few years, hasn't it?"

"I believe it was at the ceremony in Carmel," she responded, referring to the launch of the charitable foundation Frank had created in Cissy's memory a few years back, just before Tess's injury. "Time flies when you're racking up titles, darling," Aurora said fondly. "How have you been?" Had she not been in the business of noticing things, even the smallest of things, sometimes especially those, she might have missed the briefest of moments when Tess's eyes clouded over.

"Good, fine. I didn't know you were in London," Tess said, rebounding as swiftly as she did on the court, making sure no one so much as detected the wobble. "Did you come over for the wedding?"

"Vivi, Mercy, and I came over to see how Valerie was doing, running things 'across the pond,' as they say."

"Right! You opened a U.K. branch of Glass Slipper a few months back." She squeezed Aurora's hands. "How exciting. I assume it's going well?"

"Quite well, so far. Valerie is proving to be every bit as capable as we knew she'd be. You should stop in, avail yourself of some of our more pampering services."

"I definitely should," Tess agreed with seeming enthusiasm. If one didn't notice the way her mouth tightened at the corners.

So . . . something *was* wrong. It could simply be lingering tension from her contretemps with her older brother. If Vivi were here, she'd tell Aurora she was making something out of nothing. But Aurora's instincts were clamoring. She certainly wasn't going to come right out and ask. If Tess was putting up a front, it was for good reason. Aurora may be an old friend of the family, but she doubted Tess would confide in her. At least not right away.

So she'd just have to be subtle about it. She squeezed Tess's hands now and gave her her warmest smile. It wasn't hard. She'd always had a soft spot for Cissy's only daughter. Rapscallion that she was, it only made her more lovable in Aurora's eyes. "So tell me, dear, how is life treating you now that you don't have to trot all over the globe, racket in hand?"

"Wonderfully," Tess said, breezily dismissive, as expected. But when Aurora maintained her firm hold on Tess's hands, giving the younger woman her most understanding and attentive gaze, Tess relented a little. "It's taking a little getting used to," she admitted. "But I'm fine, really."

"I can only imagine, sweetheart. You've spent a lion's share of your life either playing tennis, or training to play more tennis. It's got to be an adjustment to shift your focus elsewhere. Are you playing socially? For your own pleasure?"

"Not as much as I'd like."

Tess shifted her gaze away, just for a split second, but it was telling. Aurora wondered how long it had been since she'd picked up a racket at all. The abrupt end to a career that so dominated her life had to have been, in many ways, like losing a loved one. Which Tess already knew a little something about, having lost her mother. And being back at the scene of her final triumph, surrounded by all the hoopla of the one grand-slam event she'd dominated during her career, even for such a lovely reason as a wedding, couldn't be easy for her.

"Well," Aurora said, her tone soft, soothing, but not patronizing in any way, "no one could fault you for filling your time with other activities. It's probably good for body and soul."

Tess smiled, gave a little shrug. "That's what I tell myself."

Aurora smiled in return. "No worries, then. You look marvelous, dear." *Except for those shadows chasing across those lovely green eyes of yours.*

"Thank you. I do feel better physically than I have in a long time. I don't think I realized how much the aches and pains were a part of my daily life. Being off the tour has definitely been a good thing in that way."

Which left the obvious question dangling. *Patience, Aurora, patience.* "I can well imagine. You've worked so hard, for so long, you should enjoy your time now." She fished as gently as she could. "Don't let anyone pressure you to jump into something else until you're ready."

The smile grew more forced as Tess gently withdrew her hands from Aurora's after a final squeeze. "Me? Let anyone boss me around?" She laughed, but it wasn't quite up to snuff. "Hardly. It is so great to see you again, Aurora."

"An unexpected pleasure, to be sure. I shouldn't dominate your time, dear. After all, you're here to see your brother and his lovely bride-to-be." They both glanced over to where Bobby and Andrea stood, several feet away, deep in conversation with Wade. "I'll let you reunite. But I would love to see you again while we're both in town, take some time out of the whirl and get a chance to really visit."

"I would enjoy that," Tess said, seeming sincere, although Aurora knew she was as professional about smiling her way through the constant stream of offers to claim a chunk of her valuable time, as she'd once been about winning matches.

But Aurora wasn't easily put off. "Where are you staying, dear? Perhaps I can drop by and we'll have a perfectly lovely

British tea." She smiled ever more brightly and squeezed Tess's arm again, as a sudden thought occurred to her. "I'm staying at a lovely place in Kensington Gardens. Wexley House. Belongs to an old friend of mine and Way's, Sir Robin Hargrove. He's always abroad and when he heard I'd be in town for an extended stay, he insisted I enjoy his hospitality." Aurora leaned close, eyes twinkling. "And though we're both used to five-star accommodations, darling, I must tell you, his is quite the decadent lifestyle." She took Tess's hand with both of her own. "Please say you'll come have high tea with me at Wexley."

"That sounds lovely," Tess said, obviously surprised. "I wouldn't want to put anyone to any trouble."

"Nonsense. His kitchen is fully staffed and I'm afraid they're finding me quite lacking as a guest. They love to put on quite the show and I'd feel so much better about all that work if I had someone to share it with." Her eyes widened further as the rest of her strategy fell into place. "In fact, unless you have plans to stay with your family while you're here—"

Wade stepped up just then, and leaned down to give Aurora a kiss on her cheek. "You must be joking. Tess would sleep on the street before she'd willingly room with any of the Hamilton men again. It's a pleasure to see you, as always, Aurora," he said, perfectly polished smile creasing his perfectly handsome face. He glanced at his sister. "But don't worry for her welfare. She's not excluding everyone of our gender when it comes to making sleeping arrangements." He shot a wink at Aurora.

Aurora swatted at Wade's arm, even as she caught Tess's eye roll. "It's a good thing you're a handsome rascal," she informed him. "I'd scold you myself, but I daresay your sister doesn't put up with your social commentary, nor should she."

"Now you know why I don't room with him," Tess said dryly.

"So, I have a perfectly splendid idea," Aurora announced. "If there isn't anyone special—and frankly, even if there is, Sir Robin has scads of bedrooms—why don't you consider staying with me at Wexley?"

Wade shot a smug look at his sister. "Yes, Tess, that's a lovely idea. You could make quite a slumber party out of it."

Tess gave her big brother a syrupy grin. "Aurora is wrong, you know. Your good looks don't save you. This is why you're still single."

"Dear pot, perhaps you've met kettle—" he began, but was cut off.

"Yes, but I'm single by choice," Tess told him. "I get offers. You?" Without waiting for a response, she turned back to Aurora. "I am really flattered by the invitation. And sorely tempted."

"Wonderful!" Maybe her instincts were wrong, but if not—and honestly, they were rarely wrong—Aurora couldn't have planned it better.

"If you really don't think it's an imposition." For the first time that evening, Tess's smile reached all the way to her eyes.

"Of course not." Quite pleased with herself, Aurora resisted the urge to give a little fist pump—a gesture she'd picked up from her more colorful partner, Vivian dePalma, and which always made their other partner, Mercedes, roll her eyes and shake her head.

But this moment deserved a little fist pump. Aurora didn't know yet what was going on, but judging from Tess's reaction, she'd just provided a very welcome, if unexpected, rescue of some sort. All she had to do now was find out what in the world Tess Hamilton needed rescuing from. Besides her own occasionally annoying family members. "Fabulous! I'll call over to the house and have them get ready for you."

"Thank you so much." Tess gave Wade a brief, sidelong smirk. "And contrary to popular opinion, they'll only need to prepare a room for one."

Wade winked at Aurora. "She's only been in town a few hours. Give her some time."

Bobby poked his head in just then. "Can you two retract the claws for a few minutes? It's supposed to be a party here. Tess," he said, taking her arm, "can I borrow you for a minute?"

"Gladly." She paused by Aurora. "See if you can keep him from making a pompous ass out of himself with any of the other guests. It's a tall order, but if anyone can do it, you can."

Aurora patted Tess's arm. "I'm sure he'll be fine." She glanced past Tess to Wade and shifted her body to include Bobby. "Cissy would be so happy to know you three are together, celebrating such a wonderful family event."

She had the satisfaction of seeing the oldest Hamilton child look a wee bit chastened. "Off you go," she said, nudging Tess toward Bobby. As the two disappeared down a short hallway, she saw Bobby dip his head toward his sister and whisper something, his expression serious and concerned. Hmm.

Admittedly quite curious about the exchange, Aurora immediately turned to Wade with a bright smile. "Wade, darling, would you be a doll and see if you can find me a small plate of those wonderful canapés I saw drift by moments ago? I'm afraid if I have so much as another sip of champagne without eating something, it will go right to my head." She winked at him. "And then I'll be the one who needs saving from myself."

Wade shot her a wolfish grin that reminded her of what a charming devil he could be when he wasn't busy badgering his sister. "I'm not so sure that would be a bad thing."

Aurora laughed and swatted playfully at his arm, setting her bracelets to jingling. "You're a bigger scamp than you let on."

He leaned down and kissed her cheek. "Don't tell anyone. You'll ruin my reputation as an uptight, humorless, control freak." He winked at her, then moved into the throng of guests.

She watched after him for a moment as he quite smoothly

worked the crowd with a quick smile here, short nod there, and wondered if he realized what a natural politician he was. With everyone but family, anyway. "Just like your father," she murmured. *Who happens to be the king of uptight, humorless, control freaks.* She smiled to herself as she worked her way toward the short hallway Bobby and Tess had disappeared down.

It only took a moment to hear their voices. They'd ducked into the suite's small, galley-style kitchen. Aurora paused just outside the doorway, telling herself she wasn't snooping so much as trying to help the daughter of a very old friend.

"I was a bit worried about you, that's all," Bobby was saying.

"Why on earth would you be worried about me?" Tess said with what sounded like a sincere laugh.

Aurora wished she could see Tess's expression. That her younger brother was apparently concerned about her, as well, was all the confirmation she needed. Of course Tess was going to deny it to Bobby. This was his special moment, and Tess had always taken on the big sister role with him, especially, she imagined, now that he was on tour.

"You should be focusing on your upcoming nuptials."

"Nothing to worry about there. I don't care if we're married by a clown in the middle of a three-ring circus, as long as she says yes."

Aurora could hear the honest delight and joy in Bobby's voice.

"Of course she'll say yes, she's getting the best guy on the planet. I am so happy for you."

There was a rustling sound. Hugging, Aurora surmised.

"Come on, let's get you back to your engagement party."

Aurora started to duck back down the hall, then Bobby said, "Wait," and Aurora froze in place. There was a moment of silence before he said, "I, uh, I heard Nike didn't renew their sponsorship."

"How did you hear that?" Tess didn't quite pull off a casual tone.

"So it is true? My manager was talking to one of their reps this morning about a possible deal for me, and she let it slip. I guess she figured that as your brother, I already knew. So why didn't I?"

Again Tess tried for the short, breezy laugh. "Don't be silly. You're over here preparing for Wimbledon and your wedding. It's really not that big a deal."

" 'Not that big a deal'? They've sponsored you for almost your whole career. It was one of your biggest endorsements."

"One of many, Bobby. They simply decided there wasn't anything for them to endorse anymore."

"Sure there is. Your rep is still huge and you know it. You're still a major draw. Hell, Wade told me you guys were chased all the way from the airport by the paparazzi."

"It wasn't my fault," came the automatic reply, which made Aurora smile.

"I'm sure it wasn't," he said, affection clear in his tone, but the seriousness returned an instant later. "I just don't understand the decision, from a loyalty or business standpoint."

"Loyalty has no place in business," Tess responded. "Trust me on that one."

Aurora heard the edge in Tess's voice. Maybe it was just as well she couldn't see her face. This way she wasn't swayed by Tess's acting skills. She knew what she heard.

"So it's just a little bump, then? Everything else is going all right?" Bobby asked. "I know it seems like I've vanished on you lately, but the tour and—"

"I'm the very last person you need to explain that to. And who's the older sibling here? Since when did you need to check up on me? You know I'm fine. When haven't I been?"

"Just trying to be the good brother."

"Oh, you're definitely the good brother, trust me."

"Come on," Bobby said, chuckling. "You shouldn't let Wade or Dad get to you like that."

"You didn't have to fly across the Atlantic with the two of them. You're lucky I didn't parachute out halfway across and take my chances on a passing barge."

"You have a point there," he said with a laugh. "So, have you made any decisions yet?"

"About?"

"Life. I know you, and globe-hopping or not, you've got to be going a bit stir-crazy by now. Still juggling offers, figuring out what sounds best? Anything fun and exciting?"

Aurora missed Tess's response when someone tapped her on the shoulder. She barely squelched a surprised squeal and almost spilled her champagne on the hallway carpet. She supposed she should have kept a better lookout for intruders.

"Can I refresh that for you, madam?" A tall gentleman in black serving attire held out a bottle of champagne. "I was coming to get another bottle, but there is a bit left here if you'd like me to top you off."

Aurora clasped a hand to her bosom and sighed in relief. Thank goodness it was one of the waitstaff. And not Wade or another guest wondering what she was doing skulking around in the hall. "Please," she said, pushing her glass at him as she regained her composure.

Andrea came down the hallway just as the waiter stepped past Aurora into the kitchen. "Is Bobby still back here?"

Aurora smiled brightly, thankful now the waiter had found her first. "Yes, dear, in the kitchen with Tess."

"Tim is here and wants to make a toast." Tim was Tim Robertson, Bobby's doubles partner.

Bobby stepped into the hallway. He bussed Aurora on the cheek. "Thanks for asking Tess to stay with you."

"Of course, dear. It will be a delightful chance for us to catch up."

"Do me a favor, would you?" he asked, more quietly.

"Certainly," Aurora said, admiring his continued concern for his sister. Bobby may be the baby of the family, but he was quickly growing into quite a decent young man. "Anything."

"Just . . . I don't know. Wimbledon was her favorite event, you know? It's her first time being here as a spectator instead of a player. I worried that having her come over here for the wedding right beforehand was going to make it harder on her and I feel badly about that . . ."

Aurora patted his cheek, then framed his face with the palms of her hands. "Cissy would be so proud of you." She gave him a short, noisy kiss on the cheek. "Go off and enjoy your lovely toast with your even lovelier bride-to-be. I'll watch over Tess. Don't you worry."

Bobby grinned. *Such a cute boy.*

"With you on the case?" he said, "I'll rest easy."

After he left, Aurora ducked into the kitchen to find Tess chatting up the tall waiter. Who was also a cute boy, Aurora noticed, now that she wasn't having heart palpitations. She cleared her throat gently, but Tess just smiled in her direction, not remotely embarrassed to have been caught flirting.

"John here was telling me about a wonderful party in Notting Hill that he's been hired to work later. Sounds like fun. Care to join me?"

"Perhaps," Aurora said, knowing she shouldn't be surprised. Tess's party girl reputation was only partially exaggerated. "I was wondering where you've stowed your luggage. I thought I'd call Glass Slipper and send a car to pick it up for you and deliver it to Wexley."

"It's with Dad at the Connaught. He had an emergency

conference call from California just as we were getting through customs. You don't have to go to all that trouble. I'll arrange something."

"I'm sure you can, darling. But I don't mind. Perhaps I'll head over to the Connaught myself. I haven't seen Frank in ages. We can go together, if you'd like. Then you'll have time to freshen up before heading out this evening."

Tess just grinned. "Fair warning, it will just give me more time to work on you, convince you to join me. Girls night out. Maybe we'll call Vivian and really do the town."

Aurora just smiled, thinking her little plan was going to come together even easier than she'd thought.

Wade stuck his head in the kitchen. "There you are. If you could peel yourself off of the hired help, Tim is making a toast. Come on."

The waiter flushed, but both of the women in the room just looked at each other and grinned. With Wade looking on, Tess bussed John the waiter on the cheek. "Thanks for the party tip. Perhaps I'll see you later."

The young man was so flustered, he couldn't quite respond.

Wade just rolled his eyes and walked out.

"You know, you really shouldn't torture him like that."

"Who?" Tess quipped, "John or my jerk of a big brother?"

Aurora sighed and shook her head. "Both, I suppose. You're a force to be reckoned with, Tess."

"I know. And if they'd all just realize that up front, they could make their world and mine a much easier place to live in." She laughed as she stuck her arm through Aurora's. They accepted fresh glasses of champagne from the pink-cheeked waiter, and headed out.

Once back in the throng, Tess left Aurora to go stand between the happy couple and her older brother. Aurora listened to Tim's delightfully heartfelt toast, but her smile as she sipped her champagne was as much one of triumph as it was in sincere happiness for the young couple. She didn't relish the idea of having to explain her little project to her partners and debated briefly on simply not including them in the loop on this particular case.

Of course that would never work. Her smile grew and she finished off her champagne in one long sip. Come to think of it, what with Mercy's little venture with her godson Shane some months back, and Vivi's own recent pet project, with the transformation of the delightfully sweet, if somewhat gawky Lucy Harper . . . they could hardly fault her for taking on her own little endeavor. She would secure their support. One way or the other.

All that was left was to put her plan into motion. How exciting! She waved down a passing waiter. "More champagne, please."

Chapter 5

"Honey, if I was sleeping with him, you'd be the last person I'd tell." Tess shot the photographer a naughty smile, then ducked her chin against the blinding litany of flashbulbs that erupted a moment later as she made the mad dash to her limo. *God bless Aurora and Glass Slipper,* she thought, extremely thankful for the company town car they'd insisted she use while in residence. If they only knew just how thankful she was.

The driver was pulling away from the curb in front of one of London's hottest new nightclubs before she even had the door completely shut. Well trained, she thought, wondering just what kind of Glass Slipper clients he'd shepherded around town before. A phalanx of paparazzi poured in the street behind them, some giving foot chase for a healthy block or two before giving up. Thankfully none of them opted to follow via car. No, there were bigger targets of opportunity still dancing the night away inside ZSpot. A photo of her exiting alone wouldn't fetch all that much these days, anyway. She'd need something studly and preferably famous on her arm, to be worth chasing en masse.

"Wexley House, please," she informed the driver, then slumped back against the seat, only partly relieved that no chase had ensued. Not because she missed that. She didn't. At all. It was dangerous as all hell and the thrill of being hotly pursued by crazed maniacs with cameras had worn off very early in her career. But being pursued also meant seeing her face splashed across celebrity columns on a minimum of two continents. She needed to maximize that face time if she was going to convince any of the narrow-minded, blowhard company reps that she was still a marketable commodity.

She'd been in town a full week now and had hit the pretournament social circuit like the regular she used to be—both the corporate-sponsored gigs for the tennis crowd and the ones favored by celebrities in general. She intended to avail herself of a blitz campaign of free publicity, showing up in all the right places, with all the right people. *Yesterday's news, my ass,* she thought as she kicked off her heels. She'd be damned if they'd make her into a has-been. All she needed was one endorsement deal from a major company and her immediate concerns would disappear. Companies wanted what other companies had. She could parlay one good deal into a string of smaller ones, maybe get a commercial or something out of it. From that point she could springboard herself into . . .

She blew out a long breath and blinked at the uncustomary and quite sudden stinging at the backs of her eyes. "Yeah . . . springboard yourself into exactly what?" Visions of performing a perfect dive off a platform, only to realize too late she was headed down into an empty pool, swam through her mind. "Swimming pool roadkill."

"Beg pardon, miss?" the driver politely inquired.

She waved her hand. "Nothing, just talking to myself."

Which she might as well get used to. The social hot spots had provided her with ample media opportunity, but they weren't exactly panning out as well as she'd hoped. Or at all, really. The interest was definitely there, but there was nothing new to get them going. She just had to decide what she was willing to give them in order to get what she wanted.

Bobby's wedding was news now, at least in the tennis world, but with the Championships coming up, all of England was abuzz with anything and everything tennis. Wimbledon was a cherished, almost sacred event among the Brits. She should be able to capitalize on that. But the fact that the groom's father was a U.S. senator and Bobby was marrying an Englishwoman who also happened to be a relatively well-known sports designer, made him front-page news on both sides of the pond. "Yeah, my baby brother is getting better press than me and he doesn't even want it."

"Pardon, miss?"

She just waved her hand at him.

She was truly happy for Bobby and Andrea, but admittedly their upcoming nuptials were cramping her style a wee bit. She could have easily plotted something scandalous and gotten all the coverage she'd ever desired and then some—because, really, why not? Everyone expected that from her anyway—but she didn't want to do anything that might ruin Bobby's special day. And given her rapidly approaching marketability expiration date, she doubted future sponsors would appreciate that kind of publicity at this point.

But her fistful of grand-slam titles were nothing but statistics now, trotted out during the "compare and contrast" portion of current event commentary. So, dammit, what the hell was she supposed to do to get a little attention? She was the international wild child, the bad girl of tennis. Fiery temperament and spicy scandal were her m.o. Or had been. So what if she was as tired of all of that as her former sponsors were? Being the good girl sure as hell wasn't getting her anywhere.

She'd already attended several glittery affairs, looking for the right industry insider to hook onto, but so far, nothing was popping. There was too much fresh blood for them to scent and track. No one was cutting through the crowds to make their way to her table. In fact, it was humiliating to admit, but she'd had to make the rounds of several parties herself.

"Wexley House, miss."

Tess fought a yawn as the car rolled to a stop in front of the sumptuous London digs of one Sir Robin Hargrove, complete with a private drive and huge iron gates to keep out trespassers. *I do manage to land on my feet once in a while,* she thought. Between her dad footing the plane tickets and Aurora extending her hospitality, along with her limo, Tess couldn't have asked for an easier entrée to all the London prechampionship hoopla. "Thanks, Davy," she told the driver. "Don't get out. I'll get my door."

"Thank you, miss. Have a lovely evening."

She glanced at her watch after waving Davy off. "Just past midnight." A smile ghosted her lips as the gates opened to let the limo exit. "And my coach didn't even turn into a pumpkin."

She should still be out, making the rounds. But she simply didn't have it in her tonight. She refused to admit defeat, but she was a bit disheartened at what she'd accomplished so far. Tomorrow Bobby and Andrea were throwing a dinner party for family and a few close friends. The wedding was the following day, on Saturday. The Championships began a short week later. Not exactly her honeymoon of choice, but to each his own.

She rolled her shoulders and fought another yawn as she turned toward the wide marble stairs leading to the front door. Not even thirty and she was already a party pooper. It was then she spied the other car parked a bit farther along the drive, in the deeper shadows cast by the west wing of the mansion. It was a dark, two-door sedan. Apparently, Aurora had company. She looked up, but didn't see any lights on in the east wing where Aurora's rooms were. Her lips curved then. "Well, well." Aurora might not be much for staying out late, but apparently her social life wasn't suffering because of it. "You go, girl," she murmured.

Tess climbed the stairs and, when one of Sir Robin's many employees didn't open the door in anticipation of her arrival as they usually did, she shrugged and pulled open one side of the pair of massive oak-and-cast-iron-studded doors herself. The thing weighed a ton, as it turned out, and was almost twice her height. "Just what the hell were they afraid was going to break in here, anyway? A Trojan horse?"

The dazzling crystal chandelier that hung overhead glowed softly—who knew you could dimmer switch those things?—and the hand-painted, gold-leaf sconces dotting the walls between the doorways were also turned down so the entire foyer was cast in little more than a golden glow. She'd always thought her home in Boca was ridiculously large for one person. But Sir Robin's foyer alone could be subdivided into comfortable housing for a family of four.

When nobody emerged from the shadows to take her shawl and purse, she turned toward the staircase. Maybe Thursdays were the help's night off. Which was fine by her. She liked her five-star amenities, sure, who didn't? But she'd never grown accustomed to having paid help hovering about. She was halfway up the stairs when she heard the sound of voices coming from the rear parlor. The house had three off the foyer alone, two front, one to the rear right-hand side, leaving room on the rear left for the curving mahogany staircase that wound up to the open second-floor atrium.

"I appreciate the dinner, Aurora, really I do," came a man's voice.

"Don't forget the cognac," Aurora replied.

"Of course. You're a gracious hostess, as always, and you know I appreciate the personal touch."

Tess grinned. Nice voice, deep, well modulated, confident. "Not bad, Aurora. Not bad at all." Despite being intrigued—okay, curious bordering on downright nosy—about Aurora's gentleman caller, Tess continued her climb up the stairs.

"But you're going to have to give me something a lot stronger and get me quite drunk if you want me to agree to this insane idea of yours," the man finished.

Tess paused again. Hmm. Business meeting? Or indecent proposal? Had it been Vivian dePalma back there in the rear parlor, Tess would have bet all the money she used to have on the latter. Given that it was Aurora, she reluctantly had to go with the former. Although what kind of business Aurora was conducting at home, this late at night, was beyond her. "Ah, well," Tess sighed, resuming her climb. She'd just pry it out of Aurora in the morning over breakfast. Unless Mr. Deep Voice showed up at Sir Robin's knights-of-the-round-table–sized dining-room table alongside Aurora, which would answer most of her questions right there.

She grinned. Although it would admittedly spark a number of new ones.

"It's, what, ten days before the opening round?" the man went on, his tone slightly less conciliatory. "Gabrielle will be in the main draw for the first time. I came to you because I thought she could use a little help in getting a grip on the demands that are being made of her at such a young age. I'm doing the best I can, but she's growing up fast, and, well, I thought she needed a woman's influence. But not that kind of influence, and definitely not that woman. Besides, her game is fine. Yes, she's between coaches at the moment, but that's okay. We don't need help with her game."

Tess froze. Championships? Wimbledon? The hell? Gabrielle who? And who was this guy? Her father? Manager? Agent? Tess's little voice instructed her quite firmly to go on upstairs. Obviously this didn't concern her or Aurora would most definitely have asked for her help. After all, she had someone living under the same roof who had a wealth of knowledge about the game and the pressures presented by the tour. But she hadn't asked, so Tess wasn't going to get involved. Lord knew she had enough of her own problems.

"I wasn't insinuating her game was somehow lacking," Aurora responded gently. "But you said yourself she lost her coach quite abruptly. She is young, and this is a very important event with more media coverage than she's ever had to deal with. You're right, she needs more than you can give her right now." Aurora's voice softened to that soothing, nurturing tone she used to such good advantage in her work. "Which is why you came to Glass Slipper. And I'd be remiss in doing my job if I didn't at least float this idea in your direction."

"I appreciate that, but with all due respect, Aurora, it's insane." He sounded like a man of conviction, Tess thought, but he was also still standing in the parlor. Which meant he was thinking about the offer. Whatever the hell it had actually been.

Tess was creeping back down the stairs before she'd even realized she planned to eavesdrop. Okay, so she never listened to her little voice, no matter how rational and sane it sounded. And honestly, this was just too good. Not that she planned to intrude into what was obviously a private meeting, but if she heard something that indicated she might be of some use? Tess would be remiss if she wasn't willing to do something to help repay Aurora for her kindness and hospitality. Right?

It was all the rationalization she and her little voice needed. She slid out of her heels and tiptoed closer to the parlor door.

"I understand, and I'm not ungrateful, I know most would

consider this a once-in-a-lifetime opportunity," Mr. Deep Voice agreed, "but I can tell you without a single doubt that the very last person Gaby needs mentoring her in any capacity right now is—"

"You stated quite clearly that you wanted to help her learn to deal with the off-court pressures of the tour, am I right?" Aurora interrupted. "Here we are at one of the tour's biggest events, and I'm offering you the chance to give Gabrielle every advantage possible. Off court, and on, if you're so inclined. All in one package."

Tess frowned. What in the hell did Aurora know about tennis coaches or sports shrinks? *Shit.* Maybe she was assuming Tess would hook her up with whomever it was she had in mind. Although it didn't seem like Aurora to promise something to a client that she hadn't set up first. But if she already had a coach or shrink lined up for this young girl, why not even mention it to Tess during the chats they'd had while she'd been staying here? Get her take on things? Client-godmother privilege.

Then again, maybe this client represented a lot of money to Glass Slipper and he was threatening to take his business elsewhere. Maybe Aurora was securing his continued patronage by making promises up front that she hadn't exactly backed up yet. Except, well, no. Because, first off, the godmothers were rolling in it. At this point in their lives, they only worked because they truly loved what they did. About which, one thing was very certain: They didn't roll over for anyone. Secondly, there was no other place like Glass Slipper for this guy to turn to instead. And yet . . . it was past midnight and Aurora was obviously quite serious about wanting to make things work out with this man and his protégée.

Tess wondered if maybe popping in and seeing what was what would be a good idea after all. She could go back and open and shut the massive front door again, call out as if she'd just gotten in. Aurora would certainly come out to welcome her home and Tess could work the conversation a little, get a feel for what was really going on.

"I have to think about Gaby," Mr. Deep Voice was saying, "and I just think the match you're suggesting couldn't be more problematic. It's not like mixing oil and water, it would be like mixing oil and a lit match."

"You honestly think she would be a detriment to your sister? Encourage her bad behavior? I think the exact opposite would be the case. You don't know her, Max."

His sister, huh? Tess was scooting back to the front door while still trying to hear what they were saying.

"I know enough," he said. "Everyone does. And how can we not when she's been on the cover of every pop-culture magazine, every tabloid, every—"

"Propaganda, Max. You know better than to believe everything you read."

Tess had already frozen in place. *No.* Oh, hell no. Aurora would not do this, would never promise—would she? Because, honestly . . . Tess Hamilton, the bad girl of tennis, mentor to the youth of today? What the hell was in Aurora's cognac? was what Tess wanted to know.

"I don't have to believe everything I read," this Max person responded. "I can go just by what I've seen in the accompanying photo spreads to know this would be a disaster in the making."

" 'A disaster'?" Tess murmured, finding herself somewhat affronted by this stranger's negative opinion of her, despite the fact that she essentially completely agreed with him.

A tennis coach?

She'd never considered it. Quite a few of today's best coaches were former ranked players on the tour, albeit rarely as accomplished or highly ranked as she'd been. In her case it would almost seem . . . a step down of sorts. Mostly because players of her stature didn't have to work that hard to make a good living after retirement. "The ones who invested wisely, anyway," she muttered.

Still. She shook her head. No. She just wasn't seeing it. Not that she was averse to hard work. No one had worked harder on her game than she had. She wasn't afraid of work. But she'd pictured things like the charity benefits her father had suggested, or something similar. A spot on the board of directors, an ambassador of goodwill, that kind of thing. Even working with some sports company or other to help develop a new line of gear, or . . . well . . . something. Her face and name alone had been responsible for selling a lot of rackets and tennis skirts over the years. Surely she could turn that into something profitable now.

But coaching?

And even if she did know a thing or ten about the game, Aurora was also marketing her as some kind of spiritual mentor or head shrink or something to this kid. *Was she crazy?* Please. Tess might be tired of her own bad-girl image, but even she acknowledged that she was very likely the last person who should influence today's youth when it came to managing their off-court life. Hell, she couldn't even manage to hang on to her own fortune!

Oh, shit. It all began to make a sickening kind of sense. Had that been where Aurora had gotten this harebrained idea? Had Bobby said something to Aurora at the party last week about Tess losing her Nike deal? If so, she was going to have to kill him. Which was a shame, really, with him only days away from his wedding and all. But honestly, if he'd sold her out . . .

Okay, so she couldn't even work up a good mad where Bobby was concerned. She knew if he had meddled, his heart had been in the right place. But that didn't help her much at the moment.

"Max, hear me out," Aurora pleaded calmly.

"If even half of what they've printed since she left the game is true, she's been far too busy hopscotching around the globe, spending her fortune by day and partying by night, to be interested in having an actual job, much less one as demanding as what you're proposing."

Tess stiffened. It was one thing for her to question her own viability as a coach, but who the hell did this guy think he was, dismissing her like that? He didn't even know her, for God's sake! Which was the other downfall of celebrity. People saw a few photo spreads, read a few articles, and felt like they were her best friend. Or worst enemy.

"Perhaps you weren't listening to me, dear," Aurora said, ever the unflappable one. A skill Tess was rapidly wishing she had developed somewhere along the way. Steam was already rising. "I wasn't proposing that Tess be involved with Gaby in any long-term relationship. Although if things worked out and you all wanted to continue on beyond Glass Slipper's involvement, far be it for me to stand in your way."

Tess had been ready to storm into the room and give them both a piece of her mind—a more gentle piece where Aurora was concerned, but a piece nonetheless. However, Aurora's last statement had her pausing just outside the door.

"I'm only offering you her guidance during your sister's stay at Glass Slipper."

"One week? What can Tess possibly offer her in such a short time?"

"Insight."

There was a pause, then Tess heard a long exhalation. Max's, no doubt. "She has to prepare. This is her second slam on the pro tour and—"

"I assured you Gabrielle would have ample time and access to grass courts for practice."

"She'll need me with her."

"We can discuss all that later. Are you saying you'll consider my offer?" There was a silence, then Aurora continued building on her apparent edge. "Just let the two of them talk with each other. I think you'll be pleased with the results. As for coaching her on her game, as well, I suppose that will be up to you and Tess to decide. It simply seems rather foolish not to avail yourself of what a person of her amazing stature would have to offer, even if only during Gabrielle's brief stay. Imagine having access to one of the most brilliant tennis minds of our day."

You go, Aurora, Tess thought, enjoying Aurora's very subtle set down of this Max character. Maybe she didn't have to storm the room after all. Of course, she was going to have to tell them both there was no way she was going to go along with this little deal. She had no time to baby-sit some headstrong tennis ingenue. These next few weeks were critical to her future, and though Aurora likely meant well, whatever compensation she intended to give to Tess in exchange for services rendered, it couldn't possibly be enough to be of any serious help. And there was the little matter of at least asking her up front whether she'd even consider such a deal.

"I appreciate what you're trying to do and, as I said, I'm not ungrateful," Max responded. "The kind of access you're offering is unprecedented, to be sure. On the court. However, you'll have to pardon me if I question letting Gaby talk to someone who hasn't exactly been a shining example of behavior modification off the court. To my way of thinking, she's the very last person Gaby needs to pattern herself after. It's bad enough that she constantly throws Tess Hamilton in my face as an example of why her sort of temperament isn't detrimental to her game."

Tess smiled. Ah. So the sister was a fan, was she? Despite herself, she was intrigued. If for no other reason, she was tempted to take this task on just to shut this guy down. Maybe she did have a thing or two she could say to this Gaby and set her straight about the pitfalls of fame, fortune (or lack thereof), and celebrity. Besides, it was only for a week, and all she had to do was talk to the kid? Well... she could probably work that in. What the hell, right? And if it would twist this narrow-minded jerk's boxers into a knot and make him think twice before condemning a person he'd never even met, well then, more the better.

Tess Hamilton, rabble-rouser. Her smile grew to a grin. Perhaps some things would never change.

She pushed the door open and stepped into the room, her confident, grand-slam-winning smile plastered all over her face. She strode across the room, stopping directly in front of the man presently standing next to Aurora. The one currently choking on his cognac. Very satisfying entrance, really.

In her peripheral vision, she caught the pink that rose to Aurora's cheeks, but she directed her attention to Max. She and Aurora would have a little chat later on. In the interim, it was time for a little fun.

"Hello," she said to him, smile still in place as she extended her hand. "You must be Gabrielle's brother, Max. I'm Tess Hamilton. I understand I'll be working with your sister."

Chapter 6

"Uh . . . hi." And after that scintillating conversational retort, Max found himself suddenly shaking hands with the former number-one player in the world and holder of ten grand-slam singles titles, wondering exactly just how much of their conversation she'd overheard.

Good job, Fontaine, very smooth.

"Hello," she replied, sunny, open, and very direct. Her handshake was firm. And though he'd known she was tall, in heels she was almost as tall as he was at just a few inches over six feet. Very imposing. That dress she had on didn't help, either. If the way the stretchy black fabric clung to her tight curves was any indication, she was also still quite fit despite being out of action for almost two years.

At the moment, however, he was mostly distracted by her face. Sparkly green eyes, white toothy smile, confident bordering on cocky. He'd seen that same face, that same exact expression, winking back at him from countless magazine covers. And yet, in person, she seemed far more guileless, far less calculating, though he wouldn't go so far as to say she appeared innocent or naive. She just didn't come off as brash and brassy as he'd expected her to be. In fact, her demeanor, despite her party dress, was polite bordering on downright professional.

"Not to be rude," she said, "but I couldn't help overhearing a bit of your conversation as I came in. I think it's wonderful that you're trying to help your sister. It's a big, scary world out there on tour. Even for someone who is . . . how did you say it? Not a 'shining example of behavior modification'?" She shrugged.

He winced.

"I get quoted wrong all the time, but I think it was something like that. If you'll pardon my being so bold," she went on, "I think I could probably find one or two pieces of wisdom to impart to Gabrielle." Her grin widened. "I understand we have a lot in common. Good for her."

Okay, so maybe she was a little brash. More than a little. This was more in line with what he'd expected. And a sudden resurgence of confidence rushed in—okay, crept in—as he regained his footing. "I appreciate the offer, I do. And I hope you won't take this the wrong way," he said, fighting the urge to down the rest of his cognac in one swallow. The woman had presence. In spades. It was like the room had been suddenly amped up in some way, air particles more electrified or something. He'd all but forgotten there was anyone else in the room. "Gaby idolizes you, and it's because of that, that I have some concerns. As impressive a career as you've had, actually because it's so incredible, I'm afraid that you giving her any advice would come across to her as some kind of tacit approval of the temperamental way she behaves. As a dominant junior player, she's already been the subject of some fairly intense scrutiny. Now is the time to step in and give her the tools she needs to handle that kind of pressure off court so it doesn't affect her game on court."

Aurora stepped closer. "Given the way Gabrielle pushed Serena to that third set in Paris last month, I understand your concern. She could do well here. Even without her coach," she added pointedly, not for a second giving up the battle. She laid her hand on Tess's arm and squeezed. "Of course, no one knows better than Tess how fast things can happen on tour in terms of that sudden avalanche of interest from the media. The British press can be rather intense."

Max kept his attention on Tess. It wasn't all that difficult. "I appreciate that you have a wealth of experience in that area and probably some very good advice on how to handle it. But I'd rather encourage her to find a way to cut down on the histrionics on court, focus on her game, so she can stay out of the spotlight off court. I don't want her to need your advice on how to handle the paparazzi. I'd rather steer her completely away from that kind of distraction."

Tess paused for a moment and he was half-afraid he'd seriously offended her. Then a split second later she tilted her head back and laughed. It was a full-bodied, deep-from-the-belly kind of laugh, which was as surprisingly infectious as the rest of her. She was a lot to take in. And even more to take on. It exhausted him just thinking about it.

"You can't be that naive," she said, when she finally caught her breath.

He noted from the corner of his eye that Aurora's smile had broadened and her eyes were bright as she watched the byplay between the two. Well, of course she was pleased. She was watching Tess play him like a fiddle, which meant she suspected she'd ultimately get her way. He wished he could say with any amount of confidence that she was wrong. But as he was standing there, stupidly saying absolutely nothing in the face of Tess's mocking laughter, he was beginning to feel both outnumbered and outplayed. Naive, indeed.

"Don't you realize that you can't switch off your sister's temperament on court like some kind of lightbulb? I'll admit, I haven't seen her play; I missed her match in Paris, but I've heard about her, about her game. If she's truly anything like I was, it's that very fire and determination that will keep her head in the game. Turn that off and she'll be useless out there." She laid her hand on his arm now and it was like an electrical current shot straight up to his shoulder. Any chance he'd had of regrouping and regaining the upper hand was, at the very least, temporarily derailed. And he was probably being somewhat kind to himself with that assessment.

"You're trying to protect her, which is admirable," Tess continued, "and I know you only have her best interests at heart. But she's already who she is, to some degree, anyway, and if you want her to have success on court, then maybe instead of trying to extinguish her fire, you should begin to think how best to harness all that energy so she can be the success everyone seems to think she'll be."

"That's exactly what I'm trying to do."

"But you're going about it the wrong way. You want to contain it, control it, modulate it. It doesn't work that way."

"Sure it does. It's called maturing, growing up."

"In a sense," she said agreeably, surprising him. "If she were floundering that would be one thing, but it sounds like she has a strong mental game already. Why don't you give her some credit that maybe she's already harnessing it, already directing it in a healthy way."

"By slamming her rackets and shooting tirades to the line judges?"

Tess just grinned.

Max rolled his eyes. "It's not something to be proud of."

"Oh, I don't know. Venting my wrath on a hapless racket or two was exactly what I needed to get over a bad shot or bad line call so I could return my focus to the point at hand, and my opponent across the net. If I kept it inside, it would have distracted me for who knows how many points, and just like that it'd be game, set, match to my opponent."

Which was exactly, almost verbatim, what Gaby had told him. Though he'd be damned before he shared that information. More ammunition Tess Hamilton did not need. "Other players manage to find a way to contain themselves and still stay focused. She's young. She can learn to do that. And it will help her all the way around, on the court, and off. It just seems to me—"

"It seems to me that you haven't a clue what makes your sister tick. Obviously you're a very contained sort who doesn't understand us more emotional types."

What the hell did that mean? He found himself somewhat put out by her rash assessment. Like he was a tight ass or something. Gaby's words from earlier in the week echoed through his mind. Well, they were both wrong. He was far from being that guy. He could be very spontaneous if properly motivated. Just not with his temper. Or with scheduling. Or, okay, ever, really, if he were honest. But that was because he had to be a good role model for Gabrielle. He was all she had. Otherwise he'd be a lot more . . . Jesus. Maybe they were right. He really was not liking this conversation.

"She is who she is, Max. Yes, for some people, tossing a racket is a bad thing. For some players, that's when they lose focus, not regain it. But for a very few of us, it works in the opposite way."

"That doesn't make it right," he insisted. "For her, anyway."

Tess's smile shifted, became less friendly. "You're embarrassed. That's what this is all about, isn't it? It's not about shaping Gaby's temperament so she handles her life better, it's about modifying her behavior so she what, acts like a lady at all times? So she doesn't make you look bad?" There was an obvious edge in her tone and it pricked at him.

"I'd like to think of it as instilling the principles of good sportsmanship. You don't just get to act like a spoiled brat, on court or off, and claim it's what you have to do to keep your head in the game. She needs to grow up and learn to handle the life she's stepping into. And, if you'll beg my absolute pardon, perhaps you should have, as well."

He set his glass down on the closest flat surface and turned to Aurora while he still held on to some semblance of control over his temper. No one pushed his buttons that easily. Except for his sister. Which made his decision about all this quite easy, as it turned out. "I very much appreciate what you're trying to do for Gaby. But I think perhaps this entire idea was a mistake. I'm really sorry you've gone to all this trouble, but I'm going to look elsewhere for the help I think she needs."

"You're going to do what, then?" Tess interjected. "Take a kid who doesn't even have a regular coach at the moment, and send her to a sports shrink? Oh yeah, that'll help her ten days out from her first Wimbledon. Screw with her head right now and you can pretty much kiss her chances good-bye. But hey, at least you won't have to worry about that off-court pressure; the press here will chew her up and spit her out during the first round, then forget all about her. Because she won't make it to the second round."

He grabbed his jacket off the back of the nearby sofa. "I can see myself out," he said tightly. "Have a good evening."

"I can help your sister, Max," Tess called after him. "And I'll bet when she finds out that you turned down the chance for her to work with me, you'll need a whole hell of a lot more than a sports shrink to get her temper under control."

Of course she didn't let him go without a parting shot. Of course not. Tess Hamilton always had the last shot. And, as usual, it was a winner. He knew he should just keep walking, out the door, through the front entrance, and straight to his car. *Don't let her goad you.* But there he was, turning back at the door, foolishly trying to hit a clean return when he knew he didn't have a prayer of landing the shot. Or even getting it over the proverbial net. "I'm all she has. I may not always make the right decisions, but everything I do, I do with her best interests in mind, and at heart. And so far, we seem to be doing quite well without your input. I'm sure we'll muddle through this tournament without you, too." He shifted his gaze to Aurora, who wasn't looking nearly as perturbed by all this as he'd have expected. Possibly because, having witnessed this exchange, she'd reached the same conclusion he already had. Oil and matches don't mix. "Thank you. For everything. I do appreciate it."

Only after hearing the front door shut did Aurora finally turn to Tess. "Well," she said, hoping her smile was appropriately abashed, "that went well."

Tess raised her brows, then burst out laughing. "Oh yeah. I really made friends and influenced people tonight." She picked up Max's glass and downed the final dregs, making a face as the cognac hit her throat. "How do you drink this stuff?" She shuddered and carried the glass over to the rolling cart that held an array of crystal decanters and a beautiful sterling-silver ice bucket. Exchanging Max's glass for a clean one, she made herself a gin and tonic, neat. "I'd apologize for losing you a client, by the way, but I figure it just makes us even."

Aurora smiled. There was a slight edge to Tess's otherwise affectionate tone. She knew she deserved far worse. "I'm sorry, dear," she began, quite sincerely. "It goes without saying that I owe you an apology. I regret how this all came about. It certainly wasn't how I'd have planned it, given a better chance."

Tess turned and leaned back against the cart, nursing her drink. "How did this come about? What was he doing here so late? And, if you don't mind my asking, when were you going to tell me about big brother? Overprotective much?"

"Speaking from one with experience in such matters."

Tess laughed. "Why do you think I moved three time zones away?" She gave a little shudder. "I can't even imagine dealing with Wade as my brother while on tour, much less my manager."

"The dynamic with the Fontaines is very different. Gaby lost both parents when she was little—she and Max shared the same father, Trenton Fontaine, wealthy international financier. I'm sure your father has heard of him. Way and I had spent time with him through the years, during both of his marriages. Max is largely estranged from his mother and Gaby has no other family, so they are all each other has, for the most part. He has been mother, father, manager, pretty much everything except coach for her, since right after he got out of college."

Tess nodded, sipped her drink, but didn't say anything. Aurora knew she was curious; after all, she'd put on the pretense of knowing all about Aurora's little plan when she'd crashed their party of two earlier. Aurora took that, and the fact that she wasn't reading her the riot act over her high-handedness just now, as a good sign. This wasn't how she'd planned this, but she hadn't really had time to put a plan into place. Max had forced her hand this evening. But she was nothing if not optimistic. She had to be, in her line of work. "He's not a tennis player, but—"

"Gee," Tess said dryly, "I'd have never guessed."

Aurora merely smiled, nodded. Smooth and steady. "So you can imagine the obstacles he's had to overcome."

"I'm sure he's of sterling character. Emphasis on character." Tess finished her drink and set her glass back on the serving tray. "So, why don't you tell me what your Machiavellian plan was all about." She crossed the room and, unconcerned about the designer dress she had on, plunked down on the overstuffed settee that had been positioned in the middle of a collection of high-backed chairs and a delicately carved walnut tea table, which were all arranged in a grouping in front of the parlor's main attraction, its beautiful Italian-marble fireplace. She patted the place next to her and smiled.

Aurora knew better than to be fooled by that innocent grin. But she gladly took the seat, quickly deciding how best to play this latest turn of events to her advantage. "Again, allow me to apologize."

Tess waved that away. "Your heart is always in the right place, Aurora. I know that. But why didn't you just come directly to me and ask me to help you out?"

Her own lips curved in a knowing grin. "You haven't been the easiest of butterflies to pin down of late."

Tess had the grace to look abashed. "I've been a thoughtless houseguest, haven't I?" She reached out and covered Aurora's hand with her own. "I'm sorry. You're right, and after you've been so gracious in inviting me here. It's been crazy, what with the wedding preparations and the pretournament social whirl, but that's no excuse."

The smile and the apology were sincere, but Aurora saw past that. Tess was on a fishing expedition here . . . and it wasn't entirely simple curiosity. Aurora resisted the urge to smile. She did so love it when a plan came together. She slid her hand from

Tess's and patted her knee. "No matter, dear. We're here now. As for my plans for Max and his sister, you already understand his reasons for bringing her to Glass Slipper."

Tess nodded. "Have you kept in touch with them over the years, knowing his parents and all? Did you go to him or did he come to you?"

"A little of both. Valerie Wagner, who runs our London location, came up with a rather brilliant idea to run a promotional tie-in with Wimbledon, catering to those who flock here to watch the Championships. It was geared toward providing our more standard spa amenities, with the idea of elevating our presence here, getting the word out, so to speak. She hadn't really expected to grab the attention of any of the players, but a small number of them have discovered us, and decided to avail themselves of some of our more unique amenities. Max heard about it through the tour grapevine and when he realized I was here in London, he rang me up. It was delightful to get the chance to see him again; it's been a few years, I'm afraid, but I've kept track of the two of them, much as I do your family. We got to talking about Gabrielle and he was discussing his concerns about her turning pro, and, well, it just sort of went from there."

"So what's with the late-night meeting?" Tess grinned then. "Of course, despite his less-than-obvious charm, he is quite good-looking." She nudged Aurora gently. "When I saw the extra car in the drive, I was hoping you might have had other plans for the evening."

Aurora found herself blushing. "Oh, you are quite the scamp."

Tess merely laughed. "Vivian would have gone after him in a heartbeat and you know it."

Aurora sniffed. "Which is what sets Vivi and me apart. I conduct myself with at least a bit of class and a modicum of control. Especially where members of the opposite sex are concerned."

"Oh, you don't fool me. I bet you get just as much action as she does. You're just more discreet."

Aurora gamely tried to keep her expression neutral, but Tess's impish smile did her in and she found herself grinning like a woman decades younger. "I don't suffer the lack of an escort if I so desire one," she admitted, "but unlike Vivi, I do prefer my gentleman callers to be somewhere in the vicinity of my own age."

Tess hooted. "You go, Aurora."

She blushed, but they both laughed.

"So," Tess asked, "if you weren't hoping for a moonlit tryst with a hot younger guy, what was he doing here so late?"

"Gabrielle has been our guest this past week, mostly taking advantage of the spa services. I've been trying to set something up for her, to deal with the other issues Max and I had discussed, but I wasn't happy with the individuals I'd hunted down so far, and you know we have our standards. I wanted it tailored to her specific needs. He and I met up at a charity function this evening, quite serendipitously, and I had this brainstorm! Here I am searching all over London for the right person to talk to Gabrielle and she's right here under my own roof! I was half-hoping you'd be at the party this evening and I could just introduce you both, but when you didn't show, I invited him back here to discuss it privately, and, well . . . the rest as they say . . ." She merely smiled.

"So you were out reveling in the London nightlife yourself. And here you were giving me a hard time." Tess raised her glass. "Scamp, indeed."

Aurora waved away her teasing, and found herself grinning. She had forgotten just how much she'd enjoyed Tess's company in the past. So much talent, such a wonderful career. And now here she was, embarking on a new path, and Aurora couldn't help but wonder if Tess was, perhaps, a bit lost as she tried to find her way in this new world of hers. Presumptuous? Possibly. But when had that stopped her?

"I am sincerely sorry for just winging it, as they say. I know I should have waited until I'd spoken to you. I know you're very busy, and I wouldn't have otherwise imposed on your time, but it just seemed too serendipitous not to at least try and see if we could work something out. I'd hoped to talk to you this morning, or at some point during the day, but you must have been up and out early this morning."

Now it was Tess's turn to blush slightly. "Something like that. I'm sorry I've been so scarce. It really was rude of me." She took Aurora's hand again. "You've been really wonderful, and trust me, I'm very grateful for your hospitality. I'm sorry if I screwed things up with the Fontaines."

"I don't think anything of the sort. Despite her brother's misgivings, I do think you'd have been quite good for Gabrielle."

"I'll admit that when I first overheard his comments, although I was a bit put off by the intensity of his dislike for someone he didn't even know, I thought he had a valid point."

"You handled it quite smoothly." She patted Tess's knee, smiled. "You were quite convincing. I appreciate that."

Tess snorted. "I just wanted to make him reconsider talking out of his ass without consulting his head first. Sorry," she added.

"No worries, dear. Now, I realize I have no right to ask this of you, considering everything, but would you seriously consider talking with Gabrielle?"

"Were you sipping something other than cognac?" Tess teased. "Because I'm pretty sure when Max left here, he wasn't planning on leaving his sister at Glass Slipper another day, much less agreeing to let me within restraining order distance of her."

Aurora waved a dismissive hand. "I'll handle that." She took both of Tess's hands now. "I know it's a lot to ask, and of course you'll be handsomely recompensed for your time—"

"I can't let you pay me. I've freeloaded already."

"Trust me, Sir Robin was thrilled to hear he had you as a guest of Wexley House. You owe me nothing. Glass Slipper is quite capable of providing you with adequate compensation for your valuable time, as we do anyone who works for us."

"I tell you what, why don't we consider this my charitable contribution for the year? Dad's been hounding me to get more involved in giving back to the community, so you'll give me the chance to surprise him. Trust me, that's payment enough."

Well, this wasn't at all how Aurora had hoped this would go. Newly retired and, if what Aurora had overheard at Bobby's engagement party was true, possibly not as financially secure as one would assume. What Tess needed was a new niche to fill. A life makeover was in order. And, after all, that was Aurora's specialty, was it not?

Chapter 7

Tess paced the length of the parking lot, then back again. The gravel lot was tiny, wedged at the end of an alley that ran behind two houses on the outskirts of the village of Wimbledon. It backed up to a set of private grass courts that Glass Slipper had reserved for Gabrielle to train on during her stay. Tess had tried to get Aurora to finagle her first meeting with Gaby at a tea-house or restaurant or even Glass Slipper's London headquarters. Anywhere but on court.

She'd heard the suggestion Aurora had made to Max that night, of her possibly giving Gabrielle coaching tips in addition to all the mad life-on-tour skills she was here to impart. She'd given it some thought and frankly, she wasn't all that keen on the idea. The idea of coaching had passed through her mind when her money problems surfaced, but she'd rejected it out of hand. Sure, former players retired and became coaches to the stars of tomorrow all the time. Mostly lower ranked players. Rarely someone with her track record.

Largely due to the fact that someone with her reputation, and the accompanying income that accorded, didn't need to slave away on the courts, imparting their hard-earned wisdom to someone else, doing all the exhausting travel . . . only to sit in the stands on game day and watch someone else hit the ball. Not to mention the fact that the press would have had a field day when they found out she'd resorted to coaching. She could almost hear the endless speculation by the announcers, not to mention all the whispers and tittering chatter echoing through tournament locker rooms around the world, as everyone speculated on the whys and wherefores of Tess Hamilton's swift financial downfall.

There had to be a better way back to financial security, one that was more fitting to her stature as a former superstar of the tennis world. And definitely less potentially humiliating. But, if she were honest with herself, that wasn't the only reason she wasn't seriously considering coaching as an alternative source of income. She stared through the link fence and mesh screen at the bright green grass courts that awaited her. No, it went well beyond that.

She wasn't playing. At all. Hadn't so much as swung at a ball since announcing her retirement.

She leaned her forehead against the fence, breathed in the scent of the freshly trimmed greens, and sighed. In all the ways she'd imagined immersing herself back into the game, finding a way to enjoy it again while no longer competing, this would have never even made the list. Not that she'd had a specific plan in mind, but she'd always sort of imagined being alone when she did it, just hitting balls from the machine, finding her rhythm. It wasn't going to be a fun day.

She could still hit the ball, dammit. Just not like she used to. Her shoulder couldn't withstand any kind of constant punishment. She knew that. Had grudgingly accepted it. Enough to know retirement had been her only option. But that didn't mean she had to like it.

Every time she'd looked at her courts back home, knowing it was time to head out there and get something back of the game she'd devoted her life to . . . she'd found something else to do, promising herself that tomorrow she'd go out and hit a few. Find her way back to enjoying, on whatever level possible, the game she loved. She closed her eyes against the brilliant green of the grass court in front of her, beckoning her even as it terrified her. "This was not how it was supposed to go."

The sound of crunching gravel prompted her to turn around. The same dark sedan she'd spied in Aurora's drive the other night pulled in and parked beside the low-slung Jag that Sir Robin had insisted she use while in town. Maybe Sir Robin needed a personal assistant or something, she mused, as she watched the Fontaine duo emerge. She could just sell off what little she had left, drop out of sight permanently, and live in the lap of luxury in London while running errands for a wealthy, titled Brit.

She was just warming up to her little fantasy when Max emerged from the car and slid off his sunglasses. Hmm. Dark hair, rangy build, brown eyes, casual stance. He really was quite attractive, in an earnest, boy-next-door kind of way. She usually went for guys who were more obvious with their alpha traits. Jocks, mostly. Max didn't appear to be overtly athletic, but he was hardly soft. He appeared comfortable in his own skin, but not the type who liked to draw attention to himself, either. He looked . . . sincere.

He glanced at her car, or what he presumed was her car, and seemed to barely refrain from rolling his eyes. She debated telling him it was Sir Robin's ride, but it could just as easily have been hers. She'd had one almost just like it when she stayed in

Paris. Besides, she knew he'd inherited his dad's fortune, so it wasn't like he had to ride around in that boring old sedan. The man obviously didn't know what he was missing.

She most definitely did.

"I see you found the courts okay," he finally said.

Much to your dismay, she thought. "I know the village pretty well. I used to stay in a place close by every summer for grass-court season. You should consider renting or leasing out here next time, for the fortnight. It's nice to get out of the hustle and bustle of the city. Helps keep the focus and concentration."

"Funny, I seem to recall you enjoying the London nightlife."

She added "determined" to his list of traits. Determined to keep her out of his sister's immediate circle. Determined to think the worst of her.

Obviously, he still wasn't keen on this little idea, but somehow Aurora had persuaded him to let the two of them meet for a few minutes before Gaby's practice session. She'd half-hoped the whole event was a sparkling disaster so she could be done with this charade and get back to the matter at hand, namely finding herself new endorsements. But one look at the stubborn set to Max's chin brought her rebellious, competitive nature right back to the fore. What it was about him that pushed her buttons, she really didn't know. But now she was determined, too. Determined to make this brief meeting with his sister nothing short of the Second Coming. If only so he'd be forced to admit that she really did have something of value to offer his sister. Whether he liked admitting it or not.

And then she forgot all about Max as she got her first look at Gabrielle, who was presently climbing out of the passenger side of their car. "Max, where is my other gear bag? Please don't tell me you forgot to put it in the car. I told you I needed it." This was followed by a dramatic sigh, followed by an equally dramatic petulant pose against the open doorframe of the car. "What am I going to do without my other rackets?" she whined. And not very prettily.

A shame, because she was otherwise a strikingly beautiful girl, Tess noted. Even more so in person than the photos Tess had seen of her after her loss to Serena in Paris. Quite tall, with long legs and arms, but not at all bony. Nicely muscled, strong frame, but still feminine. She had Max's dark hair, thick and luxuriant from the looks of the long ponytail that cascaded over her shoulder. She had his brown eyes, too, only hers slanted just a bit, and her skin tone was more olive in complexion. Maybe after her mother. Nice cheekbones and a full, wide mouth rounded out the picture. A mouth that was presently pulled down in the corners. Something told Tess this was not an unusual expression for the teenager.

"I needed those rackets. We had them strung with the tension *I* wanted, not Sven's way. I really needed to use those today. What am I going to do?"

"Gee, Gab," Max said, teeth gritted into a fake smile, "I don't know. Maybe use one of the other ten that are in the trunk."

"Boot."

"Excuse me?"

"In England, it's called a boot," she said, as if anyone who was even remotely cool would obviously know this.

"I can think of another boot we can discuss," Max replied, "starting with the one I'm going to plant up your—"

"Hello," Tess said as she stepped out from the shadow cast by the court fence, smiling, though not exactly sure why. Gabrielle appeared to be something of a typical teenage snot, and Tess already knew her brother was a narrow-minded prig. Maybe it was something in their byplay, reminiscent of the many verbal altercations she'd experienced with Wade in their formative years. Well, okay, even their later adult years. Or just yesterday on the phone, discussing Bobby's wedding.

Tess thought the ceremony had been a lovely, poignant, perfect affair between two people so obviously in love it even made her yearn a little, if briefly, for the ideal of matrimonial bliss. Wade, on the other hand, had thought it far too understated for someone of Hamilton stature and couldn't understand why there had been no press invited. Men. Thank God he and her dad were already winging their way back across the Atlantic. Now she could settle down to the real business at hand.

Just as soon as she got this little event over with.

Gaby's expression went slack as she noticed Tess for the first time. "Oh, Jesus," she gasped. "You're Tess Hamilton!"

Well, well. When she wasn't pouting, and with her eyes all wide like that, Gabrielle Fontaine suddenly looked like nothing more than a naive young girl. Tess already knew better, of course, but it was nice to see the teenager had some depth. She'd need it.

"Last I checked," Tess responded with a laugh. She walked over to Gaby and stuck her hand out. "Pleasure to meet you."

The teenager didn't move. She just kept staring at Tess, mouth hanging open.

Tess glanced at Max. "She seems a bit shocked to see me here." She left the remark dangling.

Max's scowl deepened as he shifted his weight a little.

Gabrielle whipped her head to Max. "You knew she was going to be here? And you didn't tell me?" That last part ended on a high squeak. She turned back to Tess. "Oh, my God, it's such an honor to meet you! I've only been a huge fan of yours since forever. I remember watching you play Steffi when I was maybe five or six and I'd just started taking lessons. You were new to the tour, like I am now, and Steffi was about a year away from retiring and you just smoked her! I can't believe you won your first grand slam during your rookie year. That's what I want more than anything in the world. But it's so much harder than playing juniors. I mean, I knew it would be, duh, but even then, it's so much harder, you know? I mean, of course you know. I want it really badly, though. Especially here. This is my favorite slam and I know it was yours, too, right? I mean, I knew when I saw you win here against Steffi that I wanted to play tennis like that, like you. Maybe have the chance to play you someday, like you played Steffi. I always dreamed of beating you. I was so upset when you retired last year and I'd never get my chance." She blushed quite prettily. "God, I'm sorry, that didn't come out right. I'm not usually such a dork, I swear."

Tess couldn't help but grin. She was anything but dorky. Gabrielle was talking a mile a minute without so much as taking a breath. Her excitement was palpable and the sheer energy she exuded was off the charts. She was a beautiful young woman with the kind of spark that would make her perfect magazine-cover fodder, even without the talent she apparently possessed. The combination of swaggering confidence and teenage innocence probably had editors and paparazzi everywhere just salivating while waiting for her to do something newsworthy.

Max definitely had his hands full. Poor older brother. Probably had zero idea what to do with his not-so-little sister these days. For a brief moment, Tess thought about her mom and dad and wondered how hard it must have been for them, watching her grow from the juniors to the main draw at such a young age. Especially her mom, who knew what lay ahead for her, but was completely ineffective in telling her headstrong daughter anything she wasn't convinced she already knew.

The world was truly Gabrielle's oyster and she knew damn well she was a very fine pearl. Tess understood that. Taking that slam off of Steffi her first year out had only cemented Tess's willful attitude. Confidence bordering on arrogance. But she'd worked damn hard at her game, and every win only made her work ethic grow stronger. And as the titles racked up, she knew she'd earned every damn one of them. So what if she was a little cocky? Okay, a lot cocky. She could back it up, couldn't she?

Only now, looking at Gabrielle, did she see what she must have looked like to her parents at that age. At sixteen, Gaby's princess-of-tennis attitude was a surefire recipe for sleepless nights and daily headaches. Good thing Tess was only here to talk with her for an hour or two and give her some advice. No way did she want to step into the middle of this family-tempest-in-the-making.

Tess could feel the almost physical pull of the courts behind her, and admitted that there might have been a little part of her that wanted to see if Gaby had the goods to back up the attitude. She'd meant to do a little more research on the girl's junior career before meeting her, but with Bobby's wedding and all, she hadn't been able to. And maybe, just maybe, there was a tiny part of her that wanted to step on that court and teach this young lady a thing or two. The little rush of competitiveness felt surprisingly good. She glanced at Gaby's gear bags and found herself wondering if she could still take her after all her time off.

It was all she could do not to laugh at herself. Apparently the cocky confidence thing never went away. So much for being the role model Aurora was hoping for.

"I'm sorry you didn't get your chance to give me a shot," Tess told her, never more sincere. "Who knows, maybe we'll get the chance to hit a few someday, just for grins."

Gabrielle goggled. *"Really?"*

Now why in the hell had she added that last part? Sheesh. Probably because Max's scowl was permanently etched into his face now. What was it about poking at him that got her going, anyway?

"Oh my God," Gaby gushed, running the words together like they were one big word. "That would be so awesome. Tess Hamilton as my hitting partner, even for an afternoon. I might die right here on the spot." She grinned. "I'm probably embarrassing you. I promise, I'm usually more polished and professional than this. I've met a lot of the great players, and I never gush. It's just that you, well, you . . ."

Tess grinned. "How do you think I felt when I first met Steffi?" She put her hand on Gaby's arm and leaned in, lowering her voice. "I sweated right through my lucky tennis dress before I ever reached the court. I was so freaked out that if I changed clothes, I'd never have a chance to beat her, but how gross was it going to be, walking out onto Centre Court in front of a box full of royals with obvious pit stains? Talk about embarrassing."

Gabrielle's eyes widened. "Did you change?"

Tess shook her head. "It made me so nervous I almost fell over doing my curtsy and keeping my arms down by my sides." She grinned. "But somehow I didn't mind so much when I was lifting that trophy over my head." She laughed. "So, thank you for the gushing. I'm flattered. Even if you didn't sweat through your clothes."

Gaby clamped her arms to her side. "Who says I'm not?"

They both laughed and Max finally stepped closer and cleared his throat. It only took one glance at him to know that bonding so effortlessly with his sister wasn't exactly endearing her to him. Which, perversely, made Tess want to try all the harder. She still agreed with Max that she might not be the best role model for his sister, but to Tess's way of thinking, an hour or two wasn't going to hurt anything, either.

"We've got the court reserved for two, which gives you about a half hour before practice."

"I thought we had it right now? And a half hour for what?"

Gabrielle looked from her brother to Tess. "I completely forgot to ask you why you were here. Not to watch me practice?"

Tess shook her head. "Although I could probably learn a thing or two."

Gaby blushed furiously. "Right," she said, trying for casual cool. "Not in this century." She glanced quickly at Max. "So . . . ?"

Tess probably should have stepped in and made it easy on the two of them, but it gave her a bit of pleasure to watch Max stutter his way through the explanation, especially since he wasn't one hundred percent behind the idea. Or any percent, for that matter.

"This is part of your deal with Glass Slipper. A chance to pick Tess's brain, ask her whatever you want to know about being on tour, that kind of thing."

"Are you *serious*?" Gabrielle goggled again. "Really?" She looked between the two of them, then hooted and clapped her hands together. "Well hell, if you'd told me this was part of the deal, I wouldn't have been such a brat about going in the first place."

"It, uh, it just sort of came together in the past couple of days."

She looked to Tess. "Are you going to be around the whole week I have left at Glass Slipper? Or just today?"

"Today for sure," Tess told her, careful to keep from looking at Max. She was surprisingly drawn to Gaby. She saw a lot of herself in the young girl. "Why don't we go sit on one of the benches and talk for a bit?" Tess motioned to the gate that led to the courts.

"Okay, sure." Gabrielle looked at her brother. "What are you going to do?"

Max managed a tight smile. "Assuming you don't want me hovering, I have some calls I need to make. I'll stay out here."

Tess wondered if his first call was going to be to Aurora.

"'Kay," Gaby said, already turning to Tess as she finished speaking. "I'll come back out for my gear later. I'm all yours, Tess."

"Right this way, then." She stepped over to the gate.

They hadn't gone a half-dozen steps when Gaby paused and said, "Wait a second, I'll be right back." Tess turned and watched as she ran back to Max and hugged him tightly. She was too far away to hear what was said, but she saw Max's tense stance relax. The smile that followed was so honest and affectionate, Tess actually felt a little tug in the vicinity of her heart.

Gaby gave him a noisy kiss on the cheek, then bounced back toward Tess with such natural exuberance and energy, Tess felt every day of her twenty-nine years.

She caught Max's gaze past Gaby's shoulder. It wasn't so tight or disapproving now. But his smile faded as he stared at Tess, and she found herself wishing she could reassure him in some way that she would never encourage Gaby to do anything rash. So she did the only thing she could think of. She grinned and popped Max a thumbs-up as Gaby stepped past her through the gate. Rather than nod in approval, or sigh in relief, the scowl came back. Tess swore under her breath and rolled her eyes. "Men," she muttered.

"What?" Gaby asked, holding the gate open for her.

"Well, then," Tess said brightly, motioning toward the courtside bench. "Why don't you tell me a little bit about what the tour has been like for you so far. You just turned pro a few months ago, right?"

"Yep. Right after the Australian Open. We decided it was too much to travel all the way down there for my opening tournament. I needed some regular match play, first. So I stayed at home and prepared for the clay-court season. I wanted to make the draw for the French Open if I could. I had pretty good results in juniors, so I got a wild card to Amelia Island."

Tess took a seat and Gaby straddled the bench next to her. "How'd you do?"

Gaby shrugged and tried to look nonchalant and humble. "I did okay. Quarterfinals at Amelia Island. Quarters over here, too, at the Italian Open."

It was all Tess could do not to snort. God, she was so much like Tess had been at that age. "Pretty good start."

Gaby's shoulders slumped. She scowled, clearly unhappy. "Until I drew Serena in the first round at the French."

Tess smiled. "Bad luck. But at least you got to play one of the stadium courts your first time out. Daunting, but kind of exciting. I missed that match. Which court did you play? Suzanne Lenglen or Philippe Chatrier?

"Chatrier."

"That's my favorite. So what did you think about the whole experience?"

Gaby gave her a sideways look. "My first match in grand-slam play and I'm on a show court with, like, five billion people watching me."

"Something tells me that didn't throw you off much."

Gabrielle fought to retain her scowl. "It was a little intimidating."

Tess grinned. "Don't be modest. You loved it."

"I'd have loved it a whole lot more if I'd played better."

Tess shrugged. "You had a good run coming in, and Serena could have had an off day."

"She played pretty well. First serve percentage was high." A hint of a smile played across her face as she gave Tess a sidelong glance. "I still got her to three sets."

Tess nudged her on the shoulder. "I call that a pretty good start."

"Yeah. I guess." Her expression smoothed. "I really wanted to do better. It was my first slam. I wanted to stay longer."

"That's good."

"What part?" Now Gaby snorted. "The part where I got wiped off the court in the third set? Or the part where I'd barely unpacked before it was time to head back to the airport?" She sighed and waved her hand. "I'm sorry, that sounded ugly."

"You just sound like an athlete who was really unhappy with her performance. That's the good thing."

Gaby looked up then. "How?"

"If you'd been completely happy with that result, that would show complacency to some degree. Which would doom you. A winner wants to win. Coming in second is losing."

Gaby grinned. "Good thing my brother can't hear you talk like that."

Tess smiled. "Yeah, well, he's not the one out there fighting for every point. You put in a lot of time on your game and so you expect it to be there for you when you need it. I hated losing. Hated it. It was like a personal insult."

"That's exactly how I feel!"

Tess shifted to look directly at her. "But you don't get mad at your opponent. You get mad at yourself. Which makes you work harder on your game so it won't let you down next time."

Gaby sat back a little, thought about it. "I never really thought about it like that."

"So, you came to London early for grass-court season. Play some warm-up events for Wimbledon?"

"One. Birmingham." She rolled her eyes. "I made it one round further before getting the other Williams sister. Fought her to a tiebreaker in both sets, but I couldn't get it to three."

"Still, pretty decent outcome for your first time meeting them. Formidable players, both of them. And Venus on grass is tough. This could be the beginning of a rivalry."

Gaby laughed. "I'm pretty sure for it to be considered a rivalry, I'd actually have to be able to beat one or the other of them at least some of the time. Or even once."

"You'll get there."

Gaby looked a bit dubious at Tess's certainty.

"You think you will, right?" Tess asked.

Gaby nodded automatically.

Tess grinned. "That's what I thought. So why aren't you playing Eastbourne this week?"

"I wanted to, but there was the whole media thing. The press in Europe has been a little crazy. It started in France, when I got Serena to three and ended her streak of not dropping a set. Then I played Venus to a pretty big crowd here and it sort of drew attention. Max panicked and decided I'd be better off taking the time before Wimbledon practicing on my own and getting 'mentally ready.' Like I can't handle a little pressure. I've waited my whole life for this!"

"So you want to come out guns blazing and taking no prisoners, and he wants you to go slower?"

She nodded. "I dominated juniors the past two years. I'm so ready for the tour, I know I am. Because of my age, I'm already restricted in how many tournaments I can play in a year, but he wants to pace me even slower, not have me enter that many events my first year on the tour, and just let my ranking improve gradually. Which is ridiculous. I'm almost seventeen!" She said this like she had one foot in the grave. "Plus he's all worried about the attention I'm getting and that it's going to freak me out." Her shoulders slumped and she looked petulant again. "He thinks I'm a baby or something. I've been playing my whole life."

"What about your coach? What did your coach say?" Tess watched her closely. "Is Max coaching you?"

"God, no. Like it's not hard enough having him as my

brother, mother, manager, and baby-sitter. I swear he'd tutor me, too, if he thought he could get away with it."

"You have a tutor on tour with you?"

She shook her head. "I worked hard the past two years during juniors so I could get my GED early. It was the only way to get him to let me go on tour instead of making me play in college instead."

Tess nodded in approval. She'd done pretty much the same thing. Except for that last part about actually getting the GED. She'd always meant to. She'd finished all of her classes. Well, most of them. But she entered the pros younger than Gaby. The age restrictions were different then, and she'd zoomed up the ranks so fast, she'd just never gotten around to it. She'd wheedled her mother into letting her dad and Wade think she'd finished, promising she'd take the test someday. Well, someday never came, her mother stopped bugging her as long as she was doing well on tour, and then her mom got sick and, well, none of that seemed all that important anymore.

"So if your brother doesn't coach you, who does?" She knew the answer to this, of course, but she wanted to hear what Gaby had to say on the subject.

She immediately ducked her chin, then put it right back up again, but didn't quite meet Tess's eyes. "I've been working with Sven Sardoz since right before turning pro. But I sort of lost him after the last match in Birmingham."

" 'Sort of lost him'? Where, at the airport baggage carousel? How do you lose a coach?"

Gaby's lips curved in a dry smile. "Oh, there are a couple of ways. At least, that I've discovered so far." She grinned a little. "You ran through more than a few yourself, right?"

"Is that the kind of role model I am to you?"

Gaby sobered a little, clearly unsure if she'd insulted her idol. "I, uh—"

Tess went easy on her. "I do know how hard it can be to find someone who understands how you see the ball."

Gaby let out a little sigh of relief. "Exactly! I've tried to tell Max that it's really important for me to have someone who totally gets the way I want to play my game, but—"

"Just out of curiosity, who makes the decision on what coach you use? If you don't mind my asking."

"We decide together. Mostly."

"And Max does the firing?"

Gaby had the grace to look a little uncomfortable. "When necessary."

Tess suspected that if what she'd heard about Gaby's on-court temperament were true, more than one coach had left of his or her own accord, rather than by the decision of either Fontaine sibling. Not that she was even remotely considering tackling the job herself. She was just curious. Because it reminded her of her own rocky path with coaches. And managers. And agents. And accountants . . .

"So, who are you hitting with?"

Gaby squinted against the sun as she peered past the fencing to where her brother was leaning against their car, talking on his cell phone. "Petra Kasyanova. She's a little older than me and plays on the doubles tour." She glanced at Tess's watch. "She should be getting here soon. We only have the courts for a couple of hours."

It was right on the tip of Tess's tongue to offer to hit the ball until her partner showed up. She was admittedly curious to see Gaby's game. The girl talked the talk, but Tess was more interested in the court skills she had to back it up.

Just then another car pulled into the gravel lot, and two women piled out of the car. One in tennis gear, the other in slacks. Gaby groaned. "Christ, not Tabitha. I'm going to kill Max."

"Not Petra, I take it?"

Gaby just shook her head. "I guess she couldn't make it."

Before Tess could ask what was so ghastly about Tabitha, Gaby was bouncing up. "It's been so great getting the chance to meet you. You have no idea what this has meant to me. I wish it wasn't over already."

"Mind if I stay and watch?" Tess had no idea she was going to make the offer until it was out of her mouth. But she couldn't deny she was quite curious to see the teenager in action.

Gaby froze, but only for a second. "Sure! I mean, no, I don't mind at all." She looked a little dazed at the proposition, which made Tess feel inordinately pleased. There was still a lot of little girl inside the sixteen-year-old phenom.

Tess settled on the bench as Gaby ran over and talked to the newcomers and Max. Tess hadn't gotten the chance to talk to her at all about the pressures of the tour or anything else Aurora had wanted them to cover. Not that they couldn't arrange to talk again, she supposed.

Sure, Tess needed to be focusing on strategizing her future survival, but surely she could squeeze in another hour or so to talk to Gaby. It would make Aurora happy and Tess owed her for the accommodations, no matter what she said. Might piss off Gaby's brother a little, but that just made the proposition that much more interesting.

Smiling, she pulled out her cell phone and dialed up Aurora to see what she could set up.

Chapter 8

"What do you mean I can't see her?" Max lowered his tone when several of the Glass Slipper employees glanced his way, clearly concerned that the calm serenity of their hallowed halls not be disturbed. "We clearly agreed that I was to accompany Gaby to all practice sessions."

Aurora, with her gracious, Southern charm in full force, didn't so much as blink at Max's heatedly whispered statement. "I assure you, she'll be fine. She's been quite enjoying herself so far."

Aurora had already detailed some of their more pampering services that Gaby had availed herself of over the past week. "I know she has. But the tournament is less than a week away now. Without a coach, I need to make sure her game is on the right track, be there for her. Don't get me wrong, I appreciate everything you're doing for her, Aurora, you know that, or I wouldn't have agreed to any of this. And if it helps her deal with the stresses of being on tour, or even the fortnight of the Championships, then I'll be forever in your debt."

Aurora took his arm and gently squeezed. "Dear Max, you know I would do that and more. I'm just so thrilled it worked out that I could be of some help to the both of you. You're so often in my thoughts and I've been so happy to see how tremendously well Gabrielle is getting along in her sport." She took both his hands. "If I haven't already told you, I'll say it again. I know you're as proud of her as you are concerned, but I hope you know she wouldn't be where she is today if it wasn't for you. She's well aware of that, too. You've done such a wonderful job."

He ducked his chin, abashed at her praise. "Thank you." Then he laughed a little. "I just wish I could believe that. I thought it had been a challenge so far. But my God, Aurora, everything just amped up about a thousand percent over the past two months. She's changing so fast, and it's not just the tour. I'm a wreck worrying about her."

She patted his cheek, as only she could. "She's becoming a woman, dear. And quite the femme fatale, too."

Max groaned.

Aurora laughed softly. "That is a good thing, trust me. In her sport, she's going to need all the weapons she can manage, on and off the court. I think she's doing just fine."

"I wish I had the same faith you did. There is so much happening so fast. It used to be all I had to juggle was her tutoring and getting her to practice, and to her tournaments. Now there are sponsorship deals being offered and endorsement contracts for all kinds of things and people wanting God knows what from her. Not to mention the media attention. She's only sixteen."

"She is beautiful and talented and spirited. She's going to attract attention whether you want her to or not."

"I know, I know. It's just, there's so much being put in front of her now. I can't be at her side every single second. I know it sounds ridiculous considering the amount of traveling she's done, but she's really led a somewhat sheltered life." He raked his hand through his hair. "Maybe she's right and I have been too overprotective. Maybe I haven't prepared her well enough for this. Maybe—"

Aurora patted his hand. "Max, darling, please. You've done a wonderful job with her, or she wouldn't be facing these delightful and exciting choices. But you're right, your job isn't done yet, which is why you've entrusted her to us for a short while. You were clever enough to realize that sometimes a girl, or a young woman, needs to hear certain things from someone other than her big brother. We're taking good care of that. Trust me, Max. Let her have some of her own time."

"She thinks she knows every damn thing and what is good for her, but trust me, she hasn't a clue half the time." He sighed in the face of Aurora's unwavering smile. "I know. It's just . . . not easy to loosen the reins, I guess."

"Don't think of it as loosening them so much as sharing them. She is going to have to make a lot of decisions for herself in the coming months. You've got to give her the chance to make some and accept that sometimes she might make the wrong ones. You've kept her under wraps as much as possible, to let her get her education and focus on honing her talent. Frankly, she's still in a controlled environment here and we're going to do our best to help give her the tools she needs to make good decisions, to keep a level head despite the insanity exploding around her, so she can stay focused on what is most important. You've given her a great foundation, we're just improving on what you've already given her. You should be proud of her."

"I am proud of her, I am. And I have great faith in her. But, Aurora, she's still just a child."

"As were you when you were handed the biggest responsibility of your life," she gently reminded him. "And look how well you've done." She squeezed his arm and pulled him into a brief hug. "It's going to be fine. She's going to be amazing." She leaned back and smiled. "You're going to survive, too. You know, if you ever need a bit of a break yourself, you can drop by."

Max sighed and smiled wearily. "Be careful what you offer. By the end of the fortnight, I might just move in."

"We'd be glad to have you." She bussed him on the cheek, then wiped away the coral smudge of lipstick she'd left behind. "Now, Gaby's practice sessions will go on as scheduled today, as will her physical conditioning. We have all your detailed notes on her routine and will follow them to the letter. But if you don't mind, I think it would be best if you sat this practice session out. She's on target, you said so yourself. One day won't derail her entire game." She walked with him to the front doors. "Go enjoy your day. London is a wonderful city. I'm sure you can find numerous things to do with your time. You need a break, too, you know."

"But—"

"She'll be fine, Max." She nudged him forward. A cloud of floral perfume enveloped him as she kissed his cheek. "Have a wonderful day. Check in with me tomorrow, okay?"

Moments later, Max found himself back in the parking lot, accompanied by a Glass Slipper employee in a peach blazer. He glanced back and caught Aurora's wave from the front porch and nodded somewhat absently in return before climbing into his car. He'd asked for this. He'd asked for her help. Why in the hell had he asked for her help?

He turned out of the long, winding drive and pointed his car toward the city, intending on going back to their hotel in town. Aurora had advised a day off, but he had calls to return, schedules to go over, not to mention checking the calendar for upcoming tour events, booking rooms, flights. He had to come up with several different game plans, each dependent on how well

Gaby did here and how he thought she'd be feeling based on that performance, not to mention what would be best for her physically. He didn't want to burn her out, body or soul.

Aurora would get her through practice and training and he could get a jump on things. So this was a good thing, his having a bit of time to himself. She was in good hands, he didn't have to worry. He'd see her tomorrow and fine-tune anything he might have overlooked. Then he could start thinking about finding a coach. The very idea made his stomach clench a little.

He started mulling over a potential list of names, but one person in particular kept floating to the surface. Mostly because she was the last person he wanted working with his sister.

Tess Hamilton.

Aurora watched Max head off with an understanding smile. "Poor man. Too many women running the show." She stepped back inside and headed to the main offices at the rear of the estate. The ones with the lovely lanai facing the courtyard. The sun was shining for a change and the courtyard gardens would be quite lovely with all the flowers still in bloom. A perfect day for an early tea, she thought. Her pleasure only increased when she found both Vivian and Mercedes waiting there for her, a sterling-silver tea service already laid out. "Hello all," she said airily, too happy with the way her plan was unfolding to care if she sounded a wee bit giddy.

Both of her partners were seated at a round, leaded glass table that took up the lion's share of the screened-in porch. She poured herself a cup of Darjeeling, helped herself to a sampling from the arrangement of small scones, then took a seat across from the other two.

Mercedes was bent over some folder or other, making notes.

Vivian was on her cell phone—or mobile, as they called them here in London. So she helped herself to her first scone and added sugar to her tea.

"You sound quite chipper," Mercy said, not looking up from her work.

It was the former girls' school headmistress in her, Aurora supposed. Yes, they were here in London on business, technically, but mostly it had been to visit Valerie and their new location. So what on earth Mercedes was working on so seriously, Aurora had no idea. Of course, she did everything seriously. Knowing her somewhat anal-retentive tendencies, she was probably double-checking the books, making sure the profit margins were as reported. Honestly, Aurora had no idea how she stayed awake looking at so many numbers.

"Well, dear, that's because I am chipper," she responded brightly, turning her thoughts back to her own little project. "Things are moving along quite swimmingly, I must say."

"Can you fax a copy to me," Vivian was saying on the phone. "Wonderful, darling." She laughed lightly. "Why, of course. I wouldn't dream of standing you up. Seven?" She paused, then laughed again. "How naughty of you. And I assure you I'm quite steady in spike heels." Another pause, an even throatier laugh. "Yes, darling, see you then. All of you." She clicked off and took a deep sigh, obviously quite pleased with herself. "I got the information you wanted," she informed Aurora.

"You're looking very cat-and-canary," Aurora replied, not meaning to sound snippy. Somehow, where Vivi was concerned, it just always seemed to come out that way.

"You're welcome," Vivi replied, a satisfied smile on her face.

"Must have been some business meeting," Aurora observed. "You're all but glowing."

"Am I?" Vivian didn't blush or bother to hide her supreme satisfaction with herself and life in general. Vivi's former life as

Hollywood fashion guru to the stars had left her quite jaded. Not that her current lifestyle had altered that reality much. Aurora swore Vivian could find trouble in a nunnery. Probably had, for that matter. God knows her age hadn't slowed her down. For Vivian, sixty-five was the new forty.

"When isn't she glowing?" Mercy commented, still focused on her forms.

As she rarely included herself in their banter, both Vivi and Aurora paused to send her a surprised look.

"What?" Mercy said, looking up. Her stern visage was enhanced by her closely coiffed silver hair and the modest-to-no makeup she wore.

"Nothing, dear," Aurora said instantly before Vivian could say anything. "You're absolutely right." She didn't need any tension marring her otherwise perfectly lovely day. "So," she said, turning back to Vivian. "What did you find out?"

"Your hunch was right. It's not just the Nike deal she lost. Every single one of Tess's sponsorship deals has expired, no renewals. She has no endorsement deals current or pending, either, that I've been able to discover. She hasn't signed with a new management agency since leaving her last one, and apparently she and her accountant parted ways rather abruptly, as well. So I did some further digging and discovered she had a rather nasty run-in with the IRS last fall and as a result, she's sold off most of her international assets. Paying this year's tab almost wiped her completely out. She's in the clear with the government now, but all she has left is her home in Boca, several cars, and whatever other personal items she might have invested in, jewelry and the like. She owns the home outright, but taxes and maintaining the grounds, along with the pool and tennis courts, are costly. Not to mention her day-to-day lifestyle. Essentially, she is hemorrhaging money just to maintain the status quo. Frankly, given the sorry state of her bank accounts and lack of any discernible income, I don't know how much longer she can last."

Aurora sat in disbelief. She'd suspected things weren't going well for Tess, but she'd had no idea the situation was so dire. She would have felt guilty for her snooping when Tess was clearly intending to keep her financial woes private, but she was only trying to help. And just as clearly, Tess was too proud to ask for help. She was well aware that Tess's extensive nightlife rounds had been made mostly at the pretournament sponsor parties. "Nothing new to report? Perhaps something she's put together since she's been here?"

Vivian shook her head. "I'm afraid not."

Aurora shook her head. "Poor dear. How did she let such a tragedy befall her?"

"Her retirement was rather untimely—perhaps she simply wasn't prepared for the sudden loss of income?" Mercy suggested.

Aurora sighed. "Perhaps. But she's a smart girl from a smart family. Why didn't she invest? Are you certain she has no other properties or the like? I can't believe she's come to this point so quickly."

"Believe it," Vivian told her. "I'm having the documentation faxed over, but trust me, she's as close to broke as she could be."

"Why hasn't she turned to her family for help? Her father—"

She was cut off by Vivian's burst of laughter and Mercedes' sigh.

"What?" Aurora asked, feeling a bit slighted. "She comes from a very close family. I happen to know that Frank is doing quite well. Wade and Bobby are financially independent. Surely any of them would help out if they knew the gravity of the situation."

"Somehow I doubt, with Tess's enormous pride, that she

would ever let her own family know how badly she mismanaged her estimable fortune," Vivian said.

Frowning, Aurora put her teacup down. "You have a point. Oh, dear." She lifted her teacup. "Thank goodness, then, that she has us."

" 'Us'?" Mercedes queried, arching one eyebrow quite formidably.

Aurora waved a hand at her. "Don't worry, I'm not asking anything directly of you." She glanced at Vivian. "I do appreciate your calling in a few favors. Your . . . contacts are aware the information is to remain absolutely secret, correct? I'd never forgive myself if I only made things more difficult for her."

"My . . . 'contacts,' as you call them, are always discreet, darling," Vivian assured her. "But you do realize that word will eventually get out? I'm sure Tess does, as well. Tennis is like any other billion-dollar industry. The people running it love nothing more than to eat their own young." She waggled a scone at Aurora. "Mark my words. She'll be lucky to stroll onto the All England Club grounds before all hell breaks loose for her. The British media are absolute fiends when it comes to ferreting out information like this."

Aurora tightened her hold on her teacup, her smile all the more determined. "I suppose we have our work cut out for us, then, don't we?"

" 'We'?" Mercedes asked.

Aurora sighed. "I'm using Glass Slipper's facilities to help accomplish my goals, so in essence, yes, we."

"She's not a paid guest," Mercedes, always the accountant, reminded her.

"At the moment she's actually a temporary employee, providing a service for one of our clients."

"The Fontaines, yes." Mercedes slid her glasses off and

looked directly at Aurora. "I'm still debating the relative merits of you taking on a personal client while we're here."

"For goodness sake, Mercy, when it was your godson—"

She waved a hand, unmoved by Aurora's argument. "Be that as it may, if you're going to be utilizing our assets here without—"

"Oh, for heaven's sake, Mercy," Vivian retorted, dabbing at a bit of wayward raspberry filling that had landed on her plate, then licking her finger. "Leave her be, will you? Aurora's little project will hardly bankrupt us."

Aurora beamed at the unexpected support. "Thanks, Vivi. And you're absolutely right. When I'm done, everyone will make out quite handily. Customer satisfaction won't be a problem." She picked up her linen napkin and dabbed at the corners of her mouth. And prayed like hell she was right.

Max whipped his car through the gates to Wexley House, thankful he didn't have to argue with the guard to gain entry. His name was still on the admittance list from the other night. There were no cars in front of the house, but then, Aurora had mentioned she used Glass Slipper limos to ferry herself about town. She'd offered him use of one, as well, but he'd declined. However, it was highly likely Tess took advantage of the service. She was the limo sort, after all. When she wasn't tooling around in one of Sir Robin's Jags, anyway.

"Must be nice," he grumbled, even though he knew it was a bit unfair. After all, he wasn't exactly hurting for money. Regardless of how well Gaby performed on tour, Max had long since made sure that their inheritance would continue to work for them for years to come. He just chose to utilize his good fortune in a less . . . ostentatious way. And he certainly didn't sponge off of people. Aurora had offered her Glass Slipper services gratis. A favor to an old family friend. He wouldn't hear a word of it. Tess, on the other hand, who had to be far more financially secure than he could ever dream of being, seemed to have no problem accepting whatever favors were tossed her way.

He looked up at the broad front to the mansion, seeing it for the first time in the light of day. The marble and stone exterior was every bit as daunting as the collection of art and priceless antiques he knew littered every room inside. Right up Tess's opulent lifestyle alley.

Shaking his head at the decadence of it all, he took the front stairs two at a time. He rapped on the door, then glanced at his watch. "Half past two. She should just be getting up." Whatever the case, he wasn't leaving until he'd spoken with her, even if he had to personally drag her hard-partying backside out of bed.

First he'd make sure she knew how much he appreciated her taking time from her oh-so-busy retired schedule to talk to his sister. Then he'd do whatever it took to make sure she opted out of any more of Aurora's well-meaning, if somewhat alarming schemes. He had enough to worry about the next couple of weeks, watching over Gabrielle. The last thing he needed was to worry about a wild card like Tess Hamilton. Emphasis on the word "wild."

Chapter 9

Tess set up the ball machine and questioned her sanity for the hundredth time in the past couple of hours. She'd woken up to a cool, gorgeous sunny day and decided to take a walk around the grounds . . . only to discover that in addition to a manicured croquet lawn that would make Alice in Wonderland drool, Sir Robin also had a lovely, quite immaculately maintained grass court.

"This is crazy," she muttered as she walked back around the net to her side of the court. She didn't even have her own rackets, for God's sake. *This is so not the way to do this,* she silently cautioned herself. Not that it was going to do any good. She was on a mission now.

Wearing beat-up sneakers, gym shorts, and an oversized Stanford T-shirt of Bobby's, she gripped one of Sir Robin's admittedly decent rackets and took her stance on the baseline. The tension of the strings was all wrong, of course, and the grip was too big for her hand. The belly was too wide for her taste, and there was no damper on the strings. But despite every possible sign indicating she should seriously reconsider this endeavor, here she stood anyway.

Well, at least if you make an idiot of yourself, the only person who's going to know is you. And Sir Robin's majordomo. She absently wondered how long it would take the tabloids to begin hounding the poor man. Not that what she was doing right now would be news. No one cared if Tess Hamilton did or didn't hit tennis balls around anymore. No, this moment only mattered to her.

But as soon as anyone got wind of her financial downfall—and even she knew it was only a matter of time, what with her little plan of fixing her problems while in London not exactly panning out—they would be all over any teeny-tiny tidbit of information that would add to their "how the mighty have fallen" story.

She aimed the remote at the state-of-the-art machine—go, Sir R!—and clicked the button. "Fuck 'em," she muttered, and, gripping the racket in both hands, bounced back and forth on the soles of her feet, focusing intently on the chute. It wouldn't be the first time she'd smacked the fuzz off a ball as a way of mitigating stress.

The hollow whooshing sound of the first ball shooting toward her coincided exactly with someone calling out her name.

Concentration shattered, the ball whiffed by her as she looked around to see who it was.

"Sorry," Max Fontaine said, looking anything but. He paused outside the fence that surrounded the court.

What in the hell was he doing here? She glanced behind him, but there was no sign of Gabrielle. They weren't supposed to meet until later. And it was supposed to be just her and Gaby today. Aurora had said she'd make that happen. Tess could only guess that big bro had gotten wind of their little plan and was none too happy about it. Tough.

He wore khaki shorts, a navy polo shirt, and leather loafers, no socks. Nonetheless, he managed to look like he'd just stepped off the pages of *Man About Town Monthly*.

Another ball whizzed by and she clicked the remote toward the ball machine. So much for her private return to the sport.

He apparently took that as an invitation and opened the gate.

It was hard to tell with the sunglasses, but he didn't look all that thrilled to see her. So what else was new?

"We need to talk." He walked to the end of the net and stopped beside the pole.

She started to tell him he should have called ahead because she was busy at the moment. But then he'd probably offer to wait while she practiced. Which was so not going to happen. *God, how far the mighty had fallen.* She'd played to crowds numbering in the tens of thousands, with millions more watching from home . . . and thrived on it. Now she was afraid of showing off her rusty, surgically repaired, less-than-world-class form in front of one measly person.

She stayed on the baseline. "About?" she asked, shading her eyes from the sun.

"Gabrielle."

Of course. Aurora had been rather vague about Max's feelings on her continued involvement with Gaby, not that Tess really cared one way or the other what he thought. She'd been so impressed with what she'd seen at practice the other day, she'd probably sounded a little gushy when talking about it with Aurora later that night. If she were honest, it was hard to be casual when talking about the teenager's game. In fact, she'd admit that it had been watching Gaby's intensity and drive during the hour of practice she'd hung around to watch, that had directly reinvigorated her own need to get back out on the court. She could all but taste the power and speed, the feel of the ball coming off her strings, all things she loved and so desperately missed.

"Your sister is quite talented," she said preemptively. "Not that I have to tell you that." She smiled, let it go a shade cocky. "Reminds me of me, actually."

He didn't so much as quirk a lip in return. Spoilsport. She was restless. And scared. She needed a diversion, dammit. And if he wasn't going to let her take it out on a few poor tennis balls, then he could suffer being the target instead.

"That's actually my concern, and why I'm here."

"Ah." She twirled her racket on two fingers. "Yeah, it must really suck to have your sister constantly compared to a former number-one player with a fistful of slam trophies to her credit. Poor you."

"It's not me I'm worried about."

She laughed at that. "Isn't it? From what little I saw and heard, Gaby seems to be holding up just fine. In fact, she has a pretty good head on her shoulders. Better than I did at her age, I'd say. I was all ready to give that credit to you." She propped her racket on her toes and flipped her hair over her shoulder. He really wasn't her type, too uptight. Yet, perhaps he could be interesting as a different kind of diversion. "But if you're going to come out here and interrupt my practice session just so you can insult me on my own tennis court—well, my borrowed court, anyway—I don't know that I'm feeling as generous now."

As flirting went, it was far beneath her usual standards, but she wasn't really on her game at the moment. She'd like to blame him, but she'd been off for quite some time now. In fact, she was out here facing her demons—or trying to—as a means to yank herself back up again. She hated—hated—feeling anything less than fully in command.

"Somehow I doubt my opinion of you causes you to lose any sleep."

She sighed inwardly. Okay, so maybe he wasn't going to be fun to play with either—too dry and sober for her tastes. Although there was that naughty little devil voice inside her, prodding her to push just a bit harder, serve and volley a little, get him to come into the net, so to speak, set him up for the perfect return winner. Not that she was going to do anything with him when she had him at her mercy, but at the very least she'd have him enamored enough that he'd have to back down from his negative stance on her involvement with his sister.

She walked closer to him, stopped a few feet away, and tapped her racket against the net. "You know, there are times when losing sleep can be a good thing," she ventured. Soft lob. She waited for the return.

"See, that right there is what I mean."

She sighed. So damn serious. And straitlaced. She was beginning to think it was a miracle Gaby had turned pro before she was thirty. "I don't mean to be rude—well, actually I do. After all, you don't seem to mind, so why should I?"

He rocked back on his heels a little, shoved his hands in his pockets. "Meaning?"

"We'll get back to my craven ways in just a moment. First I want to ask you something. Are you this uptight all the time? About everything? I mean, do you have any idea how to have fun?"

He just stared at her. It made her want to yank the sunglasses off his face. Not that it would have automatically made a difference. The guy took stoic to a whole new level.

"What I do with my private time isn't really a concern of yours," he said, sounding even more stuffy than before.

She hooted. "Question answered, then."

He frowned.

She lifted a hand in a helpless gesture. "Hey, if you're going to slander me all over God's creation without even taking five minutes to get to know me—ever think of working for one of the rags here, by the way? You'd be a natural, trust me." She shrugged, let her hand drop by her side. "All I'm saying is, you're here specifically because you're concerned with how I spend my private time, afraid I'll somehow poison your baby sister's apparent pristine persona. Well, let me tell you, she's not as pristine as you'd like to believe."

His scowl faltered. "What the hell are you talking about? What did she tell you?"

She wanted to laugh at his instant defensive posturing, but couldn't bring herself to do it. He might be a prig, but he was such a damn earnest one. It was clear he really did care about his sister. Thinking about Wade, even for a split second before automatically shoving him right back out of her brain again, she wondered what it would have been like if he'd felt even a fraction of the protective affection for her that Max obviously did for his younger sister. Sure, Bobby and she were tight, but that dynamic had her holding the older sibling card. Not the same thing at all.

Of course, she'd had a set of parents ruling her world in her formative years, at least one of which was a fabulous role model and extremely close to her only daughter. She had no idea what Max's formative years had been like, but she knew Gaby had lost both of her parents when she was quite young. Knowing how hard it had been for Tess to lose her mother as an adult, she couldn't even imagine. Max was all Gaby had.

So really, she should lighten up on the guy. But did he have to make it so damn difficult?

"Did she confide something to you?" Max pressed. "Because, as adults we have a responsibility here. You can't let her talk you into keeping secrets." He took his sunglasses off and she was treated to a pair of brown eyes that were really something up close and personal, as it happened. Especially when he was all heated up.

Made a girl wonder what they looked like when the heat came from a different source. How had she not noticed them that first night with Aurora?

"I'm serious, Tess."

"When aren't you?" she responded, having to drag her attention away from his gorgeous baby browns. "And no, she didn't confide secrets. All I'm saying is, given her lifestyle up to now, it's like she's sixteen going on thirty-five. She's traveled, she's seen the world, she's been exposed to various cultures and things that most teenagers could only dream about knowing in a lifetime. No matter how sheltered you've kept her, she's still mature way beyond her years. She has to be, to play the kind of mentally tough game I watched her blast through the other day. And that was just practice. Lord only knows what the kid is like on court when it matters."

There was a brief flicker of . . . something, that crossed his face. Pride. And such love. He couldn't hide it if he wanted to. And that was one of his best, if only, selling points.

"Yeah, I kinda figured," she said, a bit more gently, to his unspoken response. "So why don't you give Gaby some credit here? She's a sponge, soaking up so much right now."

"Exactly."

"What I'm trying to say is that not only is she soaking up this new experience, she's integrating it in a way that is allowing her to grow and become more successful. At least that seems to be her path. So why not trust her to glean what she can from me? Use what helps, discard the rest?" She held her racket up to her face and made a deep breathing sound. "Trust me, Luke," she said in her best Darth Vader imitation. "I won't take her to the dark side."

If he found her even remotely amusing, he didn't show it. Big shock there. "She idolizes you," he said flatly. "And you've managed to trot around the globe in rather scandalous fashion and still bring home the prize money. She'll think she can do the same. You say you're warning her against the dark side of being a pro on tour. I say you're going to basically hand her a guidebook, whether you mean to or not."

"Well, hey, I guess I should be flattered you're at least giving me that much credit. Would it help if I told you that I don't think it's a wise idea for anyone to carry on as I did?" She stared at him. "Yeah, I didn't think so." She sighed and let her racket drop to her side. "Then I guess since you can't find it in yourself to trust me, you're just going to have to trust Gaby."

She expected him to inform her that he wasn't going to allow Gaby to have that decision. When he merely stood there and silently stared her down, she had to fight to restrain the urge to smile in victory. So that's why he was here. Aurora had somehow gotten him to agree to let her handle things with Gaby. Forcing him to come directly to the source of his angst, in hopes he could get her to agree to let this liaison she was forming with his sister drop.

Ha. Fat chance.

His jaw tensed, then forcibly relaxed. "I'm asking you to please opt out of Aurora's plans for you and Gaby to continue seeing each other over the next week. I'm asking that you trust me to know what is best for my sister."

"And it isn't being exposed to some international disaster like me, huh?" It shouldn't have stung. She didn't know him from Adam, so why did his opinion matter? She'd suffered far worse slings and arrows from people who did matter to her.

"You say that like I'm exaggerating your exploits." He held her gaze directly then. "Am I? Really?"

He'd sort of caught her off guard with that quiet, direct question. "Perhaps not my exploits, no. But I'm older, wiser. And just because I enjoyed myself during my time at the top does not make me a bad person."

"I didn't say you were a bad person."

She snorted. "Funny, because my character is feeling quite besmirched."

He didn't respond to that. His expression made it unnecessary. He thought she'd besmirched it just fine on her own. Arrogant jerk.

"So I'm such a lousy role model, am I? As opposed to you, you mean? Traipsing around the globe after your baby sister, watching over her while she plays tennis, living off her earnings? Or worse, your father's money?" She immediately put her hand up, palm out. "I'm sorry. That was low. Even for me." She glanced up at the sky, then down at her feet. Her brief smile was one of self-deprecation. "If my mom was here right now, she'd tan my hide but good. And the accompanying lecture would be even worse."

She shook her head, then glanced up at him. He wasn't smiling, but he wasn't frowning anymore.

"You're just not the role model I want for my sister, okay? Titles notwithstanding. She'll get those on her own."

"With who for a coach? She has talent, Max. Out the wazoo. But it's raw and youthfully exuberant. It needs to be harnessed, focused, matured. And for that, she's going to need guidance. The kind that you can't give her."

"I'm well aware of that."

"But it is exactly the kind I can give her." She had NO idea where that had come from. Damn Aurora for ever planting so much as a seed in her brain. She had absolutely no business making such an offer. It was enough that she was going to be involved with Gaby for the next week or so. She'd told herself she'd have plenty of time during the tournament to roust up the endorsement offers she so desperately needed. She could donate some time for a few days. But she didn't have the time, much less the inclination, to actually coach the teenager. Hell, she needed to get on the court herself first.

"You—you're saying you want to coach? My sister?"

His sincere bafflement snapped her out of her mini-panic attack. The fact that he couldn't even seem to begin to think she'd do something like that made her want to do it all the more.

"Why so shocked? Do you really think I'm so self-absorbed that I don't think of others?"

"I didn't say that." He lifted his hand now when she rolled her eyes. "Okay. So maybe I implied it. What's in this for you?"

"The satisfaction of helping a player with so much promise?" Actually, it was a good question. Was it just because she wanted to thwart Max? To "win" this battle he'd created between them? Even with only a second or two to think about it, she knew that wasn't it. Okay, a teeny bit, that might be it. Sue her. But mostly it was because of Gaby. "I like your sister. I know you hate this, but she does remind me of me. There's just something about her." She shook her head and smiled, a bit baffled herself now. "And I'm not so much offering to coach her—I won't be around long enough for that—but what I can be is a mentor of sorts."

"Isn't that what Aurora already has you doing?"

"Off the courts, yes. I'm just offering to expand my advice and the benefit of my experience to include some on-court pointers, as well."

He still looked skeptical. "Did Aurora call in some favor?"

She shook her head. "Although she did plant the seed of

possibly working with Gaby on the court. I admit I wasn't keen on the idea."

"Why now?" His lips might have quirked a tiny bit. "Because I've made it a challenge of sorts?"

"Now you're coming to understand me." Her smile grew.

"Well, as much as I appreciate the offer—and I do, actually—I have to respectfully decline."

"Did you already find someone to work with her? At least, tune her up for the fortnight?"

She saw him hesitate, and knew he hadn't. And that made her mad. Dammit, she was tired of people underestimating her lately. She'd spent a lifetime being an overachiever and it didn't sit well with her to suddenly be looked at in any other way. "I'll take that as a no," she said, tapping her racket against the toe of her sneaker, trying to rein in her temper. "You know, the world looks at elite athletes as if they're some kind of immortal gods or something, complete with the life afforded said godlike status. You and I both know the reality of what being on tour is like. And you're going to quickly learn that juniors is nothing compared to the pro circuit, if you haven't already. Gaby has joined the upper ranks right off the bat, and the pace can be brutal. It's grueling, with lots of time spent focusing on one thing and one thing only."

"That's all I'm interested in. Maintaining that focus, minimizing distractions."

"Yeah, the tour does offer some big, bad temptations. I'm not saying otherwise." She looked him in the eye. "Did I take advantage of some of the social perks that came along with all that hard work? You bet I did. At the time I felt I'd more than earned the right and I knew what I could handle and what I couldn't." Her short laugh was flat and without any real humor. "Do I regret some of my more colorful antics?" She glanced at him again. "On court? No. That was about my game and how I stayed focused. Off court? Sure. In the big picture of it all now, yeah, I made some costly mistakes." Very costly, she thought. He had no idea.

"Tess—"

"Let me finish." She stepped closer, tapped him once on the chest with the handle end of her racket. "But I also worked my ass off and I'm not afraid to put in what it takes to get what I want. No one trained harder than me. No one prepared for matches better than me. Those trophies didn't end up on my mantelpiece by accident. So when I tell you I can help your sister, I know what the hell I'm talking about. I think we share the same vision, the same work ethic. She sure as hell has the natural talent to go all the way to number one and then some." Her lips quirked. "Might even give a few of my records a run for the money." Her expression flattened. "And the fact that we seem to have the same temperament, off court and on, will probably make our working relationship function even better. I get her, Max. I understand what's going on up here." She tapped his forehead with her finger, then tapped his chest again with her racket. "And in here." She blew out a long sigh. "I'm not the wild and crazy party girl you think I am. Not anymore, anyway. And with the benefit of hindsight, perhaps I can give your sister a perspective of tour life she could only get from someone like me."

Max held her gaze for a long time, then finally he said, "She's only going to be at Glass Slipper for the rest of the week. How much help do you think you can be?" It sounded like a capitulation. But his expression hadn't so much as flinched, so she didn't celebrate just yet.

"Which was exactly my point this whole time. Just how much damage do you think I could do?"

Now it was his turn to look away.

"Boy, your opinion of me is really lovely. You don't even know me, but you think you have me all pegged. Wait until Gaby starts showing up in the rags."

He glanced up, frowning.

"Trust me, no matter how much you keep her under wraps, when she starts winning, and we both know she's going to, they'll come after her. The more hidden you keep her, the harder they'll dig."

"They won't find anything. She hasn't done anything. And if I have anything to say about it—"

"You won't always, you know," she said, then almost laughed at the stricken look that flashed across his face. "But that wouldn't stop them. They'll just make stuff up." She widened her eyes in faux concern. "Gosh, I hope people don't start judging *your* sister by what they read in the scandal sheets."

He scowled and she knew she'd made her point. "You've already admitted they didn't make up the stories about you."

"I didn't say that. Not all of them were lies, no. However, they don't print everything, either. Reading about me only gives you a tiny part of the story." Now she smiled. It was a slow one, and she let it reach her eyes, well aware of the effect it usually had on the opposite sex. She stepped closer, but didn't touch him. "To answer your question, no, I definitely wasn't always a good girl. I'm the cliché, actually."

"What cliché is that?" His expression remained unchanged, but the tone of his voice had dropped an octave. She was getting to him.

"The bad girl with a heart of gold."

She could swear she saw the corners of his mouth twitch. If she hadn't been looking so intently at that particular feature of his, she'd have missed it. And in fact, why was it she'd never noticed what a wickedly sensual pair of lips the man had? A shame he was such an obstinate ass. The things she could do with a mouth like that.

She suddenly felt the heat of his gaze on her and slowly lifted her eyes. The knowing look in his eyes made her cheeks flush. Bad girl, indeed.

"Yeah," he said, his voice a bit deeper, a bit rougher. "I can see that. Part of it, anyway."

Her skin prickled in heightened awareness, making her wonder just who was getting to whom? She was queen of this little game and he was nothing more than a pawn. How had he managed to get the upper hand? Even briefly. "I won't ask which part." She stepped back, put her racket between them, not at all liking the fact that her pulse rate had spiked and it hadn't been calculated by her in the least.

"Probably a good idea," he said, and there was the briefest of twinkles in those dark eyes of his. Damn, but the man had an edge to him she'd have never suspected.

"You'll see that I'm right. About Gaby and me, I mean. Trust Aurora if you don't trust me. Gaby wants this week and you've agreed to it. Let us do our thing. Then she'll be starting the tournament and I'll be out of your collective hair."

"One week." He still didn't look happy about being boxed into a corner, but then, he didn't have to be happy. He just had to leave them be.

She grinned at him then, and he actually backed up a step. There. That felt a lot more like normal to her. "What's the worst that could happen?"

He held her gaze a beat too long, then turned around, raking his hand through his hair. "Jesus," he swore under his breath. "I should have never—" He cut himself off, then looked back over his shoulder. "One week."

"No chaperoning."

"Don't push it."

Oh, but she would. He knew, and she knew it. "We'll see."

"Yes," he said, looking all enigmatic again. "I guess we will."

Her pulse skipped. Damn the man, anyway. He walked toward the gate and her gaze automatically dropped to his backside. Nice. Good calf muscles, too. *Good God, Tess, snap out of it.*

"Don't look so forlorn," she called out impishly, wanting—no, needing—to end this with the final point firmly in her favor. "This could be the beginning of something wonderful."

He stopped dead, looked back. "What?"

She laughed. "Gotcha." She waved her racket at him. "Go on, go do something productive for your sister. I have to practice if I'm going to keep up with her, much less teach her anything."

He held her gaze a moment longer. And she let him. Then he finally gave her the briefest of nods, and let himself out. He crossed the entire lawn without once looking back. Only after he disappeared up the rear steps of the estate did she look away.

Walking back to the baseline, she fumbled the remote for the ball machine out of her pocket. Shifting mental gears came automatically to her. It felt good, focusing on something she understood thoroughly, trusted implicitly to be there for her like an old friend.

So it was more than a little disconcerting that it wasn't green tennis balls that had captured her attention... but a pair of soulful brown eyes instead.

Chapter 10

"Are you kidding me? That was *so* on the line!" Gaby stormed up to the net and glared down the center service line on the opposite side. "I saw the chalk fly up."

"Residue in the grass," Tess corrected her. "It was wide. Second serve." She easily held Gaby's gaze when the teenager foolishly tried to stare her down, though privately, Tess was impressed. The girl had no fear. Not even of her. Which was exactly the kind of temperament she'd need if she was going to last out the first week of the tournament.

The draw had come out that morning. Gaby, who wasn't ranked high enough yet to be a seeded player in this slam—although Tess would bet money, if she'd had any, that this would be the only time she'd come to Wimbledon in that situation—had drawn a tough first-round opponent. Davina Slutskaya, one of the many Russians dominating the scene, wasn't currently a very highly ranked player, but an older, experienced tour veteran nonetheless. A feisty player with good court coverage and a nice serve-and-volley game that was well suited to the fast grass surface, she'd been known to topple a giant or two in her day.

It was only their second day practicing together, but already Tess was pretty damn sure Gaby could take the Russian. The kid had insane natural ability and a mental game far beyond her years. She had all the tools: a wicked forehand with excellent shot placement, a one-handed backhand that was going to be trouble for any opponent, and a serve that, when harnessed properly, could be powerful enough to give Serena a run for her money.

Tess had quickly learned that, despite Gaby's supposed hero worship of her, getting her to listen was proving to be a rather formidable task. They hadn't been halfway through their first practice session before Tess began to question her sanity in even attempting to do this. She kept telling herself that it was only for a week . . . and it was making Aurora happy and Max fume. A two-for-one deal, really. How could she pass that up?

But now that she'd committed herself to this course of action, it was like anything else she committed to in her life—she wanted to get the most out of it that she could. Which meant getting Gaby to pull her stubborn sixteen-and-a-half-year-old head out of her ass long enough to listen to the voice of experience.

Just as Gaby went to toss the ball up, Tess called out the score for her. "Fifteen-forty."

Gaby snatched the ball back out of the air and shot her a look that, had there been laser beams involved, would have reduced Tess to nothing more than a small pile of soot on her own baseline. "I know what the score is," she snapped.

Tess just smiled. She'd done her research in the past few days. Gaby had clearly outplayed pretty much everyone on the junior circuit over the past year before turning pro. She rarely lost, but when she did, it was usually because she beat herself by letting her emotions get the better of her.

Something Tess knew more than a little about.

That was the downside of being the kind of tempestuous player who used her passion and quick temper to take her game to a higher level. When channeled properly, it worked as both motivation and a pressure-release valve. But when improperly managed, it generally backfired in pretty spectacular fashion.

She could help Gaby to hone that. It would take time for her to really own it, a great deal more than they had together, for sure, but for the next six days, Tess could—and would—deliberately push her, ride her hard. Get those emotions roiling, so that when they boiled over, she had the opportunity to at least try and give her the tools she needed to use all that heat to her advantage.

A lot of coaches could improve Gaby's net game, or help harness that serving power. But Tess was probably the best qualified to help her with this critical mental balancing act, so that's what she'd focus on. Where other coaches—and her manager brother—would probably try and squash that quick-trigger temper of hers, Tess believed the exact opposite. You can't change the stripes on a tiger. So why not make the distinctive pattern work to your benefit?

She swallowed a smile. If only Max could see them now.

And to think, they hadn't even begun to talk about things like media management off the court.

"Let's see if you can serve your way out of this hole," Tess taunted, pushing every button she could.

Their first day had been spent working on ground strokes, talking grass-court strategy. No rallying in any kind of real-game situation. Tess had wanted more private time on the court at Wexley first. It had been both easier and harder to get out there and hit balls again than she'd thought it would be. Easy, because it had felt good, really good, to use her body again. Hard because it was still exceedingly frustrating to face her limitations where her reconstructed shoulder was concerned.

Still, she owed Gaby a very big thank-you. Tess had gone nine months without so much as touching a racket. It might as well have been nine years. She hadn't gone more than a few weeks without swinging a racket since she was old enough to walk and swat balls around with her mother. And the only reason she'd gone that long was when she was recovering from her first couple shoulder repairs. Even then, she'd been back on court long before her doctors recommended.

The only thing that had pushed her out there, and kept her out there, her shoulder aching, her heart still breaking, was because she had to if she wanted to hit with Gaby. Tess knew now that was why she hadn't been able to step out on a court since announcing her retirement. Simply put, she'd had no reason to. Tess needed a purpose. To just go out there and hit for no reason would have been all heartbreak and no reward.

With that knowledge, she'd allowed herself to let go. And that hadn't come easily, or right away. She'd shed a few fierce tears as she'd pounded away at ball after ball, angry with herself, with her body, for letting her down. Slowly, methodically, determinedly, as the sun crept toward the skyline, she worked through her grief, one swing at a time. She moved to the ball, let her instincts take over again, losing herself in the motion of the game. And ultimately, victoriously, she'd felt her connection to her soul mate, to the sport itself begin to return.

She'd always loved the feel of the ball hitting her strings, loved being able to harness that power, redirect it, hit the mark, right on the line. The movement, the freedom, the control, even with her shoulder screaming, felt so damn good, by the time she went back inside, searching for an ice bag, the tears on her cheeks had been tears of, if not joy, then at least relief. She'd begun making peace with it. And with herself.

So naturally, today, pumped full of ibuprofen and attitude, she'd gotten a bit cocky and decided to push them both a little. Fortunately for her and her aching shoulder, Gaby was largely beating herself today. If Gaby got in any kind of groove, she could take a set off of Tess. Tough as that was to admit. But while Tess might be more than a little rusty, she was still every bit as wily.

Sometimes experience alone paid off. And if she was going to give Gaby even a small preview of what she was about to face over the fortnight of the Championships, she wanted it to be that.

She watched the toss, focused intently on body language and racket head direction . . . and when the ball came whizzing over the net faster than anything she'd ever seen, she instinctively jumped the right way, stabbed her racket to her forehand side, and solidly connected with what should have been an ace.

Well, her notorious return game was coming back nicely, she thought smugly, deciding it was worth the ice bag later. But there was no time to gloat. With those gazellelike long legs of hers, Gaby easily ran the ball down and, with a loud grunt, expertly whipped it back, crosscourt. Tess had to run full tilt, racket out in front, just to get her strings on the ball at all. Dammit. Who was running who here?

Years of running down balls had given her great muscle memory. Tess let her brain go on autopilot . . . and on a dead run, she flicked the ball back at a wicked angle so it just dropped over the net and died. An impossible get, even though Gaby's sprinting run had gotten her to within inches of where it landed.

"Dammit!" Gaby growled loudly in frustration, clearly pissed.

Tess drew in a steadying breath or two of her own, then grinned at her. "Actually, that's game. And set."

Gaby shook her head in disgust, more at herself than at Tess—something else they shared. Even at her most emotional, Tess's fire was fueled mostly by her own determination to make her game work for her, to bring in the win no matter what it took. It didn't matter who stood across the net. It wasn't about annihilating the opponent personally. It was just about winning. Proving that point, Gaby turned back toward the bench, but after only three steps, she sent her racket flying ahead of her. It hit her gear bag, then clattered to the ground.

"Losing sucks," Tess said cheerfully.

"No shit." Gaby gave Tess a sideways glance, as she had after her previous on-court tantrums this morning.

If she was waiting for Tess to comment, much less chastise her, she had a long wait coming. First off, it would be a bit of pot and kettle. A fact she was certain Gaby wouldn't waste a second pointing out. Plus there was the added satisfaction, though a bit removed since he wasn't watching, of tweaking Max a little. Not that it was her fault Gaby was throwing rackets and swearing. She'd been doing that long before meeting Tess and would likely continue long after. Tess couldn't imagine anyone telling her otherwise at that stage of the game, either.

But secondly, and more important, she saw what no one else would see. Gaby's tall, lanky form was solid, as was her game face. She was an intimidating presence on court and that's what she intentionally projected. Tess saw beyond that. It was as easy as looking in the mirror. Nerves fluttered behind that steely stare. Uncertainty about what she was going to face on those hallowed grass courts next week plucked at her insides, making her twitchy, which in turn took that critical half second off in her reaction time, just enough to make her miss her shots.

It didn't take a genius to see that the girl had pride. In spades. She wanted to win, sure. But, almost as important, maybe more so, she didn't want to humiliate herself.

Tess grabbed her towel and rubbed the sweat off her face, neck, and arms. It was a gorgeous June day by London standards. Partly sunny, mild, a light breeze, with a few heavier clouds lurking on the horizon. It would likely rain most of the afternoon, however, which was why they'd shifted her practice time to the morning. Gaby could do her indoor training circuit this afternoon at Glass Slipper instead.

"Your shot selection has been really solid. You adjust very quickly."

Gaby was wiping her own face and stilled for a moment at Tess's praise. When she lowered the towel, though, she met Tess's gaze with an unaffected expression on her own.

So much for the hero-worship portion of their relationship.

Tess wasted a second wondering if she'd been as pompous as a rookie pro. So, okay, of course she had been. But still... The fates were probably up there laughing their asses off as Tess's karma finally came full circle. And proceeded to bite her directly on the ass.

Swallowing a resigned sigh, she continued smiling at Gaby. "You've got so much promise with that serve. I hope you find someone who can really take that and fine-tune it, get your power transfer to really give you everything you can get out of it."

"What do you mean?" Gaby said, sounding a bit affronted. But Tess saw the immediate leap of awareness in her eyes. No one wanted to have a flaw pointed out to them, and there would be a moment of denial. But Gaby seemed to be the type who, like Tess, would jump past that quickly, more concerned about diagnosing the problem and immediately doing something to fix it.

"I'd say you're working at about seventy-five percent. Which is awesome and will likely dominate a lot of the lower-ranked players as long as you can be consistent with it." She let her smile spread. "But why not aim a bit higher? You're capable of playing at another level entirely. It'll take some work, but I don't see where you're afraid of a little of that."

Gaby didn't say anything right away. Her arrogance stemmed from a long reign of dominance in the juniors and was well earned as far as that went. But this was a whole new ball game. And even with only a few pro tournaments under her belt, Gaby was already well aware of that.

"This game will humble you on a regular basis. No matter how many years you play. If you let it, it can crush your confidence and rob you of every instinct you were blessed with. And the threat of that isn't such a bad thing. Players like us—" she paused to let that comment sink in, "need to have something pushing us all the time. Who knows, maybe you'll get lucky enough to develop a rivalry on tour."

" 'Lucky'?"

Tess nodded. "Sure. Fastest way to make yourself a better player is to consistently lose to someone you know damn well you can beat. You just have to figure out how. You can push yourself hard, and your game hard, but you have to be truly tested to know what it is you're reaching for."

Gaby seemed to ponder that comment. "I know my strengths and weaknesses. I'm working on them."

"I know you are. I'm just saying that sometimes you don't know what your weaknesses are until another player points them out to you. Usually in that humbling fashion I was mentioning earlier. It's not always about beating yourself, sometimes you just get flat beat."

"Tell me about it," Gaby muttered.

Ah, now they were getting somewhere. "First round, French Open?"

Gaby shot her a look that was less than appreciative. "Actually, I was thinking about Birmingham, against Venus."

"Nah, you beat yourself that game."

Gaby's eyes widened. "How do you know? You said you hadn't watched me play before."

"Aurora has strange and magical powers," Tess said with a wink. "Never underestimate a godmother." Especially one who could get personal game film from a certain manager-brother.

"Godmother," Gaby said, clearly unimpressed.

"Hey, be respectful," Tess not-so-gently chided. "And thankful." She grinned. "She brought you me, didn't she?"

Gaby had the decency to look a bit ashamed. "Yeah." She blew out a sigh. "I'm sorry I'm being such a bitch. It's just—" She stopped, looked away, clearly and quite suddenly uncomfortable.

If Tess had to guess, she'd say that Gaby wasn't used to revealing her weaknesses. On court, or off. Game wise, or personal. She had Max, just as, early on in her career, Tess had had her mother, which was great. But sometimes you needed someone else's perspective. On the rare occasion Tess had really clicked with a coach, she'd yearned for such a trusted relationship, but they'd generally been short-lived, at best. In hindsight, perhaps the demise of most of those relationships had been sabotaged by Tess herself.

"I know it's a little terrifying and a lot intimidating, what you're going to face in the coming weeks."

"I've been out there before," she said testily. "Grass is a good surface for me."

"As a junior. You and I both know how different this is going to be. You're just worried about how different. You got pushed out onto Chatrier in Paris. That was a hell of a lot to handle in your first slam."

"It wasn't the size of the crowd that threw me off."

Tess grinned. "Yeah, you'll feed off of that energy, even when it's going against you. I did."

Gaby's expression shifted slightly, became a bit more open.

"What got you in Paris," Tess said, "was Serena's backhand. And the fact that she read your game like an open book, mostly because you let her. Not that there was much you could do about it, it was all you could do to stay in the rally with her. She's got years of experience on you and figures things out that much faster because of it."

Gaby's gaze shuttered a bit then.

"I'm right and you know it. And yeah, it sucks not to be the best. So rather than pout, figure out what you have to do to fix it. You might have to lose to her several times before you grow enough and learn enough to figure out how to beat her." Tess hung her towel around her neck. "But you can beat her. And you could have beaten Venus."

Gaby looked down then, but didn't say anything.

"You didn't trust your net game."

"I don't have a net game."

"Yeah, you do. You just have to be all but dragged into it. If you'd come in on her short balls, and she gave you plenty, that match was yours. You were just hoping she'd implode like she usually does in tight situations. And she didn't. You can't wait for them to lose."

Gaby shot her a brief glance. "My net game is pretty shaky."

"Well, you weren't going to beat her from the baseline. You should have at least tried."

Gaby looked back at her feet, but finally nodded. "Maybe."

"Don't be so hard on yourself. You know, I'll lay money on the fact that you'll be able to beat every player in the top ten by the end of next year. You have the game for it. You just have to want it badly enough."

Gaby's head shot up. "Of course I want it badly enough! Why do you think I'm out here killing myself every day? For grins?"

Ah. There was the fire she wanted to see. "This is exactly

what you're supposed to do with all that frustration I've got you feeling today. Harness it. Direct it outward, into your game. Never say die while you're on the court, go for everything you can, even when it's shaky, even when it looks hopeless. Mostly when it's hopeless. It's a character builder. When you realize you're clearly outmatched, accept it, work as hard as you can to stay in the match, and do your damnedest to figure out exactly why you're getting beat. Punish your opponent where you can, and make notes of where you can't. Then, when it's over, you shake hands and thank her. Because she just gave you a major gift."

"Which is?"

"She just taught you how to beat her. If you really understood why you were losing, then you have charted a map of exactly where you need to improve your game. Everything you go through out there is fodder for doing it better the next time. When it's working, you know not to fool with it, just hone it. When it's not, then you know where to focus. When you get pissed, channel it. Don't beat yourself up. You're already getting beat."

Gaby shot her a look.

Tess smiled and shrugged. "Hey, it's fact. Faster you deal with reality, the more you're going to learn and the faster you'll improve. Don't sulk on the court. Sure, sulk like hell for a little while when you leave the court, it's human. But while you're out there, be a sponge. If you're getting beat and it's pissing you off, then focus on why. And look across the net at her and know that next time, she's going to have to work a lot harder to beat you."

Gaby didn't say anything for a few moments, then finally she shook her head and laughed a little.

"What did I say that was funny?"

"Nothing," Gaby said. "It's just... I've never met anyone who thinks like that. You're so... focused. Like a machine."

Now Tess laughed. "Hardly. The scenario I've given you is best possible case in a losing situation. You've seen me play." She leaned down and picked up Gaby's racket, handed it to her. "You know how many of these I went through."

Gaby's cheeks pinked a little as she took the racket back.

"All I'm saying is, that's what you should be aiming for. Don't squash your temper, focus it. Sometimes you'll be on top of it, sometimes it will get on top of you." She tapped Gaby's racket. "And that's what happened at Birmingham two weeks ago."

"Yeah," Gaby said, then sighed. "You're right."

"Usually am," Tess said, intentionally cocky.

"It's no wonder Max is afraid of you," Gaby said with a laugh.

"He's not afraid of me. He's afraid of what I might say to you, how I might influence you."

"Brothers." She rolled her eyes.

"He's just looking out for you." Tess couldn't believe she was defending the guy, but it was the truth. Even if she did think he needed to lighten up.

"I know." Gaby's smile turned knowing. "And you are influencing me. But I won't tell him if you won't."

Tess laughed. "I'm not even sure what all you're going to get out of this. We don't have that much time out here."

And in a blink, Gaby went from pouty, arrogant, super athlete to sincere, earnest teenager. She touched Tess's arm. "I know I've been a pain in the ass out here, but I want you to know that your spending time with me like this means everything to me. I will never forget it."

And it was because she absolutely meant it, that Tess was out here in the first place. There was just something about Gaby that pulled at Tess. Despite the obvious similarities or because of them, she wasn't entirely sure. "I'm glad I let Aurora talk me into this," she responded, giving complete honesty in return.

Gaby spontaneously hugged her. A surprised Tess took a

second, then awkwardly hugged her back. She'd never been much of a huggy-touchy person.

Gaby broke contact and stepped back, her eyes shining now with enthusiasm and a drive that Tess completely understood.

"You said something about my serve not being full strength, but maybe it's too close to the tournament to fool with something so major. You're right about me not being comfortable at net. I should have played more doubles, I guess. You had me mostly on net points today. Maybe we can work on that?"

Just listening to Gaby's intensity and focus made Tess ache to get back on the court in a real game situation. She wanted to be back out there for herself, on tour, winning matches, winning titles. She knew it was over, but this was too much a taste, too much of a glimpse of her former life, too close. It was almost, in that moment, more than she could bear. She found herself looking away from all the hope and promise she saw in Gaby's shining eyes, a little ashamed that what she felt was jealousy. It was that very shame that forced her to look back at Gaby. Face what scares you most, that had always been her motto.

"We only have a few days. I'm not sure what I can do, but I'm willing to try."

Gaby's enthusiasm was undimmed. "Well, I was thinking about that. I know you're, like, super busy and all, and that I'm the luckiest person to have even this week with you . . ."

And just like that Tess found herself stifling the urge to smile. She was being expertly buttered up here. She should be wary, and she was, but she was also intrigued, despite her better judgment. "Go on."

"It was just, I mean, I know this is going to sound like an insult and it's not. I know you have more important things to do than help a nobody like me, but—"

Tess went still. Aurora had seen this coming, had hoped for

it. Tess had been so sure that even if it did, she'd easily turn it aside. Only standing here right now, knowing damn well where Gaby was going with this, knowing damn well it was the last thing she should be contemplating, given how her emotions were all over the map at the moment, not to mention what was going on in her personal life . . . and yet her mouth wasn't opening, wasn't cutting Gaby off before she could make the offer.

"I need a coach," Gaby rushed on. "You said it yourself. And I know Max would have a cow, but we could make him see it would be good for me. He'll want this for me if it's helping me."

Tess wasn't too sure about that.

"I don't know," she began, which was as truthful as she could be at the moment. The fact that she hadn't refused the offer outright should have concerned her. But she was already turning it over in her mind, thinking about what she could do with Gaby's game. Make it be all the things she knew it could be, pour all her frustration over not being able to play into—

"It would just be for the next couple of weeks, just to get me through this slam."

That brought Tess up short. She almost laughed at herself. For someone who had no interest in coaching as a career move, it was pretty insane how she'd immediately envisioned the two of them blazing a path through the season, wowing them at future majors, sweeping the slams.

"I know you were only here for your brother's wedding, but you're staying for the Championships, right?" Gaby rushed on. "I mean, if you would work with me even a little bit, it could help." She laughed, but it was forced. "And we both know I probably won't make it past the first week anyway."

And any idiot who knew something about anything could see how very badly she wanted to be wrong about that. Tess felt this little tug in her heart. Which, in the end, proved to be her final downfall.

Gaby, with her killer instincts on closing out a game, took Tess's arm and squeezed. "Please?" Her huge eyes all beseeching. And all that damn talent, just waiting to be molded. But just in case she wasn't completely convinced, and though she couldn't possibly know it was a deal maker, Gaby sealed it by adding the one thing Tess couldn't say no to. "We'd pay you, of course. Percentage of whatever I win. Plus expenses."

And just like that, Tess Hamilton was officially a professional tennis coach.

Chapter 11

"You did *what*? Without talking to me first?" Max raked his hands through his hair. "I don't know why that should even surprise me. Except it totally proves my point. You've been around her for one week—one week!—and you're already sneaking around behind my back, doing things without getting my consent. Things you know damn well I wouldn't approve of!"

Gaby shot him the classic teenage "duh" look. "Which is exactly why I didn't ask permission. Besides, you were the one who put me in Glass Slipper to help me get a grip on handling real-world decisions and pressure." She folded her arms. "Well, I made a real-world decision."

"You made a decision while locked in fairy-tale Glass Slipper world. Not exactly the same thing."

"Aurora approves."

"I bet she does," he muttered under his breath. In fact, she was currently the very next thing on his to-do list.

Gaby slid off her bed and came to Max's side and leaned her

head on his shoulder. As tall as she was now, she had to crouch a little to do it. "Please don't be mad," she said, all wheedling voice and pouty puppy-dog face. "It's just for the duration of the tournament."

Max sighed, then purposefully ruffled her hair, which earned him a squeal of indignation.

"Max! I have an interview in fifteen minutes!" She immediately raced into her bathroom to begin damage repair.

"What happened to the girl who yanked her hair into a sloppy ponytail and had to be almost dragged into the bathroom to wash her face and hands before eating?"

"She grew up." Hair once again in place, Gaby leaned forward to inspect her skin for any imperfections that might have sprung up since the last time she checked. Which was maybe ten minutes ago.

Max felt a quick tightening in his chest. She was growing up. Way too damn fast. And he didn't know what the hell to do with her. Aside from wrapping her in bubble-pack and storing her away somewhere until she was thirty. Maybe forty.

Gaby paused in the doorway. "You should be happy. I actually found a coach I want to work with for a change. I'm not whining or complaining. God, Max, she's like the best of the best. The best don't share their secrets, they don't become coaches. But she's agreed to help me out. It's only my second slam ever. I'd be insane to turn her down."

"So you're saying this was all her idea?" Because Gaby was right. When the very best retired, they usually rested on their laurels. And very fat bank accounts. Occasionally they popped up as commentators or ambassadors for the sport in some manner. Mostly they surfaced in conjunction with charitable endeavors. Sure, Tess was young and active, and he doubted she was the type to rest on anything, much less her laurels.

Then again, Tess commentating? With her mouth, she would

most definitely put new color in the term "color commentator." Hell, it was well known that reporters used to pack her post-match news conferences, knowing—win or lose—they were guaranteed a good sound bite or three.

Charity events, maybe. Her family was certainly philanthropic enough. Far easier to imagine was her partying around the globe. At best, she'd stamp her name on some hot line of sportswear, probably designed by her new sister-in-law. Something that didn't actually require her to do anything. But coaching? It was tough, often thankless work, with a grinding schedule. "Why in the hell would she want to do that?" He didn't even realize he'd spoken that last part out loud until Gaby responded.

"Gee, thanks, bro. Maybe because she sees something in me? I don't know. I just know that after only a couple days, she was already pointing out all kinds of things I could work on. Showing me where my strengths were, and where I was going to have problems on this surface, especially against Davina. I mean, she's played her multiple times. Do you have any idea how amazing this is? Not only was Tess a number-one player, she's a recent number one. She knows everyone out there; she can give me insights into their games I couldn't hope to get from anyone else."

Max frowned. "You said it was just for this tournament."

"It—it is."

"Gaby," he said proddingly.

She ducked her chin for a moment, but it immediately came back up, with an added defiant tilt to it that he was getting weary of seeing. "She agreed to two weeks, yes, but who knows? I mean, if I do well, maybe I can convince her—"

"Wait a minute. I thought you said she asked you. What did you say to her, Gabs?" This made a lot more sense. He should have known someone like Tess Hamilton would never have just offered up her services like that. Of course, he couldn't imagine how Gaby had talked her into it, either. Unless Aurora had a hand in this. His head began to throb. He felt distinctly outmaneuvered. Up against a united front of three determined women, he didn't even know why he bothered to try and thwart their plans.

Then he looked at his kid sister, who, despite the styled hair and modestly applied makeup, was still just that: a kid. Sure, Aurora's heart was in the right place. And sure, Gaby was excited at the chance to work with her hero. He didn't pretend to know Tess's motives and didn't really care. What mattered was that, regardless of their joint enthusiasm for this venture of theirs, he was the only one who truly had Gaby's best interests at heart. Not just for the next two weeks, but for the big picture, as well. And Gaby getting in thick with Tess Hamilton at only her second slam just couldn't be a good idea.

"If you somehow talked her into doing this, then that's all the more reason to end this charade now."

"It's not a charade! She agreed to help me, Max. And I can use the help. On the court and off."

"That's what I'm worried about. The interviews are already lining up. That's pressure enough on you."

"I can handle it," Gaby insisted stubbornly.

"You know something, I think you can, too," he said, earning a surprised look from his sister. "But if word gets out that Tess Hamilton is in any way involved with you, the media attention on you will explode."

It occurred to him right then that he might have hit on Tess's angle in all this. Was she so desperate to remain in the white-hot glare of attention that she'd willingly align herself with the new up-and-comer as a way to guarantee herself continued press coverage? It wasn't that far-fetched, really.

"You want me to learn to handle that anyway."

"That's the last thing you need right now. Your focus should be on the tournament. Tess might mean well, but—"

"But you don't believe that, do you?" Gaby lifted her hands, then let them fall to her side. "Why are you so convinced she's the bad guy?"

"It's her reputation, Gaby. It exists. And it's not an altogether good one. Yes, she's earned a place in tennis history with her string of titles, and I'm not doubting she could be a great asset as a coach, but—"

"Okay, then, let her help me. It's only two weeks, Max. Or as long as I stay in the tournament. She's here in London, I'm here in London. I might never get this chance to work with her again. We both know she's too big to probably want to get into coaching full-time, so what's the danger?" She cut him off before he could explain, once again, exactly why Tess was a dangerous woman. "If it's just the media frenzy you're afraid of, I'm willing to risk it. Aurora even got Sir Robin's permission to use his court to practice on if we need to stay out of the limelight. No one has to know."

"You're crazy if you think you can keep this quiet. And from the international press, of all things."

She crossed the room until she stood right in front of him. "All I know is that I think I could get further these next two weeks with her than without her. And if I don't do well, she'll explain to me why I didn't and help me figure out what I have to do next time." Gaby took hold of his arms and squeezed tightly. "I want that opportunity, Max. It's the chance of a lifetime." Her expression was both beseeching and intensely focused. "Please don't ruin this for me. Please."

These were the moments he hated the most. The moments where all he wanted to do was make her happy and give her whatever her heart desired. She was a good kid who worked way too damn hard and earned the right to ask for a few things now and then. And yet it was the same moment where he had to decide if what she wanted and what she most needed were the same thing. "I—I don't know, Gabs," he said, tugging her close for a quick hug. "Let me think about it, okay?" He dropped a quick kiss on her forehead, careful not to muss hair or makeup.

She sighed as he let her go and he could see she was gearing up for round two, but before she could continue to plead her case, a knock came at the door. "Mr. Fontaine?" a voice called from the hallway. "They're ready for you both. Room three-eleven."

Gaby sailed past him and opened the door before he could stop her. "Thank you. We're on our way." She walked out without waiting for Max.

Swearing under his breath, he scooted out of the room behind her and closed the door. They waited with the journalist's assistant for the elevator. As was often the case in London, the lift was darkly paneled and small bordering on minuscule. The three of them squeezed in and the assistant pushed the button for them. "Enjoying your stay?" he asked brightly, apparently clueless to the tension simmering between his two liftmates.

"We always do," Max said politely, managing a tight smile.

The buzzer went off and the door slid open. Max and Gaby exited quickly, with Gaby carefully lifting her hair off her neck for a moment, before letting it fall back along her collar. Air-conditioning was not a popular commodity in the U.K. and the air in the lift was stifling even after such a short ride.

"This way," the assistant said, directing them down a narrow, pale-carpeted hallway. "Last one on the left."

"Thank you." Max put his hand on Gaby's arm before she could stride off ahead of him. "You want a quick run through the talking points? We could ask for a few moments in the hall." He knew she didn't need a review, she'd done this kind of thing often enough. But she was also tense and unhappy with him at the moment and he mostly wanted to give her a chance to smooth out a bit before sitting down with the journalist.

"I'm fine. I could do this in my sleep."

"I know, just—" But she was already tapping on the door and opening it without waiting.

"Hello!" came a jovial female voice. "You must be Miss Fontaine."

"Hi," Gaby said, extending her hand as Max and the assistant came in behind her. "A pleasure to meet you."

She was all smiles and youthful exuberance now. Max just shook his head a little. A pro at sixteen in more ways than one. He had to admit that she did handle herself well in these kinds of situations. Her meltdowns on court had thus far never translated to off-court behavior, which was largely what saved her. Most interviews were upbeat and positive in intent. She was inevitably asked about her occasional on-court histrionics—much like Monica Seles had always been asked about the loud grunting noise she made whenever she hit the ball—but they had long since developed a disarming response to that, which, delivered so genuinely from such a polite young lady, never failed to diffuse whatever negative angle the interviewer might have been gunning for.

"This must be your brother, Max." The journalist was British, probably mid-fifties, somewhat attractive, and all smiles as she extended her hand to him. "Hello, I'm Fionula Hust. Excited for your sister?"

The interview hadn't technically begun yet, but Max and Gaby had both realized long ago that the interview started the moment you walked into the room. And in keeping with that, he smiled broadly. "A pleasure to meet you. Thank you for asking for the interview." He could have gone into politics, he sounded so sincere, when in fact, if they never did another one of these, he could die a happy man. "And yes, of course I'm excited. We're both happy to be here."

"Well," she said, all smiles, "why don't we have a seat over here and we can begin. Can I get you anything?" Before either of them could answer, she looked past Max to her assistant and said, "Simon, did you order tea? Has it arrived?"

Max and Gaby exchanged looks, both knowing it would be rude to turn it down, but also knowing the token gesture was expected. "That's not necessary," Max began.

"Please," Fionula admonished, "it's the least I can do as I know I'm taking up time in your busy schedule. Simon?"

"Right away." Simon disappeared back into the hallway as Fionula led Gaby to a pair of seats that had been arranged by the window. The view was better than their own, affording a look at the small park that ran parallel to the hotel across the street. "Shall we?"

As Gaby and Fionula settled in, Max automatically took the observer's seat on the couch and made himself comfortable. Or as comfortable as one could on the rock-hard settee.

Fionula set up her tape recorder and got her pad and pen ready. "The photographer should be here shortly. I was hoping we could get a few shots, something to run with the story?" She glanced at Max, who was prepared for this, too, and simply nodded. "Excellent." All smiles, she turned back to Gaby. "So, excited to be at your first Wimbledon as a professional player?"

Gaby nodded, then said, "It feels like I've been waiting a long time for this chance."

Fionula laughed. "Sixteen—"

"Almost seventeen," Gaby corrected, then smiled.

"Almost seventeen, and so impatient. Intimidated at all? Your run through the juniors these past two years was quite impressive."

"Thank you. I was really fortunate to do so well back then. It gave me a lot of confidence in making the decision to join the WTA tour. But of course, now I'm facing players with far more experience and I know it's not going to be easy out there. I'm just hoping to play my best tennis and see what happens from there."

Max settled into his seat as Gaby recited her standard responses. Fortunately, she had the warm smile and comfortable posture to make it seem as sincere as the first time she'd said them.

"You've drawn a tough first-round opponent. Davina Slutskaya. Have you or your brother done any research on her?"

"A little. I think this Wimbledon will be a big opportunity for me, mostly as a chance to see the players in action, learn more about everyone's game, and prepare myself better."

"A big learning curve, certainly."

Gaby nodded, friendly, open smile in place. "Don't get me wrong, though"—she laughed lightly—"I want to win. I'm going out there with the idea that I'm going to do everything I can to beat my opponent. I don't know how well I'll do, but they'll have to play me to beat me."

Fionula's smile grew, her first sound bite now firmly in hand. "So, I know your first slam was the French last month. How do you feel about your result there?"

"A little frustrated. I thought I could have done better, but the draw sort of went against me."

"You took Serena to a third set. Pretty impressive."

Gaby smiled. "It would have been more impressive if I'd beaten her. She came back strong in the third and, well, it was almost embarrassing."

"How did it feel to play on the showcase court there?"

"Oh, that part was fantastic. I love the crowds, the energy."

Her grin grew a shade cocky. "I'm looking forward to a lot more of that."

Fionula laughed again. "Well, we all know how determined you are, and how focused you've been on winning. There's been a lot of talk about you, in the press and on the tour among your peers. Looks like America has their hopes set on you to be the next big thing. Does that add unwarranted pressure to you to produce big results right away?"

Gaby shook her head. "I suppose it could if I let it, but I don't really think about it that way. There has been a lot of attention since I started winning a string of major tournaments in the juniors, so I'm kinda used to it. Mostly I just use it as motivation to play better. I do want to be one of the best." She grinned. "And not just from America."

"Well, that kind of moxie will probably be a help to you as you move further into the field. What are your hopes for Wimbledon? You were quoted after Birmingham as being upset with how you performed there. You've stayed on here in London to prepare for the slam?"

"Yes, I have. It's been good for me. We're trying to pace my first year on tour so it's not too overwhelming. I've had a little rest and a lot of time to focus on my game."

As the conversation continued on, Max relaxed even more. The interview appeared to be pretty routine. Thank God. He had enough to deal with at the moment. Which was where he'd let his thoughts drift, thinking what would be the best way to let Gaby down about this whole Tess thing. The more he thought about it, the more he was sure it was the right thing to do. This kind of media attention—nonthreatening and benign, with a positive spin—was perfect for Gaby. She'd earned the spotlight, so there was no avoiding it completely, but this was the best compromise. If by chance she won a round or two, the attention would intensify, but again, in a pedestal-building kind of way. Young phenom-does-good was the kind of press she'd get, as they tried to turn her into something the fans would rally behind, a new face in tennis.

Of course, he'd been around enough to know that if Gaby grew into the kind of pro player that was as dominant as she had been as an amateur, then the claws would come out. They loved nothing more than to knock someone down after building them up. But he'd deal with that later. Much later. Another reason to keep Tess far far away from Gaby at this stage of her career. Let her have her time to shine early.

"Are you doing anything special or different to your game as you get ready for your second slam?"

"Well . . ."

Max's thoughts were drifting at that point and he wasn't really paying much attention to the interview. If he had been, he'd have heard the small pause from Gaby before she answered. Then he might have been able to stop her in time. But he hadn't. So he couldn't.

And that's when everything went south.

"As a matter of fact, I do have a secret weapon of sorts."

Fionula sat forward right about the same time Max processed the phrase "secret weapon" and turned to look at them both. But before he could open his mouth, Gaby had already opened hers.

"Tess Hamilton has been giving me a few pointers."

"Really?" Fionula's carefully styled blonde hair all but popped out of its bobby pins. Pen poised, smile sharp, her direct gaze even sharper, she asked, "How did this turn of events come about?"

Max's mouth did open then, but nothing came out. Gaby wisely didn't so much as look at him. Even smarter, neither did Fionula.

A dozen wild thoughts careened through his head. He

should stop the interview right now. *Dammit, Gaby.* Beg Fionula not to run the information. Pay her off, if necessary. Do something. Anything.

"My wonderful brother Max set me up at the Glass Slipper spa for a little break after my early loss in Birmingham. And a mutual friend of Tess's works there and sort of hooked us up. It kind of blossomed from there."

There was a rap on the door, then the photographer ducked in. "Sorry I'm late. Are we ready?"

Max used that as his cue. He knew better than to try and squash the interview. It would just make Fionula all the more determined to run it. But he didn't have to let Gaby keep talking, either. He came off the couch in one fluid move. "Yes, we are." He made a show of looking at his watch. "I'm sorry, Fionula. We have another interview scheduled shortly. I hope you don't mind if we wrap this up."

"No, no, not at all." Fionula stood and smoothed her jacket. "I appreciate you giving me your time."

He could tell she was nervous now. His mention of another interview probably had her twitching to file her story and beat everyone else to the punch. Good, that would get them out of there that much sooner. Before his idiot sister could do anything else to sabotage herself.

Photos were taken on the balcony with a backdrop of a rare blue London sky. And mercifully over quickly. They said their good-byes to the photographer and a cheery Simon escorted them back to the lift, waving to them as the doors closed between them.

Max had spent the entire photo shoot schooling himself to be calm and collected when he finally got Gaby alone. He'd also tried to figure out a way to abort the glaring attention that was about to avalanche down upon them. He wasn't too successful at the latter. And as it turned out, the former was too much to ask, as well. "What the *hell* were you thinking?" he exploded the instant the lift began its ascent. "Do you have any idea what you've just done?"

Gaby appeared to be every bit the calm, collected customer he'd wanted to be. But the mirrored side panel afforded him a view of the way she was twisting her hands together behind her back. "Yes. I made sure I got my coach for the next two weeks."

"I told you I'd think about it; you didn't need to go to that extreme."

"Please," she said. "You were sitting over there figuring out the best way to tell me it wasn't happening."

"You have no idea what I was thinking."

She folded her arms. "So you were going to let me keep her on, then?"

Max had seen that trap coming. "That's not the point. The point is that there were ways to handle this and ways not to. You couldn't have chosen a worse way. Which, by the way, is exactly why I didn't want you two working together. I know we've talked a lot lately about how you've seen and done more than most girls your age, but that right there showed your immaturity. You acted without thinking about the consequences, which won't be minimal, I can guarantee you that."

"I can handle the media. I had Fionula eating out of the palm of my hand."

The lift doors opened and they both stalked out and headed toward their rooms.

"Only because that's the kind of story she wanted from you. Fresh face, up-and-comer on the tour. She was building you, that was her angle. But you and I both know why they spend so much time on fresh meat like you early on. So they can tear you down later." Max used his card key and flung their door open, gesturing her inside first. "Well, guess what, you've moved past go and gone directly to the meat-eating portion of your media campaign. Congratulations."

If he thought his lecture would have a sobering effect on her, he was quickly disabused of that notion.

"Oh, don't be such a drama king. I doubt anyone is going to care all that much that she's helping me out. I didn't say she was my coach specifically, just that she was giving me some pointers. We can blow this off."

"Maybe you can. But did you stop to think what this might do to Tess?"

She looked at him blankly.

"This will bring attention to her, as well. Maybe she doesn't want the world to know she's helping you out. Maybe she doesn't want every young player on the tour hitting her up for practice tips."

Clearly Gaby hadn't thought about that particular angle and her expression grew troubled. "She handles media attention all the time," she said, but not with much conviction. "I'm sure this will barely register with her."

"That's not the point and you know it. The point is, you didn't give her the option of inviting this kind of attention into her life. She might not be too happy with you, either, when she finds out."

Gaby's jaw took on a stubborn tilt, but uncertainty was clear in her eyes. "I'll explain it to her. She'll understand. Sometimes a girl has to take matters into her own hands."

"Something you've learned from Tess?"

"No," she shot back, hurt and anger now blazing from her dark eyes. "I managed to figure that out all by myself." And with that, she stalked into her bedroom and slammed the door shut behind her.

He heard the lock click a moment later. Which they both

knew was merely symbolic since he had the key to her room in his pocket. But he honored the silent request. For now.

There were other things he needed to tend to at the moment. And quickly. It was a toss-up whom he wanted to see first. Aurora or Tess. A quick phone call later, he was smiling, if a bit grimly. Apparently his luck was turning. They were both presently at Wexley House.

He rapped on Gaby's door. "I'm heading out to start damage control. I'll be gone a couple hours. Stay in here until I get back. Don't answer the phone and don't answer the door. And don't even think about messing with me on this. Understood?"

Gaby might be headstrong and rebellious, but even she knew where to draw the line when they were at loggerheads. "Understood," came her muffled, if petulant, reply.

Max sighed and leaned his forehead against the door. Why did it always have to be so damn hard? "I'll call you when I'm on my way back. I'll pick us up something for dinner."

There was no reply.

With another sigh, he grabbed his key and shoved it in his pocket along with Gaby's before heading out. If Tess was so damn fond of media attention, then she was about to become a very happy woman. And since it was easier for him to let this be somehow all her fault, he felt it was only fair that she help him figure out how to keep Gaby out of the white-hot glare as best as possible. Maybe Aurora could pull another fairy godmother trick from up her sleeve, wave the proverbial magic wand, and make this all disappear.

There were several other players staying at their hotel and a small gaggle of photographers mingled out front by the shrubbery that flanked the front drive. Max pulled his baseball cap down and hunched his shoulders as he passed them by. "A magic wand would come in real handy right about now."

Chapter 12

Aurora settled in one of the high-back chairs facing the massive fireplace in Sir Robin's parlor. "I still think we should have told him ourselves. Poor Gaby. He's not going to be happy about this." Aurora sipped her sherry and sighed a little. "Stubborn man. If he'd only open his eyes, he'd see what a wonderful job you've been doing with her."

"Trust me, I tried to get Gaby to let me do it. It's genetic, that stubborn trait. And she's had many years of handling him under her belt. She'll deal with it the right way."

"You'll have to pardon an old lady's befuddlement, but I simply do not understand what there is to 'handle' about this whole endeavor. He should be grateful you're willing to step in and help her out. Most players would kill for such an advantage."

"I've explained his concerns to you."

Aurora sniffed and waved a heavily ringed hand. "Honestly. Men. When it was McEnroe or Connors, everybody smiled affectionately and called them rascals. A woman knows her own mind and goes after what she wants and she's some kind of she-devil."

Tess paused midsip and smiled rather wryly. "Yes, well, you can't honestly say I didn't deserve at least some of the names they tagged me with. But you're also right, a double standard does exist. Why do you think John has a commentating job and someone equally outspoken, like Martina, doesn't?"

"Or like you, dear. Have you considered it?"

"Let's just say no offers have been forthcoming," she replied with a laugh.

Tess sounded as if none of that mattered to her, but Aurora knew differently. She still hadn't confronted Tess with her knowledge of the dire state of her financial affairs. She'd refused to allow Aurora to pay her as a Glass Slipper employee, but now that she'd agreed to work for the Fontaines, though briefly, there would be at least some income on the near horizon for her. It wouldn't be enough to save her in any sense, but it would buy her some time. Aurora so wished she had contacts to help Tess out, and though she knew plenty of people, in this instance, she was somewhat hamstrung. She couldn't force anyone to offer Tess an endorsement deal. And with Tess no longer playing, there was nothing really to sponsor.

Watching Gaby and Tess work together, as she'd gotten the chance to do the day before—my, what a fiery duo they could be!—she couldn't help but hold on to the hope that their partnership would continue beyond this one event. She knew that in the eyes of her peers, it would be something of a humbling experience for Tess to become a full-time coach, but she couldn't help but think that maybe that could be the niche that Tess so needed. Something that would ground her, something she could really care about. And to hell with what anyone thought.

"Which, to be honest," Tess added, "is probably a wise decision. Putting a mike on me during a live match could be risky.

I'd get all involved and who knows what would pop out of my mouth. Politically correct, I'm not. I'd be the reason the sports world would have to adopt the five-second delay."

"Oh, pish posh. Perhaps if more people spoke up and told it like it is, the world would be a better place."

Tess sipped her drink. "Oh, I agree. But don't hold your breath."

Aurora sniffed. "If the public can handle Mr. McEnroe as a commentator, they can handle the likes of you."

"You're the one who brought up the double standard. Outspoken men making blunt statements are viewed as visionaries of the sport. Women, on the other hand? Hey, we're just supposed to smile sweetly and look really hot in our cute little tennis outfits."

Aurora looked rather pointedly at Tess's skimpy hot-pink spandex tennis shorts and a fuzzy lime-green sweater. The sleeves of which were so long they almost completely covered her hands, a fashion look Aurora was aware of, even if she didn't understand it. Aside from getting in one's way, it not only threatened to trail through a dinner plate, but it also hid one's hands. And all those lovely ring fingers. Ah, well. Youth.

She supposed she should have been thankful Tess had attempted to accessorize. Though using the term in these circumstances was being quite generous. Tess had conceded to the evening chill that was ever present in Wexley House by adding a pair of matching fuzzy lime-green socks. At least she'd managed to color coordinate. Everyone had to start somewhere.

"Well, dear," Aurora said, meeting Tess's amused gaze, "you definitely did your part on the latter. Some of your tennis togs—what there was of them—raised more than an eyebrow."

Tess spluttered a short laugh, then raised her glass up in toast. "Girls just want to have fun. I always thought the world looked at our sport as something played by stuffy old people at overprivileged, private club courts. I was simply trying to bring a little excitement to the game. It's an intense, demanding sport played by top-peak athletes and I just think we should celebrate that. We're not all pristine white dresses and perky ponytails."

"Mission accomplished, I dare say."

"Thank you." She laughed again. "And it's not like I was the first. Andre with his long hair and radical 'image is everything' personality started the revolution, but then he grew up, got married, shaved his head, and got all serious about his game. I proved you could be serious and an exciting trendsetter. And look at the women out there today. Shoot, Serena took what I did and exploded with it." She winked. "We're hot and happening now, baby."

"Perhaps you should consider designing your own line of tennis wear? Your delightful new sister-in-law could probably help you with that."

But Tess merely waved her drink at Aurora. "Serena has that corner covered. They're not interested in a has-been like me."

Aurora made a very unladylike snorting noise. " 'Has-been.' Hardly. You sell yourself far too short."

"Hell, I can't sell myself in any fashion," Tess said, then quickly took a sip of her drink.

Aurora leaned forward. It was the perfect opening, the one she'd been hoping for these past few evenings. "You know, Tess, I've been meaning to talk to you—"

The rest of her sentence was cut off when the double doors to the parlor were pushed open and Phillip, Sir Robin's majordomo, leaned in. "Ever so sorry to interrupt, madam, but you have a guest." He glanced over his shoulder. "Mr. Max Fontaine. He seems somewhat agitated. Would you like me to see him out?"

Aurora's gaze connected with Tess's for a moment, then they both sighed. *Well, the cat was officially out of the bag now.* "No, Phillip, please show him in."

Aurora stood. Tess stayed where she was, curled up in the chair closest to the low-banked fire. She raised a questioning brow, but Aurora supposed it didn't much matter how they faced him.

He didn't so much walk into the room as stride into it. "Aurora, I'm sorry to intrude, but we need to talk. I'd like to speak to Tess as well, if—"

"Present and accounted for," she said, lifting her drink high so it could be seen over the back of the chair.

Max had come farther into the room and glanced in her direction, then did a double take. He opened his mouth, perhaps intending to comment on her psychedelic use of color in her wardrobe choices, but wisely closed it again.

Aurora took his arm in hers and led him to the embroidered settee. "Max, darling, I know you might not be as enthusiastic as we are about Gaby and Tess teaming up, and I know we should have been the ones to approach you with this, but per Gaby's wishes, we let her handle it. I should let you know that while I'm sympathetic to your concerns, I'm afraid if you're looking for my support in dissolving that partnership, then—"

"No, that's not why I'm here." He tossed a look to Tess. "Well, it is, but at the moment we have other, more immediate concerns."

Now Tess sat forward and uncurled her long legs. Aurora sighed inwardly. What she wouldn't have given for just an inch or two more leg. All those cocktail dresses she could have worn . . .

"What 'immediate concerns'?" Tess asked. "Is Gaby okay? Did something happen in her workout session?"

Max looked a little surprised at the sincere concern in Tess's tone.

Good, Aurora thought. Once Max spent a little more time around her, he'd come to know what a loyal, decent person she was and his concerns would diminish.

Tess stood and walked over to the side table and poured herself another drink. "Or are you just here to give us some song-and-dance bullshit and be all Mr. Drama King as a way to get her out of working with me?"

Or, on the other hand, Aurora amended, perhaps it was best to keep them apart as much as possible. Then she caught Max trying not to stare at Tess's snugly encased backside and her thoughts were turned upside down all over again. Of course, physical attraction was nothing new where Tess was concerned. But she had to admit, there was an undeniable combustible chemistry between the two of them. But perhaps she'd been too hasty in negatively labeling that volatile mix. Sometimes explosive chemistry was a good thing.

My, my . . . now wouldn't that be interesting?

"Care for a drink?" Aurora asked, sounding quite innocent, though her thoughts at the moment were anything but.

Max instantly yanked his attention from Tess, and Aurora was quite pleased with the bit of color that rose to his cheeks. *You're only supposed to help take care of Tess's financial needs,* she reminded herself, *maybe a few of her emotional ones, as well. You're not here to play matchmaker.*

Of course, the thought had taken hold now, the seed planted. She made a mental note to call Vivi later and discuss.

"I'm fine," Max said.

"Are you certain, dear? Your voice sounds a bit . . . gravelly."

Max eyed Aurora for a moment, but, being well practiced in the art, she was certain she appeared quite guileless.

"Thank you, but no."

"Oh, go ahead," Tess admonished. "Might loosen you up a bit."

Max turned back to Tess. Aurora noticed his jaw twitch. "Just because I don't plan my day around happy hour doesn't mean I'm a—"

"Tight ass?" Tess tilted her head, gave him a once-over, her gaze lingering on that particular part of his anatomy. "Although, I must admit . . ."

Max held her gaze when she lifted it to his without so much as blinking, then when she merely raised her glass in silent toast, he pointedly looked back to Aurora. Who, in turn, just managed to hide her smile behind a sip of sherry.

"And this is the influence you think is appropriate for a sixteen-year-old?" Max asked her.

"Oh, come on," Tess interrupted. "Don't you think it's way past time to stop beating that poor, dead horse? You know, it's not like I have to be doing this. But I met your sister and I liked her. Be grateful for the assistance."

"I didn't ask for your assistance. We were doing just fine without your inestimable help."

"She can't keep a coach for more than two minutes and she's facing the second grand slam of her career with a first-round opponent that would make me sweat. But yeah, sure, why ask someone for help? Silly me."

"I was working on getting her a coach. Trust me, there is no shortage of very talented people out there who want to work with her."

"I'm quite sure of that, too. But that doesn't help you, much less her, right this very second. Play begins in forty-eight hours. Right now I'm her best bet in terms of getting her head where it needs to be. I'm not going to screw around with her game, but whether you like it or not, I know what she's thinking, how she's likely to handle this, and better yet, I know exactly what it's going to be like out there."

"Not entirely, you don't," he muttered.

But Tess was on a roll and didn't hear him. Aurora flashed a quick glance at Max, but any thought she might have given to that troubling aside was swept away as the volleys continued. It was rather like watching a tennis match, she thought, more amused than alarmed. Mostly because they both wanted the same thing: what was best for Gaby. So she would just sip her sherry and stand clear until the dust settled. She trusted that when that happened, they'd have a workable solution. Or she'd need to call for medical assistance.

"You know, you tried to keep us from working together once before. And we see how well that panned out."

"Exactly my point!" Max exploded. "It was one thing for the two of you to have a few chats in private. Working as her coach—"

"I'm not exactly her coach. I'm just giving her a few court-strategy pointers, the benefit of my experience. A mentor."

"Gaby said we're paying you a percentage, which means you're working for the Fontaines. I call that coaching."

"She insisted." Tess shrugged.

Aurora's attention sharpened. Tess was good, she'd give her that. All that court savvy, she supposed. To look at her right now you'd never know that she was all but financially destitute. Poor dear. Aurora wished there was a way to just put it all out there so everyone knew what was what. She was certain a reasonable solution to all their concerns could be achieved. But she also knew she couldn't betray Tess with revealing that kind of explosive information. Max was a good man, but Aurora wasn't entirely certain what he'd do with that bit of knowledge.

So she bit her tongue and let the conversation continue, although admittedly she wasn't quite as amused by it all any longer.

"You'll only have to tolerate my existence for a few weeks or until she's out of the tournament. I don't see the big deal."

"The big deal is that she told an interviewer about you today."

Now Tess crossed the room, her expression instantly all business. "She did what?"

"That's what I came here to tell you."

"What exactly did she say, dear?" Aurora asked, quite concerned. Her plans had barely started to come together, and now this.

Max raked his hand through his hair, let out a breath. "Before the interview, she was telling me about her plan to have Tess coach her during Wimbledon."

"Mentor," Tess put in immediately. "I'm just a mentor."

Both Aurora and Max ignored her.

"And your response was?" Aurora asked him.

"I wasn't happy about it, which you all obviously knew or you wouldn't have been sneaking around behind my back all week."

"We didn't 'sneak,' " Tess shot back. "We merely avoided confrontation. Besides, you gave Aurora carte blanche to help Gaby and you knew I was talking with her. So don't get your tighty whiteys in a knot."

"Now, now," Aurora said, stepping in. Maybe she'd been wrong to think the agitation between these two was really just an overload of chemistry trying to sort its way out. For once, she really wished Vivian were here. She'd toss out a few clever double entendres and the tension in the room would either dissipate, or implode. Either way they'd have their answer. Holding out a slender thread of hope that all her carefully initiated plans hadn't been dashed, she said, "Did she tell the interviewer Tess was coaching her? What exactly did she say?"

"Yes," Tess chimed, "what exactly did she say? And what did you say to goad her into such a rash decision?"

"Me?" Max said, eyebrows leaping in defense. "I stated my concerns with her plan—calmly and rationally—then told her I'd think about it."

Tess rolled her eyes. "Which meant you were against it."

"Which meant I'd think about it," he reiterated.

Aurora saw the tic surface once again in his clenched jaw. He really had quite an attractive profile. Privately, with all those sparks shooting from his dark eyes? She thought he was quite something. If she'd been a few decades younger . . . well, no point in going there.

"Not to a teenager, trust me. She did what she thought she had to do in order to get what she knew she needed to have going into this tournament. She was only doing what had to be done because you're too stubborn and overprotective to see it yourself."

Aurora snapped back to the matter at hand. "There is no point in bickering over this. What's done is done," she said calmly. "Now we have to determine what the result of this interview will likely be. When is it being printed?"

"Originally it was slated to run Monday, the first day of the tournament. But no way is she holding back. She thinks we're talking to other journalists right now, so I know—"

"Why would you tell her that?" Tess asked, incredulous. "Of course she'll rush to press with it, if they don't sell it to some other media outlet first. All they need is some film of her and—" She stopped, and both she and Aurora looked at Max's expression. "No, you didn't. You let her take pictures? Film? My God, Max, why not just hand her the story on a silver platter?"

"It was too late then," he told them. "The story was out. I had to get her out of there before she said anything else, which is why I told her we had another interview. It doesn't matter. I'm betting it'll be all over the place by tomorrow."

"Hell, tonight's news, most likely," Tess exclaimed. "At this point every broadcast is pretty much all Wimbledon, all the time. It's the freaking Super Bowl over here. Something I don't have to tell you about." Suddenly she laughed, but there was a caustic edge to it.

"What could be funny about this?"

"Nothing, really. It's just that here you are all worried about my supposed impact on all this and who goes and screws it all up and leaks it to the press? You."

"I didn't say anything, Gaby sabotaged—" He broke off, pinched his fingers on the bridge of his nose. "This isn't getting us anywhere." He looked up, his expression set in stone. "Regardless of who said what to who—"

"Whom," Tess supplied, with an ever-so-helpful smile.

Max's jaw was clenched so tight, Aurora was surprised his molars weren't ground into dust. "Whatever. What matters is that your presence in her life, no matter your intention, is about to get her dragged right into the sticky hands of the media hounds. Right before the toughest first-round match of her life."

"Listen," Tess broke in. "There will be other grand slams, there will be other Wimbledons in her future. If you're so freaked out by all this, then yank her from the tournament."

He said nothing.

"We both know Gaby can handle this. We also both know, at least if one of us would be willing to be honest with himself, that she is going to be a superstar, with or without my help. She will be facing this type of intense media scrutiny for a very long time. And of course it never starts at a 'good time,' if there is such a thing, because if she was playing the Dubai Open in the middle of freaking nowhere, and I was hanging around, no one would give a flat damn. It's only because it is Wimbledon, because it's a grand-slam event, that anyone cares. Whenever she hit the spotlight, for whatever reason she hit it, it wasn't going to be when no one was watching. It's only newsworthy when a lot of people care. So why don't you just accept the fact that now is her time and try and figure out how to use this to your best advantage." She stalked back over to the bar and made herself another drink. "And if there is anyone around here who knows a little something about how to do just that, it's yours truly."

Aurora waited a beat, let the tension in the room shift from a boil to a slow simmer, then said, "I'm sure we can do just that. And because I'm fully part of this endeavor, I want you to know you have the full power of Glass Slipper behind you. Whatever we can do." She paused then and brightened considerably as part of the solution came to her. "One thing we can do is move you and Gaby out of that hotel and move you in here. Sir Robin would love to have more company, I can assure you, and you'll have complete privacy and a private court."

Tess didn't say anything right away, but she didn't look immediately thrilled with the solution. She was probably torn between giving Gaby the privacy she needed and having Max underfoot for the next few weeks. Well, it was a big house, a very big house. All of them could retreat to their own wings, if necessary. For Aurora's part, she was quite pleased with that unexpected little bonus. If they had to be in each other's way every day, maybe they could get past this silly antagonism and see what was becoming quite plainly apparent. Well, it was to her, anyway.

"That's a very generous offer, Aurora," Max said, sounding mostly sincere. "But I doubt Sir Robin would be thrilled with the idea of media stomping around his gates and fences, or worse, camping out."

"Are you kidding?" Aurora laughed. "You don't know him like I do. I'll be surprised if he doesn't change his plans and jet home just to be part of the excitement. He'll be tickled to play a role in subverting the press in any way. Trust me on this." She laid a hand on Max's arm. "But, of course, I will run this by him, just to be certain. You can speak with him yourself if it would make you feel any better." She turned and walked to an intercom unit that was tucked next to the service dolly and pressed a button. "Phillip, could you be a dear and call over to Glass Slipper for me? I'll need a car sent to the Fontaines' hotel." She looked at Max. "Would an hour give you enough time to pack? I think it's best we move quickly, on the off chance Tess is right and they do run this story on the evening news."

Max just sighed. Tess downed the rest of her drink.

Aurora took that as a yes. "In an hour, Phillip. Thank you, darling." She looked at her two houseguests and beamed. "Don't be such worrywarts. It'll all turn out splendidly." She slid her arm through Max's and ushered him to the door. "You best head out and get to Gaby. You can pack all your suitcases into the limo and bring your car, or better yet, why don't I have the limo sent here and you can just leave your car here. Stay completely under the radar. We can spirit you in the back way and—"

Max waved a hand. "Aurora, please, I don't think we need to go to quite those lengths. It's not like she's Elvis or something. I'll be fine. And while I appreciate your offer, I really think—"

Finally Tess spoke up. "Just do what she says so we can all have some peace, okay? And to be honest, she's probably right. Let's err on the side of caution here. For all our sakes. Especially Gaby's." She walked to the parlor doors and opened them.

"I'll have chef prepare us a lovely dinner," Aurora added. "We can discuss how we should handle this, come up with a game plan, as it were. Then get a good night's rest and be ready to tackle the day tomorrow."

Max looked at them both, then finally blew out a long breath. "Fine. At least for now." He leaned down and kissed Aurora's cheek. "Thank you. I'm sorry for all this."

"No need to apologize, dear. We do what we need to for friends."

As he passed through the parlor door, Tess called out from behind him. "And to think, now Gaby will have access to me twenty-four-seven."

"Tess," Aurora hissed, reprovingly. She loved the girl dearly, but she did have a little problem with impulse control.

Max just kept on walking to the front doors.

"Just one big happy family," Tess went on, trailing out behind him.

Aurora stepped to the open doorway, unsure whether to shake her head in exasperation . . . or pat herself on the back. Tess just couldn't leave the poor man alone. And it made her wonder why. It wasn't that she didn't know how to go after a man. Lord knows she'd plucked them like grapes off a vine over the years. When she saw something she wanted, she just went after it. She was a lot like Vivian in that way.

Aurora folded her arms and leaned on the doorframe, observing the little ritual mating dance unfolding in front of her. Wondering why Tess didn't just take what she wanted this time. What was it about Max that was so different it had her behaving like something of a fifth-grade boy who tossed out taunts to the girl he had a crush on because he didn't know how to handle what he was feeling?

And that's when it hit her. Tess knew all about stalking her prey, but it occurred to her that, this time, Tess had no real idea what to do with a man like Max, who was so different from her usual conquests. And connected, as well, to a teenager that Tess was coming to care about, no matter what she said. In fact, it was her immediate insistence on diminishing that role—mentor instead of coach—that gave her away. Much like her constant baiting of Max was giving something else away entirely. Even though she'd bet money Tess wasn't quite aware of it.

Yet.

Chapter 13

"You know something else?" Tess followed Max into the foyer.

Max ignored her and kept on his straight-arrow path to the front door. "Straight arrow" being the key phrase there, she thought. He was so damn exasperating.

For whatever reason, probably because she just couldn't resist the challenge of trying to direct that straight arrow off course a little, she didn't say what she'd been about to, which was that Gaby needed a female influence in her life, and that time spent with someone as maternal as Aurora would be a good thing for her right now.

No, instead her mouth opened and what came out was, "As I noted earlier, for being such a tight ass, yours really is quite fine."

Max paused at the door; his shoulders were so tense she half-expected him to just rap his forehead straight on the mahogany panels. "You might want to take all this a bit more seriously." Without looking at her, he gripped the doorknob and slowly turned it.

"You worry too much. We'll handle the press. Hey, who knows, I'm yesterday's news now that I'm retired. We might have blown this way out of proportion."

"You didn't see Fionula's face light up like a shark at feeding time."

" 'Fionula'?" Tess swallowed the string of curse words. "As in Fionula Hust?"

"The very one."

"Jesus," she muttered under her breath, but quickly recouped. "Well, look at it this way, if Gaby's goal was to put this out there in a big way, she picked the right mouthpiece. Key word there being 'mouth.' "

He turned a little then, looked at her over his shoulder. "My point all along."

Tess shrugged off the pointed insult. She was too busy mentally scrambling, considering all the possible ways tomorrow was likely to play out. Fionula had been a major thorn in her side during her latter years on tour. When she'd been busting her ass to come back after her first couple shoulder surgeries, Ms. Hust liked nothing more than to write opinion pieces on how she should just accept that her career was over, take her titles and big paychecks and go home. Maybe Tess should have thanked her. It was largely op-ed pieces like hers that had kept Tess focused through physical therapy and driven her to return to tour in better shape than when she'd left it.

She doubted Fionula was going to be kind to her now, which meant this wasn't going to be fun for Gaby. She'd just have to do what she could to minimize the fallout. But she'd be lying if she said she hadn't already started thinking how she could play this to her advantage. She'd been trying to get press since landing at Heathrow. Here was her perfect opportunity. She wouldn't throw Gaby to the wolves, but then, Gaby had pretty much made that decision. She was old enough to start learning the hard lessons of reaping the seeds she sowed. Tess was the first to admit she'd done some stupid things in her life, but she'd always owned up to them.

"We'll get through the next couple of weeks," she told him, then raised her hand as if taking a pledge. "I'll help her through this. I know you don't want to hear it, but I'm good at this."

"For all the wrong reasons."

"Hey, I wasn't the one shooting my mouth off in the interview today."

Max's jaw flexed. You know, he really had a decent profile. She caught herself wondering what she could say to make him smile. He'd looked pretty damn hot that one time she'd caught him at it.

Shaking that thought off, she said, "She's going to shoot her mouth off, Max. She would whether she ever met me. It's who she is. You know it, I know it. Hell, if anyone was going to influence that out of her, it would have been you. And you've had years to give it a shot."

"A running battle, to be sure. Which is why I don't need you coming in here and giving her any ideas. You're right, I have my hands quite full as it is, thanks."

Tess laughed. "I don't think she needs my help with ideas. She seems to be doing just fine on her own."

Max scowled. "You don't have to look so damn—"

"Proud of her? I wouldn't go that far. But if she operates on the idea that she wants to have a hand in what's said about her, then now is her opportunity to learn how to handle the results of her little bait-throwing expedition."

So much for getting a smile out of him. She wondered if he ever eased up. And she thought she was stressed out. Sheesh.

He'd shifted and was looking at her directly now. "Something tells me having the two of you under the same roof is going to make that damn near impossible."

"Such a pessimist." She couldn't have said what made her do it. The tension screaming between them every time they got within spitting distance of each other was hardly sexual in nature. But all of a sudden, or maybe not so sudden, she wasn't looking at him as Gaby's older brother, stick in the mud, thorn in her side. She was . . . well, she wasn't quite sure what she was doing. But whatever it was, it made her take a step closer. Mostly, she told herself, just to see what he'd do about it.

Surprisingly, Max held his ground. She knew he had an edge, but perhaps she hadn't given him quite enough credit for it. Because in that little instant of time where she had to decide whether to back down . . . or go into her tried-and-true mantrap mode, she seriously considered the former. Which wasn't like her at all. The hard truth was, she wasn't a hundred percent certain she could pull it off. It was a rare thing for her, that uncertainty.

But when had she ever backed down from a challenge?

"I'm beginning to wonder about something," she said, purposely dropping her voice to something closer to a husky whisper.

"Which would be?" he asked evenly. He held her gaze rather easily.

Hmm. The surprises kept coming. But he might as well have waved a red flag in front of her. No longer thinking about Gaby, or her own greater good, her focus had zeroed in on one thing and one thing only. She shifted an incremental step closer. "Are you more worried about my negative influence on sweet, young Gaby?" Another incremental shift and she was almost breathing the same air he was. He was taller than her own five-eleven, which was nice, she found herself thinking. Really nice. She reached up and toyed with the collar of his polo shirt. "Or are you more worried about my possible negative influence on terse, not-so-naive you?"

Without breaking their gaze, he took her hand and moved it away from his collar. "Don't be mistaken. Only one member of the Fontaine family is starstruck."

"That's not exactly what I asked."

Shockingly, his mouth twitched the tiniest bit. "I know." Then he let himself out the front door and shut it abruptly between them.

Tess stood there, mouth hanging open, before turning and leaning back against the door. She let out a short laugh. "Dammit." Who knew he had such an exit in him? "Point to the tight ass."

She glanced up to find Aurora standing in the parlor doorway, arms folded over her flowing caftan, a knowing smile beaming from her expertly made-up face.

"What?"

"Don't give me that innocent look," Aurora said.

Tess merely smiled. "Yeah, I guess it's been a few years since I could pull that off." She could see Aurora was ready to pounce on her little interaction with Max—wasn't it just her luck she'd had a witness?—and she wasn't about to let her. Hell, Tess didn't even know what had just gone on there. She clapped her hands together. "I guess we'd better prepare for our guests."

"Don't worry, dear. I'll take care of that. Is there anything we should do to try and counter Fionula's interview? What do you think she's going to do with it?"

"Well, no one knows I'm staying here, so moving Gaby here tonight is a good move. The story will break tomorrow morning when the papers come out. She writes for *Good Day* and they have no direct media outlet."

"You seemed concerned earlier that it might go that way."

"With her, you never know. If I was still an active player, I'd be more worried. But, frankly, this is gossip, not news. The Brits worship their gossip rags, but this will make a little splash, then they'll move on to something else, something more sensational than a retired player helping out a rookie."

Aurora tucked her chin. "Come now. At any other time of the year, that would be true. But we're on the eve of the British Championships. It might be a blip in the gossip rags for a day or two, but it will most definitely be chewed on quite thoroughly by those in the tennis world. Every announcer will analyze it to death, and every sports journalist is going to want a quote or something. From you, from Gaby."

"I know, you're right."

"It's going to be a flurry of attention for her, the likes of which she hasn't seen yet."

"She's going to have to learn to deal with it sometime. Consequences, there's always consequences. Nobody knows that better than me."

"Whatever the case, I'm glad we can give her some respite from what will surely be, at the very least, a major distraction for her, right when she needs it least."

Tess smiled. "Maybe next time she'll think twice before playing an angle like that, with a journalist, of all people."

Aurora laughed lightly. "Darling, I know you don't believe that any more than I do."

"True," she said, looping her arm through Aurora's as they walked back into the parlor. "But look at it this way, at least she'll get her 'Handling the Hounds of Hell' tips from the best."

"Gabrielle!"

"Miss Fontaine, this way!"

"Give us a smile, Gaby!"

"Where is Tess?"

"Well, this was a mistake," Max muttered beneath his breath

as he drove slowly through the small throng of reporters milling by the side entrance gates to the grounds of Wimbledon.

"Oh, lighten up," Gaby said from the passenger seat. She went to put down the window.

Max threw his left arm across her body. "What are you doing?"

"They just want a wave. What is the harm?"

"They'll swarm the car. Let's get on the grounds and get you to the practice court, okay?"

Gaby slumped back in the seat. "I don't know why you're being such a stick about this. We could have just trained back at Sir Robin's today."

Which was exactly what Tess had advised them both to do this morning. She'd suggested it was best if Gaby laid low today, focused on her practice. She'd offered to come down to the grounds and take on whatever press or media that had shown up after the story came out in the morning paper. "It will all blow over in a day or two if we handle this right," she'd told him. "Let me handle it."

But no, he hadn't listened. He'd thought it best to tackle it head-on. Tess had said the night before that Gaby should be responsible for the consequences of her actions, and after laying awake all night, he'd come to the same conclusion. When he'd mentioned that to Tess that morning over breakfast, she'd looked at him like he was insane.

Women.

He'd never professed to understanding them, but he most definitely didn't understand this one. Like, what in the hell had that little display in the foyer last night been all about? *Yeah, and why in the hell did you respond like you did,* his little voice wanted to know. Stupid little voice. That had kept him awake last night, too.

Well, he knew better than Tess Hamilton what was right for

his sister. He tapped the brake when a more enthusiastic photographer stepped in front of the bumper and snapped a picture straight on. "Dammit, come on!" At least, he thought he knew. He was having serious second thoughts at the moment. "Dear God, there are more of them on the inside."

His hope that the hallowed grounds of the All England Club would provide them with a safe, secure haven was quickly dashed. With the Championships beginning the next day, the quaint little village of Wimbledon had already taken on a circuslike atmosphere. The roads leading down to the grounds were filled with spectators, many of them browsing along the row of vendors crammed into the various driveways of the homes lining Church Road. He'd expected that part. They'd been here for juniors, he knew what it was like. In fact, he'd been counting on the gathering fans and autograph seekers already on line for tickets to act as a shield. Deal with a handful of reporters and photographers, then get lost in the crowd, get inside. That had been his plan.

He hadn't counted on the media with grounds passes lying in wait for them.

"That wasn't too bad," Gaby said, giving him a smug little smirk. "I told you they weren't going to care about me. Yet," she added under her breath.

Max ignored her. They parked and he got out. He retrieved her gear bag from the boot while she did a last-minute check of her hair in the rearview mirror. God save him. "You look fine. It's a practice session. Come on." As he lowered the cover on the boot, he saw several people walking directly toward them. One of them had a television camera. "Gaby, stay in the car."

"What?" She barely had time to pull her foot back in before he bumped her door shut. "Hey!"

"Mr. Fontaine?" one of the trio called out. "Can we have a

moment of your time?" A short woman sporting an excruciatingly perfect blonde hairdo trotted up to him, her photographer in tow. She cornered him against his car and stuck her hand out. "Sadie Post with the *Herald.*" Her teeth were blinding white and rather oversized. She shook his hand with surprising strength. "I understand your sister is in training with Tess Hamilton." Her smile grew wider... and exponentially more terrifying. "The bad girls of tennis working together, eh? It's such a great story," she gushed. "We'd love to do Gaby and Tess's first interview as coach and player. You'll get front-page treatment with a full-color splash photo."

The gangly, shaggy-haired photographer accompanying Sadie nodded and gave his own toothy grin of agreement. Max nodded absently toward him, thinking it better to keep his attention on the reporter. "Thank you for your interest," he said, falling into the standard spiel he'd used before. "Why don't you give me your card and I'll contact you. We're a bit rushed at the moment. Court time and all."

Wrong thing to say. Sadie's eyes popped even wider as she tried to look past him into the window of the car. "Gabrielle?" she called out. "Can we have a moment?"

Max sighed. He hated aggressive women. That moment by the door last night flashed through his mind again. Tess coming on to him, playing with his collar, breathing all over him. She'd smelled good, he recalled, then immediately scowled and deliberately shut the image out of his head once and for all. "I'm very sorry. We have practice time scheduled. Now, if you'll please be so kind, we'd like to maintain some—"

The door shoved open into the back of his thighs, propelling him forward. If Sadie hadn't been quick on her feet, he might have plastered her to the ground. As it was, he managed to regain his balance, but not before Gaby had emerged from the car. "Hello," she said, all TV camera smiles and ingratiating charm. "A pleasure." She stuck out her hand. "I'm sorry, I didn't catch your name."

"Sadie Post, Miss Fontaine."

Max raked a hand through his hair and worked his way between them before Sadie could crush Gaby's serving hand in her monster grip. "Miss Fontaine is unavailable for comment at this time," he said, jaw squared. He shot a look at his sister, all but daring her to push this any further. For once in her young life, she backed down.

Smiling cheerfully, Gaby shrugged and rolled her eyes. "Sorry. Practice time, you know." She was quite charming when she wanted to be, Max noted. She gave a little wave to the cameraman, who quickly lifted his gear. A little red light blinked to life on the front of his camera. Gaby grabbed her gear bag and swung it over her shoulder, then looked back at the small ensemble. She could have been posing for a teen magazine. "Give Max your card and I'll talk to Tess. Bye!"

They weren't going to have to worry how she'd do against Davina tomorrow. Because Max was going to strangle her the very moment they were alone.

As it turned out, there was little-to-no alone time. Gaby's practice partner, Petra Kasyanova, was waiting for them on court. Along with a surprising number of other people, apparently all hoping to get a glimpse of Gaby and Tess working together. Former star coaching the young phenom. *The bad girls of tennis.* Sadie's words echoed in Max's head. He could see the headlines now. Christ.

Gaby came over to the bench and grabbed her water. Max was a few feet away, seated on the grass by the fence. "Your backhand is on today. Good approach shots."

She just shot him a look. "I could be getting all kinds of help from Tess back at Wexley House, but noooo. I'm stuck here with Petra. Who is more worried about getting in the pictures people are taking than hitting the damn ball."

Max lifted his shoulders. "You wouldn't have to worry about that if you'd been a little more—"

"I'm not worried about it. It's Petra who can't keep it together. It's all your fault, anyway."

"*My* fault? Was I the one who sat across from Fionula Hust and blabbed about her 'secret weapon'?"

Gaby tossed her water bottle on her gear bag. "If you'd been more receptive to the idea of us working together, I wouldn't have had to take such drastic measures." She lifted a hand when he went to interrupt. "And even now, you're forcing me out here with all these distractions when I could be on a private court getting help from one of the best players ever to hit a ball."

Heads were beginning to turn as Gaby's voice grew louder.

Max stood and walked over to his sister. "Unless you want even more distraction, you might want to keep it down a little."

"I just don't understand why I couldn't have stayed at Wexley House, at least for today. Even Tess thought it was a good idea."

Max had to clamp down on his jaw to keep from telling Gaby exactly what he thought of Tess and her ideas. "We're here because you have to be responsible for the consequences of your actions. You want to go blab things to the world without thinking it through first, fine. But then you have to deal with the fallout."

Like any sixteen-year-old worth her mascara, Gaby immediately switched tactics. "Come on, Max," she wheedled sweetly. "Don't be such a bear. My first match is the day after tomorrow. I know I might have been a bit impulsive yesterday, but it's just because I'm so worried about facing Davina. I want to do well here, or at least not humiliate myself like I did in Paris."

"You didn't humiliate yourself in Paris. No one expected—"

"I expected, okay? And then I come here and blow the tune-up event. I'm feeling like I lost my edge."

"You've only been on tour a few months. It's going to take time to climb the ranks. It's one game, one match, one tournament at a time."

"Yes, and I have to play well, because you won't let me play enough tournaments to get my ranking up faster."

"It's not a race."

"It is for me," she said, the heat creeping back into her voice. "An injury could end my career early, like it did Tess's."

"Which is exactly why I'm being selective in what tournaments you play, so you don't wear yourself down too soon, burn out."

"I'm strong, Max. I can handle more than this. I want to play. Anything could happen out there. I could get hurt driving here, you just don't know. I have to make my mark now, while I'm young, while I know I can."

"Gaby—"

"So either let me play more, or let me have the kind of help I need to get better as fast as I can."

She was working up a good head of steam and Max knew if he pushed, she'd explode. On this particular day, with the added awareness of the press and the group of spectators lining the fences, the last thing he needed was to create an incident. "Petra is waiting. Go finish your session and we'll talk about this on the way back." She started to rebut, but he talked over her. "I'm not going to argue this here, not now."

She huffed out a sigh. "Fine. But we're going to talk about this later. You're ruining my concentration." She flounced off, content to have had the last word. For now.

Max snagged a second water bottle from her bag and took a long swig. Gaby would be seventeen this fall. In a little more than a year, she would make her own decisions about things like tournament scheduling and coaching. In a year, he'd be rendered obsolete if she so desired. So the more she learned now, the better chance she had of making sound decisions later. Some days, thoughts of his sister finally being on her own, leaving his own future up for grabs, terrified him.

A murmur rippled through the crowd, followed by a few hoots and whistles, then a burst of spontaneous applause rang out.

"Hey, Gaby," a familiar voice shouted. Grinning ear to ear, Tess made her grand entrance on the practice courts amid a barrage of flashbulbs and shouts for her autograph. "Ready to hit a few?"

And some days, Max thought, sighing heavily, that day couldn't get here fast enough.

Chapter 14

"What are you doing here?" Max demanded.

"So nice to see you, too, Max. Miss me?"

"Are you crazy?"

"Often." Tess dropped her gear bag next to Gaby's. Max was definitely not happy to see her. Goody. "Perk up. I believe you were the one who said she should reap what she sowed." Gaby waved and Tess nodded at her, then looked back at Max, a bright smile on her face. "After some thought, I decided you were right and I was wrong. A historical moment for us, don't you think? I'll be glad to put that in writing if you'd like."

His expression remained flat. "Always a smart mouth."

She leaned down and tugged a racket from her bag, giving him a look down the front of her tank top if he so desired. She glanced up through her lashes just in time to see him quickly avert his gaze, and grinned. "You have no idea."

His eyes went dark and his pupils shot a bit wider. Simply a biological reaction to stimulation, she told herself. But immensely gratifying all the same.

She wisely straightened and turned her back on him before she could give in to the urge to see what other kind of reactions she could provoke from him. A path she was going to have to work hard at avoiding if she had any hope of keeping this rapidly escalating situation under any semblance of control. "Petra, can you stay and hit a while longer?" she called out.

Shutters whirred as cameras recorded every millisecond.

"Autographs, Tess?" someone shouted. "Come on!"

Gaby's hitting partner was young and blonde and looked like she should be on the cover of *Barbie Tennis*, if they ever came out with such a thing. Petra took in the now rapidly increasing crowd, along with the converging reporters flipping open notebooks and directing their cameramen, and nodded enthusiastically. "Definitely, Ms. Hamilton," she called back, her English slightly accented. "It would be an honor." She then immediately hurried to her bench on the far side of the court to pull a small compact from her gear bag to check her hair. Tess glanced at Gaby, who was huffing impatiently, and shared a quick, resigned smile.

"This way, Tess!" one of the photographers shouted.

"When did you start training Gabrielle?" a reporter shouted.

"How did you two hook up?" someone else called out.

"Is this a permanent arrangement?"

"Why coaching, Tess? Hard time letting go of the game?"

"Maybe she just wants to make sure the game doesn't get boring now that she's gone," someone said, causing a wave of titters to ripple through the growing throng.

"Gabrielle," a reporter called out, "you gonna take up the 'bad girl of tennis' mantle now that Tess has laid it down?"

"You got one hell of a teacher," someone else shouted. "For tennis, too."

Another wave of laughter ran through the crowd and Tess could see this quickly getting out of control. She didn't mind fielding the shout-outs, and she didn't mind exposing Gaby to it, that was why she'd come down here, after all. But exposing was one thing. She had no intention of putting Gaby directly into the line of fire. Yet. The last thing any of them needed was Gaby saying anything incendiary, intentionally or not.

Seeing Max starting to cross the court, as well as Gaby looking to her then back at the crowd, as if ready to respond, Tess quickly grinned and waved at everyone, drawing all the attention back to her. Go with your strength, right?

"Listen up, gang," she called out. "This is supposed to be a closed practice." She walked a bit closer to the wall that ran alongside the side of the court separating the court from the walkways. The wall was about seven feet high and a foot thick, with flower boxes lining the top so the people walking along the pathways between the outer courts in this section were actually looking down into the court from an elevated position. As she drew closer, she elicited another round of whistles and shout-outs. "We don't mind if you hang out and watch, but I'm going to ask that you let us conduct business here."

"Just a few minutes, Tess!"

"First round for Gaby is day after tomorrow. Have a heart, guys. Compromise with me. I don't want to have to call security."

"How about after?" one reporter shouted. "Promise us some time?"

"Deal. When we're done, you get ten minutes."

That seemed to calm them down, but no one left the area. Tess glanced at Gaby, who had taken her cue—bless her—and already walked back to the baseline. She was hitting back and forth with Petra, who was infinitely more distracted by this circus than Gaby was. In fact, Gaby seemed to feed off the energy. *That's my girl.*

Well, Tess wasn't minding it a whole lot at the moment, either, but not because she enjoyed the attention, or particularly wanted it. She did, however, need it. As long as she could keep Gaby focused, she saw no harm in trying to kill two birds with one stone. Gaby could get a much needed crash course in Media Gauntlet 101, and Tess could increase her visibility... and her marketability. It was all about balancing. And praying that when all was said and done, the balancing act paid out at least a healthy six-figure endorsement deal with someone. She no longer cared much who. She'd hawk bug spray if they'd have her.

"Okay, ladies," she said, all business as she turned back to the court. "We're going to drill approach shots." She walked over to Gaby. "Listen," she said quietly, "I want to work just like we did the other day. But you need to get more aggressive. Davina likes to come in. She's got a great net game and she's going to use that on you every chance she gets."

"So I'll hit it deep, not give her the opportunity."

"She'll make her opportunities, trust me. If you hang out back here, you're going to lose to her. She's got a good return game and some real finesse shots."

"Then why isn't she ranked higher?"

"Lack of consistency. She lets her heart rule her head."

Gaby grinned. "I can work that."

"I'm sure you can. But in the meantime, let's keep up with the net drills, okay? I know it's way too late to be introducing anything too new, but I think I have a few ideas on how you can take what you're already doing and tweak it a little. I know you don't feel comfortable yet, up at the net, but that could work to your advantage."

"How?"

"If she's done her research, she's going to know that about you, too. So she'll try and pull you in, drop-shot you, short-court you, then pass you down the line, right and left."

Gaby's mouth quirked up a little. "Sounds like maybe you know from personal experience."

Tess shot her a look. "Don't remind me." Then her own mouth quirked. "Besides, I can get my revenge through you."

Gaby laughed. "Deal."

"Don't get cocky on me, now," Tess said, but she was fighting a smile. Gaby was a handful, but she had even more promise. So much damn talent. God, she missed this game so much it hurt. "Okay," she said, shoving that emotion forcefully aside, "so we surprise her. You're going to have to pick your moments, though. Rather than push to come in on your own shots, I'm going to work a few angles for when she brings you in. She won't be expecting it. We can't do it often, but it might make her think twice about that little strategy."

Gaby's eyes were shining, and she was rocking on her feet in anticipation. "Cool. Thanks, Tess. This is, like, the perfect insider information."

"Don't thank me just yet. I can give you the information, work the angles, but it's what you do with it that counts."

"We'll make it work."

As Gaby turned back to the baseline, Tess said, "You know, if you had a regular coach, he or she would be giving this kind of information to you on a regular basis." She'd intended the remark as a pointed reminder that Gaby wasn't doing herself any favors by keeping her coaches on the revolving-door plan. Especially during slam season. Something Tess knew from personal experience.

Instead of looking chastened, however, Gaby's grin widened. "So I'll just talk you into staying with me into hard-court season. Until the U.S. Open."

Before Tess's mouth could do much more than drop open, Gaby was already prancing back to the baseline. *Brat,* Tess thought, not nearly as put out by her protégée's little machinations as she should have been. Her initial fantasy moment aside, she had no plans to prolong this arrangement beyond the fortnight here in London. She'd help Gaby find someone who was suited for her as a long-term coach before leaving. But if everything went as she hoped, she wouldn't need this gig two weeks from now.

She moved back to the sideline and directed Petra to hit a short ball. "I want you to come in, then lob it."

Gaby had been rocking on the balls of her feet in anticipation of the shot, but stopped and stood up. "What? I could come in, pass her easily down the line."

"Because you know it's coming. You won't during the game, trust me. Davina masks those shots really well. She'll expect power from you and the first thing she's going to do is dive for the nearest sideline. So you lob her, give yourself time to get back." She grinned. "Then you bring the power. Bring the pain. You run her back and forth until your shot opens up. Capice?"

Gaby didn't look convinced.

Tess just turned to Petra. "Short court." She walked over to the young blonde and quietly added, "As soon as you hit this, stab left."

"But isn't she going to lob me?"

"Just do it."

Petra shrugged. Tess smiled back at Gaby, who was watching their exchange with typical impatience. She jogged to the side of the court, and waved them into play.

Petra placed the ball in the middle of the service box . . . and just as Tess assumed, Gaby came charging in and drove it down the line.

Petra was already moving that direction, stabbed her racket out as instructed . . . and caught the ball on a sharply angled volley that landed well out of Gaby's reach, dropping just inside the line to her far right.

Tess just folded her arms. "Now can we try the lob?"

Gaby muttered under her breath and stalked back to the baseline.

She nodded to Petra and they went through the motions again, only this time Gaby popped the ball up. Petra raced back to the baseline and made a looping return . . . and from that point on Gaby owned her. She pinned her to one corner, then ran her to the other. Back and forth. Until Petra finally gave her a short ball again. This time Gaby was ready and when Petra came in behind it, Gaby lobbed it over her head and Petra had no way of reversing her direction in time to get it. The ball dropped in just inside the baseline. Gaby crowed and pumped her fist. Petra, hands braced on her hips, just shook her head.

Tess glanced over at Max, expecting to see, at the very least, a bit of grudging respect. Only to find him on a cell call, doing business or something. He wasn't even watching! She turned back to the court, not sure why it mattered what Max thought. He was butting out and leaving them to their practice session. That's what she wanted from him. Right?

"Again," she called out, much to the chagrin of a now panting and sweating Petra. *So much for that media-perfect blonde ponytail, hm?* Tess thought. Not that Gaby's hitting partner was Tess's concern, but getting the most out of her for Gaby's sake was. It wouldn't hurt Petra any to have to think about tennis first for the next hour. Do her some good.

That hour went by fast, but both players had gotten increasingly competitive as the practice progressed and they'd accomplished a lot by the time Tess waved them off the court. She turned to Max. "Hey, can you pull yourself away from whatever is so fascinating and join us for a sec?" Everytime she'd looked over at him while they'd been practicing—which had maybe happened more often than she'd like to admit—he'd either been on the phone or buried in his daytimer.

Once he was close and the two girls were in front of her, she said, "We need to coordinate our exit strategy here." The size of the crowd watching practice had ebbed and flowed a little during the past hour, but the reporters, sensing practice time was over, were congregating again. Sort of like flies on roadkill.

"I can handle the press," Gaby said.

Petra immediately started fussing with her hair.

"I know you can," Tess told her.

"Wait a minute," Max began. "You're not going to—"

"If you'd let me explain," she interrupted, "I'll tell you what I am going to do, okay?"

"I've just spent the past hour talking to what feels like every reporter in Europe. The ones who aren't here, anyway."

Gaby's face lit up. Petra started dabbing the sweat from her forehead.

"Don't get excited," Max told her. "I turned them all down."

"What?" Gaby and Tess exclaimed simultaneously.

He raised his hands in a placating gesture, to which Tess immediately faked a laugh and playfully pushed them away. Through a gritted smile, she said, "Keep the hand gestures to a minimum. We have a lot of eyes on us, more than a few with digital capabilities. One big happy family, okay?"

"You're the one who agreed to talk to these guys," Max told her. "So why don't you go engage your adoring public and I'll get the girls out of here. I've already called security to escort us to the players' area."

"You did what?" Tess rolled her eyes. "Listen, we need to play this a little differently. The more unavailable Gaby is, the more the hounds will want to hunt her down. What we're going to do is go over there, offer everyone a few photo ops of me and Gaby together. Something to splash all over the place with the stories that are already going to come out. I've learned if you give them what they want up front, the whole thing dies down much quicker because it's not a 'big get' anymore."

"She knows what she's talking about, Max," Gaby added.

"Tell me something I don't know," he muttered.

"We're only going to field a few questions." Tess turned to Gaby. "All of which you're going to let me answer first, or toss to you. But let me do the tossing, okay?"

"But—"

"I know what I'm talking about, remember?"

Gaby huffed a little, but she knew she'd been beaten at her own game. "Fine. This time."

Both adults just gave her a look and she relented, just a little. "I'll behave, promise."

"Smile," Tess advised her. "Save the pouty looks for later when we don't have a dozen cameras aimed at us."

Gaby gave her the fakest smile ever. Tess just smiled back. "Perfect. Now you're ready."

"This is a mistake," Max told them.

"No," Tess told him sweetly, "this is the pro tour. The idea is for us to control the game where we can, not let them direct it for us."

"Smiles on, girls. Everything is rosy, your outlook couldn't be cheerier. Off we go, then," she said, tossing in a bit of a British accent on that last part. She winked at Max as she ushered the girls past him. "Keep your pencil handy." She nodded at his notebook. "I might surprise you."

"Oh, of that I have no doubt," he said so only she could hear. "But for once maybe you can do me a favor and make the surprise a good one."

"Stick in the mud," she shot back.

"Instigator."

He really was the most frustrating male she'd ever met. Outside her own family, anyway. So why was she smiling for real now?

Tess walked to the far, walled-in side of the court.

"Okay, your turn," she called up to the spectators and media lining up two and three deep. She dragged a chair from the sideline and stepped up on it so she could reach up to the top of the wall and take the pens and pieces of paper being offered by fans for autographs. Might as well kill two birds with one stone. "Ten minutes. Fire away."

One reporter, a short, mousy woman with a horrible haircut, stepped forward first. Tess didn't recognize her. Must be new. Pen poised over her notebook, the young woman addressed her in a soft British accent. "Miss Hamilton, Margaret Tompkins with the *Daily Sentinel*. Would you tell us, please, how long have you been working with Miss Fontaine?"

Another reporter elbowed in front of her and stuck a microphone over the wall. "Tess, is it true you're thinking about coming back on tour? Are you going to pull a Martina Navratilova and play doubles with a younger, fresher player like Gabrielle?"

Tess watched the mousy reporter sigh a little, but give up her ground. That one was going to have to get a lot tougher if she was going to last out here. "So, is that the rumor already?" Tess asked, shooting the more aggressive reporter a cocky smile.

"Is it just a rumor?"

Tess debated briefly the merits of dodging that question and letting the speculation build for a bit, but ultimately decided against it. "Apparently, since I hadn't even heard that one."

"No plans for a comeback, then?"

Tess continued to sign autographs for fans, pausing here and there for a photograph. "Hi, Antoinette," she said, greeting the reporter by name. "You know me, I'd be playing right now if I thought my shoulder could keep me in the top ten." She grinned, posed for another picture. "So no, I won't be returning, doubles or singles. Thanks," she said to another young fan as she handed back her autograph.

"So you're taking up coaching instead?" This came from the young reporter, asked so softly Tess almost didn't hear her.

Tess paused, didn't take the next piece of paper, and looked directly at her. "Margaret, did you say? New out here, huh?" The woman blushed a little as she nodded. Boy, completely green. "Nice to meet you, Margaret. Don't let these guys push you around," she added with an admonishing little smile in Antoinette's direction.

Tess had learned early on the best way to beat them at their own game. They treated her like a piece of meat; would chew her up and spit her out without a second thought to her welfare as long as it got them an extra inch of column space. She, on the other hand, treated them like family. A highly dysfunctional one, but family nonetheless. A case of the victim humanizing herself to her attacker. Didn't stop them, but it made them think a bit more about what they were saying in print.

"No, I'm not coaching," Tess went on. "I'm just helping out a friend who happens to be in between coaches at the moment."

"Some friend to have, eh?" Antoinette shot back, eliciting a few laughs from the crowd.

"How long have you known Gabrielle?" another familiar voice asked, echoing the shy reporter's initial question, only with a sly, underlying curiosity that Tess knew she'd be wise to exploit to her advantage.

She searched the throng until she spotted her. "Hello, Fionula."

Tess had learned long ago no amount of humanizing would work with Fionula.

"Tell us how you and Gabrielle came to be such great friends," she asked, her expression bright and perky, which fooled so many. It was all in the eyes, Tess knew. Close set and snakelike.

"Didn't Gaby tell you during your interview? Oh, that's right, you were in too much of a hurry to file your story and beat out all these other hardworking souls." She shot a cheeky grin to the rest of the group, who shared a brief moment of collective angst over Fionula's consistent ability to grab the hot headline. "To answer your question, we have mutual friends here in London."

Fionula was clearly looking for the dirt angle to this particular breaking news story. She'd trumped everyone being the first to announce their partnership, but typical of her, she wasn't satisfied with that. Dirt angles could bite you in the ass if caught unaware. But if you were sharp enough to catch on early, you could use the reporter's less-than-lovely agenda to your own advantage. Tess had every intention of doing just that. The fact that Fionula was going to unwittingly be the one to help her achieve her goal was just icing on the cake.

"As you probably know, I got into town early to be here for my brother Bobby's wedding. Now I'm just looking forward to watching a couple of weeks of good tennis."

"Just 'good'?" a male reporter called out. "Not great?"

She found his face in the crowd and grinned. "Hey, Ethan. How is Mary doing?" she asked, referring to his wife, who had been a reporter before marrying him and starting their family. "You know, with me no longer on tour, pissing players off and bringing out their best game in order to beat me..." She shrugged. " 'Good' is as good as it gets."

Everyone laughed.

"Don't let Serena or Justine hear you say that," he tossed back.

"My record against them speaks for itself. You guys would love nothing more than for another rivalry like ours to spring up, and you know it." She took another piece of paper, signed another autograph. "You know, Ethan, you're getting a little soft. You should give Mary a break with the kids, let her come out here and badger me a little. She knew how to play hardball." Exactly as expected, Fionula took up that little gauntlet.

"Is it hard being here as spectator instead of player? You owned this tournament two years ago. How does it feel being on the court as coach, not player?"

It sucks ass, how do you think it feels? Tess wanted to shoot back. Bitch. She'd known the question would come, of course, but she thought she'd handle it better. Coming from Fionula, the question hit her like an arrow to the chest. It took everything she had to maintain even a semblance of a cheery facade and pretend all was well and good in Tess Hamilton Land. Like she wasn't still in mourning over the death of her career, like her world hadn't come crashing down the moment she'd landed on her shoulder, like she wasn't still trying to glue that world back together again and having about as much luck as she would reassembling shattered Humpty Dumpty pieces.

Had it not sucker punched her to such a degree, she might have had the moxie to use the visceral intensity of her reaction to her favor, let them inside, let them see her pain, work that angle, gain sympathy. It might have won her a few marketability points. But it was all she could do to maintain an even smile. Besides, no way in hell was she going to give Fionula the satisfaction of seeing the truth.

"I'm not coaching Gaby," she said tightly, opting to sidestep the issue altogether. It would come back to haunt her again, and again, but next time she'd be better prepared. "I'm just playing mentor a little. Mostly I'm here to enjoy myself. Watch my brother play." She smiled directly at Fionula, as much a test of her own fortitude as anything else. "There's nothing more to it, really."

A statement she well knew was like waving a red flag at a bull. Dirt diggers like Fionula knew that anytime a player, or any celebrity, said there was nothing more to the story, there was definitely more to the story . . . usually all juicy.

It was a risky angle to play, but what choice did she have? Tess had to make her and the other diggers suspect there was more to this arrangement with Gaby than met the eye, enough to keep the speculation very visible in the press . . . without actually encouraging them to dig in the direction that would uncover the real truth. That multimillionaire player Tess Hamilton, former number-one player Tess Hamilton, ten-time grand-slam winner Tess Hamilton . . . was now flat-busted, broke Tess Hamilton. The same Tess Hamilton who could swing a dead cat in the middle of a corporate party and not hit anyone interested in signing her to a deal.

At the moment, it was advantage Tess, and she damn well planned to keep it that way. Before Fionula or anyone else could follow up, she looked over her shoulder and called out, "Gaby?" She waved at her. "Come on over and say hi."

The reporters all pressed closer, the fans did, too, as did the photographers and cameramen, who all resumed their jockeying for position.

Tess climbed down off the chair. "You're going to want her autograph," she told the fans when they sighed in disappointment. "Trust me. You can all say you got Gabrielle Fontaine's autograph the year she made her Wimbledon debut . . . the very tournament she will go on to dominate over the next ten years."

The reporters almost wet their collective pants getting down that sound bite. "Are you predicting her success because you'll be coaching her?" Antoinette asked.

They were like bulldogs. But she was counting on that. She knew they wouldn't give up on that angle . . . and hoped they wouldn't. As long as she was connected to Gaby, she was news.

"I'm not her coach. Her record in the juniors speaks for itself. She's only been out here a few months and she's already making her mark on the tour. You watched how she handled Serena in Paris, then took Venus to two tiebreakers in Birmingham. Give her time—and not much of it. You're looking at the next American champion." She grinned again. "Number one on the charts, number one in our hearts."

Gaby shot her a smile, and started signing a sudden flurry of autograph requests.

"Gabrielle," several reporters called out. "What do you think of Tess's prediction?"

She glanced at Tess, who gave her an almost imperceptible nod, then grinned up at the crowd. "I'm hoping she's wrong."

"What?" There was a collective gasp. Pencils poised over paper.

Gaby's grin spread wider. "I'm hoping I dominate this event for the next twenty years."

Everyone laughed. Tess beamed. God, she was a natural at this. Why in hell Max wanted to subdue any part of her natural charm and energy was beyond Tess.

"Okay, guys," she said, raising her voice to be heard above the sudden cacophony of shutters whirring and questions being tossed at Gaby. "Our superstar here needs to get inside and get rubbed down."

"Gabrielle, just one more!"

"Look this way, Gaby!"

"Come on, Tess, just a few more!"

"Hey now," she admonished with a sassy wink, "you got more than your ten minutes. We'll see you all after round one."

"You predicting an upset, Tess?"

"Think she'll beat Davina?"

Tess merely responded with a knowing smile as she quickly ushered Gaby off the chair.

"Come on, Tess," she whispered, "let me stay out here. This is great press."

"First rule of good press: Make 'em want, then make 'em wait. Wave, smile, and follow me."

Gaby looked like she was going to rebel, but at Tess's steady stare, she did as asked, and quite brilliantly. "Thanks for waiting, everyone!"

As they crossed the court, Tess told her, "There will be plenty more where this is coming from."

The crowd had migrated and were trying to come into the alley that ran between the practice courts and the main building, but fortunately security was waiting for them. She ushered Gaby and Petra ahead of her. "Just keep moving," she told them, "no stopping, no talking until you're inside." Tess moved more slowly, let the girls disappear inside. She smiled easily and waved as she passed by, but didn't answer any of the additional questions shouted to her, or pause long enough for another photo opportunity. Make 'em want, then make 'em wait. Not a bad first day as the coach who really wasn't.

Until she saw who was waiting for her at the players' entrance.

She forced a bright smile. "Hello, Max. We really have to stop meeting like this. So . . . now what did I do wrong?"

Chapter 15

"We need to talk." Max turned, but Tess stayed where she was.

"We always need to talk. It never seems to get us anywhere, though. Did Gaby and Petra get inside okay?"

"They should be in the training room." Max looked past her at the crowd still hanging over the wall. He didn't need to give them any more fodder. Tess had already seen to that little bit of business. "Let's go to the players' lounge." He bit back a sigh when Petra stepped back outside. "Your mom is waiting in the training room," he told Petra, trying to stem the impatience in his voice. And failing, if the expression on Tess's face was any indication.

"Thank you, Max." Petra put her hand on Tess's arm. "Will you come back with me and talk to my mother? She watched me on court with you and she'd like to talk to you about maybe helping me with my game, too." Tess looked from Petra to Max, then back to Petra. "I have to talk to Max now, but maybe later, okay?"

Petra's expression went straight to sulk mode, but she didn't argue further. "Okay. I will tell her you said you'd talk to her." Max didn't think Petra meant that to sound like a threat. But then, with her, everything sounded petulant.

"No problem," Tess assured her, sounding far more cheerful about the prospect than Max would have.

Maybe Tess had never met Petra's mother. He should probably warn her. Then again . . .

"Thank you so much," Petra said, perky once more as she gave Tess a quick hug. Adversaries one moment, old friends the next. Whatever got Petra what she wanted, he supposed.

They both waved halfheartedly as Petra flounced through the door toward the players' locker rooms.

Max looked back to Tess. "So, what, now you're the patron saint for teenage tennis players?"

Tess laughed. "Hardly."

She leaned against the wall, her expression settling once again into that knowing smile, an image that was popping up in his mind's eye far too often lately. That he was thinking about her at all troubled him, which was why he needed to talk to her. Now that the tournament was about to begin, not to mention the fact they were all residing under the same roof for the duration—albeit a vast roof—there had to be some ground rules. And he was prepared to do whatever it took to make her take them seriously.

"You know what I think," she said, sparkly green eyes crinkling at the corners as her smile grew.

He supposed some people thought that was cute. He knew it was totally calculated, and he'd be damned if he'd fall for it.

"Maybe the younger girls like me because even though I was clearly and quite publicly not perfect, I still managed to achieve some pretty good success doing this. I've done a lot of things other tennis players only dream of, but at the end of the day, because I'm not perfect, I'm human. So I'm approachable." Her grin could only be described as cheeky. "But I will never claim to be a saint of anything. Even I don't have that kind of moxie."

"Will wonders never cease?"

"So what's got your boxers in a twist this time?"

He just looked at her.

"What? Don't tell me you're a briefs man?"

He sighed.

"Boxer briefs? I could live with that. But could you be that hip?"

"Can we go up to the players' lounge?" He nodded past her shoulder to the alley behind her. "I've had enough of your wolf pack for one day."

"*My* wolf pack?" She folded her arms. "Gee, that's funny. I don't recall being the one who summoned them. I'm pretty sure that was, wait, yes, your sister. And if I'm not mistaken, I was the one who said we should lie low, let the resulting publicity just blow over. But no, you had to march her out here and make her face the music. I happen to think now that you were right and it wasn't a bad thing to do. But you can't have it both ways."

"You should have stayed at Wexley. I had this under control."

"Oh, right. You wouldn't have had the first clue how to deal with that crew. I know them, most of them, anyway. We've been doing that dance for years."

"They only queued up and descended on us, en masse, when you showed up."

"You're kidding yourself if you believe that. Once the word got out we were working together, they were here sniffing around for the story. And of the two of us, they stood a much better chance of getting something quotable and juicy from the rookie than they did the veteran. Especially seeing as she was the one that let it slip to Fionula in the first place."

"It must be a slow news day, then, if this rates as the top breaking story."

Tess's smile was desert-dry. "Yes, I am yesterday's news, thanks ever so much for pointing that out. But the tournament hasn't started yet and nothing juicy is going on. They need to fill column space. So yes, for right now, this is news."

"Is that why you showed up?"

She opened her mouth to respond, then paused for a moment, her expression turning to one of consideration. "What is that supposed to mean, exactly? Are you questioning my motives?"

His eyebrows shot up. "When haven't I been?"

"Exactly what are you accusing me of now?"

Max paused. She looked indignant, yes, as one would be when called out on the carpet. But if he wasn't mistaken, there was more than indignation in her expression.

She cut him off before he could speak. "If you think I'm a press junkie, you are sadly misinformed. Remember, none of this was my idea. You and Aurora cooked this whole thing up and I got dragged into it."

"I didn't see you resisting that much."

"That was mostly just to piss you off."

"What?"

"You heard me. I had no more intention of doing this than, well, than I had any intention of ever coaching anyone. I didn't come to London for this. But then you were being all holier-than-thou and tight-assed about me and my supposed horrifying impact on the younger generation of tennis players and, well, you pissed me off."

"You're saying you're only coaching Gaby—"

"I'm not coaching her!"

She'd raised her voice just enough to alert the hounds. Max took her gently but firmly by the arm. When she instinctively went to pull away, and given the hard muscle he felt beneath his fingers, he wasn't so sure she wouldn't have, he leaned in. "We're attracting attention none of us needs. Smile nice and walk with me to the players' lounge."

Tess immediately relaxed and smiled at him as if he'd just told her they'd gotten a first-round walkover. It was scary how good she was at that. Like flipping a switch.

"Don't look so impressed," she told him, all perky smiles and bubbly body language. Her eyes, however, which suddenly looked ancient and weary, told the real story. "You get used to it after a few years. Gaby will, too. She's already good at it."

When he didn't move right away, she covered his hand still on her arm, and pulled it through. Outwardly, all chummy and good buddies. He was still hung up on what he'd seen in her eyes.

"Come on." She leaned closer. "You're right," she murmured for his ears only, sounding as weary of the whole process as she'd looked a moment ago. "The wolves have seen enough."

Max let her lead them inside, where, as he suspected, she dropped his arm immediately and hopped up the steps in front of him. He didn't like what he'd just seen in her eyes, heard in her voice. More to the point, he didn't like the response it had jerked awake inside of him. He didn't want to feel any empathy toward her. She'd willingly been a subject for the media all those years, using them to her own advantage as much as giving them what they wanted. She could hardly bitch now at the toll it had taken, or the price she might be paying.

And now was definitely not the time to be noticing the way her perky little white shorts clung to her backside, either. Christ. He needed a beer. Or three.

They entered the players' lounge, which was glassed in on two sides and looked down over a broad section of the grounds. The qualifying rounds were going on, so there were a few players, some coaches, a few agents, and other player personnel milling about, but in comparison with what the place would be like tomorrow, it was sparsely populated now. Neither of them spoke as he motioned them to a table in the center of the room, where the press below couldn't spot them through the soaring windows.

He pulled out her chair. When she raised an eyebrow, he pulled his own chair out with a bit more force than necessary. "I do have manners, you know."

She said nothing, merely smiled at him in that way she had of hers, like she knew exactly what he was thinking. Which was a rare feat since he didn't even know what to think at the moment. About anything. Certainly not her.

She folded her arms on the table. "So, what horrible tenet of moral decay am I being accused of flouting this time?"

"Will you cut that out?"

She leaned back, letting her hands fall in her lap, and snorted. "How can I when you keep reminding me every two seconds."

"I said nothing of the kind." *So what if he was thinking it?*

"You don't have to," she said, reading his mind again.

Was he really so obvious? And even if he was, why did that matter? He wasn't exactly hiding his feelings about her or her reputation. "I simply thought that you coming here today only served to escalate things, when if you'd hung back at Wexley House like we'd agreed, this would have just blown over faster. The first round starts tomorrow and they'd have had fresh meat to suck the life from. When Gaby showed up the following day for her first match, we'd already be yesterday's news."

"I initially agreed about letting Gaby face the music, but then I realized it was highly possible that you, or she, could make it into an even bigger story than it had to be. Inadvertently, I mean."

"So, let me get this straight, you're saying you came here to deflect the press from Gaby? To reduce the spotlight on the two of you?"

Tess's eyes narrowed and they took on a darker green tint that even he knew, after limited exposure, was a dangerous sign. "Are you insinuating I came here to do anything else? That I had some sort of personal stake in any of this?"

She was really good, Max thought. Really good. But he'd been in the world of highly competitive sports for too long not to recognize what he was really seeing here. A good offense was always the best defense. He leaned forward and folded his arms on the table, very directly holding her gaze. "Are you saying you don't?"

She didn't back down, didn't even blink. She matched him action for action, until their faces were almost inches apart. "If you're accusing me of something specific, then come out with it. Otherwise, I'm only going to say this once: I don't give a good goddamn what you think of me, my past, my rep, or anything else. But I'm not going to sit here for the next week or two and be your punching bag, either. So unless you can specifically tell me something I've done to harm you or your sister, you need to back way the hell off."

They sat there, staring each other down, neither one wanting to back off first. Finally Max said, "My one and only concern has always been Gaby. I don't care whether you like that or not."

Tess shoved back her chair, hands braced on the table as she pushed to a stand, and in doing so, moved her face even closer to his, until he could see the pupils in her eyes shoot so wide they almost swallowed all that electric green. "As hard as this might be for you to believe, she's my concern now, too, and I don't much care what you think about that."

They both seemed to simultaneously realize that the room had fallen silent. Tess eased back slightly and allowed a slow smile to curve her mouth. That electric green now took on an entirely different hue. And damn if Max's entire body didn't stand up at attention. He was only human, after all. He knew it was for show. And if only half the press about her was to be believed, she was as good at this little game as she was at painting the lines with little green balls. But even knowing that, in that split second, he was powerless to do anything about it.

"I haven't done anything to hurt her, or her chances here. I'm not going to do anything to hurt her, Max," she purred. Her voice was so low now, her words didn't reach anyone but him. He was quite aware that they were giving off another impression entirely than the one that was really taking place.

Part of his brain questioned the wisdom of playing this particular angle. Which story would look worse in the press? That Gaby's brother-slash-manager was battling it out with her mentor-slash-coach—the bad girl of tennis, Tess Hamilton? Or that there was something else going on between Gaby's manager/brother and that very same bad girl of tennis? But even though he knew it was false advertising, the part of his brain that was ruled by the bulge currently growing inside his shorts was dominating this particular argument.

Which was the only reason he gave in to the impulse to do what he did next. Fully cognizant of several sets of eyes on them, he leaned in even closer, then reached up and slowly slid an errant piece of hair behind her ear. Her eyes widened momentarily in surprise, and those pupils of hers shot wide again, only this time for an entirely different reason.

And he'd be lying if he said he didn't enjoy the little rush of purely male power that moment gave him. Probably why he pushed just a bit harder, letting his fingers trail along her jaw before dropping away. Two could play at her dangerous little game. Best she knew that about him now, before this got any further out of hand.

"Just make sure," he began, his voice so deep, so soft, she had to turn her chin just slightly to hear what he had to say. And there was a moment, when presented with that soft spot of skin along the underside of her jaw, that he wanted almost desperately to lean in and press his mouth there, where he knew he'd feel her pulse. Vibrant and alive, just like she was. The swirling fog of pheromones was quickly clouding his judgment. Before he could hoist himself on his petard—which at the moment was quite . . . hoisted—he knew he better finish what he intended to say and end this little game. "Just make sure that while you're fulfilling your own agenda here, and you and I both know you have one, that you stick to that vow. Don't do anything to hurt Gaby, her reputation by association, or her chances here." He closed the gap and put his lips right next to her ear. "Or I will make certain that whatever little game it is you're really playing backfires in the most spectacular fashion possible."

She smelled good. Like lemons and oranges. It was the worst possible time to notice that. He pulled back, taking no small measure of satisfaction in the fact that she didn't. When she said nothing, he said, "I'm going to go have a talk with the trainer, then take Gaby back to the house." He didn't ask her what she'd be doing or what her plans were. He'd played with the fire that was Tess Hamilton quite enough for one day, thank you. If he quit right now, he could escape with only a few singe marks. A win in his column, as far as he was concerned.

Carefully not looking at any of the other occupants of the room, who, judging from the sudden rush of bustling noises and sounds of chairs scraping across the floor, had all suddenly returned to whatever it was they'd been doing before their little soap opera had played out, he exited the lounge. He was three flights down before his body finally settled. And he was no longer sure who the winner was.

Do Not Pass Go, he thought. *And most definitely, Do Not Play with Tess Hamilton again.*

Chapter 16

"Thank you, I really appreciate you going to the trouble to do this for me." Tess took the stack of morning papers from Sir Robin's majordomo and balanced the unwieldy pile in her arms. She grinned up at the taller, older gentlemen. "You da man, Phil."

She almost thought he might have smiled. It was hard to tell. "No problem at all, miss." He sketched a curt bow, then pulled the door to her suite closed before leaving.

I could get used to this, Tess thought as she spread the newspapers across her bed. Right next to the breakfast tray she'd had sent up earlier. So what if she'd done so because she wanted to avoid any kind of close encounter with Max at the breakfast table this morning? Call her a coward, she didn't care.

One thing was for sure. She was definitely getting spoiled, being waited on hand and foot like this. Even five-star digs didn't have this kind of personal touch. She wasted a second revising her opinion on having staff, and wondered if she'd have been able to afford a Phil or two, had she managed her money better. She snorted. "Oh yeah, you who couldn't keep an agent or manager on payroll for more than a few months at a stretch."

There came a tap on her door before she could unfold the first paper. Sighing, she shoved them under a pillow—in case it was Max—and padded back to the double oak doors. She had a fleeting thought that she had serious bed head, her mascara from the day before was probably smudged around her eyes, her flannel pajama bottoms were ancient and baggy, and her T-shirt had seen better days. Years, even.

"Why in the hell do I care what he thinks about how I look?" she asked herself when she found herself checking her reflection in the glass on a framed print by her bedroom door.

Scowling now, more at herself than at the untimely interruption, she opened the door a crack and started to stick her head out.

"Tess, thank God you're here!" Gaby pushed past her, almost knocking her down as she sailed into her room, crossing all the way to her bed before flopping heavily across it. She was wearing her whites—the predominant Wimbledon dress code was almost a religion in Britain—and her long, thick hair had been slicked back into a tight ponytail. Her makeup was perfect. If you were sixteen and favored smokey eyeshadow.

"Dress rehearsal? Your match isn't until tomorrow morning."

"Didn't Max tell you at breakfast? They had a walkover and moved us up to this afternoon." Gaby rolled to her back and flung her arms out wide. "I'm so sick, Tess."

Tess quickly crossed the room and sat on the edge of the bed. "What's wrong?" She put her hand across the teenager's forehead, much as her mother would have done with her, only the skin was cool and dry. "You don't have a fever."

"It's my stomach."

"What did you have this morning? Have you even eaten breakfast?" *And where is your brother,* Tess wanted to know. Why was Gaby in her room, complaining to her and not to Max? She had zero experience with this kind of thing. Sure, she'd played big sister to Bobby his whole life, and surrogate mom, too, since their own had passed away, but that was easy. Bobby called for advice. Giving advice was essentially the same thing as giving opinions. And she had plenty of those. He never needed her for illness. He had trainers and managers and girlfriends for that. He had a wife now, come to think of it. Wow, that was so weird to think about, put like that. So . . . grown-up.

"Tess?" Gaby's long-suffering tone—what Tess's mom had called a "Camille dying scene"—pulled her from her wandering thoughts. "What if I can't do it?"

"Do what?" Tess's eyes widened, then narrowed immediately as her meaning sunk in. "You mean, what if you can't play? Of course you're going to play." And not just because Tess needed her to, of course. Her cell phone had lit up first thing this morning as requests for interviews started to come in. She was glad now she'd thought to pass around some of her personal business cards—complete with her direct cell number—at those corporate shindigs she'd gone to, making sure that one or two found their way into the hands of the press covering this event or that. Just in case.

It looked like all her hard work might pay off after all. She hadn't returned any of the calls yet, wanting to see what exactly had made the print editions first. Obviously something from their little impromptu press junket yesterday during Gaby's practice session had made it into print. She'd screened the calls just enough to know that the outlets wanting her now weren't just the little rags and gossip pages. No, it was network level now, baby. BBC Radio and USA Network, to name a few. She was on her way to . . . well, to something. Something that would surely lead her to . . . something. Something with a nice payout involved.

She'd figure all that out just as soon as she got Gaby in gear. She couldn't very well make a splash on radio and television talking about why she was working with America's newest tennis sweetheart if said sweetheart squandered her first-round opportunity because she was too busy playing drama queen on Tess's bed.

"Have you talked to your brother?"

Gaby groaned and put her hands on her stomach. "No. He's been on the phone all morning and he won't understand, anyway."

Tess frowned. Both at the news that Max was on the phone—hopefully not fielding the same offers she was, because knowing him, he'd turn them all down—and at Gaby's unwillingness to talk to him about what was bothering her. "Why wouldn't he understand?"

All of a sudden Gaby scrambled off the bed, clutching her stomach. "Bathroom?"

Tess immediately pointed to the door behind her. "Through there."

She followed Gaby as far as the bathroom door, which Gaby had closed behind her. A moment later came the unmistakable sounds of retching. Tess shuddered, but kept her concerns about Gaby's health in check. At least until she had the chance to ask her a few questions.

She heard water running and some splashing, then finally a somewhat paler Gaby opened the door. Tess smiled. "Feel better?"

The teenager nodded briefly, then crossed the room back to the bed. She didn't fling herself quite as dramatically as before, but she did lay down, curling up on her side. "What's wrong with me? Food poisoning or something?"

"I doubt it. We all ate from the same kitchen last night and this morning." Tess crossed the room and sat on the bed next to Gaby. Without thinking, she reached out and stroked Gaby's long, glossy ponytail. It was as silky to the touch as it was shiny to look at. The kid really did have all the bases covered. Killer game, fit body, natural good looks. She was every sponsor's dream. All she needed was a title or two under her belt, be a threat in the slams, and Tess wouldn't be surprised if she was signing endorsement deals before her first slam title was in her trophy case. "I think you have a good case of the nerves."

Gaby rolled to her back, a surprised look on her face. "I never get nervous before a match. Not sick nervous. I just get anxious to get out there and get going. I can't win sitting in the locker room. But nerves don't get to me. Not like this."

"You're not in amateur rounds anymore."

"I know that. I played in the French and I didn't puke my guts up. I played on the show court and everything."

"First-time luck," Tess said. "You had nothing to lose and everything to gain. For you it was like a field trip to an exotic place you hoped to go back to one day." She smiled. "What was there to be nervous about?"

"Oh, I don't know, thousands of cheering fans shouting things at me in French, rooting for my opponent? Who just happened to be the number-one player in the world at the time?"

"And you fed off of that because you were the underdog, and you could use it to your advantage."

"I'm certainly the underdog here."

"In the minds of the tournament directors and the other players, maybe. But not in your mind." She tilted her head so she could match Gaby stare for stare. "Playing Serena on a grand-slam show court where she's won the title is one thing. You played to win, but you understood the odds, and when she came out swinging, you hung in there the best you could and were happy to take a set off of her."

"It would have been better to beat her."

"Sure, it's always better to win. But you made her play. And for your first time out there? You turned heads, people sat up and paid attention to you. That increased attention has followed you to London."

Gaby lifted a shoulder in a half-shrug. "I guess."

"You know. You made it further in Birmingham, played Venus well, and now your association with me has elevated that attention even more."

"I don't mind that. I really don't. In fact, I kind of like it. Don't let Max hear that I said that." Her lips curved in a hint of a smile, the first one Tess had seen today. "Not that he hasn't figured it out. I wish he'd stop jumping all over you, though. I've always felt this way, always had this kind of attitude. He knows that, but I think it scares him. Well, I know it does. So it's easier to blame it all on you. I'm sorry for that." She shifted her head on the bedspread so she could look at Tess's face more squarely. "He really is a nice guy. I don't know why you two bring out the worst in each other, but normally he's a great guy, funny, charming."

Tess smiled dryly. "I'll take your word for it."

Gaby's smile grew until it almost reached her eyes, which were still too dark, too worried. "So, if I'm okay with the attention and I've handled the pressure of a slam already, why do you think this is a case of the nerves and not just some bad shrimp or something?"

Tess stroked her hair again, her smile softening a little as she remembered exactly how she felt when she'd been in Gaby's place. She hadn't gone so far as to throw up before her first round, but she knew she'd have felt a hell of a lot better if she had. Might have played better, too. "The difference here is, you want it this time. You want Davina so bad you can taste it. You know you're finally in a first-round slam match you have an absolute chance at winning. So now it matters."

"It always matters."

"True. But be honest . . . you want this one more. You're supposed to. You're supposed to want each successive one more. The more you can do, the more you want to prove it."

"I don't feel like I'm proving anything. I just started out here. I mean, I'm not dense, I know there are expectations of what kind of pro player I'm going to become, but I certainly don't feel the pressure to become a superstar overnight or anything."

"Maybe not from outside forces you don't. But then, you don't strike me as the kind of player or person who really gives a damn what other people think."

Gaby pushed up and sat cross-legged on the bed, facing Tess. "You're right, I don't. Neither did you, right?"

"Other than my family? No, I didn't care."

"I do care what Max thinks." She looked down, fiddled with the lace trim on her perfectly white tennis socks. "He's given up everything for me." She looked up, and it struck Tess how odd it was to be looking into the face of a teenager, but into the eyes of someone who seemed so much older. In too many ways, it was like looking into the mirror of her own past. "But he doesn't pressure me. If anything, he's too protective and doesn't let me push as hard as I'd like to. He's afraid I'll burn out."

"He's a wise man. And he's obviously been paying attention. It's a real fear to have."

"I can play eleven tournaments this year and he's only got me scheduled for eight. I know I am capable of—"

"I know," Tess broke in. "*We* know. But I can speak with the benefit of hindsight. I didn't burn out, but my body didn't hold up like it might have if I hadn't pushed so hard."

"But that fall you took, nothing could have helped that."

Tess shrugged. "Maybe. But maybe if I'd rehabbed my initial shoulder injuries better and not pushed to come back so quickly, it might have been reparable this last time. I don't know. I do know your brother and I are at loggerheads a great deal of the time."

"Mostly about me."

Tess grinned. "Always about you. What else do we have in common?"

Gaby went back to picking at the lace on her socks.

Tess's smile faded slightly, but she let that go and stayed focused on her message. "I'm not complaining. I'm on your side, remember? But I also think, in this very isolated incidence, of course, that he's doing the right thing by bringing you out on tour slowly."

"I'm almost seventeen. I can enter fifteen events then, and I want all fifteen. It's not that much. Do you know how many titles Steffi had by then? She'd already won her first slam. So did Chris Evert and Serena and Venus. I just want to get in and start moving up the ranks."

"Eight tournaments, not to mention fifteen, is a healthy number over a ten-month season. And you didn't start until later this year, so it's even more compressed." She lifted a hand when Gaby went to argue. "I know, I know, you're young, you're invincible. Today, maybe. But not forever. Which brings me back to that trick stomach of yours. You do want this bad. We both know that. Just like we both know you can do the math. With only a handful of tournaments this season, doing well at the slams will leapfrog you ahead in the rankings faster than doing well in smaller tournaments. Just like we both know your quarter of the draw here is probably the best you could have hoped for. One or two lucky breaks up the chain and you could have a nice run. All you need is another giant killer to take someone out above you and—"

Gaby's eyes lit up. "You think I can be a giant killer?"

"I think you gave both the Williams sisters a pretty good scare."

Gaby's lips quirked with just the right amount of cockiness. "True."

"Exactly." Tess beamed. "Now you want Davina. And whomever else you can beat here."

"I haven't told Max this, but when the draw came out and I saw my chances, I made myself a promise."

"Which was?"

"To do whatever it takes to make it to the second week."

"Pretty tall order for an unseeded player."

"You don't think I can do it?" She didn't look crushed so much as defiant.

Tess smiled. That was exactly what she wanted to see. "I didn't say that. Big goals are good to have. Mandatory, in my book. Just don't be so busy looking at the big goal that you lose sight of all the little ones you have to make to get there."

"I haven't," Gaby assured her, then smiled a bit slyly. "Why do you think I did whatever it took to get you to stick with me for the tournament?"

That got a laugh out of Tess. "God, what am I going to do with you? If I didn't know better, I'd think the tennis gods are punishing me by saddling me with a mini-me."

Gaby scooted to the edge of the bed. "That's the nicest thing you've ever said to me."

Tess stood. "Yeah, well, be careful what you wish for."

She reached for Gaby's hand and hauled her upright. "How's the stomach?"

Gaby paused for a moment, as if she had to think about it. "Fine." She laughed. "I guess maybe it was nerves."

"And now?"

"Now I want to go kick some Russian butt."

"That's my girl."

Gaby was at the door, then turned back. "You are going to be there, right? In the players' box? With Max?"

Funny, all this time, and Tess hadn't really thought about that part. She wanted to watch her play, of course. But she hadn't really thought about actually sitting in the box, looking down across the court. A court she'd played on, won on. How was that going to feel? This morning she'd been too busy thinking about how the rest of her day might be shaping up to let her thoughts go in that direction.

"I'm heading over there soon to see Bobby, catch some of the early action." Which was the truth, only it wasn't necessarily just the action taking place on the court, so much as around the courts, in the media room, the players' lounge, and the sportscasters' booth. It was possible she could be in all those locales today if she played her cards right.

Sentiment aside, she hadn't considered that, as Gaby's supposed coach, she'd be seated in the traditional spot, the players' box, which typically afforded one of the best views of the court. The very public, very high-profile players' box. Everyone would see her sitting there. And the cameras would certainly take advantage of such an easy photo opportunity. The papers reached a limited audience. Tess could make sure the entire world knew of her association with a new, young tennis phenom. "I wouldn't miss it," she told Gaby, sincere in more ways than one.

"Max will make sure you have a pass." Then she ran back across the room and engulfed Tess in a bear hug so tight she swore something might have cracked a little. "Thank you," Gaby whispered fiercely.

Just when Tess felt something akin to a lump forming in her throat, Gaby bounced back, a grin plastered ear to ear across her pretty face, eyes shining. "I won't let you down," she told Tess. "And I'll avenge your loss to Davina. Win-win."

Tess smiled easily in the face of her enthusiasm and confidence. This kind of emotion she knew how to deal with. "Just play your kind of tennis. Stick to your game. And remember what we've gone over. Use it when you need it."

"I will. I'll see you this afternoon. Oh! I almost forgot. I want Aurora to come, too. If it wasn't for her, you wouldn't be my coach. I have to go tell Max to make that happen."

"I'm not a coach," Tess said, but the words echoed in the empty room. She slumped against the door, then realized she'd better get moving if she wanted to get down to the grounds with enough time before Gaby's match to make the rounds. If Gaby didn't beat Davina, today could be Tess's only day to make as big a media splash as she could.

She glanced at the papers she'd shoved under the pillows when she'd thought it was Max at the door. A lecture from him was the last thing she needed or wanted today. It was bad enough she'd have to sit next to him in the players' box. Her lips quirked. If she played her cards right, she could squeeze Aurora in the middle between them. Which was exactly where Aurora liked to be in all things, anyway. Problem solved.

She debated at least scanning headlines, but the shower beckoned. She could read them in the limo on the way to Wimbledon, return a few calls, see what she could set up. She hadn't given much thought—okay, any thought—to what she'd wear today. Something eye-catching, of course, but what exactly...

Tess was mentally sorting through the limited remains of her wardrobe. It wouldn't pay to be seen in something she'd already worn and been photographed in, but she didn't exactly have the funds for a quick shopping trip, either. What to do. She was tapping her lip, mulling as she headed toward the bathroom, when a rather rude tapping erupted on the other door to her suite.

"Hold on a second," she shouted, changing paths and going through the door adjoining her bedroom to the sitting room next door. Probably Gaby with some new crisis. "Don't tell me," she called through the door as she grabbed the knob. "You can't find just the right shade of eye shadow to go with all white. Let me tell you, you've come to the wrong"—she opened the door—"place," she finished lamely.

Max filled the doorway.

"To what do I owe this honor?" She pasted a bright smile on her face. "No, let me guess. I talked to Gaby this morning—who was, by the way, convinced she was dying from some rare malady, known to you and me as anxiety stress—and convinced her not to quit the tournament before her first-round match. And you're here to thank me." She leaned on the doorframe and looked at the vein bulging quite impressively in Max's forehead. "No need, really. All in a day's work."

"Have you seen these?" Max asked, slapping the papers she just now realized he held in his hand.

She'd gotten all caught up with that popping vein. And maybe a little bit with the way his jaw went all rugged and square when he clenched it like that. It wasn't quite as sexy when he was mad like this, but it made a person wonder how sexy it would look, you know, if said person could make that jaw clench for other reasons. Hmmm. "What?" she asked, vaguely recalling he'd asked her something.

"These!" He unfolded one of the papers, a gossip rag called *Good Day*, and snapped it open in her face. "We're front-page news, Tess."

Tess grabbed the paper he was waving in her face so she could see the front-page photo. "What are you ranting about? You knew Gaby and I might make a little splash after our public practice session yesterday."

"'A little splash'? Is that what you call this?" He shoved the rest of the papers at her. "And who said anything about Gabrielle?"

Tess sat down on the edge of her bed and smoothed out the papers he'd given her. "Oh. Wow."

"Oh? Wow? Yeah, oh. Yeah, wow." Max was pacing the length of the room. He turned to face her. "What are we going to do about oh and wow, Tess?"

She wasn't listening to him. She was too busy looking at the grainy, blown-up photo of her . . . and Max. Chin to chin over the table in the players' lounge. Someone must have had a cell phone with a camera. Bravo to them, because they'd snapped that one moment in time when she'd been taunting him. Of course, no one else would know that she'd been faking it. There was enough sexual chemistry sizzling in that picture she was surprised the paper didn't spontaneously combust right in her hands.

Her mind was racing a million miles a minute, trying to absorb this latest turn of events and what it would mean. How she might use it to her—their—best advantage. She wouldn't do anything to jeopardize Gaby's chances here. But this . . .

She glanced up at Max and something about the way he was looking at her sparked the imp in her. And it was becoming an increasingly naughty little imp. Which wasn't bothering her nearly as much as it should, all things considered. He was awfully fun to tease. "I don't know why you're so bent," she said casually, perusing the picture at length. "We give great cover photo, you and me." She looked at him and flipped the picture around so he could see it. "You have to admit, in the words of the oh-so-complex and brainy Paris Hilton, we're hot."

His eyebrows threatened to leave his forehead entirely. He was cute when he was riled. Which was basically all the time. Or all the time he was around her, anyway. She wondered what he'd do if she just got up, crossed the room, grabbed him, and kissed that indignant look right off his face. Of course, she wouldn't actually do that. But it didn't stop her from spending a moment or two visualizing it. A girl had to get her fun somehow.

"We need to fix this," he said, voice all deep and edgy.

I know how I want to fix it, Tess thought, but she doubted Max would see it her way. When had he ever? She sighed a little and tossed the paper to the bed. "There's nothing to fix."

"But people will think—"

"So what if they do? Is that such a horrifying thing? Let them speculate. Because that's all it's going to be. But it's press, which isn't a bad thing for Gaby. And it's not directly focused on her, which is a good thing, too. She can play, stir up a buzz, and pretty much stay above the actual gossip." *If she wants to,* Tess thought. Hmm. She'd have to work on that part.

"So nice that you've thought about Gaby in all this."

"Hey!" she shot back, not liking the tone that had crept into his voice. "It's not like I planned that."

"You didn't seem to mind much yesterday when you were taunting me. You didn't care who was watching."

"Neither did you, if I recall. You gave as good as you got."

"You have no idea what I'm thinking. But even when you do, it doesn't stop you. I know you think that media attention and tennis success go hand in hand, but I don't share that philosophy. She plays her first professional match at Wimbledon in less than six hours . . . and now we have to go out there and deal with this? Are you kidding me? It might not be a big deal to you, but it is to me. And it will be to her, no matter what she says. These are people's lives here, Tess. This isn't some game for us like it is for you. We don't find this amusing."

" 'We'? Has Gaby seen these?"

"Not yet, but seeing as she'll probably get bombarded with a few questions on our way in, I have to tell her something."

Tess looked back at the photo. The cover caption read: IS TESS MAD FOR MAX? Kind of cute, really. She recalled Gaby's comments this morning, about how she wished Max and Tess got along better, sort of pumping her brother up to Tess. And she couldn't help but think this latest turn wasn't going to bother Gaby all that much. "I'll talk to her."

"Thanks, but I'll handle it."

"So why did you come to my room, then? To blow off steam? I didn't do anything to deserve this." She flicked the paper with her fingers. "There wasn't any press in the players' lounge."

"Would it have stopped you if there were?"

"Of course it would have. We went up there to get away from the press."

He simply stared impassively back at her.

"In this particular case," she amended, "yes, it would have. I know you don't believe me, but this isn't a game to me, either. Not in the way you mean. I do know those people, I know how they operate, yes. And as I know they're going to be out there doing their job whether I want them to or not, yes, I do try to make them as useful to my cause as possible."

"And what exactly is your 'cause'?"

"I care about Gaby. I want her to have a good chance here." That much was absolutely the truth. "But you're naive if you think she isn't going to garner attention with or without me. Her game is huge. In this world, playing this game, being successful, and more important, staying successful, that spotlight is going to be a constant home for her. Whether either of you like it or not. And the only one who doesn't is you."

"If you want to help her, then stay away today."

Tess's mouth dropped open, then immediately snapped shut. "She specifically came in here to ask me to sit in the box with you. And Aurora."

"It will just feed all these rumors."

"So? You can't start letting the press dictate what you will and won't do. First rule."

"I'm asking you to stay back. If she makes it through today, we'll see."

"It's the wrong way to play this. And she wants me there. That should count for more than anything. Sit Aurora between us. Don't give me the time of day. I could care less." She threw the paper on the bed and stalked over to him, poking her finger in his chest. "But don't make her pay for your stupid insecurities. She'll be fine. Trust me." Of course, Tess knew nothing of the sort. After all, Gaby had just been in her bathroom, tossing her cookies, less than a half hour ago. But one way or the other, she was going to have to go out there and face down whatever fears she had. And if she wanted Tess in her corner to help her do that, then by damn, that's where she was going to be.

Max grabbed the finger she'd poked at him, not roughly, but he held on to it all the same. "If it turns into a circus, I'm going to personally toss you out."

"I'd like to see you try."

Then he shocked her. He smiled. And there was something wild, almost wicked, glittering from those dark eyes of his. "You think you know me, Tess. You have no idea who you're fooling with."

She was still standing there a full minute after he'd left the room. Wondering where in the hell all that had come from.

And what in the hell she was going to do about it.

It didn't occur to her until much later, as she climbed into the Glass Slipper limo with Aurora on their way to Wimbledon, that during her entire exchange with Max, as she'd argued Gaby's side, she'd never once thought about her personal agenda in all this.

Chapter 17

Max paced, waiting for the players' box to empty as the match preceding Gaby's ended. To his surprise, they had been put on Court Two; though much smaller than the stadium Centre Court and Court One, it was still a show court. Of course, it was also known as the Graveyard Court, notorious for being the scene of the early demise of many highly seeded players. Davina wasn't that highly seeded, but she was the only seeded player of the two playing today. So Max would be perfectly happy if the court's curse worked in his favor this afternoon. He shifted to one side as the steady stream of fans pushed past him. He was tall enough to see over most heads, but a quick look around didn't bring any sight of Aurora or Tess. He was happy about the latter part, anyway.

He'd made sure Aurora knew she was welcome, even offering to let her ride over with him and Gaby. But she had a lunch date with her partners, Vivian and Mercedes, and had assured him she'd just have the Glass Slipper limo drop her off, which was what worried him. Tess could easily finagle herself into that situation. He'd have gotten passes for all three of Glass Slipper Inc.'s "fairy godmothers" if they could have just granted him one wish: to make sure Tess was anywhere but here this afternoon.

"Thanks for having me on, Mary, John. A pleasure to see you both."

Max froze. He could swear he'd just heard Tess's voice. But... where? He scanned the throng again. It had sounded close by. Real close by. Mary and John, who? Thanks for having her on what?

"Well, it's a pleasure to have you up in the booth with us, Tess. I hope," came a very familiar voice, followed by a short, gravelly laugh.

John. As in John McEnroe. Up in the booth? With John McEnroe? "Oh, shit." Several older women decked out for an afternoon of watching tennis in ornate day hats and crisp linen suits—only the British—paused to give him sharp looks. "Sorry, ladies," he mumbled.

Then he spied the source of the disembodied voices. A young man across the crowded alley had a handheld satellite television. Max was tempted to push his way over there and beg, borrow, or steal the thing.

Gaby was set to play momentarily. And Tess had not only openly defied his request and come down here anyway... she was apparently more concerned with getting airtime than she really was in supporting her protégée. But then he'd known that, hadn't he? Had told her as much.

So why did he feel so disappointed? Had he really been hoping she'd prove him wrong? What possible difference would it make?

No, he was pissed because he had no goddamn idea what

she was saying. On air. To millions of people. That's what had him so upset. Not some stupid hope that he'd only just now realized he'd been harboring, that maybe, just maybe, she had a point and he'd been judging her too harshly. Right. Of course he was just disappointed for Gaby's sake. She was the one who was going to suffer from all this. Not Max. If it weren't for Gaby, he couldn't care less what Tess Hamilton did or didn't do. It's not like she mattered to him otherwise.

Right. Christ, he didn't have time for this. Other than going up to the television booth and dragging her out of there, he couldn't shut her up, but he should at least know what the hell she was saying so he could be prepared for whatever fallout would inevitably occur afterward. Obviously they were going to ask about her relationship with Gaby, and her relationship with him . . . *Shit.* He really needed to get up to that booth. Maybe just seeing his face in the background by the various technicians would be enough to shut her up. Or at the very least give fair warning.

Yeah, right. When had Tess ever once shrunk away from a public display of . . . well, anything she wanted to publicly display? Exactly never. The woman didn't know the meaning of discretion, much less ever practice it. And if he'd ever been tempted, even for a split second, to think otherwise, the sight of his face plastered all over those newspapers today should have provided ample proof to the contrary.

The stands had emptied and were beginning to fill up again for the next match. Gaby's match. He had to get in there. If Gaby didn't see anyone sitting in her section of the players' box, she'd wonder what was wrong. He knew she'd be disappointed not to see Tess there, but the one constant in Gaby's life was him. As long as he was there, she'd be focused. And she'd have a damn sight better chance of staying that way if Tess wasn't there, creating a stir. *Dammit!* Now he didn't know what to expect. He raked his hand through his hair as he scoped out the crowd, but the man with the television had vanished.

"Max, darling? Why, there you are, my dear boy." Aurora materialized out of the crowd in a swirl of blue silk caftan and heavy perfume. "I've been looking everywhere for you." She smiled as she slid her arm through his. "My, my, this is really something, isn't it?" She glanced around at the hive of activity filling the grounds on opening day, then back up at him. "Thank you so much for securing me a pass. What a wonderful surprise."

"It's the least I could do," he told her.

Aurora surprised him by rolling her eyes. "Now, now, you don't need to put up a false front on my behalf. I know you're likely very put out with me due to my interference, what with bringing Tess into the fold and all." She peered at him a bit more attentively. "I suppose I don't need to ask how you two are getting on."

Max definitely didn't have time, or the heart, for this. The other two women in his life were providing quite enough stress at the moment. "We're keeping lines of communication open." Which wasn't to say they actually listened to one another, as was made obvious today.

Not surprisingly, Aurora didn't look all that convinced. "I must admit I was a bit curious after seeing the headlines this morning. Although you are quite photogenic, dear." She gave him a quick reassuring pat on the arm. "I daresay you take after your father."

Max found himself relenting a little in the face of her sincere affection. "Thanks, I appreciate that. But I assure you it was all a giant misunderstanding."

"Those gossip rags will latch onto the slightest thing and blow it all out of proportion." Her expression was all innocence as she sighed in complete understanding, but he knew her better than that. She was digging for details. "Horrible, really."

Max couldn't tell if she was hopeful he'd tell her she was wrong, or hopeful he'd tell her the gossip rags had it all right. Another cause for concern, for certain, if Aurora was in any way going in the matchmaking direction. Given her line of work, the very idea was doubly alarming. She couldn't possibly think, for one second, that a match between him and Tess Hamilton was anything other than a match made in hell.

"Yes, they certainly are. Listen, we should probably get inside, find our seats."

"Of course. This is all so thrilling." She patted his hand, banging his knuckles with the row of heavy rings she was sporting. The bracelets lining her wrist jangled as she squeezed his arm. "And don't you worry about the rest. I'm sure Tess will get it all squared away, you'll see."

Max stopped short, and had to grab gently onto Aurora to keep her from plunging ahead. "What do you know about what Tess is doing?"

Aurora blinked at him. "I'm sorry, dear, but you said you two were communicating and I thought you knew."

"I—I came earlier with Gaby. We haven't spoken since this morning."

"Well, she told me some nonsense about you wanting her to stay at Wexley during Gaby's match. I assured her you couldn't possibly mean such a thing. After everything the two of them have gone through these past couple of weeks, Gaby would be crushed if Tess wasn't here to support her." She held his gaze quite directly, making him feel like a schoolboy being stared at by Mother Superior.

And it worked, too. He felt guilty. And he wasn't even Catholic. Still, he wasn't sure what to tell her, nor did he have the time to stand around out here, stammering his way through some ridiculous cock-and-bull story. So he told her the truth. What the hell. "I did tell her to stay home, Aurora, and I meant it. Gaby will understand." Somehow. He'd make it up to her. "Listen, it's a complicated situation. Why don't we head inside so Gaby knows we're here. I'll fill you in while she's warming up."

"That's a splendid idea." Her grip on his arm tightened a little, as did the smile on her face.

Well, too damn bad if he'd disappointed her somehow, too. *Welcome to the club,* he thought, wondering, as they climbed their way into the stands, just how exactly he'd come to this place in life.

They'd just taken their seats when Gaby and Davina entered the courts with their tennis gear bags slung over their shoulders. Being on an outer court, there was no royal box as there was on Centre Court. There, if the box was occupied, the tradition was that players would turn in unison and curtsy, or bow as the case may be, before continuing on to their respective seats on either side of the court. Max would have said that he enjoyed his own country's grand slam, the U.S. Open, the best. Hard courts, rowdy fans, planes roaring overhead, night matches under the lights. The energy was wonderful, intense, and he'd always felt there was nothing like it.

He still felt that way. But sitting here now, the stands completely filled, watching his younger sister become part of the pageantry and history that was this most venerable of the slams . . . he couldn't help but get caught up in it. Just a little. And yes, maybe for a second or two, he pictured Gaby having to curtsy as she made her way onto Centre Court for the first time. She'd get that chance. Maybe not this year, but certainly that was in her future.

Thoughts of Tess, the tabloids, her saying God knows what on national television right this minute, threatened to spoil the moment, but he refused to let it.

Aurora squeezed his forearm. "She looks lovely, Max. So pretty in her Wimbledon white."

"Yes," he said, smiling as Gaby looked up, found him in the players' box, and beamed. "She certainly does." Most of the time when he looked at his sister, he saw how young she was, how inexperienced she still was. How much she still needed him. Today, however, she looked so poised, so polished, so professional. It was easy to see her future, out there on the courts, conducting business, getting the job done, doing what she loved. And he felt a little pang of something that felt a lot like grief, accompanied by a brief moment of what could only be described as sheer panic.

What was going to happen when she didn't need him anymore? What had he left himself with? Sure, he'd likely continue on as Gaby's manager and agent, handling her business affairs and such . . . but he wasn't worried about whether he'd have a job or not.

He was worried that he didn't have a life of his own to go with it.

As Gaby and Davina hit the ball back and forth, warming up, and Aurora chattered on beside him about the various outfits she was spying in the stands, and how she was dying to sample the famed Wimbledon strawberries and cream, Max's thoughts continued down that path. He remembered Tess taunting him, asking him if he had a life outside of being Gaby's brother . . . and it made him wonder about Tess herself.

He was watching his sister grow up and take on the adult responsibilities that came with being a touring professional. Tess had just walked away from all of that, from a huge life with a ton of commitments, a life that had been all-consuming since she was younger than Gaby. To what? What life did she have now?

He knew it wasn't about money. He had money. So did Tess. It was about finding your place, figuring out who you were in this new dynamic. Is that why she put herself out there in the public eye? So she could still feel vital? He had no idea, really. But for the first time, rather than look at her as a bad influence on his sister, he thought about her as a woman first, a tennis player and a party girl second. He'd seen a hint of that woman the other day, when she'd escaped the press with him. What did Tess the woman, the one who was no longer also a tennis player, want out of life?

And why in the hell did he care?

He forced his attention back to the carefully groomed green grass of the courts. In a few days' time, the grass would be worn down to the dirt along the baseline. But right now, it was pristine and perfect, having been lovingly and meticulously maintained all year, just for this hallowed event.

The umpire called time and the line judges and ball girls and boys dutifully took their places, awaiting the first serve that would begin the match. All thoughts of Tess, his life, and the future that awaited them all, faded away as he watched Gaby take her place on the baseline and prepare to serve her way into her very first Wimbledon grand-slam event. His heart rate picked up. Aurora's nails bit into the skin of his arm as Gaby tossed the ball high, then sent it rocketing over the net.

"This is so thrilling!" Aurora whispered. "She's going to do well. I can see it in her eyes. She's determined, Max."

"Yes." That was all he could manage. His complete attention was riveted on the court as the first point played out.

Davina returned the serve deep, then, using her quick foot speed, came in closer to the net on Gaby's stab return and hit a crosscourt winner.

"Oh," Aurora gasped, as the point ended and Gaby once again took her place on the baseline to serve. "That went fast." She patted his arm. "She'll get the next one."

Max was barely listening to Aurora. Davina had game, and a big chunk of it was volleying. One of Gaby's biggest weaknesses was her net game and it was going to haunt her today if that point was any indication. He knew Tess had given her a few pointers on coming in to the net, giving Davina a little taste of her own medicine, but they'd barely had time to put it into practice. Gaby was probably overwhelmed enough with the pomp and circumstance, as well as her opponent, that anything other than relying on the game that had gotten her here was going to be too much to ask.

Her first serve was wide. As she turned to accept another ball from the ball girl, she glanced quickly up at him. He gave her an encouraging smile, but nothing more. Coaching from the box wasn't allowed. But mentally he was sending her everything he had. She turned back, bounced the ball a few times, then lofted it overhead, and put the ball on the outside of the opposite corner of the serving box. Second serves being slower, Davina returned it easily, but this time Gaby was ready. She hit crosscourt, forcing Davina to run. She kept that up, rallying from the baseline, sending Davina all the way right, then all the way left, until she was forced to hit the ball long as Gaby added more and more angle to it. Point to Miss Fontaine.

He let his breath go, only realizing then he'd been holding it. Shit, it was only the second point of the first game. He needed to settle down. And he knew that was all Gaby needed. If she could hold serve here, she'd calm down a little.

But the next three points went Davina's way and she broke Gaby's serve to go one up in the first set.

Aurora continued coddling Max's arm. "She's just nervous. I mean, my goodness, look at all this." She nodded to the packed stands, and the throngs of people milling in between the courts beyond the court wall. Up above were windows lining the side of the main building that formed two sides of the court. Along with the broadcast booths, players and other industry types had access to that area. The windows were full of observers, even for a lowly first-round match such as this one. The crowds were bigger than anything they had in juniors, even for the championship games. He wondered what it would feel like to be on Centre Court. He returned his attention to the game as Davina prepared to serve, and mentally crossed his fingers that Gaby would have a chance to find out.

The second game went quickly. Too quickly. Davina served two aces to easily hold her service game at love, not giving a single point to Gaby. "Come on," he whispered under his breath. "You can do this." Coming in today, he'd just wanted Gaby to do her best and to come away, if not with a win, then with a match she could be proud of. He knew she'd be disappointed with anything other than a win, but he didn't want her to get bageled, either.

Gaby took the first point on her next serve, playing the same baseline game she'd done before, running Davina from side to side. Her serve for the second point was an ace. Max pumped his fist by his side. *Good, good.* Gaby turned then for another ball and didn't even glance up at the players' box. Her face was sheer determination now, as the crowd, the circumstance, everything else began to shrink back a little. *That's the way,* he thought. *Stay focused, settle into your game. Make her run for the money, dammit.*

She continued her punishing baseline game, not letting Davina into the net, and went on to hold serve. It was two—one, Davina, but now Gaby was in it.

In what seemed like a blink, Davina went on a tear, serving several blistering aces and attacking the net like a Rottweiler. And before Gaby could adjust, Davina was serving for the first set, up five games to two. With her serve on fire, as long as Davina kept her serve and volley game up and Gaby stayed pinned to the baseline, Max didn't see where Gaby was going to be able to work her way back into this. She was lucky to have held her serve twice. She hadn't come close to threatening Davina's.

Gaby made her work in the next game, but Davina ended up taking the first set, six games to two. It wasn't embarrassing by any stretch, but he knew Gaby had a better game than she was showing. And even after everything they'd been through the past couple of weeks leading up to today, he didn't want her experience here to end so abruptly. Certainly not like this. "Give her a match, Gaby," he murmured. "Come on, remember what Tess told you."

There came a voice by his ear. "And here I thought you'd prefer she never even met me."

Max had been so caught up in the match he hadn't heard the murmur that rippled through the crowd as a very well-known face made her way to the players' box. With all eyes and very likely one or two cameras trained their way, he could do little but welcome her.

Aurora went to scoot over, but Max squeezed her arm gently. "That's okay, Tess can sit on your right."

Smile easily in place, Tess squeezed past Max and Aurora, taking her seat just as the first game of the second set began. There was a hush as Davina served.

Max turned his attention back to the match, but his thoughts were scattered. He wanted to demand Tess tell him exactly what she'd said during her little on-air stint and why she'd done it in the first place. Right after he asked how in the hell she'd gotten into the players' box. Davina served an ace, and Max quickly glanced to his right. Tess had a press pass around her neck. And she'd apparently banked on him not making a scene in the middle of Gaby's match when she'd decided to join them regardless of his request that she stay away.

Davina sent her next serve blistering to the outside, but Gaby was ready. She stabbed left and kept the ball in play. Max forgot all about Tess as he watched the rally unfold before him. Both players were focused, both were going for every shot. *Come on, Gabs,* he silently rooted. *Make her earn it.*

Davina won the point, earning a sigh of disappointment from Aurora, and something muttered from Tess. He tried not to think about it, focus on the play. But Davina went on to easily hold serve and it was Gaby's turn again.

"Has she been pasted to the baseline the whole time?" Tess asked him, leaning slightly in front of Aurora.

"She's doing what she does best," Max replied, not wanting to get into a discussion about this. He'd save all of it for later, when he intended to have a very involved discussion with her.

"And losing," Tess retorted.

"She'll turn it around." From the corner of his eye, Max saw Aurora settle back a little, allowing them more room to talk in front of her, a small smile playing around the corners of her mouth. Otherwise, she was all innocence, simply watching a tennis match as if nothing was going on.

Which begged the question, just what was going on? She had to have known Tess was in the announcers' booth earlier. Which, he supposed, made it clear which side she was on in this little power struggle. Not that this came as a huge surprise.

"Yes!" Tess announced, accentuating the comment with a little fist pump.

Max's attention flew back to the game. Dammit, he'd missed Gaby's serve. Her second ace of the match, too. Which he neatly blamed on Tess. If she'd just kept her nose out of this like he'd asked, he wouldn't have been distracted. Hell, he didn't care if she stayed on air all day or watched every single match. Except this one. He and Gaby had worked a long time toward moments like this and he wanted to focus on it, dammit. Enjoy it. Live every second of it. Revel in it.

"Come in," Tess whispered fiercely. "Short-court her."

Max watched Gaby serve again. Davina got it back.

"Short. Short balls," Tess urged, her voice barely reaching past Aurora to his own ears.

He was so finely tuned in to her, he couldn't block her voice out. Of course, she was right on the money, which didn't make it any easier. She was only saying exactly what he was thinking.

Gaby went on to win the game, but only because her serve got her some free points. It was one game to one, second set, best of three.

"She's doing quite well now," Aurora piped up, as the serve went back to Davina.

"She needs to pressure Davina on this serve, make her think a little bit out there," Tess said, never taking her eyes from the court. "She's making this too easy on her."

At that moment, Gaby turned to take a towel from a ball girl, so she could wipe her face as the afternoon air grew decidedly humid. She glanced up to the box, and apparently spied Tess for the first time. She gave the briefest of smiles, then tugged on her earring. A signal, maybe? From the corner of his eye, he saw Tess grin. Since when did they have signals? "Be careful," he said, "or they'll think you're coaching from the stands."

"I'm not her coach," Tess shot back, not even bothering to look at him. "Make her play, dammit!" Tess said an instant later, as Davina ripped her serve right down the tee and Gaby returned it neatly at her opponent's feet.

"Right," Max said, grinning, and knowing it wasn't entirely in response to Gaby being up a point on Davina's serve for the first time. "For someone who spends a lot of time denying she's a coach, you sure think, talk, and act like one." The words were out before he realized he'd spoken his thoughts out loud.

"Well, you of all people should know looks can be deceiving. Yes!" she exclaimed a second later, pumping both fists, then grinning broadly, as Gaby finally came into the net on a second short serve from Davina and made her pay in short, brutal fashion. "Break her, baby, break her," Tess intoned softly under her breath.

And yet Max heard every word. "Bloodthirsty," he found himself murmuring back, just as quietly.

"Damnbetcha," he heard in return, while keeping his eyes riveted to the court. He was almost hyperaware of the woman seated two down to his right, who was apparently just as wired into him at the moment, despite her focus being so intently on the court below. Appearances deceiving, indeed. And he was liking it a damn sight more than he had any right to.

Two points later, all three of them were on their feet, shouting approval as Gaby broke Davina at love. Tess threw her arm around Aurora's shoulder in a quick squeeze, but as they took their seats to ready for the next point, she glanced over the older woman's head and made full, direct eye contact with Max for the first time since her arrival.

Her bright green eyes were shining and her smile was wide and beckoning. He didn't know quite what to do with that beckoning part, nor the fact that he wasn't all that averse to being beckoned.

He sat back down, smiling absently at Aurora as she squeezed his knee in excitement, and blamed it all on the rush of adrenaline. Just as soon as they were off this court, she'd be getting a piece of his mind... and nothing else. Right now, it was all about Gaby, who was up two games to one, now on her serve and on the brink of going up three to one.

Aurora clapped her hands. "Come on, Gabrielle. You can do this."

With the help of two well-placed serves, Gaby took the game quickly.

"Now take it to her," Tess muttered. "Don't stand around back there and give her the whole court to work with."

Davina's first serve was an ace.

Aurora sighed, but Tess nudged her. "She's fine. She'll hold up."

Max heard the whirring of cameras and looked down to see the field of photographers—the heretofore very small field, given the relative lack of importance of this match—had grown slightly. Tess's appearance, most likely, he thought.

Gaby returned well on the second point, forcing the error from Davina.

"That's my girl," Tess said, nodding in approval.

My girl, Max thought. Gaby was *his* girl. Sister, anyway.

Davina tried to pull Gaby out wide on the next point, but on the first short ball, Gaby came in toward the net with a vengeance.

"Yes!" Tess shouted, leaning forward.

Max was on the edge of his seat, too, as the two players traded several fierce volleys at the net before Gaby lobbed her for the winner.

Gaby's fist pump as she turned back to the baseline matched Tess's exactly. As did the grin the two of them briefly shared before Gaby once again took up her stance, awaiting the next serve.

Spooked by the teenager's surge of confidence, or perhaps just tightening up a little as it looked like the set was slipping away from her, Davina choked and double-faulted on the next point, giving the game to Gaby, who was now up four–one, with only two more games needed to take the second set.

The crowd was getting into it now, clearly rooting for Gaby, because she was the underdog, or because she had a famous face in her players' box, or a little of both. Max had no idea. But he knew never to underestimate the power of having the crowd behind you . . . or against you. He was just thankful they were rooting for her. He glanced around the court and noticed the stands had filled in almost completely. Had word gone around so quickly that Tess Hamilton was in the stands?

He turned his attention back to his sister. Or was the buzz partly for Gaby? Whatever the case, she seemed to feed off the energy that was rocking the stands now and easily held her service game at love.

"One game away from a third set," Aurora said, clapping her hands, sending her bracelets jangling.

Max found himself glancing over at Tess, and caught her doing the same to him. When she smiled, it was one of excitement and pure joy. It was the first time he could recall seeing her so open and carefree. There was nothing calculating or mischievous there. And he found himself wondering what she'd been like when she was younger, early on in her career, when she was eager and new to the ways of the tour, much like his sister was now.

Tess was still eager, and the hunger, the competitive drive that had led her to win a handful of the same trophy Gaby was playing toward today, still shone clearly in her eyes. Only now all of Tess's energy and focus was directed at his sister.

Max pulled his gaze from Tess's, and looked down at Gaby as she went into battle to take this match to a third set. He wondered for the first time if maybe Tess was helping Gaby as a means to continue her own battles on the court of play, battles she could no longer fight herself.

Wasn't that why a lot of players turned to coaching? Tess insisted she wasn't a coach. But watching Gaby out there, clearly benefiting from the brief amount of time Tess had spent with her, and watching Tess, clearly completely invested in the outcome of this match . . . he had to wonder if maybe she was protesting too much.

She might not want to coach, and Lord knows she didn't need a job . . . but maybe this wasn't about needing a job. Maybe it was about needing to be needed. And needing to have the adrenaline rush of winning, even if it was by proxy.

So why the television appearance today? Why flaunt herself, and by association, his sister, in front of the press, inviting more attention and therefore more pressure on Gaby? His thoughts flipped back the other way. Maybe she really didn't have Gaby's best interest at heart. Max felt his own heart settle firmly back in its proper spot as reality set back in. Maybe she just wanted to stay in the public eye, maybe that was her adrenaline rush now. And she was only excited about getting Gaby into the second round for the increased visibility it would bring her. A chance to continue her swan song in the public forum.

"Oh, my goodness," Aurora said, squeezing the lifeblood out of his hand. "She's going to win the set!"

And sure enough, on a short serve from Davina, Gaby charged the net again. Davina, clearly rattled, guessed wrong and stabbed right, as Gaby neatly dumped it over the net to the left.

The crowd leaped to its feet as the cool British umpire calmly called the set in favor of Miss Fontaine. Aurora hugged Tess, Max hugged Aurora, and Tess hugged them both.

Looking past Aurora straight at him, Tess said, "She's gonna take this, Max. She's gonna do it!" She hooted. "Davina will be lucky to get two games off her in the next set. Bet you."

And without knowing exactly why, he said, "I'll take that bet."

Tess cocked one eyebrow. "Oh? A betting man? I wouldn't have thought you had it in you."

Why was he smiling at her? Encouraging her? What was wrong with him? "Life is a gamble, right?" he heard himself say.

Tess's expression turned smug as they settled back in their seats. "Okay, Mr. Risk Taker, what's the bet?"

"Gaby moves on to the second round, you stick with her."

Tess looked surprised. "I wouldn't abandon her. What kind of bet is that? Except, of course, coming from you, asking me to stay on must seem like a major capitulation. But still, not exactly a wager."

"I wasn't done yet." Now Max's smile spread to a grin, and he had the distinct pleasure of watching Tess shift back a bit. Something he doubted she did very often, in any part of her life.

"Okay, what else?"

"You're getting paid to coach." She started to object, but he talked over her. "We're paying you to coach, okay? My job is to take care of the rest. So for the duration of the tournament, for however long Gaby is in it, you'll coach her, but you'll answer to me in any matters pertaining to Gaby that don't directly relate to coaching. And you'll stick with whatever I decide. That includes all press and media decisions."

Tess held his gaze, clearly not thrilled with the bet, but unable to back down from the challenge. "We have to get her past this match, first." She turned her attention back to the game.

Max kept his attention squarely on her. "So . . . we have a deal?"

Tess glanced briefly at him. "Don't look too smug yet, Risk Boy. I haven't named my terms if you lose."

"If Gaby loses, our business arrangement is over, so—"

"I didn't say if *she* loses, she won't lose. Davina is on the ropes and going down for the count. The only part left up for grabs is how badly Gaby takes her. I said she'd win six games to two or better. That was my bet. If she takes more games than that to close this deal, you win."

Then she flashed him that grin again. The one that was calculated, mischievous, and all those other things that made his stomach knot up a little. It took a little extra rationalization to come up with why his heart was knocked a bit off balance, too. Surely he'd figure that out later.

"She takes this set six–two or better, then you're dancing to my tune for the duration."

Max wasn't entirely sure how he'd ended up with the short stick again. Something of which must have shown on his face.

Aurora patted his knee, a consoling expression on her face. If you discounted the twinkle in her eyes. "You did your best, dear. But she maneuvers people around for a living. You were outmatched."

Max ignored Tess as she folded her arms and settled back into her seat, clearly certain she'd bested him once again.

"Besides," Aurora added, "Gaby is the real winner either way, right? And isn't that all that matters?"

For a brief moment, Tess and Max traded glances . . . and in that moment, he wasn't sure either one of them could have answered that one convincingly.

Thankfully, they didn't have to. "She's serving," Aurora announced excitedly, bracelets jangling as she grabbed Max's hand in one of her own, and Tess's in the other. "Oh, I'm not sure I can take much more of this."

Less than twenty minutes later, an exultant Gabrielle Fontaine all but skipped to the net to shake hands with her opponent. Her defeated opponent. Then turned and shot the biggest smile of her career straight at her brother, and at Tess, as she pumped her fists over her head in victory. Max, Aurora, and

Tess were all on their feet cheering. The rookie upstart had made it into the second round. The notorious Graveyard Court had once again claimed another victim.

Max was so damn proud he barely heard the umpire calmly call the match. Repeating what he already knew. Miss Fontaine was the winner.

Two–six, six–one . . . six–one.

Chapter 18

Can you believe this?" Gaby was springing around Tess's room like a Ping-Pong ball on crack.

"Of course I can. You've had an awesome week. You're into the round of sixteen. And, oh yeah, you're beautiful, witty, and the camera adores you. What's not to love? Of course Chris Evert wants to interview you for *Tennis* magazine. She's no dummy."

Gaby's cheeks grew a bit pink at the praise, but she was way too wound up to be completely abashed. "God, I can't believe I'm into the second week of my first Wimbledon." She squealed a little and stamped her feet. "I mean, I can, I was there, but you know what I mean? Three rounds and I'm still in it."

Tess turned back to the mirror and finished applying her mascara. "Of course you are. And you earned it, every step. Took out Davina in three, the Romanian in straights, and yesterday—"

"I know!" Gaby crowed. "I beat my first top-ten player!" She fell backward onto Tess's bed, arms spread-eagle, beatific smile on her pretty face. Then she hooted and drummed her heels on the bed. "Amelie *so* choked in the third."

Her enthusiasm was infectious and Tess found herself snorting a little, too. "Big time. But you're the one who put the fear in her." She turned away from the mirror and waved her mascara wand at the teenager. "Be warned, the word's going to get out now. I saw Elena Branch's coach scoping out your match."

"But she lost late yesterday, right? And he was probably scoping out Amelie, anyway, not me."

"Mauresmo's game is well-known, yours isn't. And you've been making quite a splash in London." As had Tess. She'd been careful not to overexpose Gaby, keeping her as focused as possible, but the media coverage had grown to include both the sports media and the more traditional straight news outlets. And Tess had taken full advantage.

The tabs were still paying attention, too, but in London, that was par for the course for any celebrity. Tim Henman, Greg Rusedski, and Andy Murray, the new young Scots player, had all bowed out early, leaving the British with no favorite sons to cheer on. In their place, they'd adopted underdog Gaby. Tess had long been a favorite here and, by extension and their working relationship, they'd happily embraced the rookie player, as well.

Keeping Gaby mostly under wraps hadn't kept Tess from making the media rounds on her own. She'd been a guest with the commentators for both the U.S. cable and major networks and the BBC. And had enjoyed herself immensely each time. To her surprise, and that of various network officials, she'd been something of a ratings boost. Apparently, her brand of somewhat sardonic—okay, snarky—color commentary had been a hit with the public. Some papers had quoted a few random listeners as saying they appreciated her insight and liked that she had the courage to say what everyone was thinking, but was too afraid to put out there. Tess had no such fear. After all, at this point, what did she have to lose? There were no sponsors to piss off, no advertisers to threaten to pull her commercial endorsements. She was free to do and say what she wanted.

As long as it worked in the network's favor, anyway. And so far, so good.

"You have to be twice as prepared from here on in, Gaby, because they're going to come prepared for you. They know a little more about your game now. They know you've got an arsenal of weapons and that you're not afraid to try them all."

Gaby rolled over on her side, facing Tess. "I want to work on my serve-and-volley game more. It's been the only thing keeping me here this long, but I'm still having a hard time coming in really confidently. After the interview later, let's get back out there. Sir Robin's court is lighted."

Tess looked at Gaby via the mirror. "You already had your practice session today, and a good workout. We're not going to overdo."

She flopped onto her back again. "Now you sound like Max."

Just what Tess didn't need, a Max reminder. Like he hadn't already infiltrated her brain on a regular basis these past couple of days.

Wexley House was huge. They could stay here weeks and never run into each other. But she'd been far too aware he was under the same roof as she was. Especially at night, when she was lying in bed with a whole lot more important things to mull over than her increasingly confusing feelings for Max Fontaine. Much less remember things she had no business remembering.

Like the way his lips had curved that tiny bit as he stared down at her, all enigmatic and intense that night by the front door, the same night he and Gaby had moved in—what now seemed like a million years ago. Or that time she'd caught him looking at her the day Gaby had won her first-round match, looking at her with such open curiosity, as if he'd never really seen her before. She couldn't get that sort of stunned look out of her mind. Wednesday hadn't helped matters any, either.

Gaby had taken out Sylvia Mariscu, the young Romanian who was trying to break into the top by doing well here. *Yeah, well, not this week,* Tess thought with a private smile. Gaby had seen to that. And when Gaby had fought a grueling second-set tiebreaker to take the match, Max had stood and dragged Tess, seated in the row behind him, to her feet as they hooted in victory . . . and then pulled her into a bear hug. That had been disconcerting enough, but instead of letting her go right away, there had been a moment—just a moment, but it was one of those moments, like in the first round, that just stuck, timelessly, in her mind—when she'd started to pull away and he'd tightened his hold.

The look on his face had been one of surprise, like he hadn't quite meant to do that, but somehow had anyway. She'd intended to smile down at him, make some smart-ass remark, anything to regain her footing which had somehow, somewhere, gotten wobbly when he'd put his hands on her. Instead she'd just smiled down at him like some kind of lovestruck idiot with a goony smile plastered all over her face.

Then Aurora and Vivian had tugged her away and into another embrace as the celebration continued, mercifully ending the moment before she did something even more ridiculous—like the afternoon hadn't already been surreal enough. Even now she had to shake her head, remembering how it had started. The Godmothers Do Wimbledon.

She wasn't sure the members would ever recover after allowing Vivian DePalma on the grounds of the All England Club, what with her rather . . . interesting tribute to their stuffy all-white rule. Somehow Tess didn't think the executive committee quite expected a wide-brimmed, feather-festooned day hat, with tiny strawberries fixed into the folds of tulle that circled the brim. A concoction that would have looked outrageous even at Royal Ascot, which was saying something.

As if that weren't head-turning enough, Vivian had added an eye-popping all-white ensemble featuring a fitted-bodice jacket—complete with a sparkling, diamond tennis-racket brooch on the lapel—worn over her version of a retro, turn-of-the-century ankle-length tennis skirt, and capped it off with strawberry-trimmed bobby socks and white leather sneakers. It was a wonder they'd let her back on the grounds again yesterday.

But even with all that distraction, and Gaby's exulted leaps as she celebrated on the court, it had been that moment in Max's arms, that brief look of surprise on his face as his hands had tightened on the small of her back, that stuck with her.

No, she didn't need any Max reminders.

"You were like the Tiger Woods of tennis," Gaby was saying. "All those stories about how you were out there for hours right after a match, practicing. So how come you won't give me a little more time? I mean, come on, what's the worst that can happen?"

"The worst that could happen is you end up like me. Injured to the point of no repair before your thirtieth birthday. Career over."

Gaby was silent for a moment and Tess continued with her primping. Finally, Gaby said, "Do you miss it really bad? Playing, I mean?"

Tess paused for a moment, eyeliner poised. "More than anything," she said finally, opting for the truth. Her voice was a bit gruffer than she'd have liked, but Gaby had caught her a bit off guard. "It was my whole life."

"Is that why you're coaching me? To feel like you're still connected to it?"

It was an obvious question, but Tess wasn't quite prepared to answer it. Mostly because, now that it had been asked, she wasn't really sure what the truth was. "I'm not coaching you." She waved her eyeliner to emphasize her point. "No matter what your brother says. I'm just mentoring you a little, while you're in between coaches."

In the mirror, she saw Gaby smile and roll to her back again.

"What?" Tess asked. In her short time around the younger Fontaine, she'd learned to be aware of that particular little smile.

"Nothing. I shouldn't be so nosy. Max is always telling me that."

"You won't know if you don't ask," Tess said automatically.

"Exactly!" Gaby agreed. "So don't think I'm not grateful for your mentoring." She made air quotes around that last word. "It's just . . ."

Tess let the sentence dangle, knowing Gaby was purposely trying to bait her. As the silence spun out, she finally looked at Tess's reflection in the mirror. Tess merely arched an eyebrow back at her. One that she noticed needed a little evening up. Dammit, she'd never get out of here on time.

Gaby sighed. She was pretty good at manipulating situations to her advantage, but she had a way to go to catch up with Tess. "So, if you don't want to coach, what do you want to do now?"

Digging the tweezers out of her makeup bag, Tess went to work on plucking errant hairs. And very specifically avoided the very same question she'd avoided asking herself for the past few days. She was thrilled for Gaby, ecstatic, but watching her play had still taken an emotional toll on Tess. Not so much in the moment, when the adrenaline was pumping. She'd managed to focus then, shut out her memories. But at night, lying in bed, it was a different story. Then she'd replay the entire match over in her mind, visualizing herself out there instead of Gaby, reliving how she'd have played each point. It was stupid torture and she knew it, but there it was anyway. And better than thinking about Max all through the night. Talk about torture. "Right now I want to finish getting ready. I have to be out of here in less than fifteen minutes."

"That's not an answer."

Tess smiled, checked her teeth for lipstick smears. "I know."

"But you said if you don't ask—"

"I never said you'd always get the information you seek, young Padawan." Gaby giggled and Tess focused on skimming a brush over her cheekbones, then turned around. "What do you think?"

"Wow." Gaby sat up. "You look hot."

Tess smiled and did a little curtsy. "Why thank you."

Gaby instantly forgot all about her own worries and became all sixteen-year-old teenager again. She scooted to a cross-legged position, eyes sparking with a whole new kind of nosy interest. "So, who's the hot date with? Trying to make Max jealous?"

"None of your—what did you just say?"

She smiled, all sly now. "You heard me."

Of course, Gaby had long since seen the headlines earlier in the week, the infamous photo of her and Max in the players' lounge. But both Tess and Max had, on separate occasions, explained to Gaby—in detail—that the papers had made something of nothing. Tess had even reminded Gaby why she'd charmed her way into the commentators' booth with Mary Carillo and John McEnroe on opening day. Well, the part of the reason that had pertained to Gaby and Max, anyway. She'd used her time with the colorful hosts to shoot down rumors and hopefully shift the focus to Gaby's game and her hopes to do well in the tournament.

She'd have probably been more successful if the camera guys on the Graveyard Court that very same day hadn't caught her and Max staring intently at each other, smiling. She could have done without the permanent reminder herself.

"Why in the world would you ask something like that? Max and I are, at best, civil with each other. You know that better than anyone."

"He hated losing that bet to you."

"Hey, I've been gentle and he knows it. And if it wasn't for me, you wouldn't be talking to one Ms. Chris Evert here shortly. Speaking of which, shouldn't you be off somewhere primping, too?"

Gaby lifted an unconcerned shoulder. "No photographers this time, just an interview. I think we're doing it by phone."

"Nervous?"

Gaby just laughed. "I've given more interviews since you started coach—sorry, I mean, mentoring me," she added dryly. "I can't think of anything she could ask me that we haven't rehearsed, like, a million times."

Tess fished her small clutch out of the dresser and popped the lipstick she was using inside. "How are you holding up?"

Gaby flung herself back, arms wide, all dramatic once again. But grinning ear to ear. "I love all of it. I love the attention, I love signing autographs." She rolled her head toward Tess. "And most of all, I love winning!"

Tess shot her a similar grin in response. She knew exactly how Gabrielle felt. "Yeah. It's pretty intoxicating." She walked to the foot of the bed and nudged Gaby's foot with her leg. "Just make sure you pace yourself. Get some rest tonight."

"Are you going to see anyone famous tonight?"

It was funny. Gaby could be worldly ingenue one second, starstruck teenager the next. Tess found herself hoping Gaby was able to hold on to that fleeting time in her life longer than Tess had. "I don't know," she replied. That was the truth. She'd been invited by the network she'd done the commentating for to a shindig schmoozing some of the tournament and commercial sponsors. She couldn't have planned that one better if she'd dreamed it up herself, but she had no idea who else would be in attendance.

"Will you tell me all about it tomorrow over breakfast?"

"You've got a very big match tomorrow, if you haven't forgotten."

For the first time, Tess spied a bit of nerves in the way Gaby darted her gaze immediately to her feet. "I haven't, trust me."

Tess sat on the edge of the bed. "We'll have plenty of time in the morning to go over strategy. You just do your normal match-day routine. I'll be there every step. I promise."

Gaby sat up and impulsively hugged Tess. "Thank you," she whispered fiercely. "I would never have made it this far without you."

Tess gently dislodged herself from the teenager's quite powerful grip. Both because she didn't want to crush the dress she was wearing, and because she was suddenly worried about just what role she truly was playing here. Yes, in addition to the boost it had given her other mission here in London, she had been enjoying her time with Gaby, and she had come to care very much about her, but she wasn't going to be a permanent fixture in the teenager's life. She couldn't have Gaby getting too emotionally attached in return, or worse, thinking she needed Tess to win matches. She took Gaby by the shoulders and stared her directly in the face. "You earned every single point out there. Any help I've given you is merely nudging the talent you already have."

"Isn't that what a good coach is supposed to do?"

"Gaby."

Her lips quirked a little. "A girl can dream, right?" She laughed. "This is all a dream, isn't it?" She lay back on the bed again. "Maybe Aurora really is a fairy godmother." The smile spread across her face.

"Don't let her hear you say that—it will go straight to her head, which is big enough, thank you." She got up and walked to the door. "Go charm the socks off of Chrissy, then get plenty of rest tonight. We'll talk about all of it in the morning."

"Okay. Oh, one more thing, can you do me a huge favor and go out through the west entrance when you leave?"

Tess turned back. "Why would I do that?"

Gaby's grin was impish. "Because Max is out on the west patio making some calls. He'll think you look hot, too."

Tess just laughed and shook her head.

"You know," Gaby called out as she left the room, "maybe Aurora or Vivian could give you what you wish for!"

Clearly, Gaby had some deluded idea that what Tess wanted or needed was a guy. Preferably, her older brother.

As Tess left the west wing, she carefully skirted around the patio, staying out of sight, but managed to spy Max sitting out there, the sun setting behind him, head bent over a notebook as he talked quite animatedly on his cell and scribbled something down. Hopefully the name of Gaby's next coach. Still, the setting sun made for an arresting shot, she found herself thinking. He was intense. It all but vibrated off of him at times. And it did draw her, in some inexplicable way she was doing her damnedest to ignore.

No, if Aurora and Vivian really had special godmother powers, she wouldn't waste her wish on romance. She'd get them to figure out how to solve her financial crisis. In lieu of that impossible miracle, it was best she get out there and make it happen herself.

In another week tops, Max and Gaby would move on to the next tournament. And she would return home to Florida. She really didn't want to think about why that made her sad. All she needed to think about was how she didn't intend to go home empty-handed.

Chapter 19

"Gabrielle, what a surprise, my dear. What brings you down here so late?" Aurora closed her book and quickly slid her glasses off. It was a small bow to vanity, she supposed, and at her age, a rather silly one, but she'd never liked the look of glasses on a woman. And she couldn't see herself fussing with contacts, either. So she kept up the pretense of good vision when she could. And thanked her close friends for allowing her the illusion. "Shouldn't you be resting for tomorrow?"

The lanky teenager strolled across the parlor and slid into the chair across from Aurora, both of which angled toward the fireplace in Sir Robin's private library. As opposed to the general library found on the first floor, this one was tucked away in his private wing of the residence. Aurora had discovered it on one of her daily walks—Vivian would say she'd been snooping, but a woman her age had to keep her health up, did she not? And what with the typical English rainy afternoons, she'd simply found it easier to do her walking indoors.

"I couldn't sleep," Gaby said. "Too wired, I guess."

"Nervous, dear? You know, I think you have a marvelous opportunity tomorrow."

Gaby lifted one shoulder in a half-shrug. "I'm as prepared as I can be. I think. I don't know . . ." She sighed a little. "I wanted to do well when I came here, but between my experience in Paris and then not doing very well in the warm-up, I wasn't really sure if I'd even be here more than a day or two. I half-expected to be home by now, getting ready for the hard-court season."

"And look what you've done with yourself," Aurora said proudly. She hadn't quite bargained on just how involved she'd ended up being with the Fontaines and Tess, but she wouldn't trade a moment of it. It had been one of her more entertaining adventures in London in ages. And the excitement wasn't over yet.

Gaby's eyes lit up a little. "I know." The corners of her mouth curved. "I can hardly believe it." She sat up, leaned forward. "Now that I'm in the round of sixteen, I really want to make it to the quarterfinals."

"Why settle for stopping there?"

Gaby laughed nervously and twisted her hands together in her lap. "If I let myself think too far ahead, I get scared. Not scared of losing, so much as scared of wanting it so badly . . . and then losing. I mean, I know I've already done better than I should, given my experience and ranking—"

"Which will shoot up quite nicely after this fortnight," Aurora reminded her.

Gaby bounced a little in her seat. "I know." But her fingers were still locked together in a death grip. "It's just . . . I've gotten a chance to know what it feels like to win, and . . ." The one-shoulder shrug again, the impudent, excited grin. "I like it."

Aurora laughed. "Why of course you do, dear. It's a good bet you have a few grand-slam trophies in your future. But you've a long career ahead of you. Pacing is everything, darling."

Gaby slumped back again, let out a long breath. "I know, I know. Everyone keeps telling me." She stared into the fire.

Aurora watched her, wondered what was really on her mind. She had no doubt it was partly the excitement of the tournament that had driven her out of bed to wander the hallways . . . but she suspected there was more to it than that. So she bided her time. And after a few, long minutes, her patience was rewarded.

"Tess looked really great tonight, didn't she?" Gaby said, flicking at the tasseled silk fringe that lined the arm cover of the chair. "Do you know what party she was invited to? I checked her room, she's still not back yet."

"I believe it was something sponsored by one of the networks covering the event."

Gaby's brows furrowed in thought. "She's been invited into the commentating booth a couple times now."

"Yes, she has." Aurora was beginning to see where this was going. "I think she brings a little pizzazz to that particular venue."

Gaby didn't say anything for a moment, then blurted, "Don't you think she and Max look good together?"

Now that one took Aurora a little bit by surprise. She suspected Gaby was concerned about losing Tess after this week, but she had no idea those kind of thoughts were going on in the teenager's mind. "In what way do you mean? You do realize the magazines and papers are just having a little fun with them. It's nothing."

"That's what they say," Gaby said, a hint of impatience creeping into her tone. "But anyone who knows anything can see they like each other."

Aurora took a considering look at Gaby. She might appear to be a typical, self-absorbed teenager, but apparently she was paying attention to something other than her own world. "They bicker constantly," Aurora responded, curious to see what kind of foundation Gaby had for her observation. Could it be her womanly intuition was as precociously developed as her athletic skills?

"I know they do," she said, "but I think with them it's almost a kind of flirting."

Aurora wanted to believe that, too, but still wasn't quite certain it wasn't wishful thinking on her part. If they would just settle down long enough to see that their differences were actually what would make them so strong and good for each other, who knew what could happen? She'd thought getting them in closer quarters would allow nature to simply take its course, but Wexley House was a veritable ocean of space and she'd yet to see any of her carefully laid plans come to fruition.

So much so she'd called Vivian and bribed her into coming to one of Gaby's matches under the pretense of watching her play, but mostly to see what her more finely tuned romance radar had to say. A total mistake, as it had turned out. First, she should have known Vivian wouldn't be able to pass up the chance to wear something totally outlandish and inappropriate. But to make matters worse, rather than use her radar to help Aurora determine the romance potential between Max and Tess... Vivian had used it for her own personal detection devices.

Aurora supposed she should have known better than to unleash Vivi on the unsuspecting and often stuffy, upper-class Wimbledon members. She was still trying to block images of Vivian flirting outrageously with a gentleman there representing one of the banks sponsoring the Championships—a man easily half her age—by asking him if he'd like to pick one of her strawberries, for goodness sake! Aurora stifled a renewed shudder at the memory.

"Don't you think they'd make a good couple, Aurora?" Gaby asked, drawing her from her thoughts.

Something about the way Gaby asked had Aurora reconsidering the teenager's altruistic intentions. "I don't know, dear. I haven't given it much thought." A complete falsehood, of course, but it wouldn't do to raise the girl's hopes. Especially when Aurora wasn't certain exactly what Gabrielle was hoping for. Or why.

Gaby slouched farther down in the chair and let her long legs stretch out in front of her. The way she repeatedly tapped her toes together belied her otherwise relaxed pose. Something was niggling at her. "I guess I was just thinking that, you know, with me almost being eighteen..."

Aurora dipped her chin to keep Gaby from seeing her smile. Only a sixteen-and-a-half-year-old would think she was "almost eighteen." Oh, to be young and foolish again... She caught herself. *As opposed to what, Aurora, being old and foolish?*

"Max needs to get more of a life. I mean, he's with me on tour and that won't change even as I get older, so I was thinking, you know, what kind of life can he have and all? And then there's Tess, who's retired and can travel and do whatever she wants..."

The light began to dawn. "Such as coaching, you mean?"

Gaby looked over at Aurora, and there was such yearning in her young face it made Aurora's heart squeeze a little. "She's so good at it. I mean, she's hardly doing that much with me, but I totally get what she's asking me to do. It's like we think the same, we see the court the same. And my game is already so improved. And that's not all. She's smart about everything about the tour, too. She's helped me a ton with doing interviews and showing me how to work the press."

So earnest, so determined, Aurora thought. "I know she has." Much to Max's distress. "So, maybe you're thinking that if Tess and Max were romantically involved, she'd stick around as your coach?"

Now she ducked her chin ever so slightly. "You think I'm being horribly selfish, I know." She glanced up through impossibly thick lashes Aurora would have killed for at any age. "But wouldn't it be a win-win for everybody?"

Aurora let out a gentle laugh. "I suppose so. But you can't really force these things on people." No one knew that better than she did.

Gaby exhaled on a long sigh and let her feet fall to their sides, limp. "I know. It's just... well, I mean, I'd love to have Tess coaching me. Because, duh, who wouldn't? But I was also kind of thinking, hoping sort of, that if they'd get a life with each other, maybe I could have one, too."

Ah ha. So the plot thickened further. "Meaning what, dear?"

Try as she might have, Gaby was unable to squash the bloom of pink that blossomed on her cheeks. And when she looked up again, there was a sparkle in her eyes that Aurora hadn't seen before, but well recognized. It was the juvenile version of the same sort of spark Aurora had been hoping to see in Max's and Tess's eyes. Instead, the closest she'd come to seeing that kind of twinkle was with Vivi yesterday. Right before she'd asked a perfect stranger to pluck her fruit.

"Nothing, really," she said.

A complete falsehood, Aurora knew, but didn't call her on it. "Did you want to get out and see more of London? Perhaps we can talk to Max about staying on a few days after the tournament. Get some serious shopping in, see a show."

"I've been getting out and about a little, but thank you," she said politely. She looked like she was going to say more, then thought better of it and fell silent.

Aurora nudged a little. "What is it you do want, then?"

Gaby paused, then looked at her. "Freedom."

"You can't really be thinking you should tackle the city alone and unchaperoned?"

She scuffed her toes into the oriental rug. "I wouldn't be completely alone." Her voice was so soft Aurora barely heard her.

"So," Aurora said, treading carefully, "can I take it someone has caught your fancy?"

A hot blush stained Gaby's cheeks, and quite prettily, Aurora thought. *Oh, Max, poor boy, you are in for some trouble now.*

"Is he another player?"

After a few moments, Gaby nodded, then covered her face with her hands and drummed her heels on the floor.

"That good, hmm?"

When she took her hands down, the smile creasing her lovely young face was big and broad and so delightful, Aurora spent a moment wondering if maybe she shouldn't be getting her own . . . uh, fruit plucked, more often these days. Ah, the magical powers of young love.

"He's nineteen. From Belgium. He's in the top fifty and drives his own Porsche." She tilted her head back and closed her eyes. "And he has the most amazing accent."

Aurora sighed a little, even as all her internal warning bells began to clang. She'd have to decide what to do about this, whether to tell Max. Or perhaps Tess. Someone had to keep an even closer eye on the young girl. She was positively glowing, swimming in an ocean of hormones, all virtually screaming for attention. And Aurora was quite certain it wouldn't take much persuasion from the young Belgian to distract Gabrielle from her real mission here in London.

Which begged the question... "So, how did you meet—I'm sorry, what is his name?"

"Rance." Another little swoon. "I met him coming out of the press room after the second round. We've only spoken a few times, but Aurora, he is just so heavenly. And I know he's interested. He asked me to go for a ride sometime!"

Oh, Aurora just bet he had. Dear, dear, this was a bit of a dilemma.

"But Max is always hovering and I can hardly get two feet away without him tugging the leash." Her eyes widened. "Maybe you could talk to him? I've thought about asking Tess to help me, but she's not around much, other than for training sessions and the matches."

Aurora wasn't sure Tess wouldn't have helped her out, either. Although she did seem rather intent on keeping Gaby focused on the tournament. Still... Max would have had a complete meltdown if that came to pass. It was better all around that Gaby had come to her this evening. And yet, as she looked at Gaby's big, beseeching eyes, she found herself wondering just how she'd gotten herself into this predicament?

Gently, so she didn't discourage Gaby from opening up to her, she said, "Well, you've got a very big match tomorrow. You need to stay focused on that—"

"I am, but that doesn't mean I can't—"

Aurora lifted one hand, setting her bracelets to jingling. "You stay focused on the reason you came to London. Yes, you've already accomplished an enormous victory here, but your work isn't done yet. You've worked hard for this chance. And if you're as much like Tess as we all think you are, you will always regret allowing yourself to be distracted and not giving each match your full attention. Your young man won't disappear just because you've got other things on your agenda besides him. And if he does, well, *c'est la vie.*"

When Gaby didn't say anything right away, Aurora continued. "Perhaps I can have a talk with Max, as well. Once you reach the end of your run here, showing your maturity with poise and dedication, perhaps I can persuade him to give you a little space." She lifted her hand again to squelch the squeal of delight she saw was forthcoming. "I'm not saying he'll let you roam the streets of London, but we could always entertain your young man here at Wexley, perhaps let you take the Glass Slipper limo out for a limited ride through town." She smiled. "I'm sure I'll come up with something that will suit you both."

She could see Gaby was torn. The young girl obviously thought she was wise enough, and mature enough, to handle a more serious, unattended date. But she was smart enough not to thwart the only hand that was presently feeding her what she wanted most. "Oh, Aurora, thank you." With a burst of energy Aurora would have loved to bottle and sell, Gaby leaped from the chair and leaned down to give her a big hug. "I really, really appreciate it. You really are my fairy godmother."

"You're welcome, dear," Aurora said, hugging her back, enjoying the moment despite some lingering misgivings. "Now, perhaps you should think about getting back to your rooms and settling in for the night. If Tess comes in while I'm still up, I'll tell her you asked about her. I'm sure she'll tell you about anything exciting on your drive over to the grounds tomorrow."

Gaby all but skipped from the room. Aurora sat back and sighed, somewhat exhausted just from being that close to so much energy packed into one young girl. "Oh, Max, darling," she murmured to the room at large, "you really are going to have your work cut out for you with that one."

She picked up her reading glasses and slipped them back on, but her mind refused to stay on the pages of the book.

Nothing was going remotely as she'd planned. But she hadn't become the successful businesswoman she had by being

rigid and uninspired. So Max and Tess weren't falling all over each other. Initially she'd simply wanted Tess to find her path to her financial solvency. And on that score, it appeared that through her liaison with the Fontaines she might indeed find that solution. Though perhaps not in the way Aurora had envisioned. Tess was in hot demand again, and Aurora had no doubt she'd find some way to capitalize on it.

However, Aurora had spent enough time with Tess over the past several weeks to know for certain that she was at a much bigger crossroad in her life than one predicated by financial circumstance. Another endorsement deal wouldn't fix what Aurora was beginning to see was the bigger problem. What was Tess Hamilton going to do with the rest of her life? Even if she invested well and modified her living expenses accordingly, she'd been too hungry, too focused, and far too competitive as a professional tennis player to be remotely satisfied with sitting back on her laurels and living off the spoils of her successes.

Gaby had raved about Tess's abilities as a coach. Mentor. What have you. The press was all abuzz with speculation as to why Tess had taken on the young phenom, though she'd yet to see anyone speculate on the money angle. Which had been a shock, really. But perhaps Tess was seen as being so obscenely successful, it simply didn't occur to anyone to dig in that direction. Besides, Tess had cleverly maintained a very high profile about the whole thing, steering the media juggernaut to her best advantage the entire time.

Of course, that whole business with the possible romantic link to Max had been quite the timely media distraction. Aurora paused in her thoughts, and she slid her glasses off her nose. "No. She wouldn't have." She slid them back on. Surely Tess hadn't intentionally created that entire thing for her own purposes? Toying with Max privately was one thing. He was a grown man, after all, and from what she'd seen, perfectly capable of holding his own with Tess. Making it more the pity that their love match wasn't real. But surely Tess hadn't been using Max or Gaby as some sort of promotional shill. Things had certainly moved in that direction, but Aurora would like to think that it all hadn't been a calculated move on Tess's part. More a serendipitous benefit from her agreeing to help out with Gaby in the first place.

Of course, Gaby was doing quite well, so whatever the case, Tess had more than kept up her end of the bargain she'd made with the Fontaines, regardless of any ulterior motive. Aurora sighed and slid her glasses off for the last time, closing her book, too, for good measure. If only Tess could see what was so plainly evident to Aurora. She stood, and because no one was around to notice, took a moment to massage her aching hip. Getting old was a stone-cold bitch, as Vivian was wont to say.

But it would be an even colder day before Aurora was too old to play fairy godmother. She hadn't come this far to give up now. Tess might need a bit more of her godmotherly skills than most, but one way or the other, they were all going to live happily ever after. She walked with a soft limp toward the library door. "Even if it kills me, dammit."

Chapter 20

"That's the way to do it, Bobby!" Tess leaped up from her seat, as did Andrea next to her, both of them pumping their fists in the air.

Andrea threw her arms around Tess. "I can't believe it! We're in the quarterfinals!"

Grinning from ear to ear as Bobby and his doubles partner, Tim, saluted the wildly cheering crowd, Tess enthusiastically hugged Andrea back. "Not a bad wedding present, huh? A nice shiny championship trophy?"

"Whoa, don't get ahead of yourself," Andrea said, laughing nervously, but giddy with the excitement of the moment.

The energy in the stands was off the charts, especially for doubles play. It had been a tough, tight, five-set match against the two Australians, ranked fourth in the world, but Bobby and Tim had prevailed in the end.

"So, are you coming out to dinner with us tonight?" Andrea asked, still a bit breathless.

"I wish I could, but with the rain delay this morning, Gaby's match won't go on until late this afternoon, if at all. I'm going to stick around here."

Andrea's expression shifted to a knowing smile, but she didn't say anything.

"What?" Tess asked, holding onto the rail in front of her as the two of them were jostled by the exiting fans. They'd wait until the stands had emptied a little before exiting. Tess tended to cause a bit of a stir, so security had asked her to arrive after matches began and leave after most of the crowd had left. It was that or hire private security, something she'd never been thrilled about and didn't intend to start now—even if she'd had the money to fund a payroll, which of course she didn't.

"It's none of my business, of course," Andrea was saying.

For a split second, Tess thought her new sister-in-law had read her mind and was referring to her financial predicament. Had Bobby told his wife about the dropped endorsement deal?

Then Andrea said, "I know it's probably all a media stunt or something, to sell papers, but I have to admit, you and Max Fontaine make a sharp pairing. He's so enigmatic and serious and you're so outgoing and—"

"Obnoxious?" Tess finished on a laugh.

"No, no, of course not. I'm just saying you two looked rather sweet together."

Tess snorted. " 'Sweet'? Trust me, nothing between Max and me falls even remotely under that heading."

Andrea waved excitedly at her new husband as Bobby and Tim walked to the far side of the court to give interviews. Tess blew him a kiss.

"So," Andrea went on, eyes still sparkling, "what is it like working with Gabrielle, anyway? Everyone is comparing her to you, and I can see the similarities. Does it feel odd at all?"

Tess was still caught up in the way Andrea all but glowed

when she looked at Bobby. What must it be like to sparkle like that because you cared about someone so fully, knowing they felt the same way? She'd entered her past relationships with all the same gusto she did her tournaments, but never with any real idea that they'd last very long. Her constant traveling schedule was very prohibitive. And even if she wanted to date a player, that was almost worse, as their tour schedules were never the same. Of course, she was retired now and could do as she pleased. Date as she pleased. And maybe she would.

Just as soon as she figured out how to earn a living.

"Not odd so much as kind of surreal," Tess said, pulling her thoughts together. "I've never been in the position of teaching or molding anyone's game but my own."

"Gabrielle is having such a marvelous run here, you must be proud to be part of that, at least."

"Oh, I don't know that I've had that big an influence on her game. We haven't been working together long enough for that. Tucking her away at Sir Robin's place, with the private practice court, has probably done more for her than anything. She's really been able to keep her focus."

"And her composure," Andrea added with a teasing smile. "All that talk of her reputation for being a rebel, slamming rackets and questioning calls, cursing herself, and the like. But other than that little dustup in the second round, she's been almost icy out there. At least from what I've seen and heard."

"Sometimes it's like that," Tess said. "She's doing well, staying on top, so she doesn't need the outlet, the release." Her smile turned wry. "But give her time, give her nerves time. She's stepping into bold new territory now, with some big guns in her immediate sights."

"I can't believe that qualifier took out Justine. Gaby caught a very lucky break there. So you think she can make the quarters?"

Tess beamed. "Oh, I know she can."

The crowd having thinned now, Andrea turned and began making her way from the stands, as Tess followed. She tossed a quick grin over her shoulder at Tess. "You are really enjoying this, aren't you? You play it down, but I can see it. You've got immense pride in your pupil, as well you should."

"She's an amazing talent," was all Tess said. "Like I said, I'm just giving her a little advice is all. She'll find herself a real coach once this is all said and done."

Andrea didn't say anything as they quickly slipped down the side path toward the players' area, flashing their passes at security as they ducked inside. "I don't know," she said, holding the door for Tess. "Seems a shame not to stick with something you enjoy. I'm betting Gabrielle wouldn't mind." She looked past Tess then, and her entire face lit up. "Hi, sweetheart!"

Tess turned to see her brother coming down the hallway, sweaty and grinning from ear to ear. "Hey there, you big winner you," she said, thankful to have that particular discussion thwarted. Just the thought of Gaby moving on had made her heart squeeze a little. Okay, maybe more than a little. And she really didn't want to think about that right now.

As Andrea moved by her, she whispered, "And I don't care what you say, I'm betting Max wouldn't mind if you stuck around, either." Then she threw herself in her husband's arms and let him spin her around as they both giggled like schoolkids.

Tess stood there and watched the absolute joy they took in just holding each other . . . and for the first time in her life, she felt like maybe she'd missed out on a big part of something important. All the accomplishments she'd made were great, but how much better might it be to share those accomplishments with someone? Fortunately, she couldn't take the time to worry about that. She had other more immediate concerns. Because unless she figured out how to get paid, the only accomplishment she'd be sharing with anyone was filing for bankruptcy.

"Okay, okay, you two, get a room already," she teased, tugging at her brother's arm. "There are hundreds of honeymoon suites in London, you know."

"Yeah, yeah," Bobby told her with a laugh. "You're just jealous."

Maybe I am, Tess thought, *just a little.* But she'd die before admitting it to him. God help her, knowing her baby brother, he'd start playing matchmaker. "In your dreams, buddy. Listen, I'd love to stick around with you guys for dinner, but Gaby's match has been delayed and so I'm going to hang out around here."

"Okay, understood." Bobby wiggled his eyebrows. "So, does this 'hanging out' involve your young protégée's very eligible brother? You guys are smokin' the pages right off the tabs. What's going on with that?"

"Absolutely nothing. It's all just hype."

Andrea slid her arm through her husband's. "So says she, anyway."

Tess opened her mouth, then shut it again. "I don't know why I bother. Just because you two are sickeningly in love doesn't mean it's for all of us, you know."

Bobby reached out and snagged her wrist and yanked her close, catching her off balance. She fell against him as he planted a big, wet, sloppy kiss on her cheek. "Come in, the water's just fine. Scaredy cat."

Tess made a big show of using Bobby's shirt to wipe off her cheek, then simply stuck her tongue out at him.

They were still laughing as she left them and went the opposite way down the hall. Once she knew they weren't following behind her, probably too busy sticking their tongues down each other's throats, she made her way upstairs. She headed over to the indoor broadcast soundstages used by the various global networks to beam updates out to the world during the tournament. She paused outside the door to the booth she wanted, ducking as a cameraman stepped out and nearly clipped her with his shoulder gear.

"So sorry, Miss Hamilton," he said, almost gushing in his haste to make sure she was okay.

"Not a problem," she answered quickly. "Good thing I still have quick reflexes." *Now go,* she silently urged. She had to step inside that soundstage and be instantly "on" and she hadn't had time to mentally gear herself up for what could be the most important moment of her life.

Rumors had been circulating for a few days now, and for once she hadn't been the instigator of them. Word was that one of the major cable networks was thinking about offering her a guest commentating spot for the rest of the tournament. Apparently the ratings had continued to spike the few times she sat in with the regular commentators.

She wasn't nervous about the guest-spot offer. She was nervous because she wanted them to offer her a whole lot more than a guest spot. She'd really enjoyed herself—well, what wasn't to love, she was getting paid to shoot off her mouth, her second-best skill next to playing tennis—but it mattered for so many other reasons. In her wildest dreams she hadn't expected something like this could possibly fall into her lap. And to think, in a way, she had Max to thank for all of it. If he hadn't been so freaked out by the tabloid coverage of the two of them together, she'd have never charmed her way into the broadcast booth that first day of the tournament.

Since the rumors had surfaced she'd given it a lot of thought, and though it meant a good deal more work than she'd had to do filming the occasional commercial or shooting a print ad for this product or that, she'd come to realize after working with Gaby these past few weeks that she needed to be working. She needed to have a specific function, something viable and worthwhile that made her feel alive.

Watching Gaby play from the sidelines hadn't been easy. In fact, nothing about being here had been easy. So many memories, many of them wonderful, but now so impossibly poignant, knowing they'd be her last. And yet, hard as it had been, she honestly didn't want to be anywhere else. It felt like she'd come home. The buzz, the excitement, this was the world she knew, the one she thrived in. She'd realized that she didn't want to leave the game completely behind if she didn't have to. Tennis was still her soul mate, her lifeblood. Sure it would take some time to truly come to terms with the reality of no longer being able to compete, she knew that and was prepared to deal with it. Or try to. All she knew was that walking away no longer felt like the right answer. She wanted to stay . . . she just had to find a new reason to be here.

Hence the broadcasting booth she was about to enter. If all went as planned, she would stay involved in the game she loved and, equally important, keep herself out of bankruptcy court.

She'd already planned out what she was going to say to Wade and her father about the job and why she'd sold off all of her other property. She'd simply explain that without the concern of investing new tournament winnings, she'd wanted to downsize, concentrate her assets. She could see her father's nod of approval as she explained that by doing so, she could focus more on her new television career, and, of course, on her charitable endeavors.

But none of that could happen until she worked her way inside the soundstage on the other side of that door . . . and made certain that they knew they were dealing with a hot commodity they should snap up now, before some other network came calling. "Ch-yeah, right," she muttered under her breath. But if anyone could pull it off, it was her. She took a deep breath, put a broad smile on her face, and pushed open the door, already preparing what smart-ass comment she was going to use to soften them up . . . only to run smack into Max.

"What are you doing here?" they both asked simultaneously.

Tess folded her arms and waited.

Max rolled his eyes. "Don't worry, I wasn't doing anything that would spoil the Tess Hamilton–London love connection."

She narrowed her brows. "Very funny. Interview? Is Gaby here?" She looked behind him.

"Yes, interview. My sister happens to be doing quite well here, in case it's slipped your attention between all the parties and television appearances. They wanted to talk to her, but with her match being delayed, she's a little frazzled by the enforced wait and I didn't want her distracted further. So I offered myself instead." His lips quirked. "I know it comes as a shock to you, but they said yes."

She had to work not to smile. Who knew he could have a sense of humor? "Funny. And I know it will come as a shock to you, but I just got done watching Bobby win his match and move into the quarterfinals. It was pretty raucous in the stands, but I wouldn't exactly call it a party. And unless there were cameras trained on me I wasn't aware of, I wasn't on television, either."

"I wasn't talking about just now. And congratulations to your brother."

"Thanks, I'll be sure to pass that along."

"And I was referring to the fact that you haven't been around much the past few nights. Or any nights, for that matter."

She offered him a false smile. "Keeping track of my comings and goings, are we?"

"You forget, being around my younger sibling is like living with *Access Hollywood* twenty-four-seven. She keeps track, and I hear about it whether I want to or not. By the way, she can't wait until she's older so she can hit the town like you do."

Tess didn't even blink. "You'll be lucky if she makes it to majority before that happens. She's young, beautiful, talented, and headstrong. What do you think she's going to want to do? I don't have anything to do with that, nor anything to say to her about it, by the way. I can hardly tell her Just Say No, can I? I'm a lot of things, but a hypocrite isn't one of them. Besides, she's doing fabulously well here. I can't believe you're still whining and pouting about all this."

He looked affronted. "I'm not pouting."

She laughed. He was pouting, and he was pretty damn cute while doing it, too. "Oh yes you are. I'm out having fun every night, and you're stuck at home, scared to death that Gaby is going to be out having fun every night before too long, and you won't have anyone to sit at home and worry things to death with anymore."

"I have responsibilities, unlike someone else I know. I can't just go out gallivanting around."

"She's a teenager. Surely she can maintain for an evening while you gallivant a little."

"Ah, the two lovebirds."

Tess turned to find one of the producers standing behind her. "Hi, Alan."

"What brings you up to our humble digs this fine afternoon, Tess? Isn't your young charge about to play?"

"Rain delay pushed her match back." She shot him a cheeky grin. "I knew you had airtime to kill, so I thought I'd drop by and give your ratings a boost."

He laughed and glanced at Max. "Ah, she doesn't pull any punches, does she? A breath of fresh air in this business, I tell you." He patted Tess on the shoulder, then scooted past them. "Sorry to leave you folks, but I have to get back there and see how much money they're draining from my budget. Come on back whenever you'd like."

"Thanks, Alan." Once he'd gone on into the studio, she turned back to Max and got right to the point. Forewarned was forearmed. "So, exactly what did you say on air earlier? I'm assuming you got asked about the rumor du jour?"

"Which one? You're the source of so many."

"Ha ha. I was referring to the one that also included you. As in us."

"There is no us."

"Exactly my point. So I assume you said as much?"

She'd expected some sort of long-suffering sigh. She still had no idea why she enjoyed poking at him like she did. Probably because he so easily gave it right back to her. Most men were affected by her presence. Usually in a mouth-hanging-open, glazed-over-eyes kind of way that did nothing for her. He was the least affected guy she'd ever met. In fact, he was the anti-affected. So it was just her perverse nature, of course, needing to get a rise out of the one guy who really didn't care.

When he let his mouth curve very slowly into that... well, "wicked" was really the word that came to mind once again. And stuck there. She knew he had it in him, but still, it was just... wow.

You have no idea who you're fooling with.

His words from that morning before Gaby's first round echoed through her mind. At the time, she'd dismissed him. Or tried to. But things had happened between then and now. There had been those looks, exchanged glances, supercharged moments that simply wouldn't leave her memory banks. Dismiss him now? Damn near impossible.

He stepped closer, planted a hand on the wall next to her

head. She was so stunned by his making the first move—any move—she stayed rooted to the spot . . . and for once in her life she was speechless.

He leaned in, until he was so close she could make out every intricate detail of his gorgeous brown irises. "No," he said, his voice deeper, a shade rough. "I told them we were having a passionate, torrid, intensely carnal affair. I told them a man would have to be crazy not to go after someone like Tess Hamilton if he had the chance. And . . ." He leaned a tiny bit closer and she found herself suddenly unable to swallow as her throat constricted. "I told them seeing as we're living under the same roof, and with ample motive and opportunity . . . well . . ." He lifted his other hand and slowly tucked a wayward strand of hair behind her ear.

It was like every single nerve ending in her body had gone on full alert.

"I left the rest to their imagination." He leaned in until his lips were beside her ear.

At some point she'd simply stopped breathing altogether.

"How is your imagination, Tess?" he whispered. "Do you think about what they're saying? Do you ever imagine . . . us?"

Was he really saying all these things? Or was she actually asleep and this was all some sort of dream? A very hot, very explicit dream. And a damn sight better than the ones she had been having about him, that was for sure.

She couldn't find the words to respond . . . not that she had any idea what her response would have been. And any chance she might have had in reclaiming even a shred of the upper hand died instantly with his next words.

"I have." He pushed away from the wall, held her gaze for the longest moment, his dark eyes completely unreadable. Then, without another word, he stepped past her and through the door.

It clicked softly shut behind her. Only then did she allow herself to sag limply against the wall. She was known for making a great entrance, but Max had the market cornered on making a killer exit.

"Jesus. He should bottle that stuff." But even she wasn't buying her own attempt to brush off what had just happened. And what in the hell *had* just happened? Was he just messing with her? Giving as good as he got?

Or . . .

No. No, no, no. She was on a mission. He was a distraction. Hell, his sister was already a major distraction. She couldn't afford another one right now. Certainly not one that came with the international complications he would.

Alan popped around the corner just then. "Thought you'd snuck out on me. Come on, I have a spot for you, if you're game."

She had to work a lot harder than she liked to admit to pull herself together.

"You okay?" he asked as she walked past him and through the studio door he held open. "You look a little flushed."

"Fine," she lied. "Just fine." She mustered one of her trademark wry grins. "I'll be even better when there's a camera on me. You know me, I'm always game."

The producer laughed. "I have little doubt."

She brushed a piece of lint off her shoulder and fluffed her hair a little. *Nonchalant, Tess. As if your entire life wasn't riding on this.* And as if Max hadn't just turned upside down what little life she thought she had.

"You know, Alan," she said, slipping her arm through his, allowing him to open the door to the soundstage for her. And shoving Max as far from her thoughts as humanly possible. "We make a pretty dynamic team."

"I can't fault you there," he said, smiling jovially.

It was the smile that gave her the courage to go for the rest. "So, maybe you should think about offering me something more permanent than an occasional guest spot at the majors." She shot him a cocky wink. "I think we could be very good for each other."

Chapter 21

Court One. Max settled into his seat and tried to calm down enough to just absorb the moment. Gaby was in the quarter-finals and playing on the stadium show court for the first time. It wasn't the famed Centre Court, but it was only one step away. And she was only one match away from playing there, as well, perhaps in front of members of the royal family. As so many tennis greats had before her.

Including the one currently sliding into the seat beside him.

"Isn't this fantastic?" Tess said, bubbling with energy and excitement as always. "I'm so proud of her."

"I thought you were supposed to wait until the match started."

She sent him a sardonic smile. "Gee, nice to see you, too."

"I just meant—"

"I know." She nudged him with her shoulder and leaned closer. "I snuck past the guards. Shh. Don't tell anyone."

Cameras were whirring, shutters were clicking, and all he

had to do was look over the rail down at the court to see that a number of them were aimed at the players' box he was seated in. "I think it's too late for that."

She shifted away from him, ignoring him as she looked out over the rapidly filling stands. She was fidgeting and tapping her toes. "God, it feels so strange sitting up here and not down there." She laughed. "I swear I'm more nervous now, though."

It hit Max again, like it had several times when he least suspected it, what this must be like for her. He was so used to giving her a hard time, thinking only of her impact on his sister . . . and lately, on him, as well, that he didn't stop to think about what she was going through. What must it be like, forced to sit on the sidelines when the last time she'd been here, she'd been down there playing for the title? It couldn't be easy.

But you'd never know it to look at her. Perhaps because she always seemed to be so on top of everything, so confident and so full of life, it was difficult, bordering on impossible, to imagine her as anything but. The words "vulnerable" and "nervous" would never come to mind when thinking of her. Something he'd been doing a great deal more of, of late.

He glanced at her now. Her eyes were sparkling, her bright smile flashing . . . and yet if anyone looked closer, they'd notice the pinched corners of her mouth, the tight lines at the corners of her eyes. And the way she played with the sunglasses she held in her hands, opening and closing them, over and over. She really was nervous.

"Are you worried she's not ready?" he asked her. So much for his plan not to engage her in any unnecessary conversation. He'd managed to avoid anything but the most mundane of business talk the past two mornings, usually over breakfast at Wexley, with Aurora and Gaby in attendance, reviewing the day's schedule. He hadn't been alone with her since their little episode outside the network soundstage the day before last.

He'd mercifully put both Aurora and Vivian between them during Gaby's match that afternoon. Cowardly? Maybe. He thought of it as self-preservation.

She provoked the hell out of him in ways that made him crazy. He was constantly doing things, saying things, he'd never typically do or say. He'd thought—hoped—to have all that in perspective before spending the afternoon seated next to her today. She was unpredictable, and he knew he provoked her, too. He had no idea what she'd say or do in one of the most public forums on the planet, considering the millions who were watching the event all around the globe. He had no doubt they'd spend some time on camera today, probably more so than usual, given the tennis royalty he was seated next to.

But it surprised him more than a little to realize that some of the butterflies in his stomach had nothing to do with that, or the fact that his sister was playing in the quarterfinals of her very first Wimbledon . . . and everything to do with the woman seated next to him. And, even more alarming, the anxiety associated with those butterflies wasn't all bad.

"She's as ready as she can be," Tess replied. "I just talked to her in the waiting area and she's nervous, but in a good way. She's edgy and antsy and wound up. She wants to get out there and start hitting the ball, get into the match. You can't ask for more than that."

"Is that how it was for you?"

She glanced at him, obviously surprised. "Is this a trick question?"

He knew he deserved that, just as he knew he should let the whole matter drop right now. But his stomach was flipping around and Gaby hadn't even taken the court yet to warm up. He desperately needed a distraction from what was, so far, the biggest day in his sister's life, and his own, for that matter. He should be reflecting on the path they'd taken to get to this point, think about what this meant to them both.

He shouldn't be thinking about Tess, much less why she smelled so damn good.

"I'm asking because of Gaby," he said, perhaps a shade more tersely than necessary. Which didn't explain why he all but held his breath waiting for her reply. So he kept talking. Although it sounded suspiciously like babbling. He never babbled. "I'm excited for her and nervous as hell. You've been out there, done that. I was just wondering what it felt like for you." *Jesus, Max, you're such a moron. Calm the hell down.* "And, uh, if you think, based on your experience, that she's going to handle this okay." *Lame. So very, very lame.*

Tess held his gaze for a second or two longer, apparently trying to figure out what his angle was this time, or more likely what medication he was on, before she finally said, "I think we'll see all facets of Gaby today. I wouldn't be surprised if we get everything she's got, highs, lows, good and bad. She knows she's lucky in some ways to have made it this far, with a few higher seeds getting taken out by other players. But she's also worked damn hard for her spot in the final eight. She deserves to be down there, no matter how she plays today. But I'm guessing her feeling was much like mine in her place." She shot him a cocky grin. "Which was, Well damn, I've made it this far, why the hell not just take the whole damn thing?"

Max couldn't take his eyes off of her.

She broke eye contact first, and looked out across the expansive green grass court below. "She's going to have a lot to juggle out there today. Nerves, stress, the magnitude of playing on a stadium court in front of this many people . . . not to mention Hilstrom's monster serve."

She glanced at him, but wasn't really seeing him. And he

knew when she looked back out over the court again, she was remembering her own triumphs out there. Which had been many. And maybe the rare defeat, as well.

"You know, when you let yourself really, really want, you're forced to open yourself up to everything inside you. You have to be willing to leave it all out there, too, no matter how messy." She looked at him again, only this time she held his gaze directly. "It's the only way to get what you want. At least it's the only way for me."

Max found himself caught up in a way he hadn't anticipated. "Yeah. I think I know what you mean."

Tess blinked, then laughed a little and shifted in her seat, looking out over the stadium once again, and the general hubbub as people continued streaming in. "I think it will be that way with Gaby, too," she added, but a beat too late.

Max was still looking at her. She was definitely nervous and antsy, but if he wasn't mistaken, he might be the cause of just a little of that edginess now. He wasn't sure how that made him feel, but then a roar went up and he was automatically surging to his feet with everyone else as the players made their way onto the court.

"Oh, dear! My goodness. Pardon me, pardon me." Aurora stumbled as she made her way down the row to the players' area.

Vivian reached out to steady her. "Darling, if you don't watch where you're going, we're both going to make a very unseemly entrance directly onto the court." She snapped open the oriental fan she carried, which Max noted on a small groan perfectly matched the red, gold, and black silk track suit she wore. Not to mention the chopsticks she'd used to hold her flame-red chignon into place. *Oh, the cameras were just going to love this.* Quite possibly the most colorful players' box in the one-hundred-plus-year history of Wimbledon.

Again, as was happening far too often of late, he wondered precisely how his life had arrived at this exact moment. He'd pictured this day, imagined Gaby going for a grand-slam title on a big stage like this. He glanced sideways and sighed. He just hadn't imagined it would come with such . . . flamboyant company.

Vivian took her seat and flipped the fan in front of her face. "Although I dare say, darling, we do spruce up the place a bit. Far too much white for my taste. And mostly cotton, too. Haven't they heard of linen?" She sighed and arranged the folds of her gold-zippered jacket just so. "Honestly, these Brits have no idea how to liven things up."

"Well, I think you both look spectacular," Tess told her, then gave Aurora a hug. "I'm so glad you could make it."

"We wouldn't have missed it. So sorry Mercedes couldn't attend. She's not much for sitting out in the sun, you know," Aurora said.

"I offered her my umbrella." Vivian pulled out the matching horror from her bag, but mercifully left it furled. "She declined. Imagine."

Max sank back in his seat, thankful now he had Tess beside him. He'd use her as a blockade with absolutely no compunction whatsoever.

Aurora leaned past Tess to squeeze his knee, her rings biting into his skin. He'd have permanent scars before this was all said and done. "It's simply all too exciting, Max, dear, isn't it? I swear, I'm becoming addicted to their strawberries and cream here. Such a delightful tradition. You must be so proud."

Of the strawberries and cream? "Certainly," he said, opting for a vague response over one of any substance. He found where conversing with any of the godmothers was concerned, the more vague the better.

Aurora squeezed again, and he swallowed the wince, and the

breath of relief when she released her hold. "I'm sure she'll do fabulously well. This is her tournament to win, Max. Mark my words."

He smiled at her and resisted rubbing his now throbbing knee. "We're just really thankful to have made it this far. We both owe you a debt of gratitude."

Aurora waved him away. "Oh, pish posh." She grinned and leaned close to Tess. "A bit of London slang I picked up. I so love their use of the language here."

Max smiled despite himself. He couldn't help it, really. She was just too much.

"Being able to come see Gaby play her matches has been all the reward I need," Aurora told him, then she leaned closer to Tess and whispered just loud enough that he heard her anyway. "We need to talk. After the match, okay?"

Tess nodded. "Sure, no problem. Bobby doesn't play until tomorrow, so I'll catch a ride back with you and Vivi."

Max forced his attention down on the courts. Gaby had already taken a freshly strung racket from her bag and walked to her end of the court, which was right below them, so her back was to them. Inge Hilstrom, the number-two seed here, and the heavy favorite today, arrived at the far end a moment later. They started to warm up, hitting balls back and forth, moving their feet, getting the blood flowing. He wished he could see Gaby's face, but she was moving well, hitting smoothly. There wasn't any sign of nerves, despite the fact that she was playing on Court One.

The winner of this match moved into the semifinals. And a place on Centre Court. One step away from the title round. *Go get 'em, Gaby,* he silently urged. He was thrilled she'd made it this far and just hoped she played well, win or lose. But the moment, the occasion, was getting to him.

And like Tess said, with only two matches to go for the finals, why not hope a little?

The match started out a little rocky, with both players losing serve and making multiple unforced errors. Apparently, both Inge and Gaby were a little more nervous than they'd first appeared. But a half hour later, after some tense, long rallies, they'd tied it five games to five, and things began to settle down and get serious.

"Rally, dammit," Tess hissed under her breath. Her fingers were curled into fists, pressing into her knees, when she wasn't pounding on them in silent encouragement. "Don't go for the winner so damn early. You've got the stamina. Make her hit more balls. Let her make the mistake."

Max leaned forward as Gaby returned what appeared to be a clean winner to move up six games to five. Then came the call from the lines person. Wide. Point to Inge, which sent the game to its sixth deuce point. And Gaby past the boiling point.

She threw her hands up in the air and, after a glare of disgust at the offending lines person, turned to the chair where the umpire sat perched above the court. "It was on the line. Chalk flew. Check the mark," she demanded.

"It was wide, Miss Fontaine," the chair umpire calmly stated in his crisp British accent. "Please resume play."

Gaby tapped her toes, then stalked to the net. "It was in. You have to come check the mark."

The umpire merely stared her down. "Please. Resume play."

Gaby stared back, then finally turned away. Max breathed a sigh of relief, but it came a moment too soon. She was stalking back to the baseline when her racket went flying to the ground, hitting the spot where she'd stood to make her last serve. The crowd collectively inhaled, not happy with her tantrum. Gaby swore under her breath, but not quietly enough, as it turned out.

"The chair assesses Miss Fontaine a warning. Another will cost you a code violation and the point. Please resume play."

Gaby appeared to consider pushing her case, but the fans, the majority of whom had been surprisingly on her side against the popular higher seed, grew more restless the longer the game was delayed. Some of them began whistling, a fan form of jeering.

"Come on, Gabs, back to the line," Max murmured. "Keep your head in."

"She's fine. She needs to blow off steam. Settle down a bit. Trust me." She looked at Max and grinned. "Besides, the ball was clearly on the line. Watch the replay later. I'll put money on it. She was right to bark. It will serve her well later in the match. They've been put on notice; they'll watch more carefully."

Max didn't engage her on that particular debate. Too many times he'd watched players lose their cool, his sister included, then lose the game because they were so distracted by whatever injustice they perceived—wrongly or rightly—had been inflicted against them, their focus was no longer where it was supposed to be: on the court, on the next point to be played.

Gaby finally scooped up her racket and stepped back to the line. Then, after taking her sweet time readying herself, she lofted the ball . . . and delivered a blistering ace to regain the advantage. Tess smirked beside him as Gaby shot the umpire a sharp smile, then glanced up at their box before moving to take her next serve. Two minutes later, the game was called in her favor. She was one away from taking the set.

Unfortunately, Inge served well and held her game relatively easily, sending the players into a tiebreaker. It was a tense rally, with both players doing well. Gaby was obviously still upset, if the grunts she was making on every ball strike were any indication. But in no other way did her little meltdown adversely affect her game. In fact, she was playing more fiercely, more aggressively . . . and in the end, triumphed to take the first set.

With a mighty fist pump and a huge shout, Gaby turned to look up at them, a fierce look of determination on her young face.

Max gave her a thumbs-up, then applauded as she stalked over to her chair for a brief changeover before beginning the second set.

"I told you," Tess crowed as she leaned forward and applauded, too. She settled back in her seat and turned to him, smug smile curving her lips. "She is so on, baby. Game is on."

It shouldn't have been so infectious, her confidence, her enthusiasm, considering she was all but heckling him. Maybe it was her unshakable belief in Gaby that drew him in when he wanted to maintain his distance the most. "She's given herself some room," he allowed. "Now all she needs to do is keep her composure. Inge isn't going to fold and quietly go away."

Tess snorted. "Which is exactly why Gaby needs to keep the fires burning. It works for her, like it worked for me."

"So you're saying that giving in to your temper out there, slamming rackets around, haranguing the lines people, the chair umpire, never cost you your concentration? Never lost you the match?"

"A game, maybe. A match? Never." She didn't even pretend she had to think about it. Of course, to be fair, she'd likely been asked that same question numerous times. Understandable, given her fiery nature on the court. The phrase "a female McEnroe" had been used more than once.

Which brought him to his next point. "McEnroe self-destructed all the time when his temper got the better of him. What's to say it won't for Gaby?"

"You call it 'temper,' I call it 'passion for the game.' John was a phenomenal player, and sure, he could be petulant and at times definitely got too focused on what he perceived as personal slights and lost his game. But that was because it mattered so much. The game mattered, points mattered. Every single one. I'd wager more often than not, it was those outbursts that allowed him to keep going in such a dazzling manner. If he'd kept it all bottled up inside, he'd have lost more often." She patted him on the knee. "I know it's hard, having a sister who is so opposite your calm, cool, supremely collected self. But as much as you want her to be like you, she's not. If you want to help her, Max, focus on helping her improve her game. But stop trying to stifle her passion. She knows what she needs out there."

So, she thought he was cool, calm, collected. Ha. If she only knew. Calm? His stomach was currently in a knot of nerves as he watched Gaby play the biggest match of her life thus far. Cool? Quite the opposite. His entire body had gone on full alert even at Tess's casual touch of his knee. And collected? His head . . . hell, he didn't know where that was at.

Which probably explained why, when she went to take her hand away and turn back to the match, he impulsively covered it with his, keeping it right where it was.

Surprised, she looked first at their hands, then at him. "What?"

Good question, really. "No signaling from the stands. She'll get called for coaching."

"I wasn't sending her any signals. I wouldn't risk that."

Now Max smiled. "You? You'd risk anything if you thought it would get you the win."

"I'm not the one out there playing."

"Are you sure about that?"

She snatched her hand away then, and turned back to the game. When he just kept staring at her, she said, "Shut up and watch your sister return serve."

He'd intended his remark to be a teasing one. Hell, he hadn't known what he'd intended really. Regardless, it had clearly backfired. The thing about Tess that he admired was that, while she could dish it out, she took it just as well. Her verbal volleying skills were as sharp and well timed as her on-court volleys. She respected you more if you could hit a clean return winner.

Obviously he'd just sliced one down the line that had managed to cut too close to something.

"Yes!" she suddenly shouted, pumping her fist... and dragging his attention back where it should have been all along.

Gaby had just earned a break point against Inge's opening serve of the second set. He shifted in his seat, attention riveted on the court... and yet simultaneously hyperaware of every inch of the woman seated next to him. He really had to do something about that.

Inge's first serve pulled wide, so Gaby moved inside the baseline, anticipating a slower second serve.

"Return deep and come in," Tess said under her breath.

And, like they were somehow mentally linked, that's exactly what Gaby did.

"Yes," Tess hissed, fist pumping against her knee as Gaby sliced a sharp angle crosscourt, causing Inge to dive to her left... and miss.

Max applauded and found himself turning to Tess, sharing a celebratory grin and a quick high five. She smacked palms with him, then turned back to the match as Gaby prepared to serve. It took Max a second longer to do the same.

Gaby held her service game with relative ease. She had a powerful serve, but wasn't always consistent with placement, and had a tendency to go for too much on the second serve, which had earned her more than a few double faults. But she was in her zone out there today and everything she hit, no matter the angle, just seemed to find that sliver of space right inside the line.

"Man, it sucks to be Hilstrom right about now," Tess said with surprising sincerity.

Max glanced at her. "Compassion for the enemy?"

Instead of getting prickly like she had last time, she smiled easily. That was more the Tess he knew. And it struck him then. He did know Tess Hamilton . . . and somewhere along the line, she'd ceased to be the spoiled, rebellious party girl and had become something far more complex. And interesting. And more than a little intriguing.

"My opponent was never the enemy. She's just out there trying to do the same thing I am. The game is the enemy. Every ball, every point, you have a chance to do something, to use your skill to control the game. Sometimes your opponent is better at it than you are, is able to influence the outcome more than you can, but I never confused the two. Because opponents change. The game is always the game."

Max just stared at her, felt the smile spread across his face.

Her own lips quirked. "What? You afraid I'll teach Gaby to play the game and not her opponent?"

He didn't say anything, just shook his head slightly and turned his attention back to the court.

"People say you're enigmatic," she said, her tone teasing. "I think you just like jerking people's chains."

He could see her staring at him from the corner of his eye. So, she thought he was enigmatic, did she? His smile grew a little and he nudged her knee with his own. "Watch the point, Gaby's serving again."

He felt her gaze linger on him for another moment, then finally return to the game.

The match grew more intense as Inge renewed her determination and held on to her serve, then went on to break Gaby's, putting her squarely back into the match.

"Oh, dear," Aurora said, leaning forward to look at both Tess and Max. "She'll come back. You watch."

Max had almost forgotten about the godmothers, he'd been so caught up in his back and forth with Tess.

Vivian snapped her fan open and flicked it almost dismissively. "Hilstrom doesn't stand a chance. And honestly, she really should reconsider that hair color." She nudged Aurora. "We should talk with Valerie about working up something with the women's tour for next year during the grass-court season."

"I believe I mentioned that almost a month ago. Of course, you want it to be your idea and, honestly, I don't care, but I've already spoken to Mercy about it and she's working up the figures. If you want to take all the credit, however, far be it for me to steal your beloved spotlight." Aurora gave a dismissive, albeit somewhat wounded little sniff.

Vivian merely rolled her eyes. "Drama queen."

"Spotlight stealer."

Tess nudged Max's knee and the two of them shared dry smiles while the godmothers bickered.

Fifteen minutes later, the second set was tied at six games all and once again they were in a tiebreaker. All eyes were riveted on the match.

Gaby won the first point, then Inge went up two on her serve. Back and forth it went like that, neither player able to get a break to widen the margin to the necessary two points. At ten points all, Gaby finally found a corner shot that Inge couldn't reach, earning her a break point and her first chance to not only serve for the set, but for the match . . . and her place in the final four.

Tess grabbed Aurora's hand with her right and Max's hand with her left, and squeezed. "Come on, Gaby!"

Max squeezed back.

Gaby's first serve appeared to be right on the center line, but was called wide. Rather than regroup and hit her second serve, Gaby immediately contested the call.

"No, no, stay focused," Tess murmured.

Max shot her a quick glance. "What? Wasn't it you who just said—"

She shushed him. "Not now."

He wasn't sure if she meant him, or Gaby.

Inge stayed on the baseline and out of the ensuing argument.

The crowd, solidly with Gaby now, began to grow a little restless and a few catcalls and whistles began to start up. The Brits loved their underdogs, but they had little tolerance for histrionics.

"It was clearly on the line," Gaby insisted. "Do you need a new prescription for those glasses or what?"

She made a dramatic gesture with her racket hand and Max thought for sure she was going to fling it. Which would have resulted in her losing the point and sending them back to the tiebreaker and, most important, giving Inge a renewed sense of purpose, along with the emotional edge.

"Come on, Gabs, don't let it get to you now," he murmured. "One point, one point is all it will take."

The chair umpire held his cool and remained impassive in the face of Gaby's glare, but she finally backed down and sauntered back to the baseline. She took extra time, asked for different balls from the ball girl, then carefully selected the one she wanted.

"That's right," Tess urged quietly, "get your head together. Kill the ball, not the umpire."

As tense as the moment was, Max found himself fighting a smile. "You teach her that particular maxim?"

She just squeezed his hand harder and said nothing. A quick glance showed her face to be every bit as battle ready as Gaby's.

He turned his attention back to the court and watched his sister bounce the ball on the grass surface. *You can do it. Come on.*

She lofted the ball in the air, and it was as if every last person in the stands held their collected breath. She swung her racket with stinging precision and sent the ball screaming over the net. Kill the ball, indeed.

Miraculously, Inge guessed right and stabbed her racket out just in time to make contact.

Gaby was forced to run hard to the opposite end of the baseline, but made a blistering return.

Inge was there, hitting it right back.

"Pace it, pace it," Tess said. "Wait for your moment, keep her pinned back there."

And once again, it was as if the two of them had some sort of mental lock. Gaby did exactly that, running Hilstrom from side to side like a master puppeteer, until she was finally given a short ball to come in on, which she did with a vengeance. A split second later it was over. Gaby had won. In straight sets. She was in the Wimbledon semifinals.

Max and Tess leaped to their feet in exultation, pumping their fists at Gaby as she leaped about in the air. Then, as she jogged to the net to shake hands with her opponent, Max caught Tess up in an impulsive hug.

Somehow, with her eyes shining up into his, smile beaming so wide with absolute joy, he couldn't help himself. He was lowering his mouth to hers before he even considered what the hell he was doing. Or more important, where. Even more shocking, she let him.

Which, perhaps, was why it went on perhaps a tad too long as the stadium rocked and rolled around them.

And it was a snapshot of that exact moment that ran next to Gaby's exultant leap in every paper in London the following morning.

Chapter 22

CONFESS, TESS!

Aurora scanned the screaming headline of *Good Day* and smiled. "Clever," she said, pushing it aside to look at the next paper. And the next. All featuring the same photo of Max and Tess in a hard-to-deny passionate kiss. Now that was chemistry. She sipped her morning tea and waited for one or the other of them to descend and join her in Sir Robin's breakfast room, still debating how she wanted to handle things this morning.

Gaby was the first to arrive. "Good morning, Aurora! Fantastic day, isn't it?" She all but skipped over to the sideboard where a buffet had been laid out for them, as it was every morning.

Now here was someone who knew how to seize the moment, Aurora mused. If only Gaby could get her older sibling to do the same. Well, do more of the same, anyway. Max had made the first move, after all. "Why, yes it is," she agreed cheerfully. "I know we've gushed and gushed, but I must say it again, that was a tremendous victory yesterday, Gabrielle. We're all so proud of you."

Gaby busily filled her plate until it was heaping. "God, I'm starving. I couldn't eat anything yesterday for fear I'd lose all of it. Then last night I just couldn't settle down enough, which is a shame since that was such a great restaurant Max found for our celebration dinner. Now I feel like I could eat a horse."

Aurora paused in buttering a piece of toast, smiled briefly, and continued. "Well, you need to keep up your strength. Tomorrow is a big day, after all."

"God, I know." She twirled around, somehow managing not to lose everything on her plate. "Semifinals, can you believe it? I'm still not believing it." Gaby pulled out the chair across from Aurora and flopped down. "Has Max been down here yet?"

"No, not yet. Nor Tess."

"She won't be here this morning," Gaby said, crunching a piece of bacon. "I thought you knew." She polished off that piece and two more, then washed it all down with a half a glass of orange juice.

Oh, to be young and have that lovely metabolism again, Aurora thought with an inward sigh. "No, dear, I didn't. Has she already gone out? I thought she'd barely gotten in."

Gaby nodded her head as she finished a buttered scone. "I was up early, couldn't sleep. I saw her heading out around seven. Said she had a meeting out at the grounds. Someone named Alan something or other." She shrugged. "Then she's going to watch Bobby and Tim play their match. I'm meeting her over there in between for some practice time. Then we might do a bit more here this evening when she gets back." When Aurora looked up, she added, "Don't worry, we have the second slot tomorrow, so I'll have plenty of time to rest."

Aurora wisely said nothing, leaving that realm to Tess. She

reached for the teapot and refilled her cup, unable not to notice that Gaby was all but vibrating while she ate. Maybe it wouldn't be a bad idea for her to burn some of that excess energy off. Just sitting across the table from her could exhaust a person.

"So, has Max seen those yet?" Gaby asked around a bite of sausage. She reached across the table and slid one of the papers closer and skimmed the headlines.

Aurora should have been more circumspect, she supposed, but it wasn't like Gaby was going to get through the day without seeing them anyway. And, after all, she'd been there to witness it firsthand. Last night over their celebration dinner, Gaby had been anything but shy in her attempts to goad Tess and Max into a reprise of the now infamous kiss. Of course, Aurora wasn't entirely sure Gaby's motives weren't a bit mixed.

She really wished she'd had the chance to talk to Tess about Gaby's little conversation with her the other evening. She planned to talk to Max, too, as she'd promised Gaby she would, but she'd wanted Tess's input first. She'd hoped to find out a little bit more about the young man who'd caught Gaby's eye. However, they'd all headed off to dinner, with Tess and Max keeping about as much distance between them as humanly possible in a party of five. Disappointing, that. But Aurora wasn't about to let them safely retreat to opposite corners. Enough was enough. Tess had left straight from the restaurant, with Vivian in tow, and disappeared for the rest of the evening, and Max and Gaby had gone off to their wing shortly after arriving home.

So Aurora had reluctantly let it go for the evening, thinking she'd have plenty of opportunity today. Now, however, that wasn't looking too promising, either. How on earth was she supposed to play matchmaker if half of her match kept disappearing on her? Perhaps she'd just have to corner Max for a few minutes at some point and have a little chat. With Gaby twenty-four hours away from playing in her first grand-slam semifinal, probably the last thing on her mind was Royce, or Rance, or whatever his name was. But Aurora would feel better knowing she'd spoken to Max about it. Besides, it would give her an opportunity to work Tess into the conversation, get the lay of the land, so to speak.

Feeling a bit cheerier about her day's prospects, she was just helping herself to a third scone when Max wandered in, fighting a yawn.

"Hey there, sleepyhead. About time," Gaby told him as she scooted her chair back.

Aurora was astonished to note that Gaby's plate was already empty. And she was heading back for seconds. Not an ounce of fat on her, either. Even as a teenager, Aurora had never been exactly willowy. Age hadn't helped in that department. She picked up her scone, then thought better of it and put it back on the tray with a resigned sigh.

"Good morning," she said to Max. "You still look a bit weary. I suppose it was hard to unwind after all the excitement yesterday." She was referring to more than Gaby's spectacular win, and Max likely knew that. Aurora hadn't been exactly shy in nudging the two together the previous night, every chance she got. And Vivian had been downright shameless. Stubborn, those two. Why they were fighting this so hard, she had no idea. Seemed like the perfect match to her. Half of England thought so, too, if the papers were anything to judge by.

Speaking of which, she noticed his gaze fall on the stack. She watched him closely, trying to gauge his mood as he skimmed over the top headline. Darn it, she wished Tess had stayed around this morning. Defenses were lower earlier in the day. Ah well, nothing worthwhile came easily, as the saying went.

"Cute headline, I thought," Aurora ventured, when his expression remained unmoved. "Though I rather liked that 'Mad For Max' line they used earlier in the week. Cheeky, those Brits, eh?"

"So are you going to ask her out or what?" Gaby said, now crunching apple slices.

Max blinked and looked up, seemingly coming out of a momentary haze.

That, at least, was promising, Aurora noted.

"Ask who?"

Gaby rolled her eyes. "Please. Tess, of course. Come on." She gestured to the papers. "You had her in a lip-lock in front of the entire country. Don't tell me that was fabricated by the papers, because I was there, remember?"

"Oh, I remember, all right," he mumbled, then abruptly turned and shuffled to the sideboard, keeping his back to both of them.

Unlike most mornings, his hair was a bit mussed and he had yet to shave. He was usually casually but crisply attired at breakfast, in khaki shorts and a polo shirt. This morning he had on a faded U.S. Open T-shirt that looked like he'd slept in it. For that matter, so did the shorts.

Aurora sipped her tea to hide her smile. All signs of a restless night. And she doubted he'd lost sleep worrying about Gaby. Aurora knew he was thrilled his sister had made it this far. Which meant it was highly likely Max had tossed and turned thinking about something else. Or someone.

"Gaby, I called a car to take you over to the grounds for practice."

Gaby paused midbite. "You're not going with me? We always drive over together."

"I'll be over there, but I have a few other things to do this morning."

Gaby shot a wink at Aurora that her brother couldn't see.

"Okay, sure. Do you have a meeting with 'Alan,' too?" she asked, making air quotes with her fingers.

He glanced over his shoulder. "Alan who?"

Gaby giggled. "Whatever. You go to your 'meeting.' I'll be fine."

Max looked at her a moment longer, slightly bewildered, then shrugged and went back to staring at the sideboard. "Good," he said absently. "That's good."

Aurora noted he'd yet to put a single thing on his plate. Restless night. Distracted. Loss of appetite. Oh yes, her morning was getting better by the moment. Now she just had to track Tess down at some point. "Perhaps I'll ride to the grounds with Gaby. Maybe Tess can get me in to see Bobby's match. I'd love to get the chance to watch him play. And, of course, any excuse for another round of their delightfully sinful strawberries and cream."

"That would be great," Gaby said, bouncing in her seat. "Give us a chance to talk." She scooted her chair back. "I think I'll go take a shower." She made silent signals to Aurora, motioning to Max, still standing behind her, and mouthing, "don't forget to talk to him about you-know-who."

Aurora nodded and calmly sipped her tea as Gaby exited the breakfast room, leaving her alone with a still distracted Max. Looked like she had her day's work cut out for her. She smiled. Her favorite kind of work, too.

"So, I can't promise who I'm going to team you up with yet. I may end up using you down in the stands, on the grounds, doing one-on-one interviews with players, their friends, family members, what have you. I want you in the booth, too, don't get me wrong. We'll just see how everything plays out." Alan grinned. "You were right, you are a hot commodity. Our ratings have never been better during the first week. I think if we play this right, we can have a long, profitable working relationship."

Tess tried to keep still in her seat, when what she wanted to do was dance and shout. "Speaking of profitable, Alan," she began, sending him her brightest smile. "You've obviously got me interested, so why don't we talk numbers?" *Play it cool, don't be too eager.* But it was darn near impossible. This was the answer to all of her prayers, and a few she hadn't even thought about.

Alan pulled his briefcase up and put it on the table between them. They were seated in a small office near the players' lounge that he'd borrowed from the Club so they could speak in private. "I was hoping to get the chance to talk to your business manager, or whoever handles these matters for you."

That brought her up short, but only for a second. "Since retiring, I've handled my own negotiations. Of course, my attorney vets all my contracts." Or would. As soon as she hired a new one.

Alan perked up at that news. Corporate types hated working directly with the talent. They wanted their legal department to work with the people on the other end who spoke the same language they did. "Well, I'll get that information from you and get the paperwork sent out as soon as the event is over and we're all back in the States."

Tess's smile took on a sharper edge. "All wonderful, to be sure, but aren't we jumping the gun here a little bit? I'd like to know what the offer is exactly."

"Certainly, certainly." Alan snapped open his briefcase and pulled out a sheaf of papers. "I had this drawn up, preliminary figures, mind you, just to give you an idea of what we're looking at. Once your lawyer looks over the contract itself, we can certainly discuss any particulars that might concern you, but I think you'll be very happy with our offer." He slid the papers across the table.

Tess kept her game face firmly in place as she skimmed past the part that outlined the various events she'd be expected to attend. They'd already gone over most of that. She'd be on the road at least two weeks out of every month during the season, which lasted almost the entire year. At times she'd have to travel more often, especially in the weeks leading up to and including the four slams. She didn't mind. It wasn't much different than her life before, when she was still on tour.

Surprisingly, it wasn't flashes of her own career highlights that leaped immediately to mind, followed by the inevitable little clutch in her gut. No, the first image that had popped into her thoughts had been one of Gaby, yesterday, leaping around on the court, exultant, knowing she'd just earned a spot in the final four of her first Wimbledon. As hard as it had been for Tess to sit in the stands while someone else was down there fighting it out, there had been something intensely gratifying in seeing Gaby win.

There had been that moment during the match, when she'd come into the net as Tess had instructed her to do, and won the point... then turned and immediately looked up into the players' box and locked eyes with Tess. That small grin they'd shared. Like no one else could possibly understand how great that particular moment felt but the two of them. And in that moment, Tess hadn't felt as removed from the battle as before. She'd felt... she'd felt as close to the game as she supposed she was ever going to feel again.

"So, what do you think?"

Tess blinked and looked up at Alan, nonplussed for a moment, before pulling herself back together. She quickly flashed him her trademark smile, then looked back down at the sheaf of papers. "I've learned not to skim the fine print."

Alan chuckled, but it was the confident laugh of a man who

knew he'd closed the deal, so was quite willing to be patient if need be.

And when Tess turned to the next page and saw the number of zeroes on the bottom line, she realized why he felt so sure of himself. She swallowed hard as the excitement of the moment once again threatened to overwhelm her. She hadn't realized just how worried she'd been that she wouldn't pull out a win when she needed it most. But now, seeing the result of all of her planning and strategizing since coming to London, and all the stress leading up to coming here, as she'd sold off everything she had to stay afloat . . . it was as if she'd just won the biggest grand-slam trophy of her entire life. And perhaps she had.

Somehow, she managed to keep her cool-and-casual demeanor, as if she fielded offers like this every day. Which, in the not so distant past, had actually been the case. "Of course, my attorney will have to go over this and decipher all the legalese and such." She looked up, flashed him a smile. "But unless there's something in here that I'm missing, it looks like we should be able to hammer something out."

She might have squandered her money once she had it, but she was no dummy when it came to making it. She was going to take this offer, and she was pretty sure Alan knew she was going to take this offer, but there would be some room for negotiation—there always was. So why settle? Neither side expected the first offer to be the binding one.

"I couldn't be happier," Alan responded. Translation: "I have a big legal department, too, fire when ready."

"Great. Can I take this with me?" she asked, picking up the stack of papers and pushing her chair back.

"Absolutely." Alan pushed his chair back, too, and they both stood. He extended his hand, and Tess enthusiastically shook it. "I'm thrilled to have you as a member of our little network family."

"I'm thrilled to have the chance to join in the fun."

"We'll get in touch sometime later next week, once this hoopla is over and we're all back home for a short break."

"I'll be sure to get you the information on my attorney before I leave London." With this contract offer in hand, hiring the best was not going to be a problem.

"Excellent." He walked around the table and motioned for her to lead them to the door. "So, I suppose you have a busy day lined up?"

"Yes, practice session with Gabrielle, then my brother is playing in the doubles semis this afternoon."

"Yes, yes, I noted that he and his partner were still very much in the thick of things here. Well done," he said, adopting the British phrase, despite the fact that he was from Los Angeles.

"I'm really excited for him," she said, as he leaned past her and opened the door.

"One thing," Alan said, stopping her just as she was about to step into the hallway. "Your business relationship with the Fontaines?"

"Yes?" Tess stepped a bit back in the doorway, as the noise coming from the players' lounge next door filled the hallway.

"I assume this goes without saying—and without knowing the exact nature of your agreement with them, you'll have to pardon me if I'm overstepping here—but we'll expect you'll be severing whatever business ties you may have with them before adopting your duties with us. Conflict of interest and all that." He smiled. "Not to mention we'll be keeping you a little too busy to be offering support to individual players."

"Of course," she said. It was something she already knew would be expected of her. "I'm only helping Gaby through this event. So by Sunday, whatever the outcome, we'll no longer be working together." Again, there was that pang. But of course it was natural to feel a little sad. Tess had grown to care about Gaby, and she would definitely be following her career with a bit more personal interest than before. Fortunately, her own new career would provide her with ample opportunity to do just that. If she was lucky, perhaps she'd even get the chance to call one of Gaby's matches in the near future. It was a win-win, really.

So why was there a lingering twinge of melancholy at the thought of Gaby being out there on the court, looking up in the stands at some other coach? Of course, Tess would do her best to help Gaby, and Max, select a really good replacement. And yet . . .

"Excellent," Alan told her. "I'd best get back to the booth. Come up and see us anytime you get the chance."

She nodded as he snapped his briefcase shut and stepped past her into the hallway. With one last hearty handshake, he headed the opposite direction, leaving her thoughts still on Gaby. She stared down at the papers in her hand, and thought about everything this contract would mean to her. "Money issues all solved," she murmured. Still, she wasn't as completely thrilled as she thought she'd be, all things considered.

"Well, well, isn't this a delicious bit of a coincidence. Was that Alan Chapman I just saw leaving you . . . and with an interesting bit of paperwork, it looks like."

Startled, Tess snatched the papers up and turned around to face one of her least favorite people. "Why hello, Fionula, who let you into the chicken coop?"

As this was typical in tone of most of their off-the-record dialogue, Fionula merely smiled. "And eggs seem to be hatching everywhere today."

Tess kept her expression seamless. "No doubt. If you'll excuse me, I have a practice session to get to. A closed practice session," she added pointedly.

"No comment on your tawdry little public display? Everyone is buzzing."

Tess bit the inside of her cheek, and hoped that it passed for a casual smile. "Only in your world would a sincere expression of emotion and celebration between two adults constitute as anything tawdry. Now if you'll excuse me."

Fionula shifted only slightly, but enough that Tess would have had to get her to move in order to get by her. "Care to comment on your little meeting? Tongues will be wagging."

By which Fionula meant that if Tess didn't explain, she would be more than happy to get those tongues wagging by speculating in print on what had gone on behind closed doors. And it went without saying her speculation would be far more sensational than anything that might have actually taken place. The word "tawdry" came to mind once again.

"No, I don't," Tess said. Alan would hold a press conference at some point, probably at the next event he was covering, to announce her joining the network sports team. He would love to do it here, however with only a few days left, they both needed more than a handshake agreement before making such an announcement. "But thanks ever so much for whatever yellow journalism you'll print to get the revenue up for your, gee, what was that word I was looking for? Oh yes, your 'tawdry' little paper."

"I'd hardly consider *Good Day* tawdry. We have a circulation of over a quarter of a million copies."

"Then I suppose we both need to reconsider our definition of the word, don't we?" Point to Tess, game over. She didn't wait for Fionula to move, but brushed past her and kept on walking. *Well,* she thought, *that was going to make for interesting reading tomorrow.*

This morning's interesting reading floated through her mind. She'd loved seeing the picture of a beaming Gaby, fists clenched in victory. She wasn't sure how she felt about the other picture. Hell, she still wasn't sure how she'd felt about the kiss itself. Or Max.

She hadn't expected it, which, along with being caught up in the moment with everyone else in the stands, was probably why she'd kissed him back. In some ways it had been over so fast, it was like she'd done it in a dream or something. But in other ways, when she let them, little things filtered into her consciousness. The way his mouth had felt on hers. Warm. Confident. Dedicated. And there was that thing he'd done again, tightening his hold on her, keeping her where he wanted her when she might have shifted back. Or would have, probably, if he hadn't been holding her so tightly. She might have clung a little, too. She had a distinct memory of digging her fingertips into his back, which was more muscled than she'd have thought. But that had merely been for balance, because he'd caught her off guard and all.

Christ. Who was she trying to kid? She'd enjoyed every last second of it. And it was pretty much all she'd thought about since. She just didn't know what in the hell to do about it. In a few days the tournament would be over and they'd all go their separate ways. She would miss Gaby. More than she'd realized, if her reaction a moment ago had been any indication. And she'd miss Max, too. She felt like maybe she was just finally starting to get to know him. But that was life, right?

So, as per her usual modus operandi when it came to personal matters she didn't feel like dealing with, she'd just avoided the whole thing. Unfortunately, it wasn't like the old days when she could escape by hiding out on a court somewhere. Even when said court was in a stadium seating ten thousand screaming fans. She knew how to solve any problems she encountered out there. It was the off-court problems that gave her a little trouble.

Dinner had been a study of awkward discomfort. They'd both gone out of their way to not even make eye contact, much less small talk. And yet she couldn't keep from darting looks at him when she thought he wasn't looking. Wondering what he was thinking, had he regretted the kiss that would surely be splashed across a front page or two . . . or did he maybe want to kiss her again?

She was being ridiculous, really. Like she was Gaby's age again, or something. But still . . . She hadn't even planned on going out last night, but heading back to Wexley, knowing Max was under the same roof thinking God only knew what kind of thoughts . . . she'd taken Vivian up on her offer to do the town. And then there was her morning meeting, so she'd avoided him at breakfast, too. But now it was practice time. She thought she'd have her act together by now and the whole matter firmly sorted out in her mind.

It had merely been a nice little interlude while it lasted, burned off a bit of that sexual tension they'd somehow managed to build up despite sniping at each other all the damn time. And yes, it got all of England and perhaps half of Europe absolutely convinced they were shacking up at Sir Robin's place. But since she'd be walking out of his life in a few days, all the buzz would die down, no doubt replaced by the next salacious bit of celebrity gossip, and they'd both be free to continue on with their lives as if it had never happened.

As it turned out, it wasn't Max who greeted her at the practice court with Gaby, but Aurora instead.

"What a nice surprise," Tess told her as she encountered the two of them waiting just inside the building doorway for the security escort through the fans to their practice court.

"I'm getting all the behind-the-scenes scoop today," Aurora bubbled. "It was so nice of Max to arrange for my pass." She took Tess's arm. "He was sorry he couldn't be here, he had some other business to attend to." She held Tess's gaze for a moment, in a meaningful way that Tess completely ignored.

"Good," Tess finally responded.

Aurora looked a little disappointed at her lackluster response. "So, what brought you down here so early today?"

Tess debated briefly about telling her, but Gaby was hovering and it really wasn't the right moment. "Oh, just a bit of business that came up. Good news, actually." She sent a telling look past Aurora's shoulder to where Gaby stood, chatting with the cute young security guard. "I'll tell you about it later."

Aurora smiled. "That would be lovely. We need to do a bit of catching up, you and I."

Tess wasn't sure exactly what that meant, but she was anxious to get through the gauntlet and out to the practice court. "Sure. No problem. I promise."

"I was hoping that perhaps you could find a way to finagle me a spot in the box with you during Bobby's match today. I would so love to see him play. And that would give us more time."

Tess's brow furrowed. Aurora seemed awfully intent on something. More than likely something about Max, given that Aurora had been almost as bad as the teenager at dinner last night, trying to maneuver them together. Well, she was going to have to wait a bit longer to try and work her matchmaking wiles on Tess today.

"I'm certain we can get you a seat, and I'd love the company."

"Are you ready, miss? Madam?" the guard asked them politely. "We should head out."

"All ready," Tess assured him, smiling in relief. "Aurora, you stay in the middle and Gaby and I will bring up the rear." She leaned close to Gaby when she stepped back beside her. "You ready? It's going to be a little crazy out there today, all things considered. Just smile, nod, but no questions, no autographs.

We'll see how practice goes, how frenzied it is out there, then maybe a few signatures afterward. Then home."

"Okay," Gaby said, surprising Tess with her easy acquiescence. She was all but bouncing on the balls of her feet. "I'm ready. Hey, where's Petra? Who's hitting with me today?"

Tess grinned, and it was the first time all morning that she felt it all the way down to her toes. "You're playing in your first slam semis tomorrow. You'll be practicing with me."

Chapter 23

The Glass Slipper limo door opened and Max automatically scooted over to make room for Gaby. Only it was Tess who slid in. He leaned forward as she quickly closed the door behind her to keep out the rain. "Where's Gaby?"

"You bumming my ride?" Tess asked at the same time, obviously just as surprised to see him as he was to see her. "Since when do you use Aurora's limo service?"

Ever since our kiss in the players' box was plastered all over England, he wanted to tell her. He'd sent Gaby ahead in the limo for practice earlier in the day so she could have the privacy she needed to stay focused. Her win yesterday had elevated her celebrity status even more. He'd known he'd get a bit more interest because of being Gaby's manager, and perhaps a lot more because of the renewed focus on the state of his relationship with Tess Hamilton, but he hadn't quite counted on just how much until he'd tried to pull his car into the car park earlier and had been all but mobbed by media and fans alike.

"I thought I'd catch a ride back with Gaby," he told her. "Where is she?"

Tess frowned. "She's going out with Aurora and the other godmothers for high tea and a little shopping. I thought you knew."

"She's *what?*" Max pressed the intercom button. "Driver—"

"Don't bother," Tess told him, "they've already gone." She leaned back in her seat, still damp from her short run through the rain to get to the limo. Her hair was stuck to her cheeks and forehead, but she didn't bother to do anything about it. She wore the same shorts and T-shirt she'd had on out on the practice court earlier, only now they were damp and clinging to her skin. Her long legs sprawled out between them, all tanned and toned.

His body stirred and he made himself look away. "Never mind," he told the driver, then released the intercom. "So, did you set up that little adventure?" His tone was a little terse, but then, wasn't that exactly the kind of thing Tess would do? "She needs to stay on track for tomorrow. The last thing she needs is to be gallivanting all over London. She could be mobbed."

Tess just stared at him, arms folded.

"Okay. All right." He made himself hold her gaze. "I'm sorry," he said. And he meant it.

"Wow. That must have hurt."

He sighed. What was it about her that brought out the worst in him? Or maybe he was just subconsciously sabotaging any chance he had to be himself with her. "So tell me, what exactly is going on?"

Tess shrugged. "You've got me. I can only guess, with the godmothers' hand in this, they're trying to play matchmaker again."

He couldn't tell from the tone of her voice how she felt about that particular idea, so he opted to say nothing.

"Gaby and I went into the players' locker room to wait out the rain, see if we could get back on the practice court," Tess went on. "When that didn't look like it was going to happen, Aurora got the idea to take Gaby out for high tea and contacted Vivian and Mercedes."

"And you weren't going to go along?"

"Believe it or not, I do have some common sense. The godmothers are very good at what they do. Spiriting Gaby out for the afternoon for tea won't be that much of a challenge. Trust me when I say that Gaby will enjoy herself in privacy. But keeping me incognito is another story. And me and Gaby in public together was just asking for trouble." She gave him a pointed stare. "As the closest thing she has to a coach, I wanted to make sure she had a nice time, got a little break, but also kept her focus. We agreed that if the weather clears, they'll get her home in time so we can practice at Wexley later on."

Max blew out a breath. He wasn't happy with this little turn of events, and Aurora's high-handedness, but he knew she was probably hoping for this exact thing to happen. Max and Tess alone together. And though he had no idea what he was going to do with the opportunity they'd presented him with... he couldn't say he was exactly upset about it. "I shouldn't have jumped to conclusions. Knee-jerk reaction. I should know better by now."

"And here I was just getting used to you always thinking the worst of me." She shifted her gaze out the window. With the rain running down the tinted glass there wasn't much to see, but apparently that was preferable to looking at him.

He couldn't say he blamed her.

Max watched her for a moment or two longer. She was right. He was always jumping to the worst conclusion where she was concerned. Initially it had been to protect Gaby. But he'd known for some time now that she had Gaby's best interest at heart every bit as much as he did. She might have different ideas on how to handle things like media scrutiny and the like, but she'd never once jeopardized Gaby's training schedule or anything else.

He'd also started to see the real woman behind the bad-girl image . . . and he was undeniably intrigued. He understood that it was a lot harder for her, this new life she'd entered into, than she let on to anyone. She was trying to find her way, just like the rest of them. And doing him and his sister a huge favor in the meantime. Yes, he was very intrigued. And undeniably attracted. Hence that stupid, impulsive kiss yesterday.

But the bottom line was, she was Tess Hamilton, tennis superstar. In a few days' time, she would flit off to some other world event and leave the two of them behind.

Gaby was going to really miss her. But even harder to admit was how much he was going to miss her, too. He'd gotten used to having her bubbling enthusiasm around, and he even liked her somewhat jaded view of the world. Yet she was always optimistic, always upbeat. Hell, he even liked sparring with her. The truth was, he looked forward to it. She kept him on his toes. He never knew exactly what to expect. Every time he was around her, he was more aware, more alive. Just . . . more.

Maybe he was still so insistent on finding that bad side of her because that would make it easier to let her walk away.

"I don't think the worst of you, you know," he said quietly. When she said nothing and kept her gaze locked on the window, he nudged her foot with his. "I wanted to. Would have made things a lot easier. But I was wrong about you."

That had her looking at him, surprise and wariness both on her face. "Oh?" Her lips quirked. "Gee. Where is the media when you really need them? This is the front-page moment right here." She laughed, but there wasn't much humor in it.

"They're trying to paint us as some hot couple. If they only knew the real story, huh?"

Just let it go, he schooled himself. *Let the moment go.* She's out of your life in three days. *You apologized, you made peace. Leave the rest alone.*

And yet, somehow, where Tess was involved, impulse always seemed to rule the day.

"What is the real story?" he asked her.

Judging from her expression, that had caught her off guard. Good. He didn't want to be the only one sitting here with sweaty palms and a heartbeat that wasn't quite regular.

"What do you mean, 'what is the real story'?"

Of course she'd lob it back in his court. He'd hoped she'd answer, at least give him some guidance on just how big a fool he was about to make of himself. "I guess what I mean is... we've been dancing around each other for the past twenty-four hours and going out of our way to pretend nothing happened yesterday. Like it was just another fabrication of the press or something. Why is that, do you suppose?"

She shifted in her seat a little, and for the first time since he'd known her, she didn't look so confident and in control. He'd seen her nervous for Gaby. He'd seen her grapple with the emotions stemming from her new view from the sidelines of a game she'd dominated in the not so distant past. But he'd never quite seen her like this—not meeting his gaze, fingers tangled in her lap, the toes of her sneakers tapping against each other.

It was on the tip of his tongue to just tell her to forget he'd brought it up. To save them both from this conversation. But it was hard to speak and hold his breath at the same time.

Finally she looked up, met his gaze. Her eyes were darker than he'd ever recalled seeing them. A deep sea-green. Christ, now he was being poetic. He was a goner. Truly a goner.

"You kissed me back," he blurted. *Oh, great move, you idiot. How smooth are you?* His teenage sister was right. He had to get a life. She probably had smoother moves than he did. God, that was an image he didn't need at the moment. "Why?" he asked, trying desperately to sound casual, as if this were nothing more than a business conversation.

She didn't look away. And when she tipped her chin up, ever so slightly, he relaxed a little. This was the Tess Hamilton he knew. That vulnerable Tess he'd just gotten a glimpse of scared him a little. He knew how to handle the bold, brash Tess. He couldn't get them back on their proper footing, but he knew he could count on her to do that for them both.

So, prepared for some smart-ass response, it was a bit of a shock when she said, "Because I wanted to."

He swallowed. Hard.

"In fact, I'd been thinking about it for a while."

Palms, sweatier. Heartbeat, thundering. Throat, completely dry. "Yeah," he managed. She'd put it out there. It was only fair he did the same. "Me, too."

And then she smiled. It was a slow, sweet curving thing that lit up her whole face and brought the sparkle back to her eyes. "God, we're a disaster, aren't we?"

"Why do you say that?"

She laughed a little, only this time it filled him with warmth. Like he wasn't already on fire. But this warmed him somewhere else, somewhere deep inside.

"It's just, here we are, successful, talented, worldly, with at least a certain amount of sophistication. We're single, not altogether hard on the eyes, and I doubt either of us ever had to work too hard to find a date on any given night."

"Speak for yourself," he said wryly.

"Oh, that's only because you don't try. And I thought *I* took my job too seriously at times." She waved away his attempt to respond. "You have dated, right? On the rare occasion?"

"Yes, but they were never—"

"Just answer the question. Were you ever turned down for a date?"

He had to stop for a second. "No, I guess not. But it was usually business."

She barked out a laugh. "For you, maybe. But this just proves my overall point."

"Which is?"

She settled back in her seat, and let her feet rest against his. "That we're both kind of screwups when it comes to anything resembling an actual relationship. Sure, we can date, we can mingle, we can socialize. Some of us can actually fling." She paused for a second. "What, no snarky comment about my less than savory social past?"

Other than the irrational jealousy he suddenly felt for a raft of guys he didn't know and had never met? No. "Just finish making your point."

The corner of her mouth tilted a bit, and she looked like she wanted to call him on that, but she went on. "I'm just saying we don't know how to have normal, long-term relationships. It's easy to date when it doesn't matter. But when it comes to figuring out stuff when it does matter, well, we are rather inept."

"Maybe. But I think the kind of lives we lead make long-term arrangements difficult. That more than anything else is why I don't date a lot. And maybe why you 'fling,' as you say. What else is there, given our schedules?"

She held his gaze for a moment, and his heart skipped a beat. But then she said, "Bobby figured it out. Other players have figured it out. It can be done."

"Maybe we've been too busy focusing on other things."

"Maybe." She glanced down at her hands, then back up at him, then back down at her hands again.

She was nervous. And for whatever reason, that helped him to relax. "So . . . are you saying that it matters?"

She shrugged her shoulders, kept her gaze in her lap. "I'm saying that maybe that's why we've been so obnoxious with each other. It's like we're suddenly in the schoolyard and you're pulling my pigtails and I'm shooting spitballs at you because we don't know what to do with this other stuff we seem to rile up in each other. So we punch the buttons we do know how to handle instead."

Max grinned now. "Are you saying I rile you up?"

She shot him a look, snorted. "When haven't you riled me up? It's like your life's mission or something."

His smile stayed in place. But he didn't. He shifted across the space between them and sat beside her. Her eyes widened in surprise, and maybe a teeny bit in alarm, but she stayed where she was. "I'm not talking about that kind of riled."

She held his gaze for what felt like an eternity. "Neither was I."

He thought his heart might pound right out of his chest. "So what are we going to do about this lapse in our social development?"

"Ignoring it doesn't seem to be working out too well."

"No," he agreed. "No, it doesn't."

"There's Gaby to consider," Tess said, clearly looking for anything to hang on to.

Max noted the way her eyes went darker as he shifted even closer. "Who is second only to Aurora in playing matchmaker."

"You know," she said, shifting toward him, "I'm not going to be around much longer."

"Only if you don't want to be." He bent his head down toward hers.

She pulled back slightly. "What do you mean?"

"Well, you could keep coaching Gaby, travel with us. But I really don't want to talk business—"

"We need to talk, Max. I need to tell you someth—"

"Tess, for once, business later. Come here." He slid his hand around the back of her head and tilted her mouth up to his. "I've been dying to do this pretty much from the moment I stopped doing it yesterday." He kissed her, gently at first. "And call me greedy, but I want you all to myself. No cameras, no crowd."

She murmured against his lips as he kissed her again, then gave up and let him kiss her. Slowly, almost shyly, she shifted a little to allow them both a better fit. He felt her fingertips skate across the back of his neck, tentatively.

This wasn't the Tess he knew. The feel of her touching him, the way her skin warmed beneath his touch, the scent of her shampoo as he pulled her to him and damp strands of her hair slid across his face, all combined to drive him wild. He took the kiss deeper, heard her make a noise, deep in her throat, which drove him to take it even further.

He pushed her back, and they slowly slid down onto the leather bench seat. And then she was opening for him, letting him take the kiss deeper, her fingertips biting into the skin on the back of his neck and shoulders as she pulled him closer.

He was never so thankful for a limo in his life. Plenty of room, tinted windows... and a discreet driver tucked safely away on the other side of a nice, opaque privacy screen.

He liked how she fit beneath him. Her legs tangled with his, all long and strong. She lifted her hips, and pressed right into his, making him groan. He buried his hands in her hair, holding her so he could continue the long, slow, torturous kisses. Then she was gripping his shoulders, kissing him back, dueling with him for control. Breathing heavily, he shifted his attention to the long line of her jaw, alternating kisses and gentle nips along the soft skin leading to the side of her neck.

She turned her head, allowing him access, groaning a little herself as he took full advantage. He buried his face in her hair, his lips next to her ear. "It's insanity, you know, how badly I want you."

"Why insane?" she asked, breathless herself, her hips still restless beneath him, driving him completely wild.

"You make me want to lose control." He nudged her, made her turn so she looked at him. "I never lose control."

A slow smile curved her lips. "Well, don't you think it's about time you started?"

He matched her smile with one of his own. "Yeah, I think maybe it is."

This time the kiss was far hungrier, and there was nothing shy or tentative about her response. Losing control was followed quickly by losing all restraint. He wasn't sure who started pulling off damp T-shirts first. He was too caught up in exploring every inch of her to care. She writhed beneath him, held his head where she wanted it, then gasped in delight when he did whatever he damn well pleased. And pleased her, as well.

Shorts quickly followed shirts. He'd seen most of her already, as had most everyone in the Northern Hemisphere. Southern, too, come to think of it. Her clothing choices on court over the years had often left little to the imagination.

She left nothing to his now.

And he couldn't help but to simply stop and stare in abject appreciation.

"What?" she asked, her gaze so needy, so hungry.

"You. You're stunning."

She grinned, but it was the pink that darkened her cheeks a little that charmed him most.

"You're pretty damn amazing yourself." She gently drew her nails up along his back, traced them over his shoulders, then down along his chest, making him shudder in anticipation. "Lucky me." Then she laughed as she buried her fingers in his hair and tugged him back down.

And he very willingly allowed her to take his mouth, only he slowed it down this time, lingered rather than conquered, until she was moving more slowly, sinuously beneath him. Only then did he slide down her body, taking time to inventory every inch along the way. She was writhing, moaning, demanding. And it was highly likely she was leaving footprints on the interior of the roof of the limo. Normally that kind of thing would worry him. However, his biggest concern at the moment was digging a condom out of his wallet, which was twisted up and tangled in his shorts pocket.

"Here," she said, her voice throaty and rough, "let me." She snagged the packet from him and ripped it open with her teeth.

For whatever reason, that look, that wild grin she shot him while she did it, made him laugh. She joined him, and somehow they ended up sliding to the floor of the limo, still laughing as they untangled themselves just enough for her to take matters into her own hands. And then he was sliding on the opposite seat and pulling her into his lap. He groaned long and deep as she slid down on top of him. "Sweet—Tess. I've never felt anything . . . you're so incredibly . . ."

"Perfect," she said, groaning as she took him deep, bracing her hands on the seat behind him as she began to move. "That you definitely are."

"Come here." He turned her head, took her mouth in a kiss every bit as binding as their bodies were.

Then there was no more talking. It was just the two of them, finding their rhythm, finding each other, mouths joined, bodies joined, moving faster, then faster still, their moans filling the rapidly steaming inside of the limo as the rain continued to drum down.

"Max," she panted along his jaw, then buried her face in his neck, her body tightening around him, little whimpers escaping her as she bucked against him once, then again.

"Tess," he said, then groaned as he felt her begin to climax. He pulled her hips down, holding on, until she cried out—and drove him right over the edge after her.

When the bucking finally stopped, both of them were breathing heavily. He slid sideways and shifted their bodies so she was sprawled on top of him. Both of them so spent, they just lay there for several long minutes, their chests rising and falling. Slowly other sounds filtered in. Rain beating on the moon-roof glass. Cars idling in the lane nearby as they rolled to a stoplight. Muted sound of a bass stereo throbbing the air. Laughter from someone, somewhere outside.

Then the limo moved on, and it was quieter again. And all he heard was his own heartbeat. And the feel of hers, thumping against his chest.

It had been sex. Wild, fun, exciting, and definitely satisfying. But sex all the same.

At least, that's what he struggled to tell himself as his hand drifted to her hair and he fought against the urge to tilt her mouth up to his and kiss her again. Only this time the kiss would be gentle, and tender. And claiming. As if he had any right. Or any hope. She was his only for the moment. He'd be wise to remember that.

She'd probably done wild stuff like this a hundred times.

He'd done it precisely once. And exciting as it had been, had it been up to him, he would have rather had her in bed. A nice big one, where they could play and taunt and tease. But also where they could fall asleep in each other's arms. And where he could wake up and watch her as she slept. Then make love to her again as the sun came up.

God, he was such a sap.

Any minute now he was going to get over this sentimental crap and sit them both up so they could collect themselves and get dressed. Then he'd figure out what the new normal was going to be between them. At least for the next couple of days, anyway.

His heart clutched a little at the thought of that. Of her leaving. So he decided not to think about it. It was going to happen soon enough, whether he did or not. For once in his life, he wasn't going to plan and schedule everything. For once, he was going to do his damnedest to live in the moment.

Tess shifted up from where she'd been nuzzling into his chest, so her lips were pressed beneath his chin. "Do you know what I can't believe?" Her voice was delightfully drowsy and soft.

Talk about a loaded question. Max could name a long list of things he couldn't believe at the moment. For once he took the safe route. "What can't you believe?"

She lifted her head and smiled up at him. "I can't believe we've been under the same roof at Wexley for weeks now, with a gazillion bedrooms, all outfitted with huge, down-filled beds—" She laughed. "And when we finally do this, it's in the back of a limo."

His arms tightened around her, seemingly of their own volition. "I was just thinking something along those same lines myself."

"Were you?" she teased, then nipped his chin.

Given the considerable effect she had on him, it shouldn't have come as any surprise that his body stirred again. Why, why did he only carry one condom? was the first thought that came to mind. "Maybe we should do a compare-and-contrast kind of study," he told her, sliding one hand up her back so he could cup the nape of her neck. "Bed versus limo."

"You think?" She didn't need any provocation to tilt her head back and invite his kiss.

Yeah, he was in such serious trouble here.

Just as his mouth brushed against her, the chirping of a cell phone filled the air.

Chapter 24

"Not mine," Tess said, slipping down, nipping his jaw along the way, before nuzzling against his chest once again.

Max groaned a little, held her closer, but the phone kept chirping. Swearing, he reached a hand out and grabbed for his shorts, fumbling in the pockets.

"Who is it?" she mumbled, quite intent on her exploration expedition.

"I don't care, I'm going to turn it off." Then he looked at the screen and flipped it open instead. "Aurora?"

Even Tess could hear Aurora's excited chatter coming through the phone, and an instant later they were both shifting to a seated position.

"What's wrong?" Max asked, gripping the phone to his ear. "Slow down, I can't understand you."

"What is it?" Tess scrambled off his lap and began gathering their clothes in a heap on the seat. "What's going on?"

He held up his hand to stall her so he could hear. "What?" he said a second later. "She *what*?"

" 'She what,' what?" Tess asked in a heated whisper. "Who 'she'? Gaby?"

Max shushed her and switched the phone to his other ear. "How in the hell did she disappear in the middle of high tea at a five-star hotel?"

Tess dug her nails into his thigh. "Gaby took off?"

"Yes, yes," Max said into the phone. "I know, Aurora. Listen, just—listen, don't worry about that right now. You think she's with who? Who the hell is Rance?" He shot a look at Tess, who shot him a look right back and shrugged.

"I have no idea," she mouthed.

"Okay, okay," he said back into the phone, "we're on our way—yes, I'm with Tess. We're . . . hell, I don't know where the hell we are, we're in the limo." He paused, looked at Tess again. "Yes, still. Look, I'll be there as fast as I can. Don't go anywhere. And for God's sake, don't talk to anyone."

Max clicked off and immediately began dialing again. "They can't reach Gaby on her phone." After repeated tries, he didn't have any better luck. He finally flipped the phone shut and threw it against the back of the opposite seat. "I take my eye off the ball for one second . . ." He swore under his breath as he took the clothes Tess handed him and began quickly dragging them on.

"Hey now, wait a minute," Tess said, not ready to be so easily dismissed. "I know you're worried, but Gaby isn't a little kid."

"She's certainly acting like one."

Tess yanked her damp T-shirt over her head and shuddered as the cold cotton clung to her skin. "She's acting like a teenager with raging hormones, who's been kept barricaded in her room for too long."

Max paused in the middle of tugging on his shorts, his expression incredulous. "Are you blaming this on me?"

"Of course not. I know you've only done what you thought was best for her. God knows, I wouldn't have had the first clue how to raise a younger sibling, much less one who is a professional athlete. Thank God Bobby was already grown when our mom died. You've done an amazing job. Gaby is a tremendous young lady. I'm just saying, she's at an age where she needs to be given a little room to take some personal responsibility, make some personal decisions—"

"Oh yeah. And look at the first one she makes! Running off in the middle of tea to race around London with some Belgian punk."

Tess tried not to smile. It would be a wholly inappropriate response at the moment. From Max's point of view, anyway. But he was being such a . . . well, a guy about this. "Of course she screwed up and did something over the top. Isn't that sort of a teenage rite of passage?"

"She could have come to me! Could have asked me—"

Tess just folded her arms and stared at him.

Max looked like he was about to pop a vein. But a moment later, he slumped back in his seat and blew out a long breath. "Hell."

"You couldn't have known, okay? This is the trial-and-error part of life." She smiled a little. "Just ask my dad. You'll both learn from this little escapade of hers." Tess saw that beneath the anger, he was truly concerned about Gaby, afraid for her safety. She leaned forward and put her hands on his knees and gripped them tightly. "Listen to me. I know you're scared for her. But despite immediate evidence to the contrary, she's a very smart girl. A very smart girl who has a lot of personal pride and very strong opinions about things. She's not about to let that 'Belgian punk,' as you call him, do anything he shouldn't be doing."

Max let his head drop back and covered his face with his hands, groaning. "I'm going to kill them both."

Now Tess laughed. Which brought Max's head back up as he glared at her. "I'm glad you're so highly amused by this. She could be out there right now—"

"In a cute little sports car, being driven around London by an even cuter young guy, and just enjoying herself. Nothing more."

"What do you know about this guy? Rance somebody. Apparently he's on the men's tour. I don't know him."

"I wish I could help you out, but I don't know him, either. As much as you don't want to, you might trust Gaby just a little bit here. I know that teenagers make stupid mistakes all the time, so do full-grown adults, but she just wanted a few hours to be young and carefree and fancy herself in love a little. It's romantic."

"Only you would think this is romantic. That's the girl point of view. Trust me, Rance isn't thinking anything of the sort."

"I think Gaby can hold her own. And if things get out of hand, she can use her celebrity to help her out. Someone would recognize her if she wanted or needed them to."

He swore again. "Christ, you're right. And we thought the paparazzi situation was bad already."

Tess smiled. "It'll be okay. We'll weather this storm just like we have all the others. And it's harmless. She's sixteen and having a spin around town with a boy. Yes, it might make the papers, but come on, it's not like she's hanging out in some nightclub and being snapped leaving at three in the morning, underage, and doing God knows what."

"Are you speaking from personal experience?"

Tess let the snide tone and accusation slide, because she

knew he was under extreme stress at the moment. And because she was still foolishly hoping to salvage at least a little of what had just transpired between them. A moment in time that was rapidly receding into the distant past as the limo continued to roll along. "If I am, then know that everything I'm saying today carries some merit. We'll find her, and you'll have your turn to jump all over her. All I'm saying is to listen to what she has to say. Sure, she can't just go taking off. But maybe you two need to talk, figure out some sort of compromise for her to have a little personal freedom, too." She paused for a moment, and when he didn't say anything else, she pushed a little harder. Someday she'd learn, but apparently that day hadn't arrived yet.

She slid across the space between them and sat next to him, tugging at his shirt until he turned to look at her. "I'm sorry. I know you're scared. She's going to be fine. And you two will work things out. But before all hell breaks loose here, I want to tell you one more thing."

He just stared at her. And she hated the distance she saw in his expression. He was pulling back, and pulling back fast.

"You need some personal freedom, too. Don't beat yourself up because you both decided to try to fit a little fun in your life. You both deserve it. And though it sounds a little self-serving at the moment"—she paused and smiled at him—"you'll both be better off if you find a little balance."

He held her gaze for the longest time, then said, "I appreciate what you're saying. I do. But she's my sister. And you're going to have to let me handle this my own way."

Anything else she might have said was cut off when the limo pulled to the curb and Aurora, Vivian, and Mercedes came rushing out of the hotel lobby to greet them. Max opened the door and went to get out, but the three women pushed their way in, instead.

Tess had a moment of panic as she looked around the inside

of the limo for any telltale signs of just what she and Max had been up to before Aurora had called. If any of the godmothers were thinking along those lines, they didn't show it. Their faces were lined with worry. And, in Aurora's case, abject apology.

"I'm so sorry, Max. I should have talked to you about her little crush sooner," Aurora said as they crammed together on the opposite bench seat, facing Tess and Max. "I never thought she'd do something rash like this. One moment we're having tea, the next she's excusing herself for the ladies' room, and—"

Vivian sighed. "Aurora, honestly. She's a young woman having her first romance with a boy. And a very handsome one at that."

Everyone turned to look at Vivian.

"What?" she said, looking innocent, or trying to, anyway. "While you were on the phone with Max overreacting, and Mercy here was making certain the hotel security kept mum about the situation, I went back and asked to take a look at the security cameras for the rear entrance to the hotel and saw him come in and meet her." She smiled. "Very cute. Nice choice."

Tess thought the top of Max's head might blow off. " 'Cute'? 'Nice choice'? Vivian, she's out there in London with some hooligan—"

Vivi reached forward and patted his knee. "Dear boy, calm down. I borrowed the security office's computer—and he was quite the charmer, I must say—and did a little search on our young Belgian. He's from a very good family and there are no scandals attached to his name."

"And yet he came to the rear entrance of a hotel and helped a sixteen-year-old girl sneak off."

"Almost seventeen, and my goodness, Maxwell, didn't you ever do anything daring when you were a teenage boy?"

"Of course I did. Why do you think I'm so worried?"

All three godmothers smiled at that. Tess, on the other hand, just looked at him. "You did daring things?"

He didn't look at her. "This isn't some little game here. She's not some regular teenager. She's God knows where. Paparazzi could be chasing them through the streets. We have to do something!"

Mercedes spoke up for the first time. "I think the best course of action is for Vivian and me to remain here, in case she returns to the scene of the crime, as it were." Her tone was well modulated and calm, as it always was. "You three should head back to Wexley and wait for her there. If any of us gets word of anything, we'll communicate accordingly."

Mercedes was always the voice of reason, and the tension in the idling limo seemed to go down several notches almost immediately.

"I think we should do more than sit around and wait," Max insisted.

"Like what," Vivian asked, "drive around London in hopes we cross paths? Call in the local constabulary? Involve the media? I think that is asking for more trouble."

"It's the middle of the afternoon, broad daylight," Aurora said, trying to sound reassuring, but obviously more worried than her counterparts. Guilt was still clearly written on her face. "Perhaps Mercy is right and we should wait her out. The police wouldn't do anything at this point, anyway."

"Overkill, trust me," Vivian said. "She's fine. You can play big brother when she gets home and send her to her room, or ground her, or take away her tennis rackets if you want. But being any more alarmist than we've already been won't resolve this situation any faster."

"I understand what you're saying, Vivian, and I appreciate all of your concern, but if you think I can just sit by and wait while she's out there—"

"There she is!" Tess shouted.

A shiny black convertible zipped past the limo, which was still idling curbside in front of the hotel. The top was down—at some point the rain had ceased—and Gaby's long, shiny ponytail flashed in the sun as they whipped into the narrow lane that ran alongside the hotel.

Max immediately rapped on the partition. "Follow that car!" he shouted.

Vivian clapped her hands together. "I've always wanted to say that."

Before they could turn into the side street, two motorcycles and a tiny Renault tucked in right behind Gaby and Rance.

"Photographers," Aurora gasped, nose all but pressed to the tinted glass of the passenger window.

"Goddamn son of a bitch," Max swore, pounding on the partition. "Get moving!"

The driver was already on it. He moved them in behind the little motorcade, turning into a rear circular drive, enclosed by a small, walled courtyard in the back of the hotel. After pulling through the gates, he turned the car so it blocked both entrance and exit.

"Nicely done," Mercedes observed to no one in particular. "I'll make sure to note that on his service record with Valerie."

Max was already lunging for the door as Vivian reached across and grabbed his arm. "Remember, she's young and fancies herself in love. Don't do anything rash. You'll regret it later. And there are cameras recording everything."

Vivian's delay gave Tess all the time she needed to flip the locks and keep Max right where he was. "We need an exit strategy."

"We need to get out there and keep those animals from—"

"Trust me," Tess said. "They have all the photos they need already. And if we all go piling out of this car, we're only going to increase the drama quotient. They're not going to give up their cameras and blocking them in here is only going to set everybody on edge."

"Open the doors, Tess."

She ignored the warning tone. "Have the driver move along into the courtyard, then let Mercedes get out and shuttle Gaby and Rance inside. She has the least recognizable profile of any of us, they won't know who she is. Once their picture-taking opportunity is over, they'll leave." She looked at Max. "Then we can get out, go inside like normal people, and you can have a talk with both Gaby and the young man who dared to take her out for the afternoon."

"Brilliant," Mercedes said, while Aurora and Vivian nodded in agreement. She pressed the intercom and directed the driver to pull around.

"Your experience in these matters is invaluable, Tess," Aurora said, patting her knee.

"Glad somebody thinks so." She held Max's gaze as she popped the locks. And she could tell it cost him dearly to sit by while Mercedes slid out of the car and made her way through the small cache of photographers who were busily snapping the young couple as a grinning Rance got out, waved to the camera guys, who kept their distance seeing as their quarry was being receptive, and went around to open Gaby's door.

"Did you see?" Aurora said, beaming at Max. "A young gentleman."

"A young gentleman asks permission." Max's hands were fists on his knees. "He doesn't sneak his date out the back door."

"Desperate times," Tess murmured, catching Vivian's wink.

"He's so proud to be seen with her," Aurora went on in a wistful tone. "He's keeping them all at bay, as well."

Mercedes walked up and Gaby had a moment where she

saw the limo and froze. It was hard to make out her expression, given the big black sunglasses she wore, but she smiled a moment later and waved one last time at the picture-taking pack, before letting Mercedes usher them past the doorman and on inside. Two of the photographers tried to follow them in, but whatever Mercedes said to the doorman worked, as he kept them firmly on the other side of the revolving door.

Max was all but clawing at the door by the time the photographers boarded car and bikes and drove off. They'd barely cleared the courtyard gate before he was out of the limo like a shot.

Tess was hot on his heels, knowing Aurora and Vivian would catch up. She wanted to do whatever she could for Gaby. And for Rance, for that matter.

"Where are they?" he demanded of the concierge, who met them just inside the door. He was well trained enough to personally and discreetly deliver the quartet to the nearby room where Mercedes, Gaby, and Rance awaited them.

"Sir," Rance said, stepping forward the instant Max and Tess entered the room. He put his hand out. "I need to apologize."

Good job, Tess thought, wondering if he'd come to that conclusion on his own, or whether Mercedes had given him a Glass Slipper crash course. How to Save Your Ass in One Easy Handshake.

Max was momentarily nonplussed by the unexpected gesture, which gave Gaby a chance to step in.

"Don't be mad at him, Max. I talked him into it. He wanted to meet you first and ask you, but—"

Max turned on her. "But what?"

She had the grace to flush, even as her chin came up. "I told him you'd be completely unreasonable about all this and I can see that I'm right."

"You should have talked to me. I understand you talked to

Aurora. We would have worked something out after the tournament was over."

Tess heard the hurt in his voice and had to curl her fingers inward not to reach for his hand. The instinctive need surprised her.

"I couldn't wait, Max. Rance lost in the doubles quarters; he's leaving tomorrow." She glanced over at the handsome young tennis player. "I didn't know when we'd ever get the chance again."

Vivian sighed. "The trials of young love," she said wistfully.

Max shot her a look, then turned back to Gaby. "You scared us all. We had no idea where you were, and wouldn't have known who you were with if Vivian hadn't looked on the security cameras—"

Gaby looked stricken. "I'm really sorry," she said to the godmothers. "I know it was wrong and I shouldn't have taken advantage—"

"No, you shouldn't have," both Max and Aurora said at the same time.

Now Gaby's chin dropped and she looked truly chastened for the first time since returning. "I'm really sorry," she said in a little voice. "I just wanted an hour or two on my own. I didn't mean to make it such a big deal."

"The paparazzi chased you, anything could have happened," Max said.

Rance stepped in then, angling his body in front of Gaby. "Blame it on me. I pushed her. She was only trying to see me and"—he took Gaby's hand in his—"we should have talked to you first, sir. I know it looks bad," he went on, his accent deepening as he spoke faster. "But I don't usually act like this, either. It's just, your sister . . . she's a really wonderful girl and I like her very much. But I would never do anything to harm her, please believe me."

Aurora and Vivian, die-hard romantics both, sighed a little at his impassioned speech. Mercedes looked to be reserving judgment.

"I come from an important family. I have handled the European press my entire life," he went on. "I know how they are, what they want. I bargained with them and they let us have our space for a little spin in trade for a few photos at the end. They waited until we were at the hotel. I wouldn't put her in jeopardy in a car chase." He looked at Gaby and his expression all but melted.

Even Tess found herself sighing a little. She glanced at Max, wholly expecting to find him on the verge of throttling the punk, as he'd called him. Only to find him looking at the young couple's joined hands like he'd been poleaxed or something. Which, she supposed, he was. He really didn't know how to handle this. Any of this.

Without thinking, just needing to support him somehow, she slid her arm through his and stepped in for the first time since entering the room. "We appreciate your need for personal time," she said, realizing exactly how that was going to sound and not caring. Gaby had pushed when it came to wanting Tess in her life as a coach. Maybe Max needed another little nudge to keep her in his. "And I know you didn't mean to scare us so badly. Can we all agree that you realize the potential severity of the situation you created and that, in the future, any and all plans to see each other will be cleared with your brother?"

Gaby and Rance, still clutching hands, quickly nodded in agreement.

Mercedes stepped up then. "And I think a formal apology for ruining tea, in writing, from you both," she added with a pointed look at Rance, "would also be in order."

"Yes," Gaby said, cheeks flushing again.

"Absolutely," Rance agreed.

Everyone, including Tess, shifted toward Max, waiting for his response. There was a long pause where it seemed everyone held their collective breath. Then, finally, he said, "The rain has stopped and I believe you and Tess have scheduled practice time." His tone was terse, without much room for conciliation. "In case you've forgotten, you're playing in the semifinals of your first grand-slam event tomorrow. You might want to put a little thought to match preparation."

She looked down at her feet. "I know. I will." She looked up through lashes suddenly wet with unshed tears. "I'm really sorry, Max," she said softly. She glanced at Tess. "I really am. I thought . . . I mean, you went out all the time, and still managed to play well—" She broke off, suddenly looking stricken all over again. "Don't blame her, Max," she said. "I didn't mean that. She didn't influence—"

Tess shushed her. But Max had gone rigid the moment Gaby had gone there. Tess slid her arm free. "Why don't we take one of the limos and head over to the grounds now, find out what the plans are. I need to check on Bobby's rescheduled match time, too."

Aurora stepped in. "That sounds like a wonderful plan, dear. Let us know what you find out and we can meet up with you later."

Rance cleared his throat. "Would it be okay if I walked Gaby out to the limo?"

Gaby's eyes lit up. But the collective impassive responses from all five adults quickly dashed her hopes. She turned to Rance. "I think it's best if I just leave now with Tess. Thank you for the ride." Her normally confident and bold voice softened a little. "I hope we can again someday."

Rance shifted on his feet and Tess found her respect for the young man growing as he grappled with what he wanted to do, and what he knew he must do, in the face of the group staring him down.

"I enjoyed the pleasure of your company, Gabrielle." He lifted her hand and pressed a very quick kiss on the back of it. *"Adieu."*

With that, he turned and stuck a somewhat shakier hand out to Max. "Again, I apologize. I hope you can forgive my impulsiveness. With your permission, I would like to see your sister again, when our schedules permit."

Max's jaw flexed, but after a moment, he said, "We'll see."

Rance seemed to understand that at times retreat was the better part of valor, and after a short handshake and another quick smile at Gaby, bid a hasty retreat.

"My, my," Vivian said as the door shut behind him. "Not a bad start, Miss Gabrielle, if I do say so myself." Then she stepped forward and slid one arm through Max's and one through Tess's and drew them together. "Speaking of which..." Her smile grew. "Where exactly did you two get off to this afternoon?"

Tess caught Max's gaze from the corner of her eye, and she wondered what he was thinking. He'd probably forgotten all about it. Or wanted to. Especially after what Gaby said about mirroring Tess's wilder, youthful behavior. What she had to figure out was whether retreat was the better part of valor for her, as well.

She gave a little laugh, as if she assumed Vivian was teasing, and slid her arm free. "We'd better get to the grounds and make sure we have a dry court."

Gaby was more than willing to let Tess get her out of there and moments later they were headed out to the still waiting limo in the rear courtyard. Mercifully there were no photographers in sight.

It was only after Tess had located Andrea on the grounds

and nailed down the match time for Bobby, then began putting Gaby through her paces on the practice court, that she remembered how she'd started the day. Her meeting with Alan. Her new job.

She looked across the net at Gaby, who would no doubt go on to tackle the world, both on court and off, with panache and power. She thought about Max, probably out there right now wishing like hell he hadn't spent the afternoon rolling around in the back of a private limo with the former bad girl of tennis. And she realized that the commentating job with the network was a blessing in more ways than one. The Fontaines didn't need Tess Hamilton's influence in their lives any longer. Once they got past this weekend, her usefulness here was done.

Funny how she wasn't as excited or settled by that prospect as she should have been.

Chapter 25

Max told himself he was too caught up in the match to care. So what if Tess had come in late, then sat on the other side of the godmothers? All three were in attendance today, watching Gaby try to make her way into the finals. He needed to focus on the match, not the confusing pile of emotions that Tess Hamilton stirred up every time she was around.

Maybe it was because Gaby wasn't playing well when it mattered most, or maybe it was because he couldn't forget how Tess had slid her arm through his yesterday, so naturally, standing beside him, supporting him, only to retreat moments later, then slip away completely. Granted, she'd gone off to help Gaby train, but that had been the last he'd seen of her until now. Yesterday had been . . . well, confusing. On so many levels. Between what had begun in the limo and ended with Rance kissing the back of Gaby's hand . . . he really didn't want to think about it.

Aurora's rings bit into his knee as she leaned closer to him.

"She seems to be a bit scattered. Do you think it's because of yesterday? I'll never forgive myself if taking her to tea—"

"No, Aurora. It's not your fault. You can't be on every day. She's nervous out there and it's affecting her game. She'll settle down." At least he hoped so. The first set was a point away from being over and Gaby was down at five games to two. "She'll come back in the second set, you watch." He prayed his confidence was warranted.

A moment later, however, the first set was over, in her opponent's favor. Max had to work at not glancing down the row at Tess. Gaby didn't even look up at the players' box before heading back to her chair. The bounce in her step was gone, her shoulders slumped. Her body language told the story. "Come on, come on. Don't give up now," he murmured. It didn't help that her opponent was having one of those days where everything she could get her racket on went in by a hair. Gaby was having to hit three winners instead of one to make each point, and coming up short most of the time. It could be demoralizing even on a good day.

The second set began much like the first and Max began to see the writing on the wall. He found himself looking down the row, anyway, meeting Tess's gaze over the heads of the godmothers. It surprised him how badly he needed to see, to feel, Tess's unending optimism right now. If only Gaby would see it and feel it, too.

Tess held his gaze. It was the first time he'd looked into her eyes since . . . well, he couldn't afford to go there right now. They needed to talk. When this thing was over, they would talk. What he wanted to say, he had no idea. But there were things left unsaid between them. There had to be. Because when he looked at her, it didn't feel finished.

She gave him the smallest of nods, and he wondered if she was reading his mind again. Or just reassuring him about Gaby.

He wanted both. But as he returned his attention to the match, he wondered if it wasn't too late. On both fronts. He told himself it was okay. Whatever relationship he thought he might have with her would have probably ended on some spectacular, internationally scandalous bad note. He didn't really believe that, but it was easier to cling to that notion than the possibility he was letting something important slip through his fingers.

Much as his sister was doing out there on the court. How much were they both going to regret this? On her first try Gaby had made it further than they'd ever expected, even in their wildest of dreams. But he also knew she didn't want to go out like this. If she had to lose, she'd want it to be on her terms, having made her opponent fight to the last breath to beat her. "Come on, Gabs. Fight, dammit," he muttered beneath his breath.

Aurora leaned closer again. "She is a fighter, Max. Don't you worry. She gets her determination from you."

He glanced down briefly, but Aurora's gaze was rooted firmly on the match. He looked down the row again, this time catching Tess unaware. He watched her for several long moments, leaning forward in her seat, attention riveted on the court, fists clenched and pressing against her knees as she all but willed Gaby back into the match.

He returned his attention to the game. And thought maybe both Fontaine siblings were about to be guilty of letting something important go without a fight.

To Gaby's credit, she did try to rally in the second set, but she was going for her shots too hard, pushing them just wide, or just long, in her determination to get herself back into this match. Her opponent wasn't going for winners at this point, but just keeping the ball in play long enough for Gaby to beat herself.

Max felt his heart sink lower, one notch at a time, as each

point went in her opponent's favor. He didn't blame her escapade yesterday. He blamed himself. Maybe he should have balanced Gaby's time better, let her have more freedom. Maybe he should have balanced his own life better, as well.

Maybe the distraction of Tess, or the distraction of Rance, of budding relationships in general, was to blame for today's result. But did that really matter? It was to be expected, he told himself. It was part of growing up. For him and his sister. On Gaby's part, she'd outdone herself here and had nothing to be ashamed of. He'd never cared about winning, just about playing. And then, only because of Gaby's love for the game. But Gaby had always held herself to both standards.

She'd be a nightmare of emotions later, humiliated by her inability to play her own game, to come up with the shots when she needed them most. Which led him to wonder how he'd feel later. When it was time to pack up and leave Wexley House behind, head home, regroup, start turning thoughts toward the upcoming hard-court season. Without Tess.

Suddenly a murmur rippled through the crowd and Max realized he'd let his thoughts wander to the point of losing track of the game. He jerked his attention back to the court in time to see Gaby's opponent march to the net to question a call. The chair umpire initially refused to climb down and check the mark, which was on the far side of the court from him. The young Russian continued to harangue him and eventually, to many whistles and catcalls from the crowd, he relented and climbed down.

Upon inspecting the offending mark on Gaby's side of the net, he let the ruling stand. The ball was wide. Second service. The crowd roared its approval of the call and Gaby's opponent stalked back to her spot on the baseline and prepared to serve again. If her expression was anything to judge by, it would be a blistering second serve.

Instead, she hit wide again. Only this time there was no arguing the point. It was clearly wide. She'd just double-faulted, and for the first time, Gaby had an edge. A very, very slight one. But an emotional one, perhaps, as well. The next serve didn't get it in until the second try and it was clear the previous point was still very much on her mind. Gaby's opponent was rattled.

Which she proved by playing very tentatively on the next point, as well. Gaby took full advantage. She won that point, and the next, finally earning a chance to break serve. Max pumped his fists and willed her on. She still had a long way to go to get fully back into this match, but he'd take any sign of encouragement.

A second later it was game to Gaby. They all leaped to their feet and Max caught Tess's gaze. Eyes shining, she was grinning and pumping her fists. Her enthusiasm was infectious and he let himself feel it, take it on. When he looked back at Gaby and caught her glancing up at the box before she went to the line for her own service game, he gave her two thumbs-up and mouthed "go get her."

Had Gaby looked worried, or too serious, he'd have worried. Instead, her mouth quirked just a little at the corners before she turned to the ball girl to request balls to serve with. That was the look he wanted. Cocky, confident, like the world was her oyster. She had nothing to lose, everything to gain. And right now, she just wanted to stay out there a little bit longer. And have some fun.

Gaby took the next two service games. And in less than twenty minutes, she had the crowd on their feet as she brought the second set even, with the threat of pushing it to a deciding third set. Her opponent had lost her edge and her mental game had deserted her. She was still fighting hard, but Gaby was finally giving back as good as she got.

By the time they got to the tiebreaker, the tension in the

stands was palpable. Max was clutching Aurora's hand, as she was Vivian's next to her, and so on, all the way down to Tess. Then, on the next point, a bad call sent Gaby stalking to the net. The crowd groaned, then held its collective breath. Max's heart began to sink again. *Not now. Not now.*

But rather than lose her temper, and possibly her focus, she calmly but directly challenged the call. The umpire slid out of the chair and checked the mark, but ruled in her opponent's favor.

"Come on," Max urged. "Don't let this get to you."

Gaby nodded, then turned back to her end of the court, which was just below them. She glanced up at the box, and winked at Tess. Aurora let out a surprised laugh next to him, but Max just sat there with his mouth temporarily hanging open. A quick glance at Tess showed her grinning right back at Gaby. Like they'd planned this or something. Which, of course, they couldn't have. But something passed between them in that moment that only the two of them fully understood.

Gaby turned and proceeded to send a missile of a second serve over the net, pulling her opponent out wide for the return, which Gaby then neatly sent zipping down the opposite sideline, well out of reach. The crowd roared. Gaby just smiled, pumped her fist, sent a look to the chair umpire . . . then prepared to serve again.

But her opponent didn't fold this time, nor quietly go away. She'd been here before, had the court experience, and more important, the grand-slam experience. She got her head back in the game and began to give Gaby the tiebreaker of her life. Both players battled fiercely. This was exactly what Max had wanted to see all along. The rallies went on longer than usual, both players trying to push the other to make the first mistake. His stomach was in knots as they traded points back and forth, neither player able to close out the set.

In the end, it was Gaby who made the fatal error, clipping the tape on a short ball, and watching it fall back on her side of the net, giving her opponent the first match point of the game. After more than two hours on the court, with the play careening from listless to some of the finest grass-court play of the tournament . . . it all came down to this.

Max held his breath, as did everyone else in the stands.

An instant later it was over. Game, set, match. To the Russian.

Gaby's Cinderella run at Wimbledon had officially come to an end.

Eyes stinging with emotion, he watched her run to the net to shake her opponent's hand. They skipped that and hugged each other, as the entire stadium stood and cheered. This was what they'd come to see, two gladiators battling it out. There was no shame in this defeat. And though he knew Gaby was disappointed, when she looked up at the players' box and gave a little shrug, there was still that little quirk at the corner of her mouth. She knew she'd done her best. Maybe not the entire match, but she'd come back, she'd fought hard. And she'd simply been outplayed.

"She fought hard, Max," Aurora told him, a soothing pat on his knee as the crowd bustled around them. "You should be proud of her."

"Oh, I am, I am." He watched as she packed her gear and waved to the crowd one last time before leaving Centre Court. The place erupted in cheers. She'd clearly won their hearts. And Max knew they'd both be back here again. Maybe next year, maybe the one after that. But they'd be back.

He stood and helped Aurora and Vivian move past him to exit the box in front of him. Mercedes followed. He needed to get down to the press room. All the players gave a mandatory press conference after each match, win or lose. He wanted to be there for Gaby, lend moral support if nothing else.

Tess came up, then. "She played her game, Max. She played her game." There was pride in her eyes, as well as disappointment. Tess didn't like to lose any more than his sister did, but there was fight there, too. And determination.

"Yes, she did." Maybe it was time he played his, too.

Tess started to move past him and descend the steps to the waiting security personnel who would escort her inside. Max put his hand on her arm, stopping her. She looked up, eyebrows lifted in question.

Had she really been naked and in his arms yesterday? He shut those images out. "I have to go down to the press room, but—"

"I was going to go back to the locker room. Talk to her, make sure she's okay before she faces the vultures. If you don't mind, that is."

He appreciated that she'd asked, but hated the sudden formality between them. "Of course it's okay. You're her coach, after all."

She just looked at him, that combination of exasperation and amusement he'd come to expect—and enjoy—clear on her face. And right then he knew he couldn't let her go. Gaby needed her. And maybe more important, he needed her.

"You can be really proud of her, Max." She started to slip free of his hold and move past him.

He didn't let her go. "You can be, too."

She paused, looked at him. "Of course I am."

"I mean—"

"I know what you meant. Listen, I need to talk to you. Right after the press conference. I—"

Vivian popped up just then. "Darlings? I think you need to get yourself to the press room pronto." She looked past Max to Tess. "Both of you."

"What?" Max asked her. "What's going on?"

Tess urged Max down the stairs, staying right behind him. "Is Gaby already in there?"

Vivian nodded and hustled them into the waiting arms of the security cadre, who turned and moved them en masse inside and down the short hall to the press room. She stopped just in front of the door and looked at them both. "So is Fionula Hust." She glanced at Tess and a brief look of despair crossed her face. "She's found out, Tess. Everything."

Max looked at Vivian, then at Tess, whose expression swiftly went from confusion to dread. "What?" he demanded. "What's going on?"

"The job offer?" Tess asked.

"That and . . . you know. About the endorsements, the taxes, all of it."

"What job offer?" Max asked. "What endorsements?" But no one was listening to him.

Tess's shoulders slumped. Max couldn't remember ever seeing her look so defeated. "You knew?" she asked Vivian quietly. "And she's badgering Gaby about it?" She was clearly upset.

Vivian nodded. "Yes, honey, we did. I'm so sorry. Aurora ducked out to tell me. I came and found you immediately. I didn't know what else to do. Aurora is just inside the door, keeping watch."

"Thank you, Vivian." Tess pushed at Max. "Let me in there." Despair had quickly turned to anger. "I can't believe she's got the balls to use Gaby to get to—what am I saying, of course she does."

Max grabbed at Tess's arm. "Do you want to tell me what in the hell is going on?"

"This isn't about Gaby, Max. It's about me. I am sorry. I—" She broke off, swore. "I have to get in there. She shouldn't have to deal with this alone, or at all. It's wrong and way out of bounds." She glanced back at Max. "I tried to tell you this yesterday. I should have told you a long time ago. I'm really sorry. I didn't mean to hurt either of you. I never meant that."

"Told me what? Hurt me how?"

But she'd already pushed inside the door. Flashbulbs were going off and there was a hubbub in the room that wasn't typical of the well-mannered way in which the Club members preferred to run things.

Max went to push in the room right behind her, but Vivian—all five-feet-nothing of her—stopped him. "Let her handle this, at least to start. You going in there right now will just fuel the fire."

"Whatever the hell is going on, I should be in there. Whatever Tess did or didn't mean to do, obviously she's done something."

"Now, Max, she was in trouble. She did what she had to do, but she's always been there for Gaby. Always. Never forget that."

Max was already pushing open the door, but looked back. "In trouble how?"

Vivian sighed.

Max's gaze narrowed. "How long have you known about whatever this is all about?"

"Tess didn't know that we knew. We've been trying to help her, behind the scenes, as it were. Help both of you, really." She sighed again and looked even more miserable. "Don't give up on her, Max. She needs us. She needs you. And she's not used to needing anyone."

Max didn't say anything, but opened the door. And stepped into chaos. Patented Tess Hamilton chaos.

Chapter 26

Tess walked into a barrage of shouted questions and flashbulbs going off in her face. Neither bothered her so much as the expression of utter relief on Gaby's face when she spied Tess making her way to the table to take a seat next to her. "I'm so sorry," she whispered, leaning over to make sure the words were heard only by Gaby and not picked up by the microphones on the table in front of them.

"I don't know what they're talking about," she whispered back, having to talk directly into Tess's ear to be heard over the continuous shouts and whirring photographic equipment.

"Don't worry, I'll take care of it. Let me handle the questions."

Gaby just nodded, looking far more the young teenager at the moment than the highly trained athlete who just held her own on Centre Court moments ago.

"And by the way, you made me proud out there today."

Gaby just ducked her chin. Tess used the moment to paste

on her cockiest grin and turned to face the phalanx of reporters and journalists seated in the rows of chairs in front of them. No point in dancing around it at this point. "Hello. I hope you don't mind my crashing the party. I understand you have some questions for me." She wagged a teasing finger. "Shame, shame, picking on a rookie player who just suffered her first major loss." She faced down one particular reporter directly, her grin turning perhaps a shade more feral. "Fionula, perhaps you could lead things off for us."

The journalist didn't even blink. In fact, Tess thought there might be some drool collecting at the corners of her mouth at the opening she'd just been handed. "Can you tell us about your financial situation at this time?"

"I thought you'd already done that research," she replied. "Seeing as you've apparently been speaking with some sense of authority on the subject today."

A light round of titters rippled through the crowd, but most shifted a bit closer, held their recorders a bit higher, waiting for the next volley.

Fionula's gaze hardened slightly, but she'd faced far worse. "I understand you've experienced a reversal of fortune with the loss of your endorsement income and an extensive payment to the IRS for overdue taxes. Is that true?"

"I wasn't aware that my financial status was the business of anyone but myself, and perhaps my accountant. Okay, and the manager at the Jaguar dealer."

Fionula ignored the chuckles of her comrades. "Your tax records are on file. Your payments to them have been quite substantial and must have created a—"

"I believe Uncle Sam and I are square," Tess said, cutting off her assumptions. "Do you have anything indicating otherwise?"

Fionula saw that for the dead end it was and quickly changed tactics. "Nike confirms that they haven't renewed your contract. As have several other major manufacturers you've represented over the past year. Can you confirm any new endorsement deals at this time?"

"I am always considering new offers and various business ventures. Again, I don't believe this is the business of the general public. Unless you'd like to discuss your salary and income tax records, as well."

The room went silent as everyone seemed to draw a collective breath.

Undaunted, Fionula said, "I'm afraid no one cares about my income and expenditures, but of course we're always curious when someone who has achieved such enormous success—"

"Might turn out to be just as human as anyone else?"

It was as if the collective unit of media personnel were themselves watching a tennis match, their heads shifting from Tess to Fionula, only pausing to scribble notes or shift their cameras.

"Meaning?"

"Meaning that just because I'm a prominent sports figure doesn't mean I have to expose every detail of my personal life. I'm not running for office. Hell, I'm not even playing tennis anymore."

"Is that why you've sold off all of your assets in several European countries?"

Tess didn't blink. "Not that it's anyone's business, but yes, I'll confirm that. I no longer travel the globe playing tournaments, so those properties ceased to be necessary for me."

"So liquidating these numerous assets wouldn't have anything to do with the tax payments, the loss of endorsements?"

Tess shrugged. "Business decisions." She smiled. "As you know, some years are better than others."

Like the pit bull she was, Fionula dogged onward. "Regarding that, can you confirm you've been offered a position as a sports commentator by Alan Chapman of the RBC sports cable network? And is it true you've accepted?"

From the corner of her eye, Tess noticed Gaby shift slightly to look at her, as well. Clearly she was surprised to hear about it this way, but it wasn't like she had signed on for life with the Fontaines. Gaby might have hoped to extend their partnership, but that agreement had never been made.

Still, she didn't want Gaby to find out like this, in such a public forum. It was exactly the kind of thing Max would expect of her, making a spectacle out of something best handled in private. It wasn't supposed to happen like this.

So, of course, it was happening just like this.

Tess should have made time to talk to Max. His offer to continue coaching Gaby had been casually made under the most extenuating of circumstances and she wasn't even sure he'd been sincere. Not that it mattered now. What had surprised her was how compelling the offer had turned out to be for her.

In fact, yesterday after the Rance Incident, when she was forced to admit that maybe Max was right after all, and Gaby would be better served being coached by someone with a somewhat tamer influence, was exactly when she began thinking what it would be like if she did stick around. Max probably didn't need to be saddled with the sort of distractions that came with the Tess Hamilton package, either. And yet, since Alan had made her the offer, she'd perversely done nothing but think about the life she might have had with the Fontaines. Both as coach to Gaby, and as . . . well, whatever Max was willing to let her be.

Of course, today's little circus had probably taken care of any future possibility there. On both fronts, personal and professional. She cringed, thinking of what Max was going to say, although she had a pretty good idea of exactly what that would be. Only this time, she deserved it. Not that she'd planned this circus, but she could have clued him in before this had a chance to happen.

All that she had left now was to pray Alan had a good sense of humor, and that he believed that any publicity was good publicity. Christ, but she'd managed to screw things up royally. Again. Only this time it wasn't just her life, this time there were others involved.

She glanced at Gaby, then back at Fionula. "As I've stated before, I field offers all the time. At the moment, I can honestly say there is nothing to report. Any and all offers are still pending." She smiled sweetly. "Of course, if that changes, you'll be the very first to know."

"One more question," Fionula said, having to raise her voice to be heard over the sudden barrage of questions being shouted at Tess. "Is it true you took on coaching Gabrielle here as a means of putting your creditors off until you could secure a more lucrative deal? And now that she's made it this far in the tournament, do you wish you'd worked a better offer with her brother Max?" She paused for just a moment, then smiled like the snake she was. "Or perhaps, given several of your very public displays, you already have. Care to comment?"

"That's insane!" Gaby blurted out, finally finding her voice. "Tess isn't using us for money. Why would she do that? She doesn't need to coach me. She was only helping me because—"

It was like watching a car wreck happening right in front of her and there was nothing Tess could do to stop it. She watched the moment unfold as if in slow motion . . . Gaby breaking off her heated defense and slowly turning to face her, confusion and hurt dawning in her eyes. Every camera in the room started shooting frames at double speed and the cacophony of voices grew to an almost fever pitch.

"Why did you agree to help me?"

Tess read the question on her lips, the noise so loud now she couldn't actually hear the words. She wanted to tell Gaby she'd done it for Aurora, and for herself, and for a lot of reasons that hadn't been there in the beginning but were there now. But the bottom line was, one of the deciding factors that day she'd agreed to stay on beyond the Glass Slipper agreement she'd made with Aurora, had been the promise of a percentage of the purse. Of course, no one could have predicted just how big a payoff that would be and certainly Tess had never seen it as an answer to her prayers. Just something to help her buy time until she found an answer.

She thought she'd found that answer with Alan's offer.

Now she wasn't sure she knew anything at all.

"Why, Tess?" came the repeated shouts from the reporters, and she could just see that four-inch headline tomorrow: WHY, TESS?

Gaby was still staring at her, her big doe eyes all stunned and confused, but still filled with hope. Hope that her idol and hero really hadn't let her down so badly. *Yeah. Why, Tess?*

"I—" Tess's defense, not that she had one, was cut off by a voice coming from just inside the side door the players used to enter the media room.

"She was helping out a mutual family friend." The deep voice easily projected over the chaos of shouts, instantly quieting the room.

Heads swiveled en masse. Tess turned toward the door, too, heart sinking, even as hope bloomed there.

Gaby spun around in her chair. "Max!"

Max made his way up to the table where she and Gaby sat and picked up one of the microphones mounted there. "Tess agreed to help a family friend and be a mentor of sorts to Gaby when I was seeking out help for her. As you know, this is my sister's first year on tour, and she's not used to any of this," he said, pointedly staring down the group, but his gaze seemed aimed directly at Fionula. "We've done our best to make Gaby available to the media, and for obvious reasons, she's enjoyed her time here in London. We achieved far greater success over the fortnight than we could have ever believed, and I think a big part of that success is due to Tess's coaching and mentoring ability."

When he paused, the entire room exploded with questions. Tess started once again to speak, touched by Max's defense of her, but knowing he was doing whatever he had to in order to get Gaby out of this situation as unscathed and as quickly as possible.

Max raised his palm to quiet the room, and continued to speak. "When Tess agreed to stay on with Gaby for the duration of the tournament, she offered to do so gratis. Gaby is right, she didn't have to help us and I sincerely doubt money was a motivating factor, as we had to insist she go on our payroll at all. Tess loves this game and I think she sees in Gaby a little of herself and . . . well, she'd have to respond to the rest. But as I am the one who ostensibly hired her, I wanted to put to rest right now any rumors that she was motivated by greed or anything else. She's been pretty selfless these past few weeks." He glanced over at her. "And I, for one, am very glad she decided to hang around."

"Max! Max!"

"Tess, what do you say!"

"Max, are you two involved personally?"

"Tess, are you staying on with the Fontaines?"

"Max, is Tess going to be Gaby's full-time coach?"

"Tess, what about the job offer from RBC?"

The shouts came from all corners of the room. But it was all white noise to Tess, who was still caught up staring at Max. He'd come to Gaby's rescue. And he'd come to hers, too. He'd gone above and beyond defending his sister to defending her, as well. Even when Tess knew he must be upset, knew he had to believe there was at least a scrap of truth to Fionula's accusations—she was too good at what she did to toss out questions like that without having done her homework—yet he'd just stood there and exonerated her anyway.

Tess had her own personal four-inch headline screaming through her mind: WHY, MAX?

Did he really believe in her? Or was this some kind of angle?

Gaby chose that moment to reach under the table, take Tess's hand, and squeeze it tightly.

Tess tore her gaze from Max and looked next to her. Gaby was beaming, confident that her hero was still high on her pedestal. "I knew it."

Tess looked into those shining, trusting eyes, then briefly back at Max's steady, reliable gaze. And she knew what she had to do.

After giving Gaby's hand a quick, reassuring squeeze, she turned her attention back to the room and to the pack of wolves seated in front of her. As much as she hated what she had to do, the thought that maybe this would be the last time she'd ever have to do something like this was a huge relief.

"I appreciate Max's defense of my rationale in taking on such a fine and upcoming player, as you all now know Gabrielle is going to be. While he is right in saying that I've come to care for her a great deal, and have found myself far more invested in, and enjoying, the process of helping her improve her game, that wasn't the only reason I agreed to help her."

A low hum started in the room as pens scratched on paper, recorders were held closer, and cameras once again began whirring.

"It is true that we were approached by a mutual friend and

that I wouldn't have been involved at all if that hadn't happened. But I must admit that I did have some less than altruistic reasons in taking on this job."

"Tess—"

She glanced at Max and shook her head. "You deserve the truth."

"Maybe." He slid his hand under Gaby's elbow. "Come on," he said. "Press conference over."

Tess felt momentarily stricken. It was bad enough that she was about to humble herself in front of what amounted to the entire world once the stories were filed, but for Max to do such a complete turnaround and abandon her now hurt more than she was willing to admit. Not that he didn't have every right to distance himself and Gaby from her at this point, but still . . .

She waited until Gaby stood and was helped out from behind the desk, then turned back to the microphone. "As I was saying—"

Max turned around, clearly surprised. "You, too," he said, holding out his hand. "Like I said, press conference over."

"But I need to explain—"

"Yes, you do. But not to them. You don't owe them anything. In fact, I think they've taken quite enough from you. Have you done anything illegal?"

"Of course not," she said, surprised at the question.

"Fine." He turned to look at Fionula. "Then what you do and why you do it is nobody's business but yours."

Her cell phone buzzed at her hip. A quick glance at the screen showed it was Alan calling. Word really did travel fast.

"Max—"

He held out his hand. "I've shared you with them enough for the past few weeks."

She glanced back at the filled rows and expectant faces. She'd become so used to living on a public stage, and she'd used that stage to her advantage every bit as much as they'd used her to sell papers. But maybe Max was right. She'd given, she'd taken. Maybe it was time to call it a match, and find another way to conduct her life. Out of the public eye. No matter what it cost her. So she did the hardest thing she'd ever done. She shut her mouth.

Offering nothing more than a smile, she slid her chair back. As if on cue, the room erupted in a renewed barrage of questions. They'd been given a taste of something juicy and she knew they wouldn't stop until they'd chewed every last bit of meat off that paper-selling bone. But that didn't mean she had to make it easy on them. Or even care what they did and didn't find out.

What was important was finding someplace private to explain everything to Max and Gaby. Once they knew and understood everything, she'd call her family and explain it to them, too. Well, Bobby and her dad, anyway. Wade would take his pound of flesh off of her eventually. After that, it didn't matter who knew what, or said what. Whatever happened after that was going to be conducted in private. She was officially out of the spotlight.

Even if that meant losing her house and living out of one of her cars. Which was a definite possibility. She didn't think Alan was calling to congratulate her on her little media blitz. And no matter how supportive he appeared at the moment, when Max heard what she had to say . . . well, she'd keep the SUV instead of the Boxster. More room for sleeping.

Max stepped out into the hall, followed by Gaby and Tess, only to find all three godmothers waiting for them. The shouted questions from the press only stopped when they closed the door behind them.

"My goodness," Aurora said, fanning herself with a program. "It sounded like a mob scene in there."

"Close to it," Max said. He turned to the security personnel standing on either side of the door. "Can you take us—"

Tess moved in. "There is an office just outside the players' lounge that I used the other day. If it's possible, we'd like to use that for a short time. And we'd appreciate any privacy you could give us."

The guard nodded, then motioned them to follow him.

Moments later, all six of them were ushered into the small office Tess had used to meet with Alan. She'd debated asking to talk to Max and Gaby privately, but the godmothers deserved to know what was going on, too. Although it appeared they knew far more than she'd realized.

"I'm so sorry it came to that, dear," Aurora said, still fretting, twisting the rings on her fingers.

"I believe I told you this would happen," Vivian said with a sniff. "Darling, we should have had this conversation weeks ago, but Aurora was convinced we had to do things her way. I knew it would end badly."

Aurora looked miserable. "I was only trying to do what was best for all of you. I know it's not much consolation, but my heart was in the right place."

"Enough, Vivi, Aurora," Mercedes said quietly. "Let Tess speak for herself."

They all shifted toward her, expectant looks lining their faces.

Tess couldn't have felt more awful. "Well... I suppose some of you know at least part of the story." She looked at the godmothers.

Aurora smiled a bit sadly and Vivian merely nodded.

"It appears that Max's concerns about me were more well founded than even I wanted to believe. Over the last couple of years on tour, I wasn't quite as forward thinking as I should have been regarding managing my income, and everything else.

After the injury, the only thing that mattered was getting healthy and getting back on tour. I didn't listen to my advisors, and, well, I did find myself in something of a pretty major bind with the IRS."

"Tess?" Gaby's face was one of innocence lost. It would have happened sooner or later, but Tess would have hoped for later. And definitely would have preferred it not to have anything to do with her.

She lifted a hand. "All taken care of, but at the loss of pretty much everything I owned. I—I honestly thought I'd earn it back when my endorsement deals were renewed, but as it turned out, they weren't. None of them. And no new ones have been forthcoming. I'm apparently yesterday's news. I lost my management team, as well, and no one wanted to take me on. I haven't had to worry about money in a very long time, so I didn't take it seriously. I'm taking it very seriously now."

"So you really are broke?" Gaby asked in a hushed whisper. "All those titles and—"

Tess didn't think she could feel any lower. That roomful of reporters could take lessons from one too-wise-for-her-years teenager. "Close enough. When Bobby invited me over to London for the wedding, I thought it was my only chance to figure things out, drum up some interest, something, anything. You thought I was out partying every night. Well, I was out, but it wasn't for a good time. Honestly, I'm tired of that lifestyle, have been since before I retired. They were mostly corporate functions. I didn't see any other way of getting the attention I needed to prove to the sponsors and various other corporate entities that I was still a viable commodity. I can't get the attention on court any longer, so . . ."

"Couldn't you tell your family?" Gaby asked. "Wouldn't they help you out?"

Tess deflated even further. Gaby and Max were so close—

Gaby would have gone to her brother if she found herself in trouble. Tess could have gone to hers . . . but hadn't. "I didn't want to do that. Not only because I wouldn't ask that of them, but because I was embarrassed and more than a little humiliated. Both of my brothers and my father are very successful—"

"So were you!" Gaby insisted. "It's not your fault that—"

"It's only my fault," she quickly corrected. "I have no one else to blame." She sighed. "And I will tell my family now, right after I get done here. Even without the help and all the lectures, I should have been honest with them." She looked them each in the eye. "And at some point, I should have been honest with each of you, too. I didn't mean for it to turn out like this, with you and Gaby being dragged into my latest drama. I can only hope that neither of you, or Glass Slipper, are adversely affected when this all comes out in the papers."

"Nonsense, dear, we've weathered far worse," Aurora said. "And I stand by my decision to hire you in the first place."

Tess felt a twinge in her chest. "Thank you for that. I'm not sure I deserve it. You know, I took you up on your offer of hospitality at Sir Robin's because I didn't have the finances to back my own mission here. I've used all of you to some degree. I'm so sorry."

"Honey, there comes a time when most of us manipulate a situation to our own advantage," Vivian said on a dry laugh. "You were doing us a favor, Gaby a favor, and Max a favor. You earned your keep with us, as you did with them. Honestly, I don't see why everyone has their feathers in a twist."

"Thank you, Vivian, that means the world to me. But normally when I get myself into situations, I can get myself back out again in a way that only affects or impacts me. I didn't do that this time and I feel horrible about it."

"So did you?" Max asked quietly. So quietly, his words startled her.

She looked at him directly for the first time since leaving the press room. "Did I . . . ?"

"Get yourself out of trouble. Was Fionula right about the network offer?"

There wasn't any accusation in his voice or his expression. It might have been easier to take if there were. It would have been far better than the resigned disappointment she found there instead.

She held his gaze. "The offer has been made, yes. I did spend time in the booth as a guest commentator the past two weeks, which you both knew about. But that didn't happen by coincidence. Once I heard how the ratings went up, I deliberately played that angle." She shook her head. "I wasn't trying to do anything other than find a niche for myself, a paying niche. It didn't occur to me that it would hurt anyone. Maybe I am the selfish girl you thought I was. I just wanted to salvage what was left of the life I once had. I never meant—" She stopped herself. "That's no excuse."

Aurora stepped closer and rubbed Tess's shoulder. "You're being too hard on yourself."

It should have made her feel better, and it did, but in an awful sort of way. Her eyes burned even as she tried to laugh. "No, trust me, I'm not."

"You are," Gaby insisted, hero worship still firmly in place despite everything. "Your whole life was tennis, on and off the courts. The whole world followed your every move. How could you know what you wanted to do instead when it all suddenly went away? You were just trying to survive. You didn't do anything wrong."

"What *do* you want, Tess?" This from Max. "Is the commentating job just a means to a financial end, or is it what you see yourself doing for the future? Will it make you happy?"

"I doubt I'm going to have to worry about that. Alan

Chapman has already left two voice mails on my phone and I'm guessing it's not to congratulate me on a successful press conference."

"You could talk your way back into it if you wanted to," he said.

He'd said it directly, without any negative inflection. Because he knew her. And because he was right. She found her lips quirking a little, which surprised her, given the nature of the talk they were having. "Possibly. I know I was lucky to get the offer. It would have given me a chance to stay close to the sport, travel, be a part of the tour, all of which are major bonuses."

"You are quite good at it, Tess," Mercedes offered, then looked at her two partners when they looked at her in surprise. She stiffened slightly. "Don't look so shocked. I might have begged off traveling to the grounds with you. The sun, even such as it is here, is so bad for the skin. But that didn't mean I wasn't watching the coverage on BBC." She looked at Tess. "I thought you brought a lot of color to the commentary. Humanized it."

"Thank you," Tess responded sincerely. "But to be honest, though I enjoyed it well enough, it wouldn't have mattered. I was being offered a very nice amount of money to get myself out of financial trouble. So I'd have probably said yes anyway."

" 'Probably'?"

That was from Max. Everyone looked at him. Tess, too.

He was looking directly at her. Only at her. "Meaning you haven't signed anything yet?"

She wasn't sure if he was getting at what she thought he was, maybe even hoped he was, but if she was going to give them complete and total honesty, then she had to be honest about this, too, even if she ended up looking like a total fool. At this point, it wasn't that big a risk to take. "I—I, uh, well, there was this other offer I was seriously considering," she said quietly. "But I wasn't sure it still stood."

"And if it did?"

"I was contemplating taking a job with a network without even mentioning it to you, although I did try. Doesn't that piss you off?"

"Did that offer come before mine, or after?"

"Before, but that's not the point—"

"It's exactly the point. If it had come after—"

"I'm not sure I still wouldn't have taken it." She ducked her chin at the hurt she saw flash across his face, but immediately looked at him again. He deserved the truth straight. "I'm sorry. I—I thought Gaby was better off without me. You, too. I seem to attract trouble." She smiled a little, her tone turned dry. "Understatement of the century, I know. And I bring it on myself half the time. I plan to work on that, I really do, but I don't have to subject you two to me while I do."

"You 'plan to work on that,'" he repeated. Now Max surprised her when his lips quirked a little, too. "On national television? Spouting opinions?" He snorted a little, but the teasing wasn't harsh. In fact, it sounded quite . . . affectionate. "Good luck with that."

Her smile grew, even as the ache in her heart grew with it. Idiot! Look at what she'd thrown away. And for what? She would sell her house, her cars, give up her courts, everything, to be even a tiny part of that. She didn't even want television spots and ratings points. She just wanted to be involved in the sport she loved, with people she loved. Do something that really mattered. Mattered to her, anyway. And, most important, share it with people who mattered.

The money mattered the least.

Max walked over to her and reached out for her hand. Her own hand was shaking a bit when she lifted it to his and let him pull her to a stand. "What if I told you the offer was still open."

There was a collective intake of breath between the godmothers.

Aurora sniffed into a silk handkerchief that had materialized out of the folds of her billowing caftan. Vivian smiled knowingly and murmured, "You go, girl." Mercedes merely held her gaze for a long moment, then nodded her approval.

Tess shifted her gaze to Gaby, who looked both like a young girl with romantic stars in her eyes . . . and a budding young professional who badly wanted the very best on her team.

Finally she looked at Max. "I'd tell you I've never wanted anything so badly in my entire life. My new life."

Max's jaw flexed, but his dark eyes gleamed. "What, exactly, do you want?"

"I want to be Gaby's—" She broke off on purpose, then looked at Gaby. "I'm not sure I make such a good mentor, but I think I can be a pretty damn good coach." She looked back at Max. "I didn't know how it was going to feel, being forced to sit on the sidelines. But watching her play, knowing I could have some impact on all that potential she has . . ." She lifted her shoulders. "It felt good. Invigorating. Exciting. Like I'm still part of what's going on out there. And I don't mean that I'm living my career through Gaby." Tess looked at her. "She's going to have her own amazing career. But it's like the next best thing to being there. It fits me."

No one said anything, but everyone smiled.

"What?" she said, as the silence grew and so did the smiles.

"We all saw that, honey," Aurora said gently. "We're just glad you figured it out, too."

She felt her cheeks heat up, but couldn't keep from smiling herself.

"So?" Max asked.

She looked at him, nonplussed. "So?"

"The job is still yours if you want it. Right, Gabs?"

Gaby leaped from her seat and ran to the two of them. "Yes,

yes, yes! Say you'll do it, Tess. I promise I won't be a pain in the ass. And I promise—"

"Not to make promises," Tess said, pulling Gaby into the hug. "Because I can't promise I won't do something stupid, either, and just having me around is likely to cause a ruckus you otherwise wouldn't have had."

Gabrielle's eyes twinkled. "Are you sure about that?"

Tess frowned. "Gaby—"

Max nudged his sister with his elbow. "Don't blow this for us," he said out of the side of his mouth. Then he hugged her, and told her to sit down, before turning back to Tess. "There's one more thing I need to know."

He took Tess's other hand, so he held them both. "Anything," she told him, meaning it. He knew the whole story, and he was still standing in front of her. Maybe she hadn't totally screwed things up. That was all she could think as she looked at Max's smiling, nervous face. She was going to get what she wanted. And, like everything else she'd ever wanted, she was prepared to work her ass off to keep it. Wait. What was he nervous about? "Are you still afraid I'm going to lead Gaby astray? Because if I'm going to do this, I can't be proving to you all the time—"

"No, that's not it. I'm pretty sure you were right and my sister is going to be my sister and there will be trouble in my future with or without you." He tugged her a little closer. "But maybe having you around will keep us one step ahead." He shot Gaby a look over Tess's shoulders.

For her part, Gaby pretended to examine her manicure and look exceedingly innocent. No one was buying it.

"So what are you worried about? I won't talk to the press except on Gaby's behalf and we'll work something out so you'll feel comfortable with that when I do. I don't plan on doing the party circuit any longer—that was only me trying to find a way out of this financial nightmare." Her eyes widened. "Oh! I guess we'll have to figure out what to do about all that, too. But don't worry about my percentage. I'll sell my cars. The house, too, if necessary. It's too big for me, anyway, and we'll be traveling most of the year and—"

"Oh, for God's sake." Max just shut her up with a kiss.

Gaby cheered. Aurora sighed. Vivian whooped. Mercedes smiled.

"What was that for?" Tess asked him when he lifted his head.

He smiled. "If you have to ask, I'm doing something wrong."

Now her mouth curved and she pulled his head back down. "No. You just served an ace." She smiled up into his shining eyes. "Right down the tee."

"Gee," he teased, as he let her pull his mouth to hers. "And I don't even play tennis."

"We could change that, you know."

Max groaned.

Mercedes turned and picked up her bag. "I think we're done here, ladies. Gabrielle, I believe you missed out on a high tea yesterday. Seeing as your time in London is short, would you care to accompany us? We can toast your success. You've really taken this town by storm."

Gaby smiled and stood, looking back at her brother and Tess. "Not yet." Her smile grew to a cocky grin. "But I'm going to."

Aurora and Vivian continued watching the kissing couple, hands over their hearts, wistful looks on their faces, until Mercedes forcibly nudged them from the room.

"Where did everybody go," Tess asked some time later, when they both finally paused long enough to take a breath.

"I have no idea. But I'm sure they can take care of themselves."

When Tess shot him a shocked look, he tipped up her chin and intently held her gaze. There was that wicked twinkle in his eyes again. The one she was definitely coming to know and enjoy.

"What? It's only fair that if you're going to get a life, that I get one, too. And I say we start right now." He tugged her to the door without waiting for an answer. "Come on, London awaits. You can show me the town."

"What about the press?"

He grinned back at her. "Let them get their own limo."

Epilogue

"They make this look so much more effortless on television." Aurora huffed and puffed as she made her way to the sideline. "Shade. I need shade."

"All you've done is practice your serve," Vivian complained. "We haven't even played yet."

"Now, now," Mercedes said from her perch beneath the awning they'd had erected next to the court. She kept her head bent over a calculator and several binders. "I told you this was a crazy idea at our age."

"You're not even out here trying," Vivian retorted.

Mercedes looked up. "Exactly."

"Oh, don't mind her," Vivian assured Aurora. "We'll find our rhythm. I always do," she added with a wink. "As I've always said, it's just a matter of practice."

Aurora only wished she believed it. What in the world had she been thinking, agreeing to Vivian's crazy idea. She should have never invited her to those matches at Wimbledon last month.

"And trust me, darling, if there's one thing I know something about, it's finding my rhythm. Besides, I think I've found the perfect solution to our learning-curve problem."

"Oh?" Aurora fanned herself.

Just then a young, extremely well-built young man, in long white shorts and a navy-blue polo shirt, sauntered over to the courts Vivian had had installed on the rear property of their Glass Slipper home base in Potomac, Maryland.

"Hello, darling." She waved. "You must be Troy."

"Yes, ma'am," he said, his voice deep and vaguely accented.

Aurora sighed and rolled her eyes. "I shouldn't be surprised. Did you know anything about this?" she asked Mercedes.

Mercy glanced up. "I learned a long time ago to adopt a don't ask, don't tell policy where Vivi is concerned."

"I think I'm having trouble with my ball toss," Vivian was telling Troy. "Perhaps you could help me?"

Aurora decided right then and there that she was destined to be a sports spectator, not a participant. She took a seat across from Mercedes, bypassed the water bottles they'd brought out, and poured herself a mimosa from the pitcher Mercedes had had sent out shortly after they'd arrived. She took a sip and sighed in appreciation. "Now this is what I call a civilized way to spend a Saturday afternoon."

Mercedes nodded, but continued tapping at her calculator. "Things seemed to be working out pretty well with Tess and young Gabrielle."

Aurora was surprised by the mention, but more than happy the subject had come up. "Absolutely. The U.S. Open starts next week and Gabrielle did wonderfully well in the warm-up tournament." She toyed with her glass. "You know, Tess mentioned that

Bobby and Andrea are throwing a big bash up there to launch her new clothing line, right before the Open begins."

"So I hear," Mercedes responded distractedly.

"I was thinking perhaps a trip to New York might be in order. It would be fun to see everyone again." To be honest, she didn't care about the tennis or the launch party. "I wouldn't be surprised if maybe Max uses the occasion to pop the question."

Mercedes stopped tapping at the calculator and looked up. "Really?"

"I've heard word he's been seen shopping in a few jewelry stores."

At Mercedes' raised eyebrow, Aurora came clean. "Vivian and I have called in a few favors, okay? But we're happy for them, aren't we? And if Frank comes to New York for the launch party, it would be the perfect time for Max to ask for her hand."

"Hmm," Mercedes said, tapping her pen on her cheek. "I rather think he is a traditionalist. You're probably right about all this." Then she went back to work. "I'm sure we could work something out to be up there."

Aurora sighed. "Such a romantic you are." But she had seen the little twinkle in Mercy's eyes. Oh, it was going to be such fun! She'd have to see about putting together some kind of engagement party. Aurora settled back with her drink, wheels already spinning.

She listened as Mercedes continued crunching numbers. And watched as Vivian put on yet another shameless display. And here she thought nothing could be more shameless than that outfit Vivian was sporting. No woman her age should wear a pleated skirt that short. Ah well, she was in too good a mood now to worry about her best friend and partner.

She lifted her drink. "To another success story." She took a sip and smiled. "Imagine. Whose life will we change next?"

About the Author

National bestseller Donna Kauffman resides with her family just outside D.C., in northern Virginia. In her dreams, she would take Centre Court by storm. In reality, she'd happily be a ball girl if it meant getting herself on the grass courts at Wimbledon. Can you be a forty-something ball girl? Ball woman? Ball Mom? Where are the godmothers when you need them?